By Elizabeth Boyle

LOVE LETTERS FROM A DUKE
HIS MISTRESS BY MORNING
THIS RAKE OF MINE
SOMETHING ABOUT EMMALINE
IT TAKES A HERO
STEALING THE BRIDE
ONE NIGHT OF PASSION
ONCE TEMPTED
NO MARRIAGE OF CONVENIENCE

ELIZABETH BOYLE

LOVE LETTERS FROM A DUKE

AVON

An Imprint of HarperCollins*Publishers*

This is a work of fiction. Names, characters, places, and incidents are products of the author's imagination or are used fictitiously and are not to be construed as real. Any resemblance to actual events, locales, organizations, or persons, living or dead, is entirely coincidental.

AVON BOOKS
An Imprint of HarperCollins*Publishers*
10 East 53rd Street
New York, New York 10022-5299

To the families who live with autism.
May your days be blessed with the kindness of strangers,
the love of friends and families, and most of all, a cure.

And to FEAT of Washington and Autism Speaks,
my unwavering gratitude to you for your dedication
and spirit of hope.
You help us believe.

And last, but far from least,
to Jamilla Kounellas and Rhoda Toulouse
for lending their names to this story
and their generosity to the charities
near and dear to my heart.

A portion of the sale of this book will go to support
Autism Speaks and FEAT of Washington.

To learn more about autism, please visit
www.autismspeaks.org
www.featwa.org

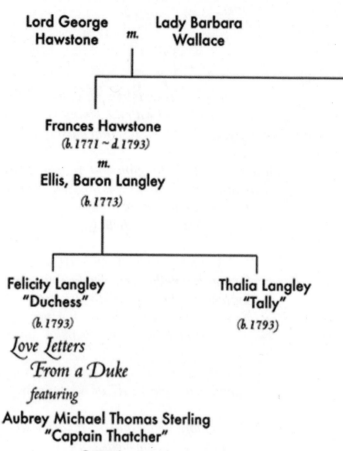

Lord George Hawstone *m.* Lady Barbara Wallace

Frances Hawstone
(b. 1771 ~ d. 1793)
m.
Ellis, Baron Langley
(b. 1773)

Felicity Langley "Duchess"
(b. 1793)

Love Letters From a Duke

featuring

Aubrey Michael Thomas Sterling "Captain Thatcher"
(b. 1780)

Thalia Langley "Tally"
(b. 1793)

For the complete Bachelor Chronicles Family Tree, please visit www.elizabethboyle.com

Elizabeth Boyle's
Bachelor Chronicles
Family Tree

Frederica Hawstone
(b. 1771 ~ d. 1800)

m.

**Bertram Knolles,
Earl of Stanbrook**
(b. 1765 ~ d. 1812)

**Lady Philippa Knolles
"Pippin"**
(b. 1793)

**Carlton Knolles,
Earl of Stanbrook**
(b. 1796)

Also Featuring:

**Lord & Lady John Tremont
"Jack & Miranda" from**

*Something About Emmaline
&
This Rake of Mine*

**The Duke & Duchess of Setchfield
"Temple & Diana" from**

Stealing the Bride

LOVE
LETTERS
FROM A
DUKE

Prologue

June 4, 1810

The Most Hon. the Marquess of Standon
Bythorne Castle, Westmoreland

My Lord Marquess,

If you would but spare me a moment of patience and allow me to introduce myself, I think you will find my forthcoming proposition quite amenable. My name is Miss Felicity Langley and I will graduate in a year from Miss Emery's Establishment for the Education of Genteel Ladies. A mutual friend of ours, Lord John Tremont, suggested I write to you and propose that we consider uniting in marriage—that is, once I've finished a brilliant Season. You see, I have every *intention of marrying a duke, and Jack thought you might prove a likely candidate despite the fact that you have yet to inherit from your grandfather. Speaking of your esteemed grandsire, how is his health . . . ?*

—*An extract from Felicity Langley's correspondence to the Marquess of Standon*

The Duke of Hollindrake's secretary laughed out loud.

This was notable for two reasons: No one ever laughed in front of the imposing and impossibly ill-tempered duke, and, who would have ever thought that his straight-backed, pinched-nosed, impeccably mannered secretary, Mr. Gibbens, even knew how?

And then he laughed again. Guffawed, really. Out loud and much to his employer's chagrin.

"Whatever has come over you, Gibbens? Have you gone mad?" the duke barked across the wide desk separating them. "Control yourself this instant!"

Gibbens struggled to do just that, but it was of no use. His gaze slipped once again to the last line of the letter he'd been reading and he broke out in a loud gale of laughter and continued until tears ran down his cheeks. It wasn't until he set aside the well-traveled post to retrieve a handkerchief from his waistcoat pocket and had a chance to wipe his eyes that he recovered enough to answer. "My deepest apologies, Your Grace. It is just that—" And then he started to stammer again, his eyes crinkling in the corners and his lips twitching rebelliously. He shook his head and pointed like a guilty child at the letter.

"Harrumph! Whatever nonsense is this?" the duke asked as he reached for it.

"A letter, Your Grace," Gibbens managed. "To your grandson."

"Standon? Whyever would someone be writing him, least of all have the nerve to send it here?" He eyed the missive in his hand as if it carried plague. "Owes more money, does he? Well, I'm not paying his debts. I'm not, I say."

Standon and his grandfather had never seen eye-to-eye, having argued years earlier, resulting in the younger Sterling leaving England and his family, without ever looking back.

Of course that had been well and good with the duke, for his miscreant grandson had been the third son of a third son, so far removed from inheriting that his foibles and follies had been nothing more than a continuing annoyance rather than any grave concern. That is, until fate intervened—and now the young buck who'd driven his family mad with his exploits and then disappeared was the heir.

So even as the old duke made his strident declaration, to anyone who knew him, there was an odd wistful note behind his words. Regret, even.

"It isn't about debts, Your Grace," Gibbens explained. "Rather, the letter is from a young lady—"

"Got himself into that sort of trouble, eh? Not going to have some wench thinking she can wrangle a fortune—"

"No, Your Grace, it isn't that sort of, um, well, difficulty," Gibbens managed, for he was a lifelong bachelor and carried an unholy fear of the female sex. "Rather it is from a *lady*. A proper one."

"A proper one, you say?" Hollindrake brought the letter up for a closer examination. "And from Bath it appears," he said, looking at the directions. "What the devil is this Miss Emery's?"

"A school, Your Grace. I believe it teaches deportment and other such qualities."

"Churning out qualified flirts and silly chits, most likely," the old man said with a snort. Yet there was a glint of curiosity in his old rheumy dark eyes. He looked up and pinned a glance on his secretary. "And what the devil did you find so amusing?"

Gibbens choked and stammered. "Miss Langley writes to ask, that is, she is under the impression that, well, apparently—"

"Out with it, man," Hollindrake barked.

The poor man took a deep breath, screwed up every bit of courage he possessed and managed to get it all out in one sentence. "This Miss Langley is proposing that Lord Standon consider her hand in marriage." Gibbens then closed his eyes and braced himself for the pending explosion.

None came. And after an indecent amount of silence, he peeked out through his lashes and discovered the old duke engrossed in reading the letter for himself.

Then the second noteworthy event occurred that day.

The duke laughed.

"Some cheek!" he said, once he gathered his wits about him. "She has the audacity to inquire about the state of my health. Probably be demmed disappointed to find me fit and hardy, I wager." He set the letter down on his desk and laughed again.

"Yes, Your Grace," his secretary agreed. "Quite presumptuous."

"Exactly!" the duke declared. "Which is why we are going to answer it."

"Answer it, Your Grace?" A sense of foreboding ran down the secretary's spine.

"Of course! Why, I suspect any chit with this much brass would make a most excellent duchess. And further, I'd wager she'd bring that rapscallion grandson of mine to heel."

Gibbens' lips flapped like a fish out of water. "You mean to accept her proposal? But, Your Grace, you can hardly accept a proposal for your grandson on a matter such as this, why it's—"

"I can and I will!" the old man said, sitting up straight and looking younger than he had in years. "So we will answer this Miss Langley—and court her in his name. One day Standon will thank me."

And eventually he did.

But not at first.

Chapter 1

Aubrey Michael Thomas Sterling,
   Marquess of Standon
b. 1780, third son of Lord Charles Sterling
Current residence: believed to be Bythorne Castle

Notes: Lord Standon poses a dilemma, for very little is
known of him (though there are persistent and unsubstanti-
ated rumors of youthful and rakish indiscretions). However,
he must have reformed upon his elevation to the marquis-
ate, for he is never mentioned in the society columns, the
Gentleman's Magazine or any other reliable form of gossip.
As such there is very little to recommend him other than the
indisputable fact that he is the Duke of Hollindrake's heir.

—An excerpt from the Bachelor Chronicles

Mayfair, London
January 1814

"Oh, heavens, Tally, this is terrible news," Miss Felicity
Langley announced to her sister Thalia, who was seated
across the sitting room.

"What is it?" her twin replied, looking up from her sketch pad.

Felicity set down the copy of the *Times* she'd been reading and sighed. "Lord Garner died."

"No!" Tally got up from her chair by the window, and as she rose, her little black dog, Brutus, rose as well, stretching out his legs and yawning before he followed his beloved mistress as she crossed the room to see the account for herself. "A riding accident! How dreadful."

"Terrible luck," Felicity muttered as she dipped her quill into the ink pot and proceeded to strike Lord Garner's name from the open journal before her.

"Heavens, that's the fifth bachelor this winter to expire," Tally said as she watched her sister draw a series of lines through her careful reckoning of the now deceased baron's life and holdings.

"Actually the sixth."

After giving her head a few woeful shakes, Tally asked, "This Lord Garner, he was rather old, wasn't he?"

"Nearly forty."

Her nose wrinkled. "Positively ancient. You should have crossed him out years ago." The twins had just turned one and twenty not a fortnight earlier, and Tally especially considered any man not in his twenties to be nothing short of a Methuselah.

"Ancient or not, one cannot overlook twelve thousand a year."

Her twin shrugged, then glanced back at the paper. "An heir worth noting?"

"A lad of seven."

A *tsk, tsk* was her sister's only reply, for she knew this meant that the new Lord Garner would have to wait another ten years before he could even be considered eligible for inclusion in Felicity's infamous *Bachelor Chronicles*.

Not that any man in his right mind would want to find

himself inside the pages of such a journal. The *Bachelor Chronicles*, as they'd been dubbed by her classmates at Miss Emery's school, was far from being the giggling, foolish musings of a title-mad young lady, but rather a meticulously researched encyclopedia of every eligible bachelor in the *ton*.

A volume of *Debrett's* could give you lineage and a family motto. The *Bachelor Chronicles* could tell you if the man had a penchant for drink and late night rambles through the wilds of Seven Dials. Mr. Billingsworth's guidebooks and histories would give you an effusive and flowery travelogue of the man's holdings and properties, but Felicity's encyclopedia of dilettantes and Corinthians revealed the true condition of the roof and whether or not the walls were buttressed by mortgages or mortar.

Dukes to barons, knighted gentlemen and even a few men of means were given her discerning perusal. Even second sons and distant heirs found their way into the *Chronicles*, because, as Felicity was wont to say, "One day a spare, the next an heir."

To accomplish all this, she spent the first few hours of each day scouring the *Times*, the *Globe*, and of course the *Morning Post*, as well as the latest volumes of the *Gentleman's Magazine*, the *Ladies Magazine*, and *The Ladies Fashionable Cabinet,* looking for information that would necessitate addendums or corrections to her *Chronicles*.

What she couldn't glean from the regular publications, she gathered by contacting Miss Emery's former students. A voluminous correspondence with these ladies, most of them having married into the loftiest families in society, gave her insights into her quarry that unfortunately never found their way into print.

"Tally, I am rethinking Pippin's future again," she said after she'd carefully blotted the wet X running across Lord Garner's entry.

"Oh, Duchess, not again," Tally protested, using her favorite nickname for her sister.

Felicity waved off her sister's objection. "I'm more inclined to see our cousin with Lord Elmsley than the Earl of Darlton. I've just been informed by the viscount's mother's second cousin's wife that Elmsley carries a bit of the romantic tragic about him, which would fit quite nicely with Pippin's current state—"

Tally groaned. Loudly. "Don't do this," she told her sister. "Leave Pippin be."

"Whyever for?"

"Because our poor cousin hasn't been the same since . . . well, you know."

Felicity heaved a sigh. "Her father's death was untimely to say the least, and the shocking state of his finances even worse, but I daresay it is high time that she—"

"Stop!" Her sister threw her hands up. "Sometimes I wonder if you even have a heart. I'm not talking about her father. I'm talking about *him*." Tally lowered her voice to a whisper. "Captain Dashwell."

"That pirate?" Felicity exclaimed. "I won't hear that name mentioned again. Not in this house. Oh, how I wish the devil would take him to the bottom of the sea! Pippin was such a sensible creature before that wastrel kissed her."

Four years earlier, during Felicity's first matchmaking endeavor, she, Tally, and Pippin had become entangled in more than assisting their teacher, Miss Porter, find her heart's desire with the rakish Jack Tremont—rather, they'd discovered themselves in the middle of an elaborate network of spies and espionage, and had stood in for Jack when their misadventures accidentally landed him in prison.

And that one night had changed their lives forever—ending with Pippin being kissed by a young American sea captain, Thomas Dashwell, as they exchanged gold for passengers from France. It had happened in the flash of an eye, but to hear their cousin recall the night, it was as if she and Dash had spent an eternity in each other's arms.

Nonsense, really, Felicity had told them both on numerous occasions. Captain Dashwell was a murderous, ruinous, dreadful pirate. Best forgotten, or better yet, hung from the nearest yardarm. For not long afterward the brash American had gone from being their ally to their enemy, as their two countries plunged into war. And, since then, his daring and audacious pirating had cost England dearly.

Tally's blue eyes sparkled. "You're just jealous he didn't kiss you."

"I am not!" Felicity told her. "I'd have shot the scallywag before he'd come close enough to dare."

"Oh, come now, you don't want to end your days never having been kissed, do you?" Tally gathered her dog Brutus into her arms, fluffing the mane of fur that ringed his monkeylike face.

Felicity's hand came to rest atop her volume of *Debrett's*, its thick weight just the right foundation from which to launch her argument. "Tally, kissing is out of the question. If I thought for a moment either of you two were going to run about kissing every pirate and rapscallion you cross paths with, I would never have gone to such lengths to get us to Town for the Season. Can't you see that this house, Aunt Minty, our very reputations, are at stake? If any of us are impugned, if anyone were to discover the lengths we've gone to . . . well . . ."

"*You've* gone to," Tally corrected. "I'm not the one getting transported for any of this. Besides, I'm with Pippin on this, Duchess. I'd prefer to find my own husband, not one of your approved dullards. I want a man like Captain Dashwell, who will kiss me senseless and leave me willing to dare anything."

Well, of all the ungrateful . . . Felicity drew an even breath. "Please do not wax poetic about kissing pirates in my presence!

Why, it isn't done. Not by us. You both must marry well—for how can I have a cousin, least of all a sister, who isn't as well-connected as I am when I am Hollindrake's bride?"

Tally set Brutus down. "When? Don't you mean *if?*"

Felicity shot her sister a hot glance. "I will marry the duke and no one else."

"But dearling—" Tally was cut off by the bell at the front door, the insistent and unexpected clamor causing them both to start. "Heavens, who could that be?" Then she froze, her face growing pale as she glanced around the salon that served as their day room. "You don't think . . . that someone has discovered—"

"Certainly not!" Felicity said, though not completely convinced. "But I suppose we must see who it is."

"I'm not going to jail, Duchess," her sister repeated, as she had every day since they'd come to Town.

"Yes, Tally, I know," Felicity replied. She gathered up her shawl from the back of the chair and tossed it over her shoulders before she left the warmth of the upstairs sitting room—the only warm room in the house, Tally liked to grumble—to do what one usually left to a servant.

Only they hadn't any.

Tally followed hot on her heels, and where Tally went, so did Brutus, who never let his mistress get too far out of his sight. He barked and growled, setting up a loud ruckus that echoed through the mostly empty Mayfair mansion they'd taken for the Season. Though of noble breeding—his grandsire, Tally liked to tell anyone who would listen, had belonged to Marie Antoinette—Brutus possessed the manners of a spit dog.

Felicity glanced over her shoulder at the parade behind her and shook her head. "Keep him from chewing on whoever it is, will you, Tally? I am still trying to determine how we will pay for the damage to Mr. Elliott's boots."

Her sister groaned. "Some solicitor. Served that old pinch

purse right." She cleared her throat and when she spoke again it was with the man's stoic pitch. "'A Season? Why, a dreadful waste of money. Economize, dear girls. Now that's the best course of action given your situation—'" she sputtered and growled, not unlike the noise Brutus was making. "That cheap, wretched bast—"

"Thalia!" Felicity heaved a beleaguered sigh. Not that she didn't share her sister's sentiments about their solicitor, but she preferred to take a more ladylike stance on the matter. "Remember what Nanny Bridget always said. 'The rare man is the one who looks toward a lady's future.'"

"Yes, well Nanny Bridget wasn't living in an empty mansion scratching by on her pin money, now was she?" she muttered back, but still she scooped Brutus up as they turned at the landing and soothed the little beast with some softly spoken assurances.

Another pair of boots would cut dearly into their already meager budget.

As the bell jangled with yet another insistent and discordant peal, Tally heaved a sigh. "Heavens! How terribly rude they are. Why don't we have Mrs. Hutchinson get that?"

"Mrs. Hutchinson . . . is . . . indisposed," Felicity supplied.

There was a indelicate snort from behind her. "Mrs. Hutchinson isn't indisposed, she's tangle-footed."

"Could you be a bit more discreet?" Felicity said over her shoulder as she rounded the second landing. "What if someone heard you? How would it look if word got out that our household has some . . . some . . . irregularities?"

"We live in an empty house, my dearest Duchess," Tally replied. "It won't be long before *someone* notices. And that housekeeper you hired does us no favors. The woman is a tosspot, a drunkard, top-heavy, a high goer—"

"Yes, yes, so she's got a slight penchant for brandy, but her wages are what we can afford."

"Nice of her to work for brandy, I suppose," Tally said. "And thank God we were able to liberate so many bottles from Uncle's cellars before we left Sussex or we'd be up to our necks in debt with the spirit merchant's bill."

Felicity did her best to ignore Tally's lamentations. "Don't be so dramatic. Mrs. Hutchinson is merely unavailable to answer the door. And that is all it is."

"Yes, if only that was all," Tally said, sharing a skeptical glance with Brutus.

The bell jangled again, and whoever was on the other side, had an annoyingly persistent way of yanking it into such a discordant clamor, it was getting on Felicity's nerves. "When I am the Duchess of Hollindrake . . ." she muttered as visions of an endless supply of coal, servants, and respectable housekeepers danced before her eyes.

"Yes, wouldn't that be lovely," Tally agreed quickly. "We'll be living around the corner on Grosvenor Square, warm and snug without the least bit of economies." She paused for a moment and let a wicked little grin tip her lips. "And most likely employ a housekeeper who doesn't drink. What do you think? Do you think the duke's housekeeper drinks, because—" She stopped mid-sentence, her mouth falling open in a wide moue. "You don't think that perhaps *he* drinks and that's why you haven't heard from him in so long? With his grandfather's death, maybe he's fallen into a dark and dangerous decline. Oh, dear, Felicity, what if he's turned into a rumpot and intends never to marry?"

"Piffle!" Felicity declared. "Aubrey Michael Thomas Sterling, the tenth Duke of Hollindrake, would never turn into a rumpot. He hasn't such a nature." With her nose in the air, she did her best to set aside the niggle of doubt her sister had managed to plant inside the armor she wore when it came to all matters pertaining to the duke.

"How do you know?" Tally argued. "You've never met the man."

Felicity wheeled around. "Not know him? What a ridiculous thing to say. I've been corresponding with him for four years. I believe that counts as 'knowing' him."

Tally reached over, took her sister's hand and squeezed it. "Dear Duchess, he hasn't written in months. Not since his grandfather died. Even you must admit that something has . . ." To her credit, she didn't say *gone wrong*. ". . . changed," she finally finished.

"Of course his situation has changed." Felicity set off again for the door. "He's a man with vast responsibilities now. He can hardly be expected to be writing to me constantly."

"As you say," Tally agreed. "Perhaps that's him now. Come to call, to sweep you off your feet and take us all to his glorious house. Would be quite convenient, since we haven't enough coal to last the week."

For a moment Felicity gave herself over to Tally's fanciful prattle. Coal. And candles. And enough tea in the chest to make a decent pot of pekoe. And the sugar to go in it, as well. But as a draught raced past her, the chill—along with her sister's dire words—brought her back to her senses.

Why had he suddenly stopped writing? Not even a response to her perfectly penned note of condolence. It was as if he was the one who'd gone aloft, not his grandfather.

Oh, whatever had gone wrong?

As the bell jangled again, Tally groaned at the clamor. "Sound as presumptuous as a duke, don't they? Should I check the window for a coach and four before you answer it?"

Felicity shook her head. "That could hardly be Hollindrake." She nodded toward the bracket clock their father had sent them the year before. "It's too early for callers. Besides, he'd send around his card or a note before he just arrived at our doorstep. Not even a duke would be so forward to call without sending word."

Sweeping her hands over her skirt and then patting her

hair to make sure it was in place, Felicity was actually re-lieved it couldn't be her duke calling—for she still hadn't managed a way to gain them new wardrobes, let alone more coal. But she had a good week to solve those problems, at least until the House of Lords reconvened . . . for then Hol-lindrake would have to come to Town to formally claim his title and take his oath of allegiance.

"So who do you think it is?" Tally was asking, as she clung to a squirming Brutus.

Taking another quick glance at the clock, Felicity let out a big sigh. "How could I have forgotten? The agency sent around a note yesterday that they had found us a footman who met our requirements."

Tally snorted. "What? He doesn't need a wage and won't rob us blind?"

Felicity glanced toward the ceiling and shook her head. "Of course I plan on paying him—eventually—and since we have nothing worth stealing that shouldn't be an issue."

The bell jangled again, and this time Brutus squirmed free of his mistress's grasp, racing in anxious circles around the hem of Tally's gown and barking furiously.

Well, if there was any consolation, Felicity mused as she crossed the foyer and caught hold of the latch, whoever was being so insistent was about to have his boots ruined.

Taking a deep breath, she tugged the door open and found herself staring into a dark green greatcoat, which her gaze dismissively sped over for it sported only one poor cape. The owner stood hunched forward, the brim of his hat tipped down to shield him from the wintry chill.

"May I help you?" Felicity asked, trying to tamp down the shiver that rose up her spine. It wasn't that she'd been struck by a chill, for this mountain of a man was blocking the razor cold wind. No, rather, it was something she didn't quite understand.

And then she did.

As this stranger slowly straightened, the brim of his hat rose, revealing a solid masculine jaw—covered in a hint of dark stubble that did little to obscure the strong cleft in his chin, nor hide a pair of firm lips.

From there sat a Roman nose, set into his features with a noble sort of craggy fortitude. But it was his eyes that finally let loose that odd shiver through her limbs with an abandon that not even she could tamp down.

His gaze was as dark as night, a pair of eyes the color of Russian sable, mysterious and deep, rich and full of secrets.

Felicity found herself mesmerized, for all she could think about was something Pippin had once confessed—that from the very moment she'd looked into Captain Dashwell's eyes, she'd just known he was going to kiss her.

A ridiculous notion, Felicity had declared at the time. But suddenly she understood what her cousin had been saying. For right now she knew there was no way on earth she was going to go to her grave without having once had her lips plundered, thoroughly and spectacularly, by this man, until her toes curled up in her slippers and she couldn't breathe.

She didn't know how she knew such a thing, but she just did.

"I'm here to see Miss Langley," he said. His deep voice echoed with a rough, smoky quality. From the authority in his taut stance, to the arch of his brow as he looked down at her—clearly as surprised to find a lady answering her own door as she was to find him standing on her steps—he left her staggering with one unbelievable thought.

And her shiver immediately turned to panic.

This is him, her heart sang. *Please let this be him.*

Hollindrake!

She struggled to find the words to answer him, but for the first time in her life, Felicity Langley found herself speech-less. She moved her lips, tried to talk, tried to be sensible, but it was impossible under this imposing man's scrutinizing gaze.

Yet how could this be? What was *he* doing here, calling on her? And at such an unfashionable hour?

And no wonder he was staring at her, for her hair wasn't properly fixed, her dress four years out of fashion, and her feet—dear God, she'd answered the door wearing red wool socks!

Tally nudged her from behind. "Felicity, say something."

Reluctantly wrenching her gaze away from his mesmerizing countenance, composing herself, she focused on what it was one said to their nearly betrothed.

But in those few moments, Felicity's dazzled gaze took in the coat once again—with its shockingly worn cuffs. *Worn cuffs?* Oh no, that wasn't right. And where there should be a pair of perfectly cut breeches, were a pair of patched trousers. *Patched?* But the final evidence that cooled her wayward thoughts more thoroughly than the icy floor that each morning met her toes, was the pair of well-worn and thoroughly scuffed boots, one of which now sported the added accessory of a firmly attached small, black affenpinscher dog.

Boots that looked like they'd marched across Spain and back, boots that had never seen the tender care of a valet. Boots that belonged to a man of service, not a duke.

And certainly not the Duke of Hollindrake.

She took another tentative glance back at his face, and found that his noble and arrogant features still left her heart trembling, but this time in embarrassed disappointment.

To think that she would even consider kissing such a fellow . . . well, it wasn't done. Perhaps, she conceded, it was. But only in all those fairy tales and French novels Tally and Pippin adored.

And that was exactly where such mad passions and notions of "love at first sight" belonged—between the covers of a book.

"You must be the man we've been expecting," Tally was saying, casting a dubious glance in Felicity's direction. Obviously unaffected by this man's handsome countenance, she bustled around and caught up Brutus by his hind legs, tugging at the little tyrant. "Sorry about that. He loves a good pair of boots. Hope these aren't your only pair."

Aubrey Michael Thomas Sterling, the tenth Duke of Hollindrake, eyed the damage to his boots first, then looked back up at the pair of young ladies before him. Twins, he guessed, though not identical. The one catching up the mutt of a dog in her arms was a lithe beauty, but it was the one still holding the door latch who caught and held his attention.

Her hair held that elusive color of caramel, something to tempt and tease a man. Especially one like himself who'd been gone too long from the company of good society—and young women especially.

Twelve years at war. Three months on a transport sailing back from Portugal. A month of riding from one end of England to nearly the other, with enough snow in between to make him wonder if he'd been dropped off in Russia instead of Sussex. Then the shock of arriving home and finding himself not just his grandfather's heir, but the duke.

The Duke of Hollindrake.

Gone in an instant was Captain Thatcher, the *nom de plume* he'd taken that long ago night when he'd disavowed the future his grandfather had cast for him. Instead he'd used the winnings from a night of gambling to buy a commission under a false name and fled to the far corners of the world where no one would interfere with his life.

The Duke of Hollindrake. He shuddered. It wasn't the mountain of responsibilities and the management of all of it that bothered him. He'd shouldered that and more getting his troops back and forth across the Peninsula. No, it was the title that had him in the crosshairs. He wasn't a duke. Not in the mold his grandfather and eight generations of Sterlings before that had set down. Stuffy and lofty, and trained from birth for the imperious role that was theirs by some divine ordinance.

Oh, to be Thatcher still. For even with his arse freezing, his nose nearly frostbit, and his fingers stiff from cold, his blood suddenly ran hot at the sight before him. And Thatcher would have stolen a sweet kiss from her pert lips, while the Duke of Hollindrake, well, he had to assume a more, *shudder*, proper manner.

Too bad this fetching little minx wasn't the miss his grandfather had wooed on his behalf. No chance of that, certainly not the social climbing bit of muslin who'd written quite plainly of her intentions to attain the loftiest of marriages—well, shy of a royal one.

"I'm here to see Miss Felicity Langley," he repeated.

By the way this miss was eyeing him—as if he were some ancient marauder, having arrived on their front steps to pillage and plunder—he realized that perhaps his aunt had been right. He should have made himself presentable before arriving on the lady's doorstep.

Well, perhaps he would, as Aunt Geneva had declared, send Miss Langley running back to Almack's at the sight of him.

"I'm Miss Langley," she said, pert nose rising slightly.

This was his betrothed? Since his grandfather had had a hand in all this, he'd expected some snaggle-toothed harridan or some mousy bit without a hint of color. Not one who'd answer the door wearing bright red socks.

"Miss *Felicity* Langley?" he probed. Certainly there had to be a mistake. His grandfather would never have chosen such a pretty chit. Breathtaking, really.

But to his shock, she nodded.

Fine. So this was Felicity Langley. He took a deep breath and consigned himself to the fact that while she hadn't the dental afflictions he'd imagined, given time she'd prove him correct about the harridan part.

"My apologies, miss," he said, bowing slightly, "I've come to—" But before he could say anything further, the lady found her tongue.

"Heavens, sir, what are you thinking?" she scolded. "Arriving at the front door? Hardly a recommendation, I daresay. Speaks more of your cheek than your experience." She paused for a moment and glanced at him, as if inspecting him for . . . well, he didn't know what. He'd never had a woman look at him in quite this way. Or scold him in such a fashion. At least not since he'd stopped wearing short coats.

Certainly he'd had his fair share of women casting glances in his direction, but this imperious Bath miss had the audacity of giving him a once over as if she were measuring him for a suit . . . or shackles.

"Now that we've settled the fact that I am Miss Langley," she was saying, "may I introduce my sister, Miss Thalia Langley."

Thatcher bowed slightly to the girl who thankfully still held her vermin of a dog, for he was wearing his only pair of boots. At least until Aunt Geneva could order up twenty or thirty new pairs. Enough to keep a room full of valets fully employed just with the task of polishing and shining them.

Miss Langley opened the door all the way, and eyed him again. "Are you coming in or are you going to stand there and let that draught chill the entire house?" One hand rested now on her hip and the other one pointed the way inside. "Or worse, you catch your death out there before we can come to some arrangement and I'll have to start this process all over."

Arrangement? Start this process all over? Well, there was arrogance if he'd ever heard it. She might be a pretty little thing, but he was beginning to see that she was also mad as Dick's hatband.

She huffed a sigh. "Now are you coming in or must I assume that you are as witless as the last one?"

He wasn't sure if it was the authority behind her order—er, request—or the draught of wind that blew up the street that finally propelled him into the house. "Yes, oh, so sorry," he said.

Then it struck him. *The last one?* Wait just a demmed moment. She had more than one ducal prospect?

And she had the nerve to call *him* cheeky?

Miss Langley closed the door, shivered, and drew her shawl tighter around her shoulders, then turned and led the way up the stairs. Her sister flashed him a saucy grin, while the oversized rat in her arms continued to look down at his boots with an eager eye. "Come along then," Miss Langley told him. "As you can see, we need your services."

His what?

But before he could ask her, she and her sister had already scurried up the flight of stairs. By the time he caught up with them, they'd turned down a narrow hall and entered a small parlor. The room was cozy, with a decidedly female air about it—a discarded basket of knitting, an open and forgotten novel on the floor near the grate. A small pile of coals glowed in the hearth, and off to one side sat a large overstuffed chair where an old lady snored most indelicately. Her lace cap sat askew and a lap robe lay on the floor at her feet.

Without missing a beat, Felicity set things to right. The book was closed—a bit of braided thread to mark the page—then the throw was settled back over the lady's lap, and she even had a moment to put a bit more coal on the fire.

"I hope Aunt Minty finds you acceptable," she said as she went about the routine tasks. "I'd wake her, but she likes a good doze this time of day, and bears no one any favors if they rouse her before she's ready." Dusting her hands off, she turned to him and sighed yet again, shaking her head as she went. "I suppose a good chaperone should be a bit more alert, but Aunt Minty is . . . well, she's quite perfect for us, for we are very aware of our tenuous circumstances and haven't the tendencies for romantic misalliances—"

"'Cept for our cousin Pippin," Miss Thalia added. "But you'll meet her later."

Her sister shot her twin another scathing look, and he took the interruption in this nonsensical conversation as his chance to wrestle some control over the situation. "Uh, yes, well, the point of my visit—"

In a flash, the chit outflanked him. "Oh yes, the point. Exactly," Miss Langley said, not even batting an eye over the fact that she had just cut him off. "Though I must say, you hardly look proper." She tipped her head and measured him yet again from the toes of his boots to the top of his head. There was another sigh and then she said, "I daresay the livery will be a tight fit."

Livery? He shook his head. Whatever was she talking about? She wanted him in livery? What sort of wanton nonsense was this?

"You look surprised. But yes, we have livery for you," she assured him. Not that he found it the least bit assuring.

"Nanny Jamilla always said a footman should be well-dressed," Miss Thalia added.

"A footman?" he stammered.

"Oh, dear," Miss Langley said. "They didn't hint that you may have the butler position, did they? I told them quite plainly we sought only a footman who could—"

He waved his hands at her. "Miss Langley, there's been some sort of—"

She didn't let him get any further. "Yes, of course, you would want the more elevated position, but we are such a small household, and really only temporary at that, so we could hardly employ a butler and a footman, now could we?"

She flashed him a smile that did something odd to his chest—left him a bit breathless and unable to jump into the opening she'd offered. Oh, this Miss Langley was an able opponent. As quickly as she'd feinted to the right, she closed ranks and turned in another direction. "You have some experience managing things, do you?"

Twelve years in Wellington's army. Commanding the 95th Rifles at Corunna, Badajoz, and Salamanca. Marches across Portugal and Spain with ill-trained, ill-fed men and having to find them not only the sustenance to keep them moving, but the bullets to keep them alive.

"Yes. A little," he answered wryly. "But Miss Langley, that hardly bears—"

"Well, of course it does," she told him. "We might be a small household—not by choice, mind you—but I am determined not to let anyone discover the truth of our situation . . ."

The truth of her situation? What the devil did that mean?

". . . and having a proper footman is one of the things that will put just the right outward appearance on things. Not that our circumstances will remain like this, I assure you. With the Season approaching, changes are afoot." She paused, but only briefly. "It is no secret that I will shortly be married to the Duke of Hollindrake—so yes, my sister and I, as well as our cousin, will not be living here for long, I daresay."

Care to place a wager on that? "Miss Langley, if you would but—"

"Please don't think our current situation will affect your position," she rushed to add. "We are quite solvent enough to afford your wages—though you look as if you could use some decent meals."

She reached over and pinched his arm. "Dear heavens, you are quite starved. Well, we will just have to see about that." She gave his sleeve a warm pat and smiled up at him.

The maneuver effectively disarmed every discordant

thought he'd been holding about her. For when she smiled, the lady looked like an angel, and her touch sent a shock of warmth through his limbs.

He struggled to fortify his position by remembering his carefully wrought speech.

Miss Langley, this betrothal was made without my knowledge and I find it impossible to—

Yes, yes. That was supposed to be how it was going.

So he opened his mouth and began, "Miss Langley, I believe there's been a—"

He was cut off yet again, but this time by the other Miss Langley. "Duchess, dearest, I fear he will never do."

"Duchess?" he managed. So she was already using the title? And without the benefit of marriage. The warmth from moments earlier fled in the face of this newest audacity.

She shook her head slightly. "I fear it is a childhood nickname. My sister still insists on using it."

Even worse. She'd been set in this course since infancy. He suddenly had an icy sort of premonition that it might take more than an ill-cut suit and a curt dismissal to rid himself of her.

In the meantime, she'd turned from him to her sister. "Whatever are you nattering on about?"

"He's too tall, Duchess. He'll never fit the livery."

Her hands went to her hips. "Of course he will." She slanted a glance back at him, sweeping her measure of him like an experienced tailor. "Well, it might be a tight fit."

There was his out. The livery wouldn't fit and he could be away from here. Then he'd order his grandfather's—nay, *his* secretary—to write Miss Langley a nice note of condolence and let her know that he'd gone completely and abruptly stark raving mad.

At least she could understand such a situation, since she seemed to be so afflicted.

But an ill-fitting livery turned out to be the least of his worries.

Miss Thalia set down her dog, which immediately renewed his acquaintance by sinking its teeth into his boots. Instead of retrieving him, the chit smiled and said, "You must love dogs."

Dogs, yes. Leather loving rats, no.

"Do you drink?" she asked, circling around him.

"Excuse me?" he stammered, shaking his boot to no avail.

"I asked if you drink. Do you have a fondness for spirits? More specifically, large quantities of brandy?" She gazed up at him, wide blue eyes very much like her sister's.

"I do not drink brandy," he replied. But he was beginning to think he should start.

Both the girls heaved a sigh, and Miss Langley rushed to explain. "I fear our cook is a bit of a tippler and we can barely afford her habits, let alone if you were inclined to partake."

"Miss, I can assure you that I have no intention of—"

"Excellent!" she declared, clapping her hands together. "Now with that settled we can get on with more important matters."

Settled? Nothing had been settled. Why, they hadn't even got to the point of his visit.

"I still don't think he can wear the livery," Miss Thalia remarked, her gaze once again raking over his body with a calculating eye. "It won't do to hire him if it doesn't fit."

"If you are so convinced, then go fetch it," her sister told her.

"I will," she shot back, turning on one heel and marching toward the door. She stopped for a second and turned around. In a flash she bent over and scooped up her dog, detaching the little brute from his boot. She glanced up at him. "You look terribly familiar. Have you been in service long?"

"Not long at all," he replied. "In fact—"

But the chit wasn't listening. She'd shrugged him off and was out a side door and off to fetch the now infamous ill-fitting livery. And with her, thankfully, went her dog.

Before she returned, he needed to rectify this entire mess, starting with straightening out Miss Langley as to *who* he was and *why* he was here.

That proved to be impossible.

"I suppose you'd like to know your duties around here," she was saying, settling down on a chair nearby.

"Duties? No, Miss Langley, I think I need to make something perfectly clear—"

"Miss Langley! Miss Langley, if you please," came a sharp, strident cry from somewhere in the bowels of the house.

"Oh, dear," she said, rising from her chair. Her shoulders straightened ever so slightly, and if he didn't know better, he'd say she was bracing for battle.

And so she was.

"Miss Langley!" This time the cry came with piercing clarity.

"In here, Mrs. Hutchinson," Miss Langley replied in an all-too-pleasant voice that belied the steel set to her spine. "Our housekeeper and cook," she said in an aside.

Ah yes, the aforementioned Mrs. Hutchinson. Of the brandy bottle fame. This was turning out to be quite a visit.

He hadn't realized how much so until he met her.

Mrs. Hutchinson was a tall, lithe woman, with dark auburn hair and sharp eyes. If she had a fondness for drink, it wasn't obvious. "Well, Miss Langley, that grocer fellow is downstairs. Full of cheek over his bill and all. Badgering me like I keep the purse strings. What should I tell him?"

Miss Langley shot him an apologetic glance, and stepped between him and the housekeeper. Lowering her voice, she advised the woman, "Tell him that our solicitor, Mr. Elliott, handles all those matters."

"Harrumph. Used that one last week and it won't do no better this week than it did then." She shot a glance over her mistress's slim shoulder. "And who's this?"

"The new footman," Miss Langley told her, obviously happy to change the subject.

Another loud *harrumph* followed. "Not much to him," she said, maneuvering herself closer and reaching out to take a hold of his arm.

Thatcher was starting to feel an affinity for the horses over at Tatt's.

The housekeeper sniffed and gave him one more pinch. "More meat on 'em than it appears, but still, he'll need feeding up a bit." She cast a glance over him as if she too was measuring him, then looked at the side of his head where the line of a scar still remained. "In the army, were you?"

He was so startled by this astute observation, he could only nod.

"Thought so. Got that 'hungry, ain't been fed since I left home' sort of look. Well, I've got a good kitchen, when the grocer ain't badgering me, and we can use the help around here. But there will be no cheek in my kitchen, do you hear me? No pinching my arse when you think I'm not looking, no chasing after my Sally, or I'll show you the business end of a cleaver, I will."

"Madame, I have no desire to—"

"Madame, he says." Mrs. Hutchinson snorted. "Nice manners, but just see that you don't."

"I have no intention of pinching you or your Sally," he said quite honestly.

"Harrumph! Mind that you don't. Then again, iffen you had the brains the good Lord gave a goat, you'd skiddle out of this asylum as fast as you can."

"Mrs. Hutchinson!" sputtered Miss Langley.

"Just giving the poor man a bit of advice, miss," she huffed. "'Sides, he knows I'm teasing." And when Felicity turned away, the lady shook her head and jerked her thumb toward the door.

"I found it," came Miss Thalia's triumphant cry as she re-entered the room, the aptly named Brutus at her heels. The mongrel reattached itself to his boot with a determined snap of his teeth.

When no one else noticed his predicament, the ladies busy laying out the livery, he bent over to pluck the determined canine off his boot. The dog growled and snapped at this interruption to his afternoon snack.

"Oh, look at you!" Miss Thalia declared. "Making friends with Brutus. Aren't you a dear man."

If she'd known what he was thinking—that the dog would most likely solve their problems with the grocer—she might not have been so effusive.

Miss Langley, on the other hand, had unfolded the silver trimmed jacket and was holding it up to survey it.

"What happened to the other footman?" he asked, having no doubt he could find the man happily ensconced in Bedlam.

"There was no other footman," Miss Langley said as she shook out the jacket.

"And this livery?" he asked, suspiciously regarding the jacket the pair of them looked determined to shove onto him with nothing less than suspicion.

"Was our father's."

He shook his head. "Your father was in service?"

"Heavens no," Miss Langley said, "a diplomat. 'Twas a costume he had made while he was assigned to the Russian court."

"No, Duchess," her sister argued. "'Twas Nanny Jamilla who had it made for him when we were in France."

"Whyever would Nanny Jamilla want Father to dress up like a footman?"

"I daresay it was a jest. You know how she liked to tease him–and she did have a fondness for footmen."

Miss Langley snapped her fingers. "Yes, now I remember. You are right. I distinctly recall Father being such a good sport about it."

Both girls nodded as if that made perfect sense, while Thatcher regarded the costume with newfound horror. They might not understand, but he had some idea what this Nanny Jamilla had in mind when she'd commissioned this faux livery.

"I daresay it seemed a waste not to put it into use," Miss Langley told him.

Practical, and insane to boot. But he rather suspected this livery had been put into service—just not the kind these two minxes intended.

Then in a flash, before he could protest, his coat was tugged from his back, along with the jacket beneath it, and the used-only-once livery with the silver trim shoved up into place.

Thankfully, Lord Langley wasn't a small man, for the jacket fit, mostly—the chest was a bit tight, but he could still breathe.

Miss Langley stepped back and surveyed her work. "Yes, yes, indeed. You almost look a proper footman." She went over to a desk and dug into a cubby. The jingle of coins echoed through the room as she returned. Gathering up his hand, she dropped a few pennies into his palm. "Please see about having your hair trimmed and obtaining a decent razor, and with that done, I think we'll all get along splendidly."

What about new boots? he almost asked, as he found himself being skillfully propelled out of the room and down the hall. "But Miss Langley, I don't think—"

"I'm sure we can settle any questions you might have in the coming days," she said quite blithely, as Brutus rose to assist her by nipping at his heels and herding him down the stairs like a hapless sheep.

He'd been routed by the French with less efficiency.

"Do you have lodgings?" she asked as they turned on the landing.

"Uh, yes," he replied, hurrying along before their infernal dog could claim his heel for a souvenir.

"Excellent. For we can't have you live in as yet." She waved her hand around the foyer, which he'd failed to notice before was devoid of decoration and furniture. With a not-so-subtle shove, his coat and hat and jacket were returned to him and he was maneuvered out the front door. "I fear the house wasn't as well-furnished as we were led to believe when we took it. But it is convenient to the square," she said, nodding toward the corner, around which sat Grosvenor Square.

And Hollindrake House.

Why, the chit had deliberately encamped within firing range of his home. He was of half a mind to move. Not that he could right this moment, not with Brutus having found a firm grip on his boot. Again.

He gave the dog a shake, but there was no removing the determined mutt.

Miss Langley flinched and shot him an apologetic glance, even as she reached down and retrieved her sister's pet. "I'm sorry about Brutus. I hope he doesn't deter you, Mister . . . Mister—" She stopped and glanced up at him, a stray strand of hair having fallen loose and curling at her shoulder.

That pair of wide blue eyes stopped him. They held an unexpected surprise to them, like a patch of bluebells adrift in a lonely wooded grove. And for a moment, she made him stop in wonder and try to figure out how on earth they'd come to this unexpected, unintended moment.

Her lips pursed, like a woman did just before she offered herself up for a kiss . . . or more. And those eyes, those extraordinary blue eyes, called to him, called to some unknown part of his heart that he didn't even know he possessed.

He could see her suddenly, tumbling backward onto the great bed in Hollindrake House wearing nothing but the duchess's coronet and those eyes looking up at him with longing, with needs she wanted only him to claim. To conquer.

But her fair lashes fluttered and she stammered again, "I hope Brutus doesn't stop you from helping us, sir. You will help us, won't you?"

Her question snaked right through his newfound livery and into his chest. It left him breathless and unsteady and wondering what the hell had just happened.

"Yes, well, Miss Langley . . ." he replied, without even realizing what he was saying. Try as he might, he couldn't quite shake off the vestiges of whatever she'd just done to him as she began to close the door in his face.

And then it struck him. The chit had beguiled him into—

"Oh, dear," she said, opening it up again. "I forgot to ask you one thing."

"What is that?" he asked, taking a cautious peek at her.

The hands were fisted on her hips again. "Your name, sir. Whatever am I to call you?"

Chapter 2

I know you asked to hear more about my school, yet I have to believe you are being more polite than truly curious. But since you professed an interest, I will say with all honesty life at Miss Emery's is a dreadful trial. The dear lady, who is purported to have groomed some of the finest ladies in Society, must be suffering from an early form of dementia, for last year she admitted an impossible girl. An American, of all things! I suppose we all have our crosses to bear, and I fear mine is Miss Sarah Browne, a most odious creature who just last week . . .

—An extract from a letter to the Marquess of Standon from Miss Felicity Langley, November 1810

"Gracious heavens! Listen to this, Staines." Lady Geneva Pensford pointed down at the paper unfolded on the table before her. "Lady Bellinger was accosted on the Thames. How terrible for poor Winifred."

"Disgraceful," the poised butler replied as he refilled the lady's cup with a steaming and fragrant pekoe.

"On the Thames?" Thatcher asked from the doorway of the opulent dining room. With a flick of a glance he took in the trays overflowing with breakfast delights, and the abundance of liveried footmen standing poised and waiting for the slightest indication that their services were needed—even though the only two people currently living in the splendid Hollindrake mansion were himself and his aunt, Lady Geneva. "Pray tell, however was Lady Bellinger accosted *on* the Thames?"

"Why, you are up far too early, Your Grace," his aunt replied from the far end of the long dining room table, a place she had sat at for as long as Thatcher could remember. In an elegant pink day gown, with her red hair still untouched by gray and done up in a formal knot, she looked the perfectly fashionable lady. She had taken after her mother's side of the family, much to the old duke's chagrin, but Geneva had made up for her lack of dark hair and eyes by perfecting the Sterling stare and being the Sterlingest of all the family. And right now she was giving him her most elevated look of disapproval. "Yes, you are up too early. Especially when Staines informs me you didn't return home until an unseemly hour. Whatever were you doing out so late?"

"Staines, you old dog!" Thatcher said, nodding to the family butler. "I would have thought you had gotten too old to carry tales to my aunt." As for Geneva, she wasn't the only one who could pin someone with a glance. "As to my whereabouts, madame, and the hour of my return, do you really want me to tell you?"

"No," she replied, adjusting her napkin. "But really, Your Grace, I do hope you don't intend to take up with your old friends and spend your hours idling about those horrid haunts of theirs."

He laughed, for that was exactly what he'd done when he left Miss Langley's. He'd gone off in search of any of his old friends—Mad Jack Tremont, Temple, even Lord Stewart Hodges would have been welcome company. But all his "horrid haunts" were either shuttered and closed or filled with young cubs and loungers he didn't recognize. And he'd realized in an instant he was far too old to join their youthful company.

Truly, his only bright spot the entire day had been those fifteen minutes in Miss Langley's madcap company.

Miss Langley. Answering her own door. In red socks, no less! He'd spent most of the evening trying to fathom how this blindingly pretty chit could be the woman his grandfather had chosen. Living in a nearly empty house, with a sleepy chaperone and a dog his troops would have viewed as a nice treat with tea.

He even considered that he'd called on the wrong Miss Langley, and would still be dwelling on such a reassuring notion if the scent of bacon wasn't tickling his senses. Taking a glance at the overladen buffet, he happily ambled down the long table until he reached the chair opposite Geneva's.

When he went to settle into it, she arched a brow and tipped her head down toward the other end, where a footman stood beside his grandfather's chair at the head of the table.

His chair now.

Oh, no. He wasn't ready yet. Couldn't he just put this off for a few more days . . . until he got used to the notion that his life—and freedom—were over?

"Your Grace," she said, "Staines has already set your place."

"Aunt Geneva, please call me Thatcher. Everyone else does."

"I shall not. Now take your place, Your Grace," she said, scolding him as she had when he'd been the child no one would have ever thought stood to inherit the dukedom.

"I won't sit down there all alone," he told her, folding his arms over his chest.

"Don't be so stubborn. It is your chair. Yours whether you want it or not."

Not. Life had been much simpler when he'd been merely Mr. Aubrey Sterling and his uncles, father, and elder brothers all stood between him and the esteemed title of Hollindrake.

But even if he had told her so, she wouldn't have heard him anyway, for she was still nattering on. ". . . you simply must sit there. Otherwise the servants will talk."

He eyed the distance between the ducal throne, because that's what it was in comparison to the other chairs around the table, and her chair. "I'll have to shout at you just to converse."

"I'm quite used to it," she replied, taking a sip from her tea. "Father quite adored bellowing at all of us down here below the salt."

"I'll go only if you come with me," he insisted, holding his ground.

She took a deep breath, then rose. "Staines," she said, addressing their butler, "His Grace would like to make some changes to the seating arrangements for breakfast."

"Yes, my lady, Your Grace," the man replied, his lips pursed with displeasure.

Lady Geneva walked down the long row of chairs with the air of an early Christian martyr. Had she been born a Papist, he suspected she'd be a saint by now.

"So now that we have all that settled," he said. "Do explain poor Lady Bellinger's predicament."

"Not until you tell me how you left Miss Langley. Is the poor dear broken-hearted?"

He shook his head. "Ducal privilege. You have to tell me first."

"Well, if you hadn't been in such an ill humor yesterday and had come home early enough to dine with me," she replied, adjusting to her new chair and position at the table, "you would know that the Thames has frozen quite solid. Has been for over a week now."

"Like it was in '95?" he asked, remembering his boyhood joy at such an event.

"Yes, I daresay like it was then," she replied. "A regular country fair—food stalls, trinkets, all sorts of entertainments, merchants ready to separate you from your coins. Why, they've even got a printing press down there and you can have your name printed on a pretty little engraving of it all." She paused as she glanced over at his coat, having finally taken in the costume he'd chosen for today, and her brows furrowed. "Everyone is mad to go," she finished, her gaze still fixed on his choice of jackets.

"Have you?" he asked, ignoring her inquisitive glance.

"Of course," she replied, straightening in her seat. "Though the company is quite rough. Certainly not someplace you would go without a proper escort."

"And who did you go with?" he asked. "Apparently not your husband, since you are still living here. By the way, how is Pensford these days?"

"Don't be so rude," she replied. "You know very well that subject isn't spoken of in this house."

So the subject of Aunt Geneva's scandalous marriage was still taboo. He wanted to point out that while that rule had been his grandfather's edict, this was now *his* house, and the subject could damn well be broached whether she liked it or not. Then again, the last thing he needed was his aunt getting her petticoats in a bunch and deciding to move out. Leaving the job of hostess wide open for say . . . someone else . . . like his mother.

Thatcher shuddered, realizing that perhaps they both had plights that were best left unbroached.

Meanwhile, Aunt Geneva sat waiting, her hands folded primly before her. "Now tell me about your visit to Miss Langley. I daresay she's probably seen fit to leave Town by now." Much to his surprise, she sounded quite worried at the prospect. Then he discovered why. "I do hope you didn't leave her in a state of decline. I don't want to see her name listed in the obituaries next month."

Of course. Such a thing would put a blight on their good name, and the one thing a Sterling never did was bring scandal down upon their family's golden reputation. With the possible exception having been him.

Aunt Geneva sighed. "Still, I suppose she was quite undone by her loss."

Thatcher glanced up from the laden plate that had just been put before him. "Hardly. When I left her, I do believe she was quite elated. She offered me a fine salary for my troubles."

She paused, her teacup halfway to her lips. "A salary? To be her husband?"

"No. To be her new footman." He paused and waited and then it came.

Geneva coughed and sputtered, nearly dropping the Wedgwood piece. "Her what?"

"You heard me perfectly," he replied. "I am Miss Langley's new footman."

Aunt Geneva laughed. "And here I thought the army had tamed that wretched sense of humor of yours. Truly, Your Grace, now that you've inherited, you need to remember who you are." She glanced over at Staines and shook her head, as if to signal to the man that His Grace wasn't truly a footman, nor mad, like the fourth duke had been rumored to be.

"'Tis no joke. This is the Langley livery." He held out his arm and smoothed his hand over the sleeve. "I fear the jacket is a little snug in the shoulders. Do you think Weston could do the alterations?"

"I think not!" she declared.

Probably also wouldn't do to let his aunt know about the jacket's rather questionable past. So instead he tucked back into his breakfast, happily chewing a large bite of ham.

"The Langley livery, indeed!" Geneva huffed. "Now tell

me what happened yesterday, and none of this falderal about footmen and livery."

"But it isn't falderal," he told her. "Miss Langley mistook me for some fellow an agency was sending over." He tried the bacon and found it to be perfect. Mrs. Hutchinson had been right about one thing—it had been a while since he'd had a good and filling meal. "Apparently you were right about me calling on her before I'd had a chance to change into something more . . . more . . ."

"Respectable? Fitting of your station?" his aunt suggested. "Your Grace, tell me you are joking about all this."

"I fear not," he told her, taking another bite of bacon.

"But Your Grace, this is ruinous. I warned you something like this would happen."

"So you did, and it has, but I don't see anything ruinous about it," he said, slathering a large helping of marmalade on his toast. "There might be a bit of a dustup, some good laughs at my expense, but I hardly see it worth this Cheltenham tragedy of yours."

"Have you thought for a moment how this will reflect on Miss Langley?" *Hence on us*, her words implied.

He glanced up. "Miss Langley? What has this to do with her? I was the one who looked like a regular beggar."

Aunt Geneva drew a deep breath. "Why, her name will be cast about in the most unflattering of manner. She'll be ruined."

"Really, Aunt Geneva, ruined?

"Utterly, Your Grace! You must go over there as soon as you are properly outfitted and set matters to right."

He waved his hand at her. "There is no need to wait for the tailor to make me decent, I must have some old togs around here somewhere in the attic. Besides, if you must know, I had every intention of going over this morning and setting matters to right, as you say."

"Good," Aunt Geneva announced. "'Tis best settled quickly. What Father was thinking when he encouraged that girl, I know not. The Langleys are hardly good *ton*." This was punctuated with a very disapproving sniff.

That his aunt looked askance at Miss Langley actually gained the chit some small favor in his mind. He'd always found the people Aunt Geneva disliked, well, interesting. And there was no arguing the point . . . Felicity Langley *was* interesting.

"And once we have this distasteful matter finished," she was saying, "we can get to the business of finding you a proper bride. I've gone to the liberty of drawing up a list of likely candidates, and I think you'll discover—"

"Aunt Geneva, I have no intention of getting married," he told her. "These bumble-brained chits they pass off in London society hold no interest for me." Empty conversations, worries about the latest fashions, or whether or not one possessed the latest *on dit*. He shuddered at the very idea of spending the rest of his life listening to such mindless prattle.

She sniffed and waved a hand at him. "You'll have your choice of brides, any woman you want. Why, they'll be lined up around the square before the end of the week."

"Yes, because they want the title," he shot back.

"So? Whatever is wrong with that? In the end, the choice is yours."

Still, even that concession didn't set well. Pick of the litter might seem a boon to some, but they were still all mewling kittens with sharp claws in his estimation.

"Your Grace, you must marry," Aunt Geneva persisted. "You are the last of the Sterlings."

"Nonsense. Isn't there that second cousin, old Bertie's boy, who's next in line?"

"Tristam?" Her regal brow furrowed.

"Yes, that's the fellow. He'll produce an heir or so and leave me to my peace."

She threw up her hands. "That will never happen. The man is most unsuitable."

"More than me? I find that hard to believe." Thatcher had been the family's black sheep for so long, he hadn't considered that there could be someone more inappropriate to inherit. "Go find him a likely bride—that ought to do the trick."

He dug back into his breakfast, which was steadily growing cold. Perhaps there was a reason beyond her ill-conceived marriage that had resulted in Aunt Geneva's banishment to the end of the table.

Like not letting the old duke finish his breakfast in peace.

"We can gain him whatever bride you want, but she'll never bear a child," his aunt told him.

"Whyever not?" he asked against his better judgment.

"Suffice it to say he is incapable of providing the line with an heir."

"An accident of some sort? Or is he just too shy around the fairer sex?" Thatcher reached over and added several lumps of sugar to his coffee. "If he's a bit of wallflower, I can fix that—I'll send him out with my old friend Tremont, or perhaps Temple, they ought to be able to introduce him to the sort of—"

"Your Grace," she said through gritted teeth, "it is nothing that your old rabble can cure," she said, heaving a sigh and then dropping her voice to a low whisper. "His inclinations tend elsewhere."

Thatcher shook his head and stared at her.

"Oh, must I spell it out?"

"Apparently so," he told her. "Especially since it means the difference in me having to marry or not."

"Your heir apparent prefers men over women."

"Oh."

"Quite so," she replied, wiping her lips with her napkin and setting it aside.

"That puts an entirely new wrinkle on all this," he admitted.

"Yes, and it was most likely why Father agreed to your alliance with Miss Langley. But since you've decided against her—which is for the best, considering her entirely inappropriate lineage—"

"Aunt Geneva, if she is so improper, whyever would the duke have chosen her?"

"How am I to know?" she declared. "I begged him to end their correspondence, but he would not listen to reason. Why, when one of her letters arrived, he and Gibbens would closet themselves away for days composing an answer."

This took Thatcher aback.

Whatever could Miss Langley have written that had turned his gruff and unruffled grandfather into some sort of quixotic Byron? Now he wished he had taken Gibbens up on the offer to read them. No, instead he'd been in such a hell-fire rage over the discovery that he was all but betrothed, he'd ridden from Bythorne Castle, leaving the man to follow in the carriage.

Which would most likely take another three, probably four, days to reach London, what with the entire country buried in snow.

Aunt Geneva, meanwhile, was doing her Sterling best to orchestrate his new life. Given that the old duke was gone, she obviously felt it her duty to move him about the family chessboard. ". . . then I suggest we throw a ball—after the Setchfields' masquerade, of course. Yes, that is perfect. It would give you the opportunity to find . . ."

He heaved a sigh and let her plan away until her final words pierced his thoughts.

". . . I suppose it would be best that I go with you this morning, to ensure that there is no lasting damage to Miss Langley's reputation."

Thatcher dropped his fork and waved his hands at his aunt. "Oh, no, you don't. I think I can handle this matter without all the falderal you'll add to it. Miss Langley's reputation is safe enough. Besides, that responsibility hardly lands on my plate, I'd say the chit's father should bear some of the duty—he's the one who's let those harebrained girls loose on London."

"Their father?"

"Yes, Lord Langley. Isn't he in service to the King? A diplomat, if I remember correctly."

"*Was* in the service," she replied.

"He's here in England, then?" he asked. "Really, the man should do a better job of minding his daughters."

"My dear boy, Lord Langley isn't keeping an eye on his daughters because he's dead."

The new footman was late.

"Oh, whatever was I thinking, hiring that man," Felicity muttered as she checked her pocket watch for the third time.

"Worse yet," Tally complained as she bundled her cloak tighter around her shoulders, "you gave that Mr. Thatcher our only set of livery."

"And three pence to get his hair cut," she admitted.

They stood on the front steps of their house, awaiting Pippin and Aunt Minty to join them. Felicity had finally consented to a trip down to the Thames to view the frozen river, but only because they now had a footman to escort them.

A footman who was two hours late to work, she mused. Not a very good recommendation for the fellow. Not to mention the fact that the carriage Pippin's brother promised them had yet to arrive as well.

"I wonder if Mr. Thatcher pawned our suit to fund some nefarious deeds," Tally muttered, more to herself, and Felicity knew her twin well enough to realize when she was starting another of her epic novels. "Do you think our footman is suffering from his time at war, like Mrs. Hutchinson said he might be? I wager he spent the night gambling excessively and drinking heavily to forget the horrors he's seen."

"On our livery and three pence? It would have been a short and dull evening, indeed."

Tally ignored her, having paused to take a swipe at her red nose, but also, Felicity knew, to give herself time to compose her next outrageous conclusions about the poor man. "Perhaps he has a mistress he is trying to keep in diamonds."

Felicity blanched. "Really, Tally," she scolded. "The man's coat was patched, his boots nearly worn through. A mistress? Wherever do you get such notions?"

Tally shrugged and sighed. "Well, he's handsome enough to have a mistress. Diamonds or not. Didn't you think him very handsome? Despite that scar, I mean. Do you think he got that from a knife or a saber? Whichever it is, he is still handsome enough."

Well used to Tally's rambling dissertations on whatever subject currently held her fancy, Felicity shook her head. "Handsome? Such a ridiculous notion. He is far too unkempt. And besides, he is a *footman*." She glanced up the block again. "And not a very good one."

"If you let him live in, we wouldn't have this problem."

"Live in? Are you mad?" She shook her head. "No, we must keep an extremely respectable household, and having a man who looks like that would only give rise to unseemly talk."

Tally grinned, rocking back on her heels. "So you *do* think he's handsome."

She flinched. *Botheration. Not just handsome. Too handsome.* Felicity tugged at her mittens and glanced again down Brook Street. The empty block left her unsettled for reasons she couldn't comprehend.

Well, it was of no matter if they never saw the too-handsome-for-his-own-good Mr. Thatcher again, she told herself. What had the agency been thinking sending him over? She had specifically requested they find an average sort of fellow who was too old to inspire any foolishness.

"It doesn't matter what he looks like," she told her sister. "When he arrives, I intend to send him packing."

"No, Duchess! You mustn't!" Tally protested. "However can we go down to the fair without him? Let him escort us to the river, and then sack him tomorrow. I so want to see this Frost Fair."

Felicity drew up her shoulders into a taut line. "We can't do that."

"Whyever not?"

"Because then I would have to pay him," she whispered, even though there was no one around to hear.

Tally heaved a sigh. "Oh, there is that." She glanced back at the door to see if perhaps there was any sign of Aunt Minty or Pippin yet. "How long do you think he'll continue with us once he discovers we haven't the money to pay him?"

"With any luck, long enough for me to secure Hollindrake," Felicity replied. That was why they had come to London, leaving behind the little cottage that Pippin's mother had left her and pooling all their funds to stage this Season. She'd known that Hollindrake would have to come to London for the opening of Parliament, if only to take his seat in the House of Lords. And she'd been bound and determined on being there to make sure no other debutante interfered with her carefully planned, and now all-too-tenuous, courtship.

Behind them the door finally opened and Aunt Minty and Pippin made their late appearance.

The old woman shivered and screwed her wrinkled face into a moue of protest. "Blasted hell! What are you gels trying to do? Freeze my arse off with this sammy idea?"

"Dear Aunt Minty," Felicity said, trying to sound as sincere as possible, "would you mind curbing your tongue? Someone might hear you and think less of you as our esteemed chaperone."

"They won't think much of me when they find me in the spring, still trying to thaw me garters off."

Pippin leaned over. "Aunt Minty, ladies don't mention their . . . well, unmentionables."

"They don't?" the lady asked, her eyes now wide open. "And why the bloody not? They wear them, don't they?"

"Please," Felicity said, now resorting to outright begging, "Aunt Aramintha, remember who and what you are. This is Mayfair, and we are all ladies of good breeding." *Well, three of us are.* "And as such, we don't use the words 'bloody,' 'arse,' or mention anything beneath one's gown."

Tally reached out and took the lady's hand, patting her thick, red woolen mitt. "I'll teach you some lovely phrases in Russian, Aunt Minty. They'll do the trick when you find yourself at a loss for proper words. Besides which, everyone will think you quite in the pink for being so Continental."

The lady's nut brown eyes sparkled at such an offer, and so she nodded her agreement to Felicity. If there was one thing Aunt Minty loved, it was a good bit of profanity.

"Besides," Tally added, "I don't think we're going to the Frost Fair today, since neither the carriage nor our new footman have deigned to show up, and the Duchess intends to send him packing when he does arrive."

"Who—the driver or the footman?" Pippin asked. "For I doubt you can fire poor Mr. Stillings, since he has been in our family for more than thirty years."

"I have no intention of sacking Mr. Stillings. It is that Mr. Thatcher I intend to dismiss. He is entirely unsuitable, never mind his obvious disregard for punctuality. Besides, there is such a thing as a man who is too handsome for his own—" Felicity's blustering came to a sudden halt when she spied the sly smile on Pippin's lips.

"And I say we keep Mr. Thatcher," her cousin said, "if he does deign to return. He has you in a fluster, and that is a good thing."

"I am in no such state. And certainly not over a footman!" Felicity crossed her arms over her chest. Why, she had never heard such nonsense!

"He was a looker, that one," Aunt Minty declared. Apparently she hadn't been as asleep as she appeared. "Seems a shame to send him packing. Thought he might be something nice to take a gander at when he came in to tend the fires and such."

"Aunt Minty!" all three girls said.

The old woman shrugged. "I ain't blind. And I ain't dead. I've had me fair share of fellows in my life, and I tell you the handsome ones always had a way about them. I remember a highwayman who used to come around the inn from time to time. Now what was his name? Gentleman, he was, and that was all that mattered. He had a way about him, he did. When he was to cast an eye in yer direction, there was little chance you'd be saying no."

Felicity closed her eyes and rubbed her brow. "Oh, heavens, Aunt Minty, this is exactly what I was saying before! You mustn't say such things. If anyone was to find out that you are—"

"Good God!" Tally said, adding a curse in Russian that brought Felicity's gaze up. "Look who's coming down the street!"

Felicity glanced up and her gaze landed on the tall, solitary man strolling toward them. There was something so commanding about his gait, the set of his shoulders, the tip of his hat, that she found herself mesmerized, much as she had been yesterday when he came to their door seeking employment.

Thatcher. The man had to be some nobleman's by-blow, for if you didn't know better, you might mistake his hawkish visage, Roman features, and height for that of a baron or even a viscount.

"That isn't who I think it is?" Pippin was saying, squinting her eyes to get a better look.

"It is," Felicity muttered. "Mr. Thatcher, our new footman. And carrying our livery, I might add."

"No, no, Duchess," Tally said, tugging at Felicity's elbow and pointing in the opposite direction. "There."

Felicity turned around and instantly her heart sank.

There was no mistaking the lady in the grand carriage approaching, despite the thick stack of blankets and bundles of furs. Miss Sarah Browne rode forth like the Queen herself, being drawn by four matched white horses.

"Only that pretentious American would ride about in the middle of winter in an open carriage so all could see her new hat and gown," Tally declared, though there was no missing the note of envy in her words.

"Whatever is she doing in London?" Felicity whispered. "I thought she'd gone back home for good."

"Well, she's here now, so you'd best fortify yourself, Duchess," Tally said, reaching over and squeezing her sister's hand. "We could always let slip to Temple that we suspect her of spying for the Americans."

Felicity shook her head. "Wouldn't work. No one would ever think her smart enough to carry out such a deception." Especially not their good family friend, Temple, now the Duke of Setchfield, whose connections with the Foreign Office went all the way to the top. "Still, we must be cautious, for what she lacks in intelligence, she more than makes up for in sheer spite, and if she discovers a hint of what we've done, well . . ."

"I don't see that you've done all that much—"Aunt Minty began.

"Not a word!" Felicity shook her finger at the woman. "Not one word out of you or you'll find yourself back in—"

"Miss Langley, I must speak to you," came the deep voice that sent a tremble down her spine.

Thatcher! Oh, the devil take the man and his now inconvenient arrival! How had she forgotten him? But now that he stood towering beside her, he was impossible to ignore.

When she turned to face him, the same deep fluster that afflicted her yesterday arose anew, leaving her once again tongue-tied. She didn't know what had her more unnerved by him—those dark eyes, or the expanse of his chest. Why, the man was like a mountain, so tall and sure of himself. And while Felicity never lacked for confidence or words, this man, this footman, left her, as Pippin had so astutely pointed out, completely flustered.

"Miss Langley," he said, tipping his head down to look at her. "Are you well?"

"Yes, of course I am," she snapped back, immediately wishing she could recall the words. "It's just that—"

"Stop the carriage! Stop it immediately!" Miss Browne was calling to her driver.

Felicity's gaze jerked in that direction and her only thought was that this entire scenario could have only been made worse if Hollindrake himself was to arrive and witness her impending humiliation.

"Miss Langley, if I could have a minute of your time, I really must—"

"Not now, sir!" Felicity glanced over him. She conveniently set aside the fact that she'd planned on sacking him, because suddenly he was a valuable asset. "Why aren't you wearing your livery?" she asked, pointing at the jacket in his hands. "And your hair, sir? Would it have been so much trouble to have it trimmed, like I asked? Well, at least you're clean-shaven—for the most part. I daresay we'll be able to brazen this out once you're wearing your livery."

"Miss Langley," he repeated, "I really must speak to you. Privately."

"Can't you see that I am in the midst of a social crisis?" she told him. "That woman could ruin me."

His gaze turned up and eyed the approaching carriage.

"But she appears to be quite friendly. Why, even delighted to see you."

"Like a hungry she-wolf," Felicity shot back. "If she discovers the truth, finds out what we've done—"

He straightened, his dark eyes now narrow gleaming slits. "What have you done?"

"That is hardly any of your concern, sir," she replied, growing rather impatient with his overly familiar air. "Please, I need to think, I need to figure out how best to send her packing before she finds a way to ruin everything." Then she turned an eye toward him, her gaze landing on the livery in his hands. "Mr. Thatcher, why are you still wearing your coat?"

"Because it is the middle of winter," he replied, thick, muscled arms crossing firmly over his chest.

"What has the weather got to do with this? Take it off, right this minute. That is an order."

Chapter 3

John Robert Bruwin, Marquess of Herrick
b. 1774
Current Residence: London and Herrick House, Kent

A most excellent candidate who is said to possess a fortune
of twenty thousand a year. Has properties in three counties,
connected to nearly every first family in society. Known to
have exquisite taste in horses, fashion, and architecture. In
other words, a perfect gentleman.

Addendum, 23 March 1812: betrothal announcement in
the Times. To Miss Sarah Browne. Disregard above note
about his exquisite taste.

Addendum, 7 July 1812: notice in the Times of Lord
Herrick's sudden death last week when his horse threw him.
Disregard note about good taste in horses and send Miss
Browne a sincere note of condolence.

—An excerpt from the Bachelor Chronicles

Take off his coat? Obviously Miss Langley had failed to notice that it was snowing. Or she was simply mad.

Never mind. One look at the wild light in her eyes and Thatcher knew the answer to his question. "Miss Langley, I will not—"

His protest fell on deaf ears, for suddenly he found his topcoat being yanked off, his jacket following, and the livery he'd been carrying tugged up onto him.

"Help me, Pippin," the impossible little chit was saying. "This coat is devilishly tight."

For the second time in less than a day he wished that Lord Langley had been a bit larger in the chest, because right now he couldn't breathe—but perhaps it was the fact that Miss Langley's fingers were rifling up his chest as she frantically worked the buttons.

As the two ladies set to work getting the coat on, Felicity made a hasty introduction. "Mr. Thatcher, this is my cousin, Lady Philippa Knolles. Pippin, this is our new footman."

This Pippin, like the Langley sisters, was fair and blue-eyed, but taller, with a reserve about her that her cousins would never be able to claim.

"Nice to meet you," Lady Philippa said, slanting him a bemused glance as Miss Langley pushed her cousin away so she could finish the task to her liking.

He couldn't remember a woman ever doing such a simple thing as buttoning his coat. And yet while Miss Langley worked with the efficiency and speed of the finest valet, her proximity left him reeling, for to stand so close to her was to catch a whiff of her perfume—a sensual, romantic scent that held more promise than a chit of perhaps twenty should ever know. To have her hands roaming over him with such abandon was to also feel the heat of her breath on this frosty day reach through the starch of his linen shirt and tease his skin. This close, he couldn't avoid spying the pink of her cheeks and a wisp of hair escaping the prison of her bonnet, leaving him to wonder what the rest of her would look like, freed from the confines of her proper dress.

This beguiling creature couldn't be the woman his grandfather had chosen for him. It was impossible.

And there was one other plaguing question. What the devil had she meant by *finds out what we've done*?

Really, what could a former Bath miss have done to inspire such a panic?

"Please, sir," she whispered. "If you could just be a footman, a silent one, for the next few minutes, I would be ever so grateful."

He had told his aunt the truth, that he was coming over here to set the record straight with Miss Langley, but the plaintive glance in those blue eyes turned out to be his downfall.

"I can try," he replied. Really, what would it hurt to continue the deception for a few minutes longer? Besides, there was another piece to this coil: If their father was dead, who was watching over the Langley sisters?

Not that he cared. Not that it was any of his concern.

"There," she said, patting his chest and tossing him one of those devastating little smiles of hers. "You almost look proper now."

"Almost?" he managed to say, wishing he could look away from the starry depths of her blue eyes.

She sighed, a bit more color to her cheeks than the crisp weather could be blamed for. "I fear, Thatcher, you will never be a proper footman."

He didn't know whether to be insulted or relieved. Not that there was much that was proper, he had to imagine, about Miss Felicity Langley. And to his shock, that part of her intrigued him.

More than he cared to admit.

Meanwhile, Miss Langley had turned to face her adversary with a stance that would have impressed Wellington. And the closer the carriage got to her, the straighter the line one could have drawn across her shoulders.

"Who is she?" he asked, ignoring the fact he was supposed to be an anonymous, and more importantly, silent, servant.

"Miss Sarah Browne," Felicity shot back, even as she pasted a smile on her face. "We went to school with her. Wretched, horrible girl. *American*." She emphasized the last word as if it explained everything.

"She's quite the bird, isn't she," Aunt Minty said, her eyes squinting to catch a better sight of the carriage and its occupants. "Got more money than sense."

"Unfortunately so," Miss Thalia muttered.

His aunt's voice echoed through his thoughts, *a proper bride*, someone like this Miss Browne, he had to imagine.

He glanced up at this chit and shuddered. She was everything he dreaded about London society. With dark hair and a fair complexion, she was pretty, but there was a predatory air about her that sent the hackles on his back rising.

"Oh, Mother, I told you! It is the Langley sisters and Lady Philippa! As I live and breathe, it is my dearest friends from Miss Emery's," Miss Browne gushed. Half rising in her seat, she waved her hand at them, a flowing gesture that swept from one side to the other.

Thatcher had never seen anything so affected and convoluted in his life. "Whatever is wrong with her?"

His answer was a pair of giggles from Miss Thalia and Lady Philippa.

"Look! She's still doing it!" Lady Philippa whispered.

Miss Langley managed better than her sister or cousin, for she stood with her lips pressed together, though she trembled from head to toe as she did her best not to laugh as well.

"Oh, she looks like a pea goose," Miss Thalia said, sounding all too triumphant.

"You've only yourself to blame," her sister whispered. "Marie Antoinette, Tally! What were you thinking, telling her that?"

"Marie Antoinette?" Thatcher had to ask, staring first at the grandiose Miss Browne, and then back at Miss Langley.

She heaved a sigh. "My sister told that silly nit that when we were in France, Marie Antoinette liked to greet her subjects thusly, and in French aristocratic circles being able to master such a wave was considered a sign of superior breeding."

Taking another glance at the ridiculous flutter of the girl's hand, Thatcher found himself squarely in Miss Thalia and Lady Philippa's camp—choking back a fit of laughter.

"And that ninnyhammer believed me," Tally said quite proudly, waving back at their old schoolmate with the same affected gesture.

Pippin turned her head and managed to say between chuckles, "Just be thankful she never made very good marks in history or mathematics because then she might have realized the poor Queen died the same year we were born."

"Oh, delightful friends!" Miss Browne called out, her hand still fluttering about like a cat with fits. "It is true! You have come to Town from your dreadful *exile*. But how is this possible? The rumors I've heard as to your dire circumstances! Your trials!"

Exile? Dire circumstances? Trials? Yet another layer of mystery fell down around Miss Langley. And as he watched her jaw work back and forth, he knew this Miss Browne had hit a nerve, a raw one.

"Rumors?" Miss Langley replied. She glanced at her companions in wide-eyed innocence, as if such a thing must be as much a shock to them as it was to her. "I can't imagine why we would be the subject of rumors. And further, I can't believe you would give credence to gossip, dear Miss Browne. You know Miss Emery thought little of those who carried tales." This was followed by a cold, plastered smile that looked capable of cracking the icicles hanging from the eaves.

"Yes, yes, I must have you confused with three other misfortunates," the girl declared, all smiles as well, but her narrowed gaze suggesting otherwise. "But here you are in Mayfair, and you haven't called on me. How can this be?" She finished by making a perfect moue.

"We'd heard that you'd returned home . . . after poor Lord Herrick's demise," Lady Philippa replied, her words sounding more like wishful thinking. "But now that we know you are here, we will be assured to keep you in our utmost thoughts."

Thatcher watched these volleys and felt like he was witnessing something more akin to an American privateer and a trio of English frigates happening upon each other at sea.

Miss Browne preened. "But of course you will, for I am received in all the finest circles, despite this ridiculous war. I daresay, you will be quite riveted when I relate the story of our return—Mother and I went through a terrible trial at sea . . ." She paused, her hand at her brow, obviously waiting for one of them to ask the question that should be rising to each of their tongues: *Oh, do tell, Miss Browne, whatever happened to you?*

But her audience remained mute, so eventually she had to give up her stance. "Well, I suppose it is too cold to share the awful details now, but soon we will have a good coze and catch up, now won't we?"

"When hell freezes—" he heard Miss Thalia begin to mutter, until her sister gave her a less than delicate, albeit subtle, jab in the ribs.

Meanwhile, Miss Browne had taken in her surroundings and her pretty face wrinkled, especially as she looked up at the grand house behind them. "Whoever are you visiting?"

"Visiting?" Miss Langley glanced over her shoulder. "Hardly visiting. This is our house."

For all Miss Browne's obvious wealth, apparently in the world of London debutantes a Mayfair address trumped a matched set of horses and a new hat.

"Here?" Miss Browne's statement was tinged with disbelief. "But Mother and I were told there were no houses to let for the Season . . . well, none so close to Grosvenor Square, that is."

"You could say we quite happened upon this one," Lady Thalia told her, rocking in her half boots and smiling like a cat before a bowl of cream.

"How fortuitous," Miss Browne said, glancing again at the mansion behind them and then at the three of them in turn, looking none too convinced. "It's just that we—I mean, Mother and I—had heard . . . well, that is to say everyone was speculating that you've had some difficulties . . ." She smiled, a feral narrow sort. "But happily I see I was misled. And you are here for the Season and the four of us will all shine together. Miss Emery will be so pleased when we all make splendid matches. Of course, I haven't your little *Bachelor Chronicles* to help me—"

"*Bachelor Chronicles?*" Mrs. Browne quizzed.

Her daughter turned to her. "Haven't I told you of them? No? Well, Miss Langley maintains the veriest encyclopedia of eligible men from which to find a husband. Has so for *years*."

Mrs. Browne cast the same simpering smile down at Felicity, "Has it helped, dearie?"

"That remains to be seen," Miss Langley replied.

"Now where are you off to?" Miss Browne asked, changing the subject and drawing all the attention back to herself. "If there was room I'd offer you a ride, but I can't take all of you, so I fear you must fend for yourselves, but you Langleys have always been such resourceful creatures, tramping about as you do."

It didn't sound like a compliment to Thatcher's ears, and

from the look on Miss Langley's face, her false smile had been replaced by a slow boil.

"We've calls to make this morning," Miss Langley told her. *"Important ones."*

"Then we're off to the Frost Fair," Lady Philippa added, winding her arm into her cousin's.

"To the Frost Fair?" Miss Browne repeated. "And you haven't been yet? I've been thrice. So very quaint—though now I hear it is thronged with such common sorts. But I suppose your cousins are quite used to consorting with such people, Lady Philippa, having traveled so much of the world as they have, so you'll be in good company."

"No worse than your average Americans, I would venture," Miss Thalia replied, her smile more teeth than lips.

Thatcher glanced at the two sisters. They'd traveled the world? How much more was there that he didn't know about this pair? Obviously quite a bit.

Miss Browne had let the insult float past her like a snowflake. "There's to be an assembly of sorts down there in a few nights, perhaps you heard? That is, if the ice holds. How unfortunate it is on the same night as the Setchfield ball." She paused. "You were invited, weren't you? The duke and duchess always include us on their guest list." She held out her hand to admire her gloves, and smiled slightly at the pretty embroidery decorating the rich, supple leather while she waited for their reply.

"But of course we were invited," Miss Langley told her. "His Grace is a very close friend of our family."

"Of course he is," Miss Browne returned, as she smoothed her hand over the thick mantle of fur that ringed her cloak. Then she leaned over the edge of her carriage and said, "I am surprised you are going out today. I would have thought you'd be too distracted."

"And why would we be distracted?" Miss Langley asked.

"Well, because of Hollindrake. He's arrived." Those cold

eyes narrowed further as she scanned the girls to gauge how her latest sally had landed.

As cold as it already was, Thatcher's blood turned to ice. So his aunt had been right. The gossips were already at his doors.

"He has?" Miss Thalia blurted out, then covered her open mouth with her red mitten. Her twin turned and cast a glare in her direction that looked capable of striking down a French column.

"You didn't know?" Miss Browne exclaimed, quite possibly loud enough for it to be heard around the corner in Grosvenor Square. "Oh, heavens, and here I thought the three of you were being such sly creatures! And now to find out that you didn't know. Yes, the duke came to London yesterday, but I would have thought that you, Miss Langley, given your special relationship with the man, would have been the first to learn of his arrival." The girl let her words unfurl like a noose. Slippery little chit that she obviously was, she knew she was on to something and was as determined as the hangman to collect his shilling. Rolling back in her seat, she tipped her head. "How very interesting, indeed. As it is, Mother and I were off to leave our cards with Lady Geneva, his aunt. But I still don't understand how it is you didn't know. Perhaps you two have had a falling out, which would mean His Grace is quite available for—"

"Miss Langley," Thatcher blurted. "I do apologize. But you will be late to call on the marchioness if we don't continue on. Her man said she expected you promptly this morning."

Miss Browne turned her sharp gaze on him. "And who might you be?"

"This is Thatcher," Felicity said. "Our footman." She slanted him a quick glance and smile, as if to say, *Thank you.*

There was no thanks necessary, he would have told her. He'd stopped Miss Browne's dissertation lest she give away enough information to have the agile and astute Miss

Langley adding up his timely and coincidental arrival into her life.

"Oh, you have a footman!" Miss Browne replied, taking another glance at him. "A cheeky sort of fellow, I think."

"Yes, but he came highly recommended," Miss Langley replied. "We quite stole him away from his previous employer."

Thatcher listened to the girl lie without a qualm or a bit of conscience and decided it was time to send Miss Browne packing before he found himself with an entirely new history. "The marchioness, Miss Langley?"

She turned and stared up at him, as did the others. "Yes, *the marchioness*," she finally managed to reply. "How could we have forgotten? It would be dreadful to be late to see *Her Ladyship* when she's done so much for us." She pressed her lips shut and shot a triumphant look at Miss Browne.

The ill-mannered Yankee heiress looked them over, as if gauging where to send her next sally, but happily for all, other quarry caught her eye. "Oh my, look," she said, pointing at an approaching carriage, "here come those horrible Hodges! I can spot their carriage anywhere. Oh, what mushrooms they are. The eldest Miss Hodges is completely unsuited for society for all she can converse upon is horses and hunting!"

"I always found them to be quite nice," Miss Langley said, her hands fisting to her hips.

"My dear Miss Langley, this isn't Bath," she said as she fluttered a handkerchief in front of her nose. "Why in London the coal dust from their grandfather's mines just seems to follow them." She took another glance at the other carriage. "Probably out shopping, for it is all they have to recommend them. What a triumph it will be for Miss Emery when *I* . . . oh, I mean to say, when *we* all contract lofty marriages and those Hodges creatures return home in the summer, spinsters still." Turning to her mother, she said, "What do you say we lurk after them to make sure we don't patronize the same modistes? I've always thought they looked so common." Matron and daughter cackled with much the same note of venom, and that was enough to signal their driver to depart.

Miss Browne leaned over the side. "See you at the Setchfield ball! I will be quite easy to find, for I shall be dressed as Pocahontas. Quite savage, Mother thinks, but I'm of the opinion that my feathers and tomahawk will make me stand out."

"I know what I'd do with her tomahawk to make her stand out," Miss Thalia muttered.

"Sounds perfectly suited for you," Miss Langley called after her, drowning out her sister's continued muttering. "We'll look for you."

"But Felicity, we weren't invited," Lady Philippa whispered.

"Not yet," she shot back, even as she kept the bright smile pasted on her lips until the carriage turned the corner.

"Whew! That was close," Miss Thalia said. She glanced over at him. "And that part about the marchioness—Mr. Thatcher, that was brilliant. You had her quite green with envy and she'll spend the rest of the day trying to determine who you meant."

Miss Langley turned around as well and was about to say something when Lady Philippa announced, "Oh, finally. Here comes Stillings with the carriage."

The plain-looking coach pulled to a stop and the driver hopped down from his perch and greeted them like long lost friends. "Lawks, look at all of you! Young ladies, if ever I saw them." He shot a wink over at Miss Langley. "You aren't up to your usual matchmaking mischief, now are you?"

If it was possible to believe, the chit blushed. "Mr. Stillings, I don't consider my efforts mischief."

He doffed his hat and grinned. "If you say so, miss." He

slanted another broad wink at Thatcher. "Best keep a careful eye on these three! Caused me a fair bit of trouble a few years back and nearly lost me my position."

"Go on with you," Aunt Minty told the fellow. "These girls are the finest ladies I've ever met. Now give me a hand up, you handsome rogue." Their aged chaperone reached over and pinched the driver's backside as she toddled past him.

"Aunt Minty," Miss Langley scolded, her cheeks growing even rosier.

"What?" the old woman shot back, shoving her cane into Thatcher's chest, so he had no other choice but to take it with one hand, while Mr. Stillings helped the miserable crone, er, chaperone, up into the carriage. Once seated, she grabbed her cane back and finished her retort by saying, "I told you afore, I ain't dead yet."

Miss Langley groaned and followed the lady into the carriage, with Lady Philippa and Miss Thalia following until each of them had found a seat.

"Well?" Miss Langley said, nodding up toward the empty spot beside Mr. Stillings. "Are you with us or not, Mr. Thatcher?"

There were several important things Thatcher had learned in the last half an hour.

First of all, his arrival into Town hadn't gone unnoticed, as his aunt had quite astutely foreseen.

Secondly, these chits had enough secrets to keep an entire battalion of Bow Street runners employed with the task of uncovering them.

And thirdly, Miss Felicity Langley was one dead cool liar, a sharpster you wouldn't want to meet up against across the green baize without anything less than a hefty pile of coins in front of you and God's own luck with cards. The chit could bluff her way out of Hell's gates.

But most importantly, whatever these three daft girls had up their sleeves to make their way into Society, well, frankly it would never work.

Like every other responsibility his grandfather had left behind, some part of this travesty was his to fix. And all of a sudden he knew that crying off and leaving Miss Langley wasn't right. Not until he'd gotten to the bottom of what was amiss in this household.

If it had been just a nagging sense of duty to the chit, he could have put Gibbens in charge of the entire situation and washed his hands of any guilt he may have felt over the obligation.

If only it was that, he thought. No, it was all about this minx. This unlikely lady his grandfather had chosen. He still wasn't utterly convinced this was the *same* Felicity Langley the old duke had courted.

She couldn't be.

Yet when this Miss Langley looked down at him from her seat in the carriage and asked him in her usual forthright manner, "Are you with us or not?" he suddenly found himself in one of those moments where one's life teeters on a precipice. For she slanted a wayward glance at him, and in those blinding seconds, he found himself caught by the spark in her eyes, by the tip of her lips.

Quite honestly, it had taken every bit of military discipline he possessed not to turn tail and run all the way back to Westmoreland to the safety of Bythorne Castle and its high impregnable walls.

Especially considering that Miss Felicity Langley, the nearly betrothed of the most lofty Duke of Hollindrake, had just sent him—Thatcher the footman—a flirtatious look of invitation that would have made a Lisbon courtesan weep with envy.

And like a raw recruit, her siren glance disarmed every plan he'd had about her, especially the one about crying off.

Instead he found himself nodding and climbing up beside the driver.

As they drove away, Thatcher realized he was not only in her employ, he was also falling under her unfathomable spell.

"You minx!" Tally whispered across the carriage to her sister.

"Whatever are you talking about?" Felicity shot back, fully intending to bluff for as long as she could hold out.

"You just gave that new footman Nanny Jamilla's look." Tally sat back in her seat and grinned. "And don't even deny it."

Felicity did anyway. "I did no such thing."

"You did something," Pippin chimed in. "And whatever it was, it worked like a charm."

"I did nothing," Felicity averred.

Tally snorted. "You used Nanny Jamilla's look on that poor man and now you'll have to pay the consequences."

"Oh, what is this look?" their cousin asked, leaning forward in her seat in all eagerness.

"There is no such thing," Felicity told her.

"There was something to how you looked at that fella," Aunt Minty declared, "and I know my fair share of Seven Dials whores who'd pay good money to be able to coax a man like you just did."

"Aunt Minty!" Felicity protested, glancing up at the closed hatch that sat between them and the two men above. "Will you keep your voice down? And how many times must I ask—please, no improper statements."

"She's improper?" Tally said, sitting with her arms folded over her chest. "You just used the most dangerous look known to the female race, and you're worried about Aunt Minty? Felicity, you were flirting with our footman! Oh, what would Nanny Jamilla say? Or better yet, Hollindrake?"

"Oh, do show me!" Pippin begged. "What is Nanny Jamilla's look?"

Tally made a moue, her eyes rolling back in her head, a strangled sort of expression that made everyone laugh.

"I didn't do that," Felicity protested, pulling the lap blanket higher and glancing out the window to gauge their progress. In her opinion, they couldn't get to the Thames quick enough. Flirting with a footman, indeed!

It wasn't like that in the least . . .

"You should have just sacked him," Tally said, settling back into her seat. "Now you have the poor man befuddled."

"He is not," Felicity retorted. "Besides, I didn't do it for *those* reasons. I only wanted him to stay on so we could go to the Frost Fair." If she could have bit back those words, she would have, for this always happened when she started arguing with her sister.

"So you did use the look on him," Tally said, pouncing on her sister's confession and sending a triumphant glance toward the others. But as quickly as her victory occurred, she paused and then turned slowly and cast a dubious glance at Felicity. "Nanny Jamilla said it only works when you have a *tendre* for a man." She took a quick glance up at the roof and then back at her sister. "And if it worked, then I must surmise that you—"

"Thalia Langley, you take that back!" Felicity said, rising out of her seat, that is until the carriage bounced over a pothole and she flew back with a rude thump.

"You like Thatcher?" Pippin whispered, her words aghast.

"No!" Felicity exploded with more vehemence than was necessary. Worse yet, she felt her cheeks run hot, adding more flames to Tally's imaginative bonfire. "I just met the man yesterday, and the notion that I am in love with him is utterly ridiculous." She turned on her sister. "You've read too many French novels of late—they've turned your mind to a pot of romantic mush."

Her twin only preened under the admonishment. "I know what I saw, and you gave that man Nanny Jamilla's look. And it worked."

"Which one was this Jamilla?" Aunt Minty asked. "The Russian doxy or the bit of skirt from Italy?"

Felicity shook her head. "Neither. Nanny Jamilla was with us when father was attached to the embassy in Paris. And really, Aunt Aramintha, none of our nannies were a 'bit of skirt,' as you so indelicately put it. Father took great care every time we moved to a new posting to choose lovely women of good breeding to keep our household and bring us up while he went about his duties as His Majesty's representative."

Aunt Minty blew out a long breath. "Sounds like a fine bunch of gammon to me."

It was, Felicity knew. At least she did now. While it was true her father had been a diplomat, he'd also been one of England's most apt spies—something she and Tally had only learned in the last few years.

And their nannies? Well, with a bit of hindsight and the perspective that being one and twenty gave a lady, Felicity had come to realize that perhaps their nannies' obligations may not have ended when she and Tally were trundled off to bed. But she wasn't about to admit to such a thing and only add to what was already considered an unconventional upbringing.

Why, the gossips and old cats of the *ton* would have a field day if it was bandied about that they'd been raised by their father's romps.

So instead Felicity raised her defenses. "Oh, heavens no, Aunt Minty! Take our Nanny Tasha—she was a distant cousin of the tsar."

"A what?" Aunt Minty asked.

"The tsar," Pippin repeated. "Like a king or an emperor."

"Harrumph! Most of them are half mad, so it's hardly a

recommendation to my way of thinking," Aunt Minty declared.

Tally chimed in. "And Nanny Lucia was a respectable widow. Her husband was a duke who'd been the finance minister to the King of Naples. Papa adored her because he said she made him laugh."

Pippin joined the chorus of approval. "Wasn't your Nanny Jamilla the daughter of a famous Arabian doctor?"

"She was," Felicity nodded. "And her mother a lady-in-waiting to the Swedish court. When her father was summoned to Paris to serve Napoleon, Jamilla married the Duc de Fraine, one of Bonaparte's advisors." She sat up straight in her seat and folded her hands in her lap. "So you see, our nannies were ladies of quality, and therefore, any look I sent Thatcher was purely of a practical nature."

"Practically flirting," Tally muttered, casting a wink at Pippin, who grinned back.

Felicity chose to ignore them.

For in the last half hour, Felicity Langley had discovered something far more startling than the fact that her almost betrothed was back in London. No, Felicity had discovered that she shared more with her twin than just the same honey-colored hair and their mother's blue eyes.

Because when she'd glanced up into Thatcher's strong features as he'd outflanked Miss Browne, she'd felt a wild, very insensible, most decidedly improper romantic notion—the same lament that had risen from the depth of heart yesterday when she'd answered the door and found him standing on her steps.

Why couldn't this intriguing man be her duke?

Chapter 4

It seemed to Thatcher that all of London had turned out to make merry on the frozen Thames. With the happy exception of Miss Browne and her mother.

Apparently, the Langley sisters and Lady Philippa didn't share their former classmate's horror of common folk. The ladies looked quite delighted to be amongst Miss Browne's rabble. Even sleepy Aunt Aramintha's eyes were bright with excitement as she watched the crowds around them.

Thatcher took a deep breath of the cold, crisp air and smiled as well.

Far better than being poked and prodded by Weston and the countless other tailors and bootmakers and milliners his aunt surely had lined up by now outside his Grosvenor Square residence.

"Come on, Duchess," Miss Thalia was saying, tugging at her sister's hand. "Look over there! A great swing! Don't you remember the one Papa took us on in Geneva? Hurry along so we can get in line."

"I will not," she replied. "I hardly think it is proper at our age to be whirled about in such a fashion."

"Bah!" Miss Thalia replied. "Proper, indeed! 'Tis fun, Felicity. And I haven't seen you smile in an age. Come along and laugh with us."

Miss Langley shook her head and stood firm. "I will not. 'Tis for children. Besides, it is a waste of money."

"I'll forgo an extra candle tonight," was her sister's reply, and off she went arm in arm with her cousin and aunt.

"As if that will happen!" Miss Langley huffed. "She'll forget her promise and be begging for more tapers so she can 'read one more chapter.'"

Thatcher laughed, and then found himself the subject of a glare from his unlikely employer.

"Please do not encourage her," came the haughty order.

"You should have gone with them," he said, nodding toward the contraption that now had the others swinging back and forth in a grand arc over the ice. "It does look like fun."

"Harrumph." Miss Langley straightened, and while her stance was convincing, he swore he could see a tiny, envious light in her eyes as she glanced over at her sister.

"Is it about the money?" he asked, though for the life of him he couldn't understand why the daughters of someone as highly placed as Lord Langley or the daughter of an earl would be in such reduced circumstances—even if both their fathers were gone. "For if you would like to go, I have a few spare—" He began to dig around in his pocket.

"I think not!" Her gaze fluttered up to meet his, and then her fair lashes shuttered him out. "It wouldn't be proper to take money from you." She heaved a sigh. "It's just that we incurred a few more expenses than we thought we would moving into Town and our solicitor is forever forgetting to send over a draft. Why just the other day he called on us, apologizing quite profusely . . ."

She nattered on, but he didn't believe a word of it. Miss Browne might be a pea goose, but he wasn't.

". . . as for going on swings, as I said before, I hardly think it proper—"

"I could escort you back to Mayfair," he offered. "Perhaps we can catch up with Miss Browne and her mother. They seemed a proper pair."

The chit looked ready to level him, but then her face softened and she laughed. "I suppose I do deserve that much." There was another sigh from her, and then finally a softly spoken sentence. "I want to thank you for your help this morning."

"My help?"

"Yes," she replied. "With Miss Browne." As she said the other chit's name, he could almost hear her teeth grinding.

He chuckled. "Apparently not your special bosom bow, as she would have led us all to believe."

"Never," Miss Langley said with a shudder. "She's well . . . I don't like to say anything ill about a fellow graduate of Miss Emery's but . . . she's . . . oh, she's . . ."

"A wretched bit of baggage?"

Her lips twitched, but only for a moment. "Mr. Thatcher!"

"What?" He leaned against the rail that separated them from the swing.

"You shouldn't say such a thing about a young lady."

"Why not?"

Her hands went to her hips. "Servants aren't supposed to speak ill of their betters."

He frowned and rubbed his chin. "They aren't?"

Shaking her head, she said, "No. Absolutely not."

"Whyever not?"

That stopped her, but only for a moment. "Well, it just isn't done."

"Of course it's done."

"It shouldn't be," she countered. "It isn't proper."

Proper. He hadn't known Miss Langley for twenty-four hours, and already that word was starting to wear on him. This chit and her proper notions.

"Tell me you weren't thinking the exact same thing."

"Thinking what?"

"That your Miss Browne is a wretched piece of baggage."

"I was not and she is not 'my Miss Browne.'"

"Oh yes, you thought the exact same thing when you saw her waving like a . . . like a . . ."

"Pea goose," she supplied.

He snapped his fingers. "Yes, that's it. Thank you."

"You're welcome," she said, nose tucked in the air. "But I will aver for the remainder of my days that I never thought of her as a 'wretched piece of baggage.'"

Thatcher leaned over and peeked beneath the rim of her bonnet. "Truly?"

"What I was thinking was far less charitable," she admitted.

They both laughed, and he wondered if she would be so free and easy with him if she knew who he was. He had to imagine not, for he couldn't remember anyone joking with his grandfather. Or for that matter, his grandfather ever laughing.

"I daresay Miss Browne will no longer vex me when I am married," she said, tugging at her red mittens, which were the same color as the socks she'd worn the day before. Red wool socks on a debutante! He had been away from London too long. Though he had to guess they weren't the pink of fashion, especially compared to the expensive rigging Miss Browne had sported. "Nothing will, I suppose."

"How so?"

She arched a brow. "For I shall be the Duchess of Hollindrake."

Presumptuous little chit. Especially when Gibbens had assured him that there was no formal betrothal in place. "You will be?"

"Yes, I told you so yesterday."

"I was a bit preoccupied in saving my boots," he reminded her.

She flinched. "Brutus! He is a horrible animal, but Tally thinks the sun sets at his feet, so I fear we are stuck with him. I hope your boots weren't ruined."

He held one out for her inspection. "Just a few reminders of our meeting, nothing more." Of course, the marks had left his grandfather's valet in horrors, especially when he had instructed the man not to attempt to repair the damage. "What if Miss Browne were to marry some other duke?"

"Unlikely," she said, full of confidence. "I have conducted a thorough study of all the marriageable dukes—"

"A wha-a-t?" he stammered.

"A study of marriageable dukes. I wasn't about to leave my prospects to chance."

"Of course not," he managed to say. "But a study?"

"Not really a study, per se, more of a chronicle."

"The *Bachelor Chronicles*," he said, remembering the odd remark Miss Browne had made earlier about a journal.

"Yes. Miss Browne and her ilk christened it thusly. Not that they understood the importance of such a work—for they only saw it as a directory of eligible men."

"And it's not?" He was more inclined to view it like Miss Browne. Hell, what man wouldn't?

"Gracious heavens, no. Finding the right marriage partner isn't just a matter of title and wealth." She paused for a moment as he arched a glance at her. "I won't lie and say those things aren't essential."

"Of course," he agreed, not meaning a word of it.

Felicity continued on as if the mocking tone in his voice held all the agreement of a fervent *amen.* "Titles and wealth aside, a true marriage requires a meeting of minds, of temperaments, of natural inclinations."

Had he heard her correctly? "Natural what?" he sputtered against his better judgment.

"Natural inclinations," she repeated. "Oh, not that nonsense that Tally and Pippin go on about. Romance and passion and such foolery. For anyone of good sense knows that when a couple is well matched, they share a . . . well, it will be . . ."

He supposed he could have nodded for her to continue without explaining it in excruciating detail, but it was much more fun to stand by mutely and watch her cheeks pink.

"Suffice it to say, the marriage will be beneficial for both parties," she managed to finish.

"Sounds as such." Sounded dead dull to his way of thinking, but he wasn't about to argue the point. "As you were saying, your *Bachelor Journals*—"

"*Chronicles,*" she corrected.

"Yes, these *Bachelor Chronicles* are a study of all the eligible dukes?"

She bit her lip and shook her head. "Well, it was that at first, but I found I needed to expand my studies."

"And how far did you expand them to?"

"To all the noblemen in England," she confessed. Proudly, he thought.

"*All?*"

"Well, not all of them. Only the unmarried ones. And of course I didn't include those who weren't up to snuff. You would be surprised how many terrible rogues there are out there."

"Yes, so I've heard," he said, wondering why his reckless past hadn't gained him such immunity. "But I thought you were only interested in ducal candidates."

"I am," she replied adamantly. "But sadly, there is a regular dearth of dukes—"

"No!" he teased.

"There are currently only three eligible dukes in the Marriage Mart."

"Only three?" A one out of three chance, and of course *he'd* won her matrimonial lottery.

She ignored him. "Yes. I fear they aren't a very prolific group, and worse still, most of them are half mad."

That should have taken the Sterlings off her list—he could cite a full list of ramshackle relations, starting with his grandfather.

"With so few ducal candidates, I added marquisates during my second year. And then earls and on down."

He closed his eyes for a moment. "And what exactly do you 'chronicle'?"

"Oh, the usual," she said. "Date of birth, lineage, residences—"

"Couldn't you glean all that with a copy of *Debrett's* or *Stockdale's*?"

She shook her head. "Why no! They don't get to the heart of the matters."

No, of course not.

"My *Chronicles* cover the important things. Tendencies toward drink, gambling, charitable associations, family connections, financial status . . ."

As she went on with her laundry list of nearly every sort of fault or folly a man could profess, he realized something very important.

He was in those pages. Chronicled and dissected with the same efficiency that marked everything she did.

So how the hell had she ever come up with him as her choice?

She'd finished and now stood waiting for some sort of response from him. Lord knows he was trying, but he couldn't make his mouth move for it had grown as dry as the Spanish plains in August. But he managed the question that was tolling in his brain like the bells of St. Paul's. "Why Hollindrake?"

"Actually, I would never have considered him if it hadn't been for Lord John Tremont."

"Mad Jack?" he blurted without thinking.

"You know him?" she asked, suspicion rising immediately in those all-too-intelligent eyes of hers.

"I know of him," he said quickly. "Who in London hasn't heard of Mad Jack Tremont?"

"True enough," she conceded, casting one last speculative glance in his direction.

Thatcher made a note to himself to kill Tremont the first chance he got. Leave it to the same man who'd convinced him that the army was his only way out of his grandfather's machinations to send this marriage-mad little chit in his direction.

"I might not have met His Grace in person," she was saying, "but I know him well enough. We've spent the last four years exchanging a veritable panoply of ideas. While he is quite opinionated . . ."

She didn't know the half of it. His grandfather had probably been the most inflated and overbearing person who'd ever lived.

". . . he expresses himself with an eloquent style that leaves any proposition up for a fair and open discourse . . ."

Thatcher slipped from where he was leaning against the railing. It was hard to remain upright—ice or not—when anyone used the phrase "fair and open" to describe his grandfather.

". . . our letters convinced me he was the perfect choice for my marriage partner . . ."

Those letters! He needed to get his hands on them. Curse Gibbens and the man's fear of riding.

In the snow, Your Grace? Oh, no, I couldn't, the bespectacled man had squawked at the very suggestion of riding.

So now while he waited for Gibbens and the carriage to arrive, he could only speculate as to what the devil his grandfather and Miss Langley have been writing about.

". . . even before I'd settled my affairs with His Grace, I knew my *Bachelor Chronicles* would prove useful. For you see, my sister and cousin are not as discerning about their marriage partners," she was saying. "And if I am to be a duchess, I must see that they succeed to their rightful places as well."

"But of course." He glanced over at Tally and Pippin, who obviously held propriety with no little regard, for they were both laughing uproariously. "I imagine you have your work cut out for you."

"If you only knew!" Felicity said, glancing skyward. "Truly, if Miss Browne marries above either of them, all my work will have been in vain. She'll bedevil me to no end."

"That may be true, but could you imagine Miss Browne's humiliation if those Misses Hodges outdid her?" he said entirely in jest.

Felicity laughed. "She would be beside herself, but I doubt Lord Stewart's daughters are going to have much luck finding lofty marriages. Their father is a bit of a . . . a . . ."

He let her falter on, for he knew Lord Stewart, or Stewie, as he was known. The toady little man in his brightly colored waistcoats had been hard to miss—and hard to divest oneself of—when Thatcher had been cutting his swath through society. The man's daughters could be paragons, but the idea of having that nincompoop for a father-in-law most likely drove away all but the most desperate fortune hunters.

"I have to imagine that Lord and Lady Stewart would shower gold down upon your head if you helped their daughters make lofty matches. Your *Chronicles* would be worth a fortune overnight," he said, thinking it all a fine jest, that is, until he spied the mercantile light blazing to life in Miss Langley's eyes. *No! He hadn't meant . . .*

"Thatcher, that is perfect."

Demmit, what had he just unleashed? "No, Miss Langley, no!"

"But I will! That is the most perfect idea." She clapped her gloves together. "I've never thought to use my *Chronicles* thusly—well, other than for Pippin and Tally—but do you really think they would reward me for helping them?"

"I—I—I—" he stammered.

"But of course they would! Think of it! Using my *Chronicles* to help unlikely ladies find husbands could change matrimony forever! Not only that, it could reverse our current situation." She clapped her hands together as if that settled it. "And I have you to thank."

"Oh, no, don't thank me!"

"But I must," she asserted.

"No, really, leave me out of this," he told her. If it was nosed about Town that he'd inspired Miss Langley's scheme, every bachelor in England would be vying for the right to put a bullet through his heart.

"Duchess!" Miss Thalia cried out, as the ride finished and her cousin was in the midst of negotiating with the man for a second turn. "Have a go?"

Miss Langley shook her head.

Her sister, cousin, and aunt climbed back into the swings and in a few moments were being rocked skyward again.

"Why does your sister call you that?" he asked.

"Call me what?"

"Duchess."

Miss Langley shook her head. "Oh, 'tis an old joke."

"Willing to share?"

A little blush stole over her cheeks. Was it from embarrassment or the icy wind racing across the frozen river? He didn't know, but it softened her features and made her look like a young lady of twenty should, instead of the little general who normally inhabited her slippers.

"Our uncle Temple christened me that when I was about seven," she finally confessed.

"Temple?" he asked, wondering if it could be his old friend, Templeton. "Do you mean the Marquis of Templeton?"

"Oh, yes, the very same. But he's the Duke of Setchfield now. He inherited several years ago, but he's still Uncle Temple to Tally and I. He's not really our uncle, but a good friend of Father's and he often visited us when we lived abroad." She eyed him again. "Do you know him?"

"I've read of him in the papers," he said, realizing he was going to have to guard his tongue around her.

She didn't look all that satisfied with his answer, but finally, much to his relief, continued with her story. "Well, if you must know, Uncle Temple told my father and half the court in Naples that I had the temperament and bearing of a future duchess. From then on I was known as *la duchessa piccolo*. She paused for a moment and then translated. "'The little duchess.' Even after we left Naples, I fear the name stuck."

"You lived in Naples?" he asked.

"Yes," she said. "My father was a diplomat and we lived many places: Constantinople, Naples, Paris, Geneva, Vienna, and St. Petersburg, until we came home to go to school."

"And did you always want to be a duchess?"

A strange, wistful look crossed her face. "When I was younger, I thought of it only in terms of the coronet and the jewels," she said, smiling. "But now, I fear I've become so eminently suited for the position that there isn't much else for me to do."

"How does one become 'eminently suited' to be a duchess?"

"Years of training."

"You trained?" If it took years of training to be a duchess, there was little hope of him becoming a proper duke.

"But of course. Deportment, social engagements, household management, diplomacy—though of course that comes naturally to us Langleys."

"But of course," he agreed, thinking how diplomatic she and her sister were with Miss Browne. "But a duke? Why wouldn't a nicely landed marquess or a long-lined earl do?"

She shook her head. "You don't understand—a duke is so much more than any of them. A duke is heroic, and noble, a knight errant, if you will. The kind of man who is handsome and carries himself with a self-assurance that commands the respect of one and all. And above all, he is a proper English gentleman who expects a proper English lady for his bride." She shook the snow off her cloak. "Really, what else is there left for me to do but become a duchess?"

"I haven't the faintest idea," he mused, for really all he'd done to become the duke was be the next available Sterling, and he certainly possessed none of the characteristics she'd listed.

She huffed a sigh and glanced over at the passing throng of visitors on the ice. "I think what I will like the most is the respect that comes with being a duchess. I won't have to endure Sarah Browne's slights ever again. She won't dare." And then, when she realized she'd revealed something too personal, she turned and ended the discussion just as one might expect from a real duchess, tipping her head so the rim of her bonnet hid her face from him.

A cut direct and well done, he had to admit. But he wasn't finished. "I'm sorry if I said something offensive."

"It's not that," she replied. "It's just that it isn't proper for a footman and lady to be chatting so publicly. I have a reputation to guard."

Thatcher leaned over and glanced beneath the rim of her bonnet. "Is that one of Miss Browne's rules or yours?"

"Miss Emery's," she informed him. "She was our teacher in Bath. She always said that 'a lady never expresses any familiarity with her lesser.'"

Her lesser? Oh, if she only knew. Thatcher straightened, rising to his full height, towering over this suddenly imperious miss at his side. "And you think of me as *your* lesser?"

For a moment there was no reply from beneath the little blue bonnet, but finally it tipped back and she glanced up at him. "No."

Her straightforward answer took him aback. "And why is that? I'm a servant after all."

"But I daresay not by choice," she offered. "You were in the army. You fought in the Peninsula, did you not?"

He nodded.

"And you were on the battlefield?"

His eyes clenched shut—the movement was involuntary, but he did it every time someone mentioned the fields. Ciudad Rodrigo, Badajoz, Salamanca. The images were enough to make a man mad. "Yes, I served in the field."

"Hollindrake once wrote to me that the men who fight for a cause, a noble one, have more honor than any mere gentleman. That you have seen things, done things, that can rend apart even the stoutest of hearts. And since you are here, and appear to be whole, I must conclude you are a brave and honorable man, and therefore hardly my lesser, even if you are our footman."

She turned around at the sound of her sister's gay laughter and watched the trio as they swung back and forth, merry and giddy.

Thatcher stared instead at this woman at his side. Every time he thought he knew her, had a picture of some marriage-mad miss fixed in his mind, another facet of her turned and sparkled like a diamond, leaving him blinded and dumbfounded.

But even more so because she'd quoted his grandfather. What had the old codger written to her?

The men who fight for a cause, a noble one, have more honor than any mere gentleman.

Perhaps she had misunderstood what he'd said, for he doubted his grandfather, the man who held nothing but contempt for anyone who had no holdings and lineage behind him, would share such an opinion regarding military service.

And honestly, he didn't know how honorable he was for it.

She was right, though, he had done things that weren't fit to remember, but it had been his duty to see the war won and Napoleon stopped, and those memories were the cost he bore.

"You should have gone on the swing with your sister," he said after some time. "Those things are fun."

His question teased her out of her silent reverie. "You've been on one of those?"

He grinned at her. "Of course! In fact, it was at the Frost Fair in '95. I was a lad of—"

Almost immediately he saw her set to work calculating his age. Demmit, if he gave her much more information, she was going to discover who he was without any trouble whatsoever.

"How old?" she ventured, trying to hide the curious note in her question.

"Let's just say a lad old enough to like trouble," he demurred.

"No doubt," she replied as her gaze swept over him from head to toe. "Was the fair then like all this?" she asked, waving her hand at the booths, the makeshift shows, as well as the circle where the snow had been smoothed and swept clean so skaters could make elegant turns about the ice.

He nodded. "And more—there was also a wild animal show. I remember someone brought the elephant from the

Tower out on the ice to prove to everyone it was safe." He laughed, at both the memory and her shocked expression. "I came every day—learned to dice at a tent not far from there." He pointed at a pavilion to their right.

"Don't tell Tally that," Felicity warned. "She'll be mad to learn as well."

"I don't think she will when she finds out I diced away my only pair of skates."

"Then it was a good lesson to learn early," she observed.

"What was?" he asked.

"Losing your skates. I'm sure it taught you the dangers of wagering," she said. "I have to imagine you never gambled after that."

"Oh, no, never," he teased.

After a woeful shake of her head, she said, "Were you any good?"

"At dicing?"

"No! I believe I know that outcome." She reached over and nudged him with her elbow. "At skating, I meant." Her gaze traveled over to the ring, where an older couple were gliding arm in arm over the ice.

"*Oh*, skating. Well, yes. Yes, I was," he told her. "Though I haven't done so in years. There weren't a lot of opportunities for it in Spain." He too looked over at the agile pair. "Do you skate?"

"Oh, yes," she said, an enthusiastic yet wistful note to her words. "We were in Russia for three years with Papa and spent every winter skating to our hearts' content."

"And your father took you skating all those times?" he asked, posing the question with an innocent air.

She shook her head. "Of course not! Papa had his responsibilities at court. Our foot—" Her eyes narrowed and she glanced up at him. "You tricked me."

He pushed off the rail and winked at her. "I did no such

thing. I merely asked if your father took you skating, and you said he did not. Then you seemed to have some problem remembering who it was who took you skating."

"I remember," she ground out.

"And who was it?"

She blew out a long breath, which was only exaggerated by the cold, leaving the little cloud hanging in the air like an exclamation point. "Our footman," she muttered.

"Your footman?" He folded his arms across his chest. "Wherever would you find one of those?" And before she could make another response, he pointed over to the other skaters. "Shall we?"

"Oh no, I couldn't . . . It wouldn't be . . ."

"Proper?"

"Exactly!"

"Why not?"

"Because I am about to become betrothed."

He let his brows rise in a wide arch. "You are?"

"Well, of course. Haven't you been listening to a word I've been saying?"

He'd been trying not to. "Miss Langley, I can't see how a few turns on the ice will affect your betrothal. Does this gentleman have objections to skating?"

She heaved a sigh and glanced back at the skaters. "Oh, 'tis nothing like that, it's just that he's a . . ."

"A curmudgeon?" he offered. "For he must be to deny you something you enjoy."

"It's just that I am to be a duchess, and you don't usually see such ladies out skating." There it was again. That wistful note. But she was right. Skating wasn't exactly a ducal pastime. He was positive his grandfather never had. And so he found himself sharing her envious glances at the people gliding over the ice.

"You should go skating," he urged her. "We could both go."

She shook her head. "I haven't any blades. Nor do you."

"Leave that to me," he told her as he took her hand and towed her toward a booth near the skaters. The red mitten now encased in his hand felt small, and oddly vulnerable.

"Really, I don't think—" she protested.

"Miss Langley, you aren't a duchess yet."

"But I will be quite soon and then—"

"And when you are, you may find yourself looking out the windows of your gilded prison wishing you'd gone for one last turn around the ice with your improper footman."

"I doubt—"

He held up his hand to stave off her protests, and by some miracle it worked. "Freedom, Miss Langley, has its advantages, and those ducal glories you long for will still be there tomorrow, but ice doesn't last forever."

She set her mouth in a stubborn line.

"Do you really want to spend the rest of your life without ever having skated again?"

"You sound like Tally," she shot back, and he had to imagine she wasn't offering him a compliment. "She was going on and on just yesterday that we'll both most likely end our days without ever being kiss—" Her eyes widened as she realized what she'd nearly confessed.

"Without ever being what?" he asked, bemused by the pink blush on her cheeks.

"Skating," she told him, her lips pursing shut and her gaze turning back to the skaters.

"Then come along," he coaxed. "Just a few turns. Besides, if your Miss Browne is right, no one of any consequence is down here and therefore your proper reputation is quite safe."

"She is not my Miss Browne," she shot back, her gaze on a couple who, hand in hand, were making an elegant and graceful circle around the ice. "Oh, it does look fun, and I suppose—"

He didn't give her a chance to reconsider. "Then skating it is." And he towed her toward the booth where a man stood hawking blades to passersby. This was madness, but he couldn't resist. Most likely she was right, duchesses and dukes weren't likely to be found skating. So they might both take this opportunity while they had the chance. He owed her that much. Before he took his place as Hollindrake and ruined all her expectations by crying off.

Besides, there were two other eligible dukes out there, and who knew how they felt about skating.

"Mr. Thatcher, I haven't any money—"

"Leave that to me, Miss Langley." And to his surprise, she did.

"Oh, look, a magic show!" Tally exclaimed. "Let's watch—for he has a monkey as well!"

She drew Aunt Minty along with her, while Pippin hung back, her gaze still fixed on the chestnut vendor across the way. Her stomach growled in protest as it had been a good three hours since they'd eaten their breakfast and she was well past her mid-morning tea and scones. "I'll be right back," Pippin told her cousin.

"Don't eat them all," Tally teased as she used Aunt Minty's age and sudden infirmity to gain them a front row vantage point from which to watch the man and his animal do tricks.

Absently, Pippin made her way through the crowd—Felicity was nowhere to be seen. But it was doubtful she was seeking out any amusements, so intent was her cousin on remaining a proper miss until she married her duke. And Tally . . . well, Tally was more concerned about having fun at the moment, with little thought of her future.

And Pippin, well, she was stuck between them—conscious enough of her position as the Earl of Stanbrook's daughter to keep her properly subdued, but dreaming of a love that could sweep her away from everything that was so very *tonnish.*

With a sigh, she stopped before the chestnut vendor. "One bag," she said as she dug into her reticule to find the coin she had tucked into the bottom.

"Is that all you want, little Circe?"

Those few words sent shivers down her spine, gooseflesh along her limbs.

Circe? Only one man had ever called her that . . . not that she ever thought of him . . .

Oh yes, she did. Had dreamt of him nearly every night for four years, and right now she couldn't even find the will to lift her gaze to see him again for fear he'd be like one of those ethereal visions that taunted her.

"Come, my sweet Circe," the man said as he circled around from behind the stand. "Don't tell me you've forgotten me?"

Her growling stomach no longer mattered. Her cousins, Aunt Minty, and the rest of London fell into an odd hush as she looked up into a pair of green eyes she never thought she'd see again.

The only thing that seemed to make a sound was the hammering of her heart.

"No," she whispered. "No, Captain Dashwell, I haven't forgotten you."

"I thought you said you could skate," Felicity said, laughing as she whirled around Thatcher. Oh, good heavens, she'd forgotten the freedom and fun of skating.

"I can," he said, as his feet went in opposite directions and he landed less than gracefully on his backside. He pointed at the blades strapped to his boots. "These are most ill-fit."

Felicity couldn't help herself. She laughed again. "You were the one who offered to dice for them. Perhaps next time you can win a pair capable of keeping you upright." She laughed again and did another quick turn around his prone figure. "Mine seem to be just fine." Gliding around him in a circle, she added, "I will point out that our former footman could skate backward."

"I was skating backward," he said. "I just went back farther than I'd planned."

Felicity giggled, and wondered when was the last time she'd done that! Just laughed for the pure merriment of it. There had been very little to laugh about over the last few years. Pippin's father's death just before they were to start their Season three years ago had kept her and Tally at their cousin's side during her mourning period, rather than go onto London with their chaperone, Lady Caldecott, as planned. Then their father's disappearance, Lady Caldecott's death, and finally Mr. Elliott's refusal to allow them to come to Town.

And she'd known that another year, let alone the four more years that Mr. Elliott threatened, would leave them veritable spinsters.

Yet here was this man making her laugh, when truly there was very little to find amusing. So how had he done it? By shaking her out of her proper mold with his ominous words.

. . . you may find yourself looking out the windows of your gilded prison wishing you'd gone for one last turn around the ice . . .

Ridiculous, really. For when she was a duchess, she'd be able to afford real skates, rather than ones they rented by dicing for them. Nor would she be constantly worried about filling the coal bin, their larder, or how they were ever going to get gowns enough for even a week of events, let alone an entire Season.

So for right now she'd take Thatcher's advice. What harm could there be in a little skating? If only her companion would . . .

"For one thing, you need to tighten the clasp," she said. "It's too loose." Skidding to a stop, Felicity knelt down before him and tugged the leather strap until the buckle held firm.

Having not given a thought to what she was doing, she glanced up the length of him, from his long, muscled legs, to the breadth of his chest, to the dark glittering gaze of his flinty eyes.

"Thank you," he said, an odd tilt to his lips.

A shiver ran down her limbs that had nothing to do with the cold. *This man is going to kiss me.*

Kiss her? Heavens, no! Where were these ridiculous notions coming from? Perhaps it was the warmth of his body beguiling her hand where it rested on his leg, sending a shiver of something else down her spine.

Oh, come now, you don't want to end your days as a spinster who's never been kissed, Duchess. Do you?

No, she didn't. But if there was going to be any kissing done, she'd do it with her betrothed. *Nearly betrothed,* she corrected as she stole yet another glance at Thatcher's lips.

"That should help," he was saying as he finished adjusting his buckles.

"I hope so," she said, getting to her own now shaky feet. Skating away from him, she let the icy air run across her flaming face, and hoped it could cool the ardor of her wayward thoughts. Stealing a glance back in his direction, she watched as he too gained his feet, his greatcoat falling away to reveal the length of his legs, the tight fit of his rough breeches, the way they encased his thighs, the lines of his . . .

And as luck would have it, he turned his head just then and caught her staring—well, gaping, actually—at his, ahem, buttocks. A slow grin spread over his lips, that is, until his foot slipped yet again and he fell. On that perfectly sculpted . . . backside.

"Miss Langley?"

She pressed her lips together and glanced up at the gray skies overhead. "Yes, Mr. Thatcher?"

"Is that proper?"

Oh, dear heavens, he did know her thoughts! That she'd been thinking of, oh, staring at . . . his derriere? Why, she might as well turn in her certificate from Miss Emery's school!

"What, Mr. Thatcher?" she replied, nose in the air and an imperious tone to her words that left no doubt as to her superiority.

"Skating like that?" he asked as he got up from the ice and pointed at the couple they'd spied earlier whirling past, their legs moving in tandem, their bodies swaying together as if they had been born skating. They held hands, and the smiles on their lips were only for each other. And most amazing of all was that they must have been nigh on eighty—and when they turned a corner, the old man leaned over and stole a kiss from the lady's lips. "Because if it is, I'd like to concede defeat and beg for your assistance."

With the skating or the kissing part? she nearly asked. Oh, curse these ridiculous notions, she chided herself as Thatcher skated up and came to a shaky stop beside her.

He nodded toward the couple. "Perhaps you should interview them for your *Chronicles*. I do believe they have more than just natural inclinations going for them," he said just as his knees started to buckle yet again.

She reached over and caught him by the elbow. "They do seem well matched, as if they know what the other needs before they know it."

Thatcher glanced down where her hand still held his elbow with steady assurance. "Do you think you and your duke will be so well matched?"

She was about to answer him just as the old couple turned in front of them and the lady smiled widely in their direction.

"I used to have to help my Henry like that, dearie," she said, winking at Thatcher. "But I think he tottered about so I would hold his hand." She laughed and skated off with her husband.

"Oh, I'm not . . . he's not my . . ." Felicity stammered, letting go of Thatcher so abruptly that he nearly lost his balance. She heaved a sigh and turned to steady him yet again. "Come along and practice, for you'll never get the hang of it again if you just stand about."

"Yes, Miss Langley," he said. They made a good turn around the ice, without a word between them.

"You didn't answer me before," he finally said.

"About what?"

"Your duke and those natural inclinations you seem to think are so important."

"Essential," she corrected.

"Yes, essential." They moved around two young girls, one of whom tossed a saucy look over her shoulder at Thatcher, their giggles following them over the ice.

Felicity pursed her lips, but said nothing.

"So do you and your duke share these natural inclinations?" he asked.

"Yes, of course."

"So why isn't he here skating with you?"

"He's just come to Town," she told him. *Without a word to me.* Oh, the embarrassment of it! Learning of his arrival from, of all people, Miss Browne.

"And I suppose he'll be renewing his natural inclinations quickly."

"Well, certainly," she said, even though doubts niggled at her once stalwart confidence in Hollindrake's affection for her.

"You know this even though you've never met?"

She swung around. "How did you know that?"

"You said as much earlier," he offered.

"I did?" She didn't remember telling him that, but then again, they had been talking about so many things, it was hard to recall.

"So how is it that you know you'll share these natural inclinations with a man you've never met? Great passion cannot be found in letters, Miss Langley."

Passion? Why was it that the word had never had any meaning to her until he said it—sending tendrils of something so delicious down her limbs that she felt *her* knees buckle. Oh, this was utter nonsense, she chided herself, straightening up and saying, "Duchesses aren't inclined toward great passions. 'Tis another reason why I am eminently suited."

"You're not even curious?" he asked.

"Not at all," she lied, looking away from the firm line of his jaw, those mysterious, dark eyes. At least she hadn't been curious before he'd arrived in her life.

"I've always held the opinion that you can't really know a woman unless you've kissed her," he said. "So how do you know you and your duke will suit if you've never even kissed him?" He glanced down at her, those perfectly carved lips of his looking ready to give her any experience she wanted in "natural inclinations."

And worse yet was that errant voice that had come alive within her since the moment she'd clapped eyes on this improper, impertinent man. *Kiss* him, *Felicity* . . .

"I don't think that is any of your business," she replied, letting go of his elbow abruptly enough to send him floundering. She skated away with her nose in the air, and made it a few feet before the inevitable happened—the great *swoosh* of his coat and the loud *thump* of his backside as he hit the ice.

She turned around, hands on her hips.

Unfortunately he didn't look any worse for the experience and had the cheek to wink at her. "Not offering to help me up?"

Help him up? "You got yourself down there, I daresay you can get yourself up." Then she skated off, trying to ignore the way her fingers curled inside her mittens as they ached to touch him yet again. To explore this annoying notion of passion that he'd sparked to life within her.

* * *

Thatcher did manage to get up, and he caught up with her as fast as he dared.

"That man over there is twice your age," Miss Langley said, pointing at Henry and his wife as they gracefully skated together. "And you haven't half his skill."

Thatcher looked over at the man, who was eighty if he was a day. "How old do you think I am?" Well, this was a fine kettle, if she thought him over forty.

"Ancient," she said with all seriousness. Until, that is, he spied the slight tip to her lips. "Truly, I am sorry, for it is hardly fair to judge your skating when it is apparent you are getting on in years and approaching a mature infirmity."

Why, the teasing little minx. "You think me that old?"

She nodded and proved her point by skating off, dashing a glance over her shoulder that dared him to catch her.

He winked back at her and pressed forward, realizing full well that he'd most likely end this race on his arse, looking like a fool.

But the spark in her eyes egged him on and had him forgetting what he was supposed to be doing. Instead of flirting with the gel, he should be casting her aside. Setting her straight that she and he did not suit. Making it clear that all her notions of natural inclinations were based on letters written by a seventy-two-year-old man and his equally unfit and romantically challenged secretary.

Nor had that kept him from considering, during all the time she spent lecturing him on what was proper, giving this miss a lesson in passion.

So he continued across the ice, his arms swinging wildly to propel him forward, his legs wavering beneath him, forging ahead as he'd done in the blindness of Badajoz. Except instead of the French, he was chasing after a lady who was most undeniably mad.

That, or he was going around the bend, for he could have

sworn when she'd been down on her knees redoing the buckles on his skates that she had looked up at him as though she wanted to be kissed.

But Felicity Langley had a way of looking at him that made him see her in all sorts of ways that were hardly proper—with her honey-colored hair pulled free, with those red socks she'd worn to the door tugged off, and with those wide, gorgeous blue eyes of hers pleading with him to do more than kiss her.

Thatcher stumbled on the ice but caught himself before he fell. His floundering about was followed by her laughter.

"What is so amusing?" he asked.

"You," she giggled. "I thought you were going to kill yourself trying to catch me." She skated around him, ending with a pretty little pirouette, her lips parted and looking perfectly kissable.

"I demmed near did," he said. "How would you feel knowing you'd killed me before I'd ever been kissed?"

Her eyes widened. "You've never been kissed?"

He leaned forward, close enough to catch a hint of her perfume, a wild note of flowers that was at odds with their wintery surroundings. "No, I've never been kissed," he told her. "Not by an almost duchess."

Well, perhaps he had overestimated the part about her flirting and wanting to be kissed. And the part about her being a proper English miss.

For Miss Langley's eyes grew wide, not with interest, but indignation.

And one other thing he'd underestimated. Just how proper Felicity Langley truly was.

For in an instant the lady's hand reeled back and came crashing into his gut in the form of a well-aimed and well-fashioned fist.

"Ooof—" he gasped as the air went whooshing out of his

chest. And to add insult to injury, his feet flew out from beneath him and he went flying up into the air and down on the ice with a great *smack*.

For a time all he could do was lay there, eyes closed, counting his blessings she hadn't blackened his eye or bent his nose. How would he ever return to his house and explain not only to Aunt Geneva, but Staines and his batman, Mr. Mudgett, that his nearly betrothed had wrecked such havoc upon him? He was demmed lucky she'd merely flattened him, with no outward evidence of his miscalculation.

Besides the bruises on his pride and ass.

"Mr. Thatcher?" she called out.

He lay there, still as stone, as unmoving as death itself. He heard her skate back, slowly. Most likely to crow over him in triumph.

"Mr. Thatcher?" This time her plea came with a little more urgency, even, one might hope, a measure of concern.

"Oh, bother!" she whispered as she knelt beside him. "I've killed him!"

Thatcher felt some smug satisfaction in her distress. Good, let her think of him as on his way aloft.

"Mr. Thatcher?" she whispered. "Dear sir, please get up."

Now he was her "dear sir." It took all his self-control not to "wake up" and point that out to her. But his gratification turned out to be short-lived.

"Gracious heavens, Mr. Thatcher," she was saying as she knelt down beside him. "You can't die, not on your first day." There was a pause as she took his hand and gave his arm a tentative shake. When he didn't move, she continued, "Oh, dear, the agency will hardly be willing to send another footman if they find out I've gone and killed you."

The agency? His eyes almost fluttered open. She was worried about them?

"Why did I ever let Mr. Jones teach me to box . . ."

Thatcher made a note not to ever cross this Mr. Jones, because if this was just a paltry example of his skills . . .

". . . for now I've most likely killed you! And worse yet, what if this accident is reported in the *Times* or, oh, heavens no, the *Morning Post*? I can just see it now: 'Deceased yesterday, a Mr. Thatcher on the Thames, a footman in the employ of Lady Philippa Knolles and the Misses Langley of Brook Street.'" There was a gasp from the lady. "That would be terrible. Someone might wonder what house we were at, and if they were to come and check . . ."

She shook him, this time without any concern for injuries. "Mr. Thatcher, Mr. Thatcher." When that didn't work, she gave him a good solid nudge. "Mr. Thatcher, this will not do! You cannot die here in front of the entire city." After a few more frantic shakes, she stopped, and suddenly he felt her bare fingers brushing back the stray strands of his hair that were falling into his face. "Please, sir, wake up! Someone will notice and it is hardly . . . oh, it is just not . . ." She reached over and traced a line over his cheek, and was nearly to his lips when they moved to form one word.

"Proper?" he finished, bracing himself as he opened one eye.

Chapter 5

Hubert Moorby, Earl Lumby
b. 1789, only issue of Lord and Lady Lumby. His mother
*   is related, albeit distantly, to the Duke of Sheffield*
Residence: Moorby Park, a house on Berkeley Square
*   and one on St. James*

Notes: According to Billingsworth, Moorby Park has a fine
vista and good shooting, which translated means it is a
Tudor relic most likely lacking a decent roof. The earl is ru-
mored to be overly fond of hounds and horses and is a poor
dancer. Maintains the town house on Berkeley Square for
his mother, which shows his good sense, according to those
who know the countess.

—Excerpt from the Bachelor Chronicles

Felicity stumbled back, landing on her backside. "You devil!" she sputtered as she scrambled back up. "How dare you
let me think you were . . . were . . ."

"Injured?" he supplied.

"Yes, and . . . and . . ."

"Dead?" he prompted.

She pointed a finger at him. "That as well. How dare you!"

He sat up and grinned at her. "But I wouldn't have discovered the depths of your feelings for me if I hadn't."

Even as Felicity's fingers curled into a fist, as if catching hold of the last vestiges of the warmth from his cheeks, her reliably practical nature overtook her mouth. "*Depths of my feelings?* I have no idea what you are talking about."

"Your fears over my apparent demise," he teased, extending his hand toward her in a request for help. "One might have found your statements quite passionate."

Passionate? Oh, dear. She had been. And worse, he knew it. What had compelled her to pull off her glove and touch him? Let her bare fingers trace the warmth of his cheek, search for the heat of his breath? For the only one who hadn't been breathing had been her—she'd never touched a man so intimately, felt the hint of stubble from his beard, harsh and wondrous beneath the tips of her fingers. And his lips, so firm and hard. All the while, one question had tolled inside her head louder than any other.

How would she ever find out what it was like to be kissed by him if he were dead?

Her gaze flew up toward him. No, she hadn't thought that. She couldn't have.

"Don't look so alarmed, Miss Langley," he was saying. "Your secrets are safe with me. Now will you help me up?" His outstretched hand tempted her like nothing ever had before. Not even the French wine Tally had been wont to steal from Miss Emery's larder, or even the thought of besting Miss Browne once and for all, could match the lure before her.

In that second, her passion found its freedom at long last. Like anything that had been withheld for so long, it poured forth a bevy of images like those she might find in the pages of one of Tally's novels.

Her hand enfolded in his, the warmth of his palm filling her veins with an tremulous heat. Instead of helping her up,

*he was tugging her into his arms, until they fell together in a
tangled jumble of intertwined limbs.*

But it wasn't onto the ice of the frozen Thames upon which
they fell . . . No, her newly freed imagination raced along,
skipping ahead of her good sense, carrying them to a warm,
deep bed and a room cast in shadows. Her essential winter
layers disappeared, and Felicity envisioned herself wearing
only her chemise, and Thatcher . . . well, the man was as
naked as the day he'd arrived in this world.

Magnificently so.

*"Thatcher, kiss me," she whispered to him in a husky,
womanly voice that surely couldn't be hers. And just as his
head dipped down to cover her lips with his, as his hand
cradled her breast, as he murmured something completely
untoward . . .*

"Miss Langley? Are you well?"

She could tell by the arch of his brows that this wasn't the
first time he'd asked her. Nor the second. Oh, heavens! She'd
been woolgathering! About *him.*

Felicity closed her eyes, her hands going to her head. Perhaps she'd been the one to fall to the ice and this was the
result of a very serious concussion. There had to be a lump
somewhere, for how else could she explain that he'd gotten
to his feet without her noticing? But there he was, leaning
over her and looking up under her bonnet, so that they were
nearly nose to nose, so close her gaze fell to his lips—firm
and well set and oh, so very masculine—as tempting as hot
chocolate or. . . . or . . .

Her first kiss.

She felt her lips purse, her eyes fluttering shut, as he asked,
"Miss Langley, are you well? You look rather odd."

Her eyes sprang open and all her fantasies went flitting
away, caught in the icy wind. "Quite well," she managed as
she shook off his offer for help by scooting away from him.
What was she thinking?

Kiss him? Why, it was absolutely ridiculous. She'd rather kiss a knighted merchant.

And that would be the extent of her matrimonial prospects if she didn't stop making a cake of herself over this wretched man.

"Hollindrake," she muttered to herself as she clamored to her feet and skated away. "Hollindrake. Hollindrake. Dearest Hollindrake," she chanted like an Eastern swami. "Sensible Hollindrake." Oh, she was feeling better already.

"Pardon?" he asked, as he caught up with her, his hand catching her by the elbow—mostly because he was teetering again, but his touch sent a shockwave of panic through her. No, not really panic. Something else. Something warm and tempting and, dare she think it? Wonderful.

Oh, this would never do. Shaking him loose, she said, "I need to go home. We all need to go home. Now! I just realized that if Miss Browne is correct and His Grace has come to London, then I should be at home awaiting his card, getting prepared . . ." *Oh, that didn't sound right.* "Making myself ready for his arrival." She paused in her rambling and chanced another look into Thatcher's dark eyes. "Imminent arrival," she added.

"Yes, of course," he said, shrugging his shoulders, and following her to the bench near the skate merchant where they sat down to unstrap their blades.

"Don't you think it unusual that the man didn't let you know that he was coming to Town?" Thatcher asked as he undid the buckles holding his blade to his boot.

Felicity tugged at her own strap to no avail. "He's a tremendously important person."

To her chagrin, he reached over and quickly and easily released her skate. "Too busy to inform his betrothed of his plans?"

"Well, we aren't actually . . . that is to say . . . well, we are nearly betrothed, so that doesn't require the same sort of familiarity one might expect if one is entirely betrothed."

The man let out a low whistle. "Nearly betrothed. Sounds like a slippery slope, to my way of thinking." He reached over to help her with her second skate, but Felicity brushed his hand aside and did it herself. "He could cry off at any moment."

"Cry off?" She rose to her feet, her entire body trembling at such a notion. "The Duke of Hollindrake is a man of honor. He would never do such a thing."

"How can you be so sure of him?" Thatcher rose as well, once again towering over her, and Felicity realized that she'd suddenly lost her advantage. "How do you know he's a man of honor?"

It was on her lips to tell this impudent man just exactly how honorable Aubrey Michael Thomas Sterling, the 10th Duke of Hollindrake was, when a shrill cry rose from the stalls behind them.

"My purse! My purse!" a woman shrieked. "It's been stolen!"

Felicity spun around. "Oh, heavens, Aunt Minty!"

"That doesn't sound like your aunt," Thatcher said, listening as the lady continued screeching.

"That woman there! She took it," came the cry. "I want the watch called. A constable summoned!"

"Oh, Aunt Minty," Felicity said under her breath as she began to lope through the crowd, pushing her way toward the knot of people gathered around the growing scandal. *This wasn't happening.* Having one's footman nearly go toes up in front of all of London was bad enough, but an aunt who was a . . .

Felicity shivered to even consider such a notion. "Oh, she just couldn't have!"

"I don't see the hurry," Thatcher called after. "I don't think it was your aunt's purse that was stolen."

"If only it was," Felicity replied.

* * *

"Captain Dashwell, whatever are you doing here?" Pippin said, taking a step back from the man who had haunted her dreams for far too long. Her hands fisted at her sides to keep them from trembling.

A dream lover was one thing, but a living, breathing one was an entirely different problem.

"So you do remember me, little Circe," he said, coming up to take her hand and kiss the fingertips of her mitten. His face was more weathered than she remembered, but those green eyes were still as sharp and keen as ever. "I must say, you have grown up since last we met, though you still blush quite prettily."

"Captain Dashwell—" she protested even as she felt the telltale heat on her cheeks rising.

Oh, heavens, Pippin, she scolded herself. *Steady. You aren't sixteen and he's no danger to you . . .*

As he had been that dark night so long ago.

Caught up in one of Felicity's madcap marriage schemes, their interference in Lord John Tremont's life had landed the poor man in jail, and it had been up to her and Tally and Felicity to continue his work for the King and country. She had found herself on a lonely stretch of beach near Hastings, the sort of secret inlet that was the haunt of smugglers and reckless coves—like Captain Thomas Dashwell. And when he rowed to shore, stepped out of the surf and into her line of sight, she knew her life would never be the same.

Her heart would never beat so fast as it did when he'd flirted with her, teased her, and eventually stolen a kiss from her innocent lips.

But in the four years since, so much had changed. Their countries were at war now, and they stood not united against France, but enemies.

Well, nearly enemies, she told herself. "Captain Dashwell, you shouldn't—"

"Sssh, Circe. Thomas, plain and simple, if you don't

mind." He leaned forward, pulled her even closer, then whispered into her ear, "The name Dashwell isn't much loved in these parts. Most of England and a good part of Scotland, for that matter. There's a rich price on my head—"

"Yes, I know," Pippin said.

"So you've been following my adventures, have you?"

"They are hard to avoid, sir," she told him. "You've caused a great number of merchants to lose their goods."

"Better they lose their tea and silks than I my head." He leaned forward. "For however would I steal another kiss from your sweet lips if I were to find my head stuck up on a pike?"

Pippin whipped her hand out of his and stepped back, looking left and right to see if anyone else was looking at them. "Then whatever are you doing here?"

"Stranded, I fear. At least until this ice melts," he told her. "I came in, to do some business, you might say, and have found myself landlocked." He waved at the ships held fast in the ice. "And without a friend to be had. At least until now." He tried again to take her hand, but this time she was quicker and tucked it safely under her cloak.

Not that such a thing would stop Captain Dashwell, she realized, as he slanted an assessing glance at her elbow, which still poked out.

Pippin took another step back. "I daresay you haven't done yourself any favors on that score. There is no doubt why you are friendless. Lady Josephine says you're a scurvy, dishonorable, wretched—"

Oh, there was no use going on. The scoundrel only preened under her scolding tones.

"But sweet Pippin, I thought that was why you liked me."

"I don't," she lied. "I don't even know you."

He tipped his head back to gaze at her, and she could see the shadow of a tawny beard on his face. For a moment as he studied her, she swore she could smell the sea on him—the tar and the pitch and the salt that had been his calling card that long ago night they'd first met.

Yet, he'd changed as surely as she had. His shoulders had grown in breadth, and now he loomed even larger over her—not like the popinjays and pampered Corinthians of London that Felicity constantly pointed out, but as a man used to living by his wits and fighting—or stealing, most would say—for what he wanted.

"So you've been reading about me in the paper? Seen the accounts of me and the *Circe*? Given any thought to that kiss of ours? When was that, two, nay, three—"

"Four years, sir," she told him. "I was but a child then, and you a regular villain to be so bold."

"A child! With a gun in her hand and doing a man's job for her country. Little Pippin, you were no more a child than you are now. And might I say you've grown into quite a fine lady. As pretty as I am dishonorable." He reached over and with one finger gently tipped her head up. "I've never forgotten those eyes of yours. As blue as my heart is black."

Pippin's heart lurched. He'd thought of her? Remembered her?

His rough fingers held her gently and there was almost a sad light to his eyes as he gazed at her. "Tell me you haven't gone and married someone else."

"No, I'm not married," she said, before she thought about it.

He grinned at her as he came closer and whispered, "I'd be sorely disappointed to discover that you hadn't waited for me—all those long years at sea for naught."

"I haven't been—"

"No, of course not," he agreed, but a mischievous light danced in his eyes as if he knew the truth. Knew her secret. "No, I have to suppose you are living in Mayfair in some grand house," he said, in a voice that held not envy, but . . . well, pity. "With servants aplenty to do your bidding."

She shook her head, unable to speak, mesmerized by the intimacy of being with him again. Just as she had dreamt. Imagined. *Desired.*

"Not in Mayfair?" he teased.

"Oh, it's in Mayfair, on Brook Street, though hardly grand," she whispered. Right this moment she was willing to tell him anything. "It's empty and cold. And it isn't even ours. Since we've no money, we had to steal it."

He stepped back from her. "You stole a house?"

"Sssh!" she warned him. "'Borrowed,' is how Felicity likes to explain it."

Dash let out a low whistle. "You stole a house? And here I thought myself a fine pirate." Then he cocked his head and studied her. "But what do you mean, no money? You're still an earl's daughter."

Apparently stealing—er, borrowing—a house wasn't such a grievous transgression in his world. But then something else struck Pippin.

You're still an earl's daughter. He knew who she was? "How did you—"

"I asked. Tremont told me. Last time I saw him. Just before this war broke out. Threatened me with a bullet through my heart if I ever came near you again." He chuckled at the memory, as if it was fondly held. "I think he thought your lofty state would frighten me away."

"Apparently it did," she said, "for it has been four years and naught a word from you . . . Not one word, 'cept what one reads in the papers." She paused again, feeling a bit tossed about. "Not that I've looked."

He laughed, loud and clear. "You little minx. You almost had me convinced you didn't care—but you do. Not looked, have you? I'd wager you've scoured the columns for me. And tell me, little Circe, how was I supposed to come calling when our two countries are at war—that, and there's been the sea and a good part of the British navy between the two of us, or are these facts that you've gone and ignored?"

"Hasn't stopped you from coming to London," she pointed out. "And selling chestnuts like some beggar."

He grinned again, stepping back to doff his ridiculous hat at her. "'Tis a fine cover, lass," he told her, nodding at his little cart. "Gives me a chance to hear all kinds of talk. The merchants can't get their wares out to sea, so they come down here and, well, wagging tongues . . ." He shrugged, then drew closer, lowering his voice to say, "When this ice breaks up, I'll be sitting off Shoebury Ness waiting for them like flies to honey."

"But you can't do that, 'tis wrong."

He laughed again. "Care to come with me and see just how wrong I can be?"

Oh yes! Please take me, she nearly said.

But somehow, Felicity's practical voice invaded her thoughts. *How can you trust this bounder, Pippin? He's a pirate. An American.* To her cousin's way of thinking, the latter was equal to the former.

Yet, what he was offering was far too tempting, tugging at her very soul. Panicked by the realization, she drew on every lesson in deportment she'd ever learned from Miss Porter at Miss Emery's school and took a firm and decisive step back. "Come with you? Why, you aren't even a proper gentleman, and I shouldn't even be—"

He moved much as he had four years earlier, sweeping her into his arms and hauling her up against him. Pippin struggled, but only a little and only to avoid a scene. Oh heavens, if Felicity saw her thusly, she'd have her hide for a wall hanging.

But oh, the devil take her, Dash was warm, and still smelled of the sea, and this time she wasn't some wide-eyed girl on the beach. Her body thrilled to be so close to him, to let her breasts press up against him, her legs and hips drift of their own volition up against him.

And just as he had the first time she spied him, walking up out of the surf on that beach near Hastings, he reminded her of Neptune's own temptation.

Her temptation.

And he knew it. The sparkle in his eyes and the wry twist of his lips said more than his brash American manners could.

"Now tell me you haven't thought of that kiss in all this time," he whispered in her ear. "Tell me you haven't wished for me to come ashore and steal you away?"

"I—I—I—" she managed to stammer, before there was a shriek from nearby.

"My purse! My purse! . . . Someone has stolen my reticule!"

Pippin's stomach lurched. "Aunt Minty!" she gasped, wrenching free of him—the chill racing across where he'd warmed her, the cold air hitting her like a slap in the face.

She turned toward where she'd last left Tally and their chaperone, only to find a strident matron shrieking, "Summon the watch! Call a constable!"

"Oh, no," Pippin said at the same time Dash cursed from behind her, "Demmit, not the watch."

She spun around, only to find the spot where Captain Dashwell had been standing was now empty, his cart abandoned.

But on a wisp of wind she swore she heard him say, "I'll find you, Circe. Mark my words, I'll find you again."

Thatcher followed behind Miss Langley as quickly as he could. For a miss so preoccupied with propriety, decorum seemed to be the last thing on her mind as she vaulted her way through the crowd at a tight clip.

What the devil had her petticoats in such a knot? So someone had pinched a purse—it wasn't her aunt's reticule that had gone astray. Really, given her reaction, one would think—

He slid to a thundering, skidding halt on the ice as one damning thought tumbled atop the other.

No! It couldn't be. Aunt Minty?

Bah! It was a ridiculous notion. Some aged chaperone who preferred dozing before the fire a pickpocket? Now he was the one going mad.

He glanced up to find that one of the city's officers had made his way to the matron's side. The only bit of Miss Langley he could still see was her bright blue bonnet bounding up and down as she made her frantic way through the knot of curious onlookers.

"That woman took my reticule!" the elderly lady trilled, one gloved hand pointing an accusing finger at Aunt Minty, while the other remained firmly tucked into an expensive ermine muff. "I'll have it back and see you hang for this effrontery!"

Tall enough to see over the crowd, Thatcher continued to push his way toward Miss Langley. She'd managed to gain her chaperone's side, while Miss Thalia stood nose-to-nose with their accuser.

Lady Philippa wasn't immediately visible, but as he drew closer, her lithe figure appeared on the other side of Aunt Minty, completing the triangle of support.

No, he had to be wrong. Their respectable chaperone couldn't be a thief. Whatever was he thinking? But that said, he wasn't so out of Society that he didn't know the ruin that even the merest hint of impropriety could cause, leaving the Langley sisters and their cousin far beyond the pale.

Then it occurred to him there was another way to save Miss Langley—*save all of them,* he corrected.

He could announce himself and reveal his identity.

That was it. All he had to do was announce himself. Then calm this matron with the veriest and most handsome apologies, followed by an invitation to Hollindrake House for the soiree or ball or whatever nonsense his aunt was determined to throw, and the promise of patronage to whatever charity she favored. That alone would no doubt curry enough goodwill to get her to overlook this obvious case of mistaken accusations.

"*I* am Hollindrake. I am *Hollindrake*," he practiced, muttering in a low voice to himself, still unwilling to make the loud and lofty public statement and leave his freewheeling life as Thatcher behind.

It would mean saying farewell to Miss Langley, he thought, taking one last glance into her lovely eyes. For once he uttered those words there would be no turning back. And despite her assurances that Hollindrake would never cry off, he would.

For while she was an intriguing minx, with all her contradictions and naive notions of inclinations, he wasn't ready to throw himself into the parson's trap just yet.

Taking a deep breath, he tried to remember how his grandfather had reduced any and all with the most withering of glances. Something with the brows and a flare of the nostrils, he thought.

"Do you realize who I am?" the aggrieved matron was saying to the constable who'd arrived to take charge of the situation. "My good man, I am Countess Lumby, and I will not be trifled with! And that woman—" She pointed at Aunt Minty. "—stole my reticule."

"I did no such thing!" Aunt Minty shot back. "She's half-crocked, is what she is! I'm a respectable lady, I am."

Lady Philippa's fair face turned even paler, and she waded in to try and smooth things over. "Dear sir, I am Lady Philippa Knolles, and this is my great-aunt, Miss Aramintha Follifoot. I believe there must be some sort of mistake, for my dear Aunt Minty could never have done anything such as this kind lady is suggesting."

"No mistake, not in the least," Lady Lumby cried out. "I daresay I know when my purse has gone missing. It was there, and then *she* bumped into me and then it was gone. Your aunt is a thief!"

"Why you old—" Aunt Minty started to say, her fists balling at her sides.

If he didn't know better, Thatcher would have sworn the old girl was ready to launch herself at the other woman.

Lady Philippa caught her by the arm and stopped her. "Auntie, please, this isn't helping. If you would just remain calm—"

But the old lady wouldn't be coddled. "Don't shush me! I won't be called a thief by some bird in paste!"

Lady Lumby's face turned such a dark shade of red, Thatcher thought she was going to fall over with apoplexy at the very suggestion that her jewelry wasn't real, never mind being referred to as "some bird." She turned to the constable and demanded, "Search her! Search her immediately! You'll find my reticule and see that I am telling the truth. 'Tis yellow velvet with gold trim and inside is a miniature of my dear, departed husband, Earl Lumby. God bless his soul, good and lawful man that he was." She followed this with a great sniffling bellow into her handkerchief.

Thatcher drew himself up and was about to press past Miss Langley and into the middle of this fray when he caught a look pass between Miss Langley and her sister. The twins shared an unspoken language, that much was obvious, and even though they were different in temperaments and nature, they were of one accord in that moment—a sense of determination—that let loose a chill of foreboding down Thatcher's spine.

What the devil were they up to now?

Miss Thalia stepped forward and began to weep . . . wail, really. "Oh, this is a tragedy! Your husband's miniature? Such a terrible loss for you, my dear lady! No wonder you are so distraught! So mistaken!"

The diversion was enough to give her sister the time to rectify the situation.

Now if Thatcher hadn't seen the glance between the twins, he too may have been mislaid by Thalia's dramatic performance. But his gaze stayed focused on Miss Langley with an instinct that had saved his life in Spain on more than one occasion.

If he'd blinked he would have missed it entirely, for in a flash Miss Langley's hand shot into Aunt Minty's cloak and whipped back out—bringing with it something he couldn't believe he was seeing.

A bright yellow purse. Gold trim and all.

The countess's reticule! Just as the woman had said.

And here he'd been ready to cast forth his name, title, and very reputation based on the assumption that this was all a mistake. Thatcher reeled back as the last few minutes took on an entirely new light. Miss Langley hadn't set off at a dead run because she feared her aunt had been robbed, but because she feared her aunt had been up to some mischief.

But that wasn't the worst of it. His almost betrothed wouldn't have reached into her chaperone's cloak and plucked out the countess's purse if she hadn't known exactly where to look—and done so with the skill that would leave a Seven Dials cove envious—if she hadn't known that the countess's claims were entirely true.

Thatcher doffed his hat and raked his fingers through his hair. Oh, this was the devil's own tangle. He glanced from the bellicose Lady Lumby to the constable who looked annoyed enough to cast them all into Newgate and let his superiors deal with it. And if the purse was found in Miss Langley's possession, she'd end up—right along with her aunt—on the next ship to Botany Bay.

Of course, that would end all your problems, a niggle of

a voice whispered in his ear, one that sounded suspiciously like Aunt Geneva's.

Here he'd thought his aunt's protests about Miss Langley's character had been just more of her top-lofty nonsense, her Sterling sense of greater worth. Yet somehow she'd seen through Miss Langley's proper veneer.

But what about his grandfather—the most Sterling of them all? Had he known?

Of course not, Thatcher told himself, dismissing such an idea outright. His grandfather would never have wanted the family linked with such scandal.

So if the old duke hadn't known—which was the only likely conclusion—that meant Miss Felicity Langley had conned the formidable Duke of Hollindrake like the veriest of rubes.

She'd gammoned my grandfather?

Thatcher knew he should be outraged, but for the life of him, such a skillfully wrought deception only left him looking at Miss Langley in a new light.

And he knew exactly what he needed to do.

Chapter 6

Felicity nearly had the purse beneath her own cloak when a solid hand clapped down on her wrist.

"I think not, Miss Langley," ordered a dark, dangerous voice that barely rose above the angry din around them. "Give it to me. Now!"

Much to her chagrin, Thatcher held her fast, despite her attempts to wrench her hand free.

"Give it to me," he repeated, quietly but firmly as he moved closer to her, so that now not only did he have her in his grasp, but his body pressed up against hers.

Instead of being furious at his overbearing intrusion, Felicity trembled with a different emotion. One more dangerous than the fear of being caught holding Lady Lumby's missing reticule.

"Don't be a little fool," he whispered. "You'll find yourself on the next transport if you are caught with that reticule."

She cast a glance over her shoulder and immediately wished she hadn't. Thatcher's eyes held an unholy fury. She'd never seen a man so irate in her life. With the possible exception of her papa when Nanny Jamilla had contrived to have him arrested in Paris so they'd be unable to leave for their next posting.

She dared another glance back. No, her footman was entirely past fury, and if the fire in his eyes ever reached his grasp on her hand, she had to imagine he'd pull her hand from her wrist.

But whatever was he doing wading into her tangle like some knight errant? Like a gentleman of honor come to save her reputation?

Like she might expect Hollindrake would.

"I won't be alone before the magistrate if you don't let go," she shot back under her breath, making another last desperate tug at his hold. Well, she might as well have tried to stop the tides. "Leave this to me," she told him. "I've the perfect plan to fix all this."

"I will see her hanged!" Lady Lumby bellowed.

"My lady," Tally was saying, using every bit of Langley charm she possessed to cosset the outraged woman. "If only we could all go get some tea and—"

"Search that woman!" Lady Lumby demanded of the constable, pointing a long, accusing finger at Aunt Minty. "Search her immediately or I will see you brought up on charges as well!"

"Miss Langley, give it to me right now." Thatcher's order held a threat worse than the countess's screeching.

Give it to him? Bah! She didn't know him, didn't trust him. Couldn't trust her feelings when it came to this unexpected man.

She spun around and pulled at his fingers. "Leave this to me," she ground out as she tried to pry his hand from her wrist.

"Miss Langley, be reasonable—"

"You've no business to be—"

"If you'd just let me handle this—"

"*My purse!*"

Felicity stilled as the words cut through her distracted rage. Her glance turned toward the countess who was pointing a thick finger at the tug-o'-war over the lady's reticule. And then she looked up at Thatcher, who had the temerity to glare at her.

At her? *Oh, the devil take him.* It wasn't as if she'd gone and ruined everything. She, after all, had possessed a plan.

"Arrest them all!" the countess cried out. "Why, these people are a veritable gang of cutpurses."

A murmur ran through the crowd.

"This is not what it looks like," Felicity said. "If only you would—"

Much to her dismay, in her distraction she found the purse finally wrenched from her grasp.

"Madame, if I can just explain," Thatcher began, holding out the reticule. "I am—"

"A blackguard!" the lady declared, recoiling in horror from him. "You're probably the leader of this gang! Your kind are all the same!"

Louder whispers of agreement rippled around them, and Felicity's blood ran cold—but that didn't stop her from continuing her defense. "My lady, I'll have you know that would be a terrible mistake," she argued. "This man is our footman, and—"

"Footman! Bah! How dare you speak to me, you devilish little tart. Arrest them, sir, or I will call on Mr. Stafford myself."

The constable nodded to the other officers who'd since arrived to start moving in, for none of them wanted the countess ringing a peal over their superior.

That is until a voice called out from behind them, "What the devil are you thinking? You'll be making the worst mistake of your life iffen you arrest the cap'n."

All heads turned at this interruption, and the crowd parted as a large man pushed his way forward. "I'm a telling ye this man no more stole that there purse than I'm the rightful King of France." He shouldered his way up to the constable and planted his feet in a wide stance. "Do you know who 'e is? Well if you did, you wouldn't be listening to this yapping crow here!"

"Mr. Mudgett, please," Thatcher warned him.

The man ignored him. "This here is Cap'n Thatcher, late of His Majesty's Rifles. A real war hero he is, saved an entire brigade at Salamanca, not to mention what he done at Badajoz. Arrest me good cap'n," he said, jerking his thumb at Thatcher, "and you'll have Wellington himself at your door."

Felicity wasn't the only one to turn an astonished gaze toward her footman. *Wellington?* Her footman knew Wellington?

Oh, this was going to make Miss Browne green with envy.

Then she shook off that wayward thought and considered the rest of what this uninvited stranger was saying. Thatcher was a war hero?

Her words from earlier came back to haunt her. *A duke is heroic and noble, a knight errant, if you will . . .* But Thatcher?

The constable repeated the question poised on every lip. "Is this true?"

Her footman jerked his head quickly.

"So how is it, sir, that you came by the lady's reticule?" the constable asked Thatcher.

"Well he found it," Mudgett huffed. "How else would the

cap'n come by it? Most likely he's about to return it, but being the modest sort that 'e is, he probably wanted the miss here to do it for him." The man thrust up his chest, his pride evident in the wide smile on his lips and the admiring light in his eyes. "This man would no more be dishonest than I would kiss a crow." He shot a hot glance at Lady Lumby. "I'll have you know, milady, you were about to accuse the—"

"The wrong man," Thatcher said, stopping the soldier's words with a sharp glance before the man could say anything more.

Whatever had just passed between the two, Felicity hadn't a clue, but she had every intention of ferreting out the truth the first chance she got.

"Madame," Thatcher said with all the grace and dignity of a gentleman to the manor born. "Your reticule. As my good batman said, I did indeed find it—your brave cries most likely scared off the villain who dared steal it."

The countess stood in stony silence while everyone awaited her verdict. But as quickly as she'd been willing to toss out her accusations, her forgiveness arrived just as readily. "You served with Wellington?" she stammered like a schoolgirl.

"Yes, madam, it was my honor," he said as he placed the reticule in her hand and curled her fingers gently around it to ensure its safekeeping. He held her hand for a moment longer, but then found she wasn't ready to relinquish him, latching onto his sleeve and holding him fast.

"I daresay, if Wellington depended on you," she twittered, "I can as well. Perhaps you could remember me to him, if you chance to meet him again. I was introduced to him once myself and it was a most memorable night."

"I'm sure it was," he demurred, trying to pull his arm free.

"Whatever are you doing working as a footman, good sir?" Lady Lumby cooed. "I daresay you should come work for me. 'Twould be a fine sight more respectable company, I daresay. The Lumbys are an old and respectable family. Why, my dear son, Hubert, is the 14th Earl Lumby." She shot a narrowed glance in Felicity's direction.

Felicity bristled and was about to open her mouth to give this woman a regular recitation of her very respectable and lofty lineage when suddenly the lady's words echoed through her ire.

Why, my dear son, Hubert, is the 14th Earl Lumby.

Her very single son, Felicity recalled. Then just as urgently, Thatcher's suggestion to use her *Bachelor Chronicles* to help their coffers—and the Misses Hodges—came hurling to the forefront of her thoughts.

She took a deep breath. Perhaps this encounter could have some fortuitous benefits. Why, if she could match . . . Oh, it was brilliant. Inspired! And it would be if she weren't too modest to confess, the best solution to their immediate problems, short of seeing Miss Browne packed off on the nearest merchant ship headed to the farthest tip of Africa.

Striking what she hoped was a contrite and convincing pose, she took hold of the countess's hand and said, "Dear Lady Lumby, how can you ever forgive us for all that has been said these past few moments?" The sincerity of her statement left her cousin and sister, and even Thatcher, gaping at her. "We are unused to Town ways, and when this terrible misunderstanding unfolded, I fear we behaved wretchedly, an embarrassment to our dear teacher, the esteemed *Miss Emery.*"

"Miss Emery, you say? Miss Emery's Establishment in Bath?" the lady asked. Felicity nodded. "Well, why didn't you say so before, gel? I was an Emery's girl myself!"

"You were?" Felicity replied, having known when she'd dropped the name that the lady was a graduate of the school. "Such gracious happenstance! How lucky we are to find you. Especially when we've come for the Season." Felicity knew from her *Chronicles* that the Lumby title was indeed an old and respected one, but one in need of cash, and she knew just how to make that happen.

And then they'd have the patronage of Lady Lumby, as well as the Hodges undying gratitude, to tide them over.

The lady preened for a moment longer. "I always said if I had a daughter, she would have gone to Miss Emery's. Alas, I have only my dear Hubert."

Felicity smiled and moved in to separate the lady from Thatcher before he caught a whiff of what she was about to do. "'Twas my mother's dying wish to see my sister and I attend her beloved school," she told her, eking out a small tear to add to her performance. When she glanced up she spied Tally's astonished features and shot her sister a look of patience. *She can help us.*

I'd like to help her into a crack in the ice, Tally seemed to be saying with her pursed lips and tight expression.

"And you're here for your Season without a mother's guidance?" Lady Lumby asked, casting a glance at the others.

Thankfully, Pippin and Tally caught on and both made appropriately woefully lost expressions over their motherless state.

"Only our aged aunt, who I fear," Felicity said, casting a small, sad glance over in that direction, "hasn't had the many benefits of Society as you seem to exemplify."

"Dear heavens, this is terrible!" Lady Lumby declared. "No guidance! And just think what could have happened if your dear footman hadn't found my reticule! I could have ruined your chances with my reckless accusations." The lady paused and once again sniffed loudly into her lacy handkerchief. "And here you are being so kind, so understanding. Then again I would expect no less from graduates of Miss Emery's Establishment." She paused to stow her handkerchief and pull her reticule strings tight. "I owe you a favor, I believe. You have but to ask and I shall grant you any boon."

Felicity let out a deep breath and smiled, linking her arm into the crook of the countess's. "I believe you mentioned a son, my lady. Might he be in need of a wife? Say, a wealthy one?"

Now what was the chit doing? Thatcher wondered as he followed the party off the ice. He couldn't quite hear what the suddenly mollified matron and Miss Langley were discussing, what with their heads bent together and studied looks on both their faces.

Plotting the demise of some helpless bachelor, he had to imagine.

At the quay, her ladyship's carriage awaited and the countess wouldn't hear of them waiting for a passing hackney to take them home, since the Stanbrook carriage had only been theirs for the trip to the river.

So the ladies were all bundled inside and Thatcher found himself outside with Mudgett on the tiger's perch at the back.

"What the devil are you doing here?" he asked his batman. "I thought I told you to keep to the house."

"Seems a good thing I was. Fine sight it would have been if I hadn't arrived when I did."

"That doesn't answer my question," Thatcher said.

"I told you I couldn't stay in that house. All that fancy gold and such." The man shuddered.

Thatcher laughed. "So you followed me. Disobeyed a direct order and came sneaking after me."

"You ain't me cap'n any longer," Mudgett shot back. "'Sides, I can't see that a duke needs a batman. You've got that fancy valet to lay out your clothes and do things up proper."

"That may be, but I prefer your honesty, my good man," he said. "And your company." He paused. "And your reinforcement, as well. I thank you."

Mudgett snorted. "But why didn't you just tell them all who you were? I'm thinkin' being a duke would have smoothed over that crow's feathers."

"That is exactly why I didn't," Thatcher replied.

His batman shook his head. "I don't see that at all. If you told that countess and those gels who you were, they'd be bowin' and scrapin' at your feet—and we'd be inside this here carriage instead of riding about on the outside. In this cold wind, I might add."

"So you do like a bit of luxury on occasion?" Thatcher teased.

"I ain't opposed to being warm, iffen that's what yer askin'. 'Tis a far sight colder here than I remembered and me bones ain't used to it." True enough. Mudgett had served in India before arriving in Spain—it had probably been twenty years since the man had set foot in his native land. "I still say you should have told them."

Thatcher shook his head. "Not yet. I've too many questions left unanswered."

Such as why didn't the Langley sisters and Lady Philippa have any money? Or what was so secret about their house on Brook Street? And most importantly, what was the woman his grandfather had chosen doing with a pickpocket for a chaperone?

"So ask yer questions," Mudgett was muttering. To his batman everything was black and white. French or English. Officer or soldier. Noble or not.

Thatcher shook his head again. "I'll not show my cards just yet. If I were to tell her who I was, she'd duck back behind some proper facade and then I'd never discover the truth about this Miss Langley—or how it was she deceived my grandfather so thoroughly." It had nothing to do with her lithesome body and fleeting, winsome glances, or the way her touch sent his blood on a hot and heated race through his veins.

"I still say it would be easier to just toss her over and be done with it."

Thatcher agreed, but that didn't mean he could. Not with his curiosity so roused. Not to mention the other parts of him that found her . . . well, demmit, rousing as well. He shook off those thoughts and told his batman, "If I want my answers, I have no choice but to continue taking reconnaissance under the cover of this livery."

Mudgett snorted. "You ain't going to cast yerself into the briars over this gel, are you?"

"Have you so little faith in my skills as a spy, Sergeant?"

"Just 'cause you got a uniform on, don't mean you won't get shot," his batman muttered.

Lady Lumby's carriage deposited the girls in front of their house on Brook Street. "Promise to call upon me, my dears!" the lady begged. Then she leaned out the door and caught Felicity by the sleeve. "And I will entertain your proposal for Hubert, Miss Langley. 'Tis an interesting proposition—one I certainly would never have thought of. But more to the point, I tend to agree that the pair may suit."

Felicity smiled. "My only wish is to see them both happy, my lady."

The lady let go of her, waving her hand at such a notion. "What is it with young people these days? 'Tis all romance and starry eyes. I say bah! Love and marriage under one roof is an impossible proposition, but no one can tell you young people otherwise." She sat back and thumped her cane onto the ceiling. "Home, Crackell!"

As the Lumby carriage rolled away, a dark cloud crossed over Felicity's shoulder, and despite her best efforts—and the vow she made during the carriage ride home to ignore the man—she trembled at the thought of him so close.

"Matchmaking, Miss Langley?" Thatcher asked, his question sending another shiver down her spine. "Is that a proper occupation for a future duchess?"

"I'm not a duchess yet," she shot back, tipping her nose in the air and dodging out from his lofty shadow and heading in a determined path toward the door. She had a thousand and one things that would need be done, and quickly if everything was going to work. Oh, and if it did . . . well, visions of new gowns and furniture and coal danced before her eyes.

Not to mention the ducal coronet atop her head.

"If you must know, I am only following your suggestion. I am going to find the Hodges sisters brilliant matches."

"My suggestion?" Thatcher's sharp outburst was matched by the thick trod of his boots following close behind her. "I'll have you know, no man appreciates being caught in a female's trap."

She turned around. "It is my experience that most men don't know what it is they want, even when it is right beneath their nose."

And there she stood, right beneath his nose, and a tiny voice niggled in the back of her heart. *That applies to you as well, Felicity.*

Applied to her? Not in the least.

Doing her best to ignore the strong set of his jaw and the obsidian glint of his eyes, she continued, "Men make this great pretense of not wanting to be caught, but in the end they usually beg for a lady's hand."

"Pretense? Have you ever considered that such a defense might be deliberate?" He looked up and down the street. "And if your theory is correct, Miss Langley, where is your duke? Why isn't he here on bended knee begging for *your* hand?" His brows waggled at her, and Felicity felt a hot flush rise on her cheeks. "Or could his delay mean he is currently fortifying his house against your wiles?"

"M-y wha-a-at?"

"You heard me, your wiles," he said. "The ones you were practicing on me today."

"Ooh!" she blustered. Shaking a finger at him, she fired back, "I did no such thing." Perhaps she had, but she wasn't about to admit anything to this arrogant, intolerable . . . "Yours, sir, is exactly the attitude that leaves women—whose fates, I might add, are entirely at the whims of men—to fend for themselves by whatever means possible."

"Whatever means possible?" Thatcher's brows drew dangerously together. "Is that what you did to secure your precious duke? Used any means possible?"

Tally, Pippin, and Aunt Minty all stepped back like spectators on a battlefield—far enough away to be out of the direct line of fire, but close enough to hear every shot. Even Mr. Mudgett, the battle-hardened veteran, edged cautiously out of harm's way.

Felicity's mouth gaped until she remembered Miss Emery's hours of lectures on the uncouth nature of such an expression and pressed her lips shut. Tight. More though out of fear of the very uncouth expression rising in her throat like bile. "Mr. Thatcher, your services are no longer—"

"Duchess!" her sister cried out, rushing down the steps and pulling Felicity out of the fray and out of earshot. Tally gave her a less than gentle shake, which worked to pull Felicity's furious gaze off Thatcher. Lowering her voice, her twin started a hasty lecture. "Don't! You can't sack him." Tally moved them both a little farther away and around a snow bank. "Have you not considered the cachet of having one of Wellington's war heroes in our house?"

Felicity did her best to ignore the image of Thatcher in a sharp uniform, standing bravely in the face of enemy fire, his only thoughts of home, and country and King . . . *and her* . . .

Oh, botheration! She was turning as mad as her sister and Pippin!

And worse, Tally wasn't done dangling Thatcher before her

like some prize. "Did you see how Lady Lumby tried to lure him away? We shall be beset with offers for his services, not to mention he is the only bit of glamour we have at present."

Felicity made a low growled protest. "He will ruin our plans."

"Your plan," Tally pointed out, "consists of a proper house with servants—neither of which we have. Given our situation, I fear he's about as close to proper as we are going to get." Felicity went to open her mouth, but her sister hastily continued on, "Don't you remember what Nanny Jamilla always said about footmen?"

"Handsome, dangerous, and capable of making every other lady envy you for their services," Felicity replied, reciting it like one of their school lessons.

"And Mr. Thatcher *is* devilishly handsome . . ." Tally let her words dangle, not that Felicity needed to be reminded of how Thatcher looked.

"Perhaps," she offered, glancing over her sister's shoulder at the man. That was one of his problems.

"And he was in the war, a hero if you believe this Mr. Mudgett, which makes him dangerous, and Lady Lumby has proven the third rule. So whatever you do, don't dismiss him. Not yet. At least not until you've gained your betrothal to Hollindrake."

"But Tally, he's—"

"Not a very good footman, I agree, but we can make do. Think of how envious Miss Browne will be when it is nosed about Town that our footman served with Wellington."

"I had rather thought of that," she admitted.

Tally caught hold of that thread and pulled. "See now, if you let him go, how would that reflect on us? Tossing a war hero out in the street?"

Her hand covered her mouth. "Oh, dear, I hadn't thought of it that way."

"Yes, I noticed that. You let your temper get the better of

you," her sister chided. "Now you'd best apologize to the man so he doesn't up and quit on us."

This was enough to jolt Felicity right out of whatever guilt she'd been feeling. "Apologize? To him? Never!" She set her jaw and shook her head. "Tally, he is the most provoking man. He was insinuating that I deceived Hollindrake into our arrangement. Why, that is entirely—"

"Correct, and that's what has you in such a temper." Tally glanced over at the glowering footman and grinned. "It appears we'll have to watch ourselves around him or he'll discover all our secrets."

Now it was Felicity's turn to make an indelicate snort. "Not likely." But still, he was rather observant and too smart by half. That in itself made the prospect of outwitting him tempting. But Tally had the right of it. They couldn't send a war hero packing.

Oh, why couldn't the man have been a cook in the war? Or a requisitions clerk? He would have to be a hero, with his darkly handsome looks and his noble features.

Not that it mattered to her, she told herself as she took a deep breath, pasted a smile on her face worthy of the finest Covent Garden thespian and trudged through the snow toward him.

As Tally so eloquently said, she needed this man. No, *they* needed him, she corrected. After all, appearances were their only currency at present.

"Tally points out, and rightly so, that I was being exceedingly rude, Mr. Thatcher. My apologies." She paused and shot a glance at Tally. *There, I did it*. Her sister smiled and nodded for her to continue. *More?* Felicity cringed. "It has been a trying day," she ground out, "and I still have much to do and I would be ever so grateful if you would continue your services with our household."

A collective and expectant sigh moved through the rest of the spectators.

He looked about to refuse her, to quit on the spot, when his friend Mr. Mudgett coughed a bit and offered some comment she couldn't hear. Whatever the man said, it was followed by a grimace on Thatcher's part.

Then he took a deep breath and bowed. "At your service, Miss Langley."

Good, now that she had his word, she couldn't resist lobbing one last ball in his direction. "Most excellent. I intend to send around a note to the Misses Hodges. Will you be so good as to run it by their house?"

Thatcher's face turned red, but Pippin rushed in to turn the tide before the man exploded. "Well, now, seems we've fixed all that," she declared. "Time for tea. 'Tis been an age since we ate."

Tally laughed and edged herself between Felicity and their footman. "Aren't you forgetting your chestnuts?"

Pippin's brows furrowed for a moment. "Oh, yes. How could I have forgotten those? Still, doesn't tea sound nice?" She set a hasty course up the steps, and when she got to the top she turned to Thatcher. "Did you truly serve with Wellington?"

He nodded politely.

Then to Felicity's dismay, Tally reached over and caught Thatcher's sleeve, pulling him along with her. "Oh, you must come up and have tea as well. My sister's note can wait. I'd love to hear tell of some of your more dangerous duties. Pippin and I have been thinking of writing a war epic."

"*Thalia!*" Felicity's horror ran all the way down to her boots. "One doesn't invite their footman to tea."

"There really isn't anything to tell, Miss Thalia," Thatcher demurred.

"Nothing to tell?" Mr. Mudgett shot back. "Nothing to tell, he says. Why, that's a fine one."

"Mr. Mudgett!" The warning rang clear to anyone who was listening. But no one was.

"Then you must join us for tea," Tally said, discarding Thatcher and pulling the other man up the steps, shooting a look at Felicity that dared her sister to come up with a reason against this invitation. "I would love to hear all about Mr. Thatcher's years of bravery." She paused at the door and then smiled sweetly at the man. "And yours as well, sir,"

"Oh, I too," Pippin declared, helping propel Mr. Mudgett inside the house.

"Well, there was that night at Badajoz, when the cap'n . . ."

Had they all gone mad? The last thing Felicity wanted to hear was that their footman had saved an entire battalion due to his courage. Or that Thatcher had stopped the French from looting and defiling poor defenseless Spanish women and children. Or anything that might shine a favorable light down on him.

Well, she just wouldn't listen to their prattle. "I have far better things to do. Such as invite the Hodges to tea," she declared as she marched past all of them.

"The Hodges?" Tally asked. "They aren't exactly high *ton*. Have you forgotten your plan?"

"No, but they have something we haven't," Felicity told her.

Her sister's fair brows drew together. "Whatever is that?"

"Coal."

Tally shook her head, confused.

"Well, we can't have the tea freezing when the Duke of Hollindrake comes to—"

"Hollindrake?" Mr. Mudgett said. "The Duke of Hollindrake, you say?"

"Well, yes, I am betrothed . . ." She flitted a glance over at Thatcher, who looked ready to make some comment, so she amended herself. ". . . *nearly* betrothed to him and I don't want—"

"Oh, miss, you don't need to worry a bit about the cold,"

Mr. Mudgett told her. "I doubt Himself will mind a nip in the air all that much."

Felicity turned and eyed the shabbily dressed man, who at present had tracked in a considerable bit of mud into their foyer. "*You* know the Duke of Hollindrake?"

"Of course I do, and if you don't mind me saying—"

"Mudgett—" Thatcher started to interrupt, but Felicity stepped in front of him and cut him off, literally and figuratively.

"How, sir, is it that you know His Grace?"

"Well, I was the duke's—"

"*Valet,*" Thatcher interjected. "Mr. Mudgett was the duke's valet."

"Valet?" both Felicity and Mr. Mudgett said together.

"Yes, valet," Thatcher asserted. "*His valet.*"

Mr. Mudgett eyed Thatcher again before he agreed, "Oh, aye, his valet."

"Before he became my batman," Thatcher said, more like he was instructing the man. "Mr. Mudgett was the duke's valet."

"Afore he was a duke and all toplofty, iffen you know what I mean," the man added.

"I don't believe it," Felicity declared.

"Why, some days I hardly believe it meself," the man told her, tipping his head to wink at Thatcher. "Oh, the stories I could tell you of *Himself*. The things I could tell you about the man, why they'd curl those fine blond locks of yours."

"Mr. Mudgett!"

Thatcher's sharp retort jolted Felicity—and she turned an inquisitive glance first at her footman and then at his former batman. "Mr. Mudgett, I would love to hear more about His Grace, but I fear Mr. Thatcher objects. Whyever do you suppose he does?"

"Oh, he would. Probably doesn't think it's a proper thing

for ladies to hear about such craven tales. Why, I could tell you anything you want to hear about the man, right down to the scar on his—"

"Mr. Mudgett!" This time Thatcher's interruption held a warning note that stopped his friend cold.

"What?" the forthright man said, a wry tip to his lips.

"These are young ladies, not new recruits."

Mr. Mudgett glanced over at his audience and shrugged. "I suppose they know men 'ave got bums, don't they?"

Tally covered her mouth to keep from laughing, while Felicity colored at the thought of her nearly betrothed with a scar on his . . . well, his posterior.

"Be that as it may," Thatcher told him, "it isn't a proper subject for young ladies." He paused and leveled a stern gaze at the man. "Besides, there is the *valet's code* to remember."

"The valet's what?" Mr. Mudgett and Felicity asked.

Thatcher took a wide stance and said in a firm voice, "The code. The valet's code. An employer's secrets are a valet's secrets."

Mudgett worked his jaw back and forth. "I suppose next you'll be telling me that goes for a batman as well."

"Especially for a batman," Thatcher told him.

"What about footmen?" Pippin ventured.

He bowed slightly to her. "Your secrets will travel with me to the grave, Lady Philippa."

Felicity noticed he didn't include her in his vow. She wove her way between her cousin and their footman. "Not that we have any," she interjected. "Secrets, indeed!" Pulling off her cloak, she thrust it into Thatcher's hands and then turned her back to him. "Mr. Mudgett, are you in London to regain your position with the duke?"

The man waved a meaty paw at her. "Nay. 'E's gone all toplofty now. I doubt he's got a place for old Bob Mudgett in that fancy house of his."

She sucked in a deep breath. "Mr. Mudgett, this cannot be.

The man I've corresponded with would never be so mean as to not help out a former employee, especially one who had spent so many years serving our dear King and country. No, Mr. Mudgett, you must have it all wrong!"

"I daresay I know the fellow better than most," the stubby fellow declared.

This stopped Felicity in her tracks. Here was the closest opportunity she'd ever had to interview a firsthand source as to the duke's character—well, other than Lord Jack Tremont, but he'd never been all that forthcoming about his old friend— still, she wasn't about to waste this golden opportunity.

"Dear sir," she said, wrapping her hand around his elbow and leading him toward the stairs. "There must be some mistake! I am certain the Duke of Hollindrake, if he knew of your plight, would be most generous in a settlement or in finding you a proper position."

"A settlement? Now doesn't that sound nice!" the man said, smiling over his shoulder at Thatcher. "Maybe you do know best, miss."

She wasn't about to let her impossible footman derail this man with all his "valet's code" nonsense. "Perhaps some tea would warm your spirits, sir, or even a spot of brandy. And then if you feel inclined, you could indulge me with a few reminiscences about the duke."

"Mr. Mudgett!" Thatcher warned, the hard thud of his boots coming up from behind them. "The code!"

Felicity ignored him and sent a broad smile in Mr. Mudgett's direction. "I have it on good authority that this code hardly applies to *former* employers."

"Oh, right she is," Tally enthused. "Think of the book you could write!" She waved her hands in the air, like a magician revealing a trick. "'The Life and Loves of the Duke of Hollindrake.'" She shivered. "A best-seller, I assure you."

"Brandy, you say?" Mudgett replied, the idea of writing a book quite lost on him. But brandy . . .

Felicity nodded. "We have a lovely vintage. A gift from the Earl of Stanbrook." The man needn't know that they'd liberated all of the brandy in the earl's cellars to pay Mrs. Hutchinson—not that she didn't have every intention of re-stocking the shelves once she was married.

"And cakes," Pippin added.

"Cakes, eh? I like cakes," he said.

Felicity sent up a fervent prayer that they had any cake.

"I can't see what harm there is in a few proper stories," he told them.

"Mudgett!" Thatcher warned again, but it was far too late, for Felicity had led her willing victim up the stairs and was ready to begin plucking him like a fat pigeon.

Not that she had forgotten her footman. At the first land-ing, while everyone else was hurrying up to the warmth of the sitting room, Felicity paused and turned to him. "Mr. Thatcher?"

"Yes?" he ground out.

"Please fetch the tea tray from Mrs. Hutchinson. You'll find her, hopefully, in the kitchen."

"Miss Langley—"

"Oh, yes," she said, cutting him off and ignoring the dark tremble in his voice. "Make sure she includes our best cakes on the tray."

Then, for some inexplicable notion, she cast in his direc-tion that infamous glance, the one Nanny Jamilla had cau-tioned to use sparingly, if at all.

To her shock it worked, for he stepped toward her, a blaz-ing look in his eyes that held little propriety, little ceremony.

And just as easily as she'd cast it, she found herself en-twined by her own net. For one look into his dark and stormy countenance, one glance at the set of his jaw and the firm line of his lips now pressed together in a hard line, sent a ripple of goose flesh down her arms. Beneath her skirt her knees wavered as she considered the raw, hard power of

those devilish lips, the rough shadow of his beard, the muscled strength beneath his patched coat.

He came crashing up the steps, taking them two at a time,
until he stood on the step below her, indecently close, so that
his very breath mingled with hers.

All too quickly she realized why it was Nanny Jamilla had
cautioned the girls to never use the look indiscriminately.
For it could tangle a man's honor, his good sense, and let
loose the hungry animal that lurked beneath even the most
civilized noble veneer—let alone the rough-edged, war-
hardened man before her.

"Anything else you would like, Miss Langley?" he asked,
his voice now mocking, as if he could see her thoughts, could
feel the wretched coil of want trembling inside her.

"Nothing but the tea tray," she replied curtly, turning on
one heel and fleeing up the stairs. Oh, she should just fire the
man and be done with it. She had no need for heroes in her
life. She had Hollindrake—who would, hopefully, possess the
same arrogant self-assurance that made her heart beat wildly.

Yet even with dreams of Hollindrake in the forefront of her
thoughts, she took one last casual peep down the stairs, and
found her beastly footman grinning up at her, as if he were
the one with the upper hand. She straightened and continued
up the steps, shaking off the last vestiges of passion that the
man seemed to awaken in her with the easy frequency of rain
in Scotland.

No, she didn't need a hero.

Nor his kiss. Or his steely embrace.

When she was the Duchess of Hollindrake, she would have
no need for such an ethereal and flighty notion as passion.

Or would she?

Thatcher made his way down the stairs toward what he
hoped was the kitchen. While he suspected he'd given the
little teasing minx a piece of her own medicine on the stairs,

that didn't mean her winsome glances hadn't put his loins into a heated rush.

If he didn't know better, he'd suspect there was a well-practiced courtesan hidden beneath Miss Langley's innocent muslin gown. A proper duchess, indeed!

And more to the point, how the devil had this chit pigeoned his grandfather? Oh, he was going to get his answers and then he'd—

He pushed the door open and found Mrs. Hutchinson at the worktable in the middle of the room, pouring herself a hefty measure of what was most likely the Earl of Stanbrook's prized brandy.

"A bit to keep the chill off," she told him, nudging the glass toward him and reaching for another, which she filled up to the top. No half measures for their housekeeper.

He took the proffered glass and raised it in a mock toast. "Mrs. Hutchinson, what the devil is going on around here?"

"So you noticed, eh?" she said, taking a gulp of the brandy.

"Just a bit," he said, taking a more cautious sip.

"You wouldn't believe the half of it," she said with a shaky wave of her hand. Obviously this wasn't her first glass of the day.

"Try me," he said, settling down across from her and pouring her another measure. "Starting with this Aunt Minty."

The lady sputtered over her drink. "She didn't get nicked, did she?"

"Nearly," he told her. "Tried to lift Lady Lumby's reticule."

"Tried?" The housekeeper shook her head and sighed. "Now that is a sad one. There was a day when Aramintha Follifoot was the finest knuckler in all of London." She sighed again and took a drink. "I tol' her not to try no more. Her eyesight ain't what it used to be, and she's not as light on her feet."

Thatcher blinked and tried to determine whether he had

heard the housekeeper correctly or if he should set aside the brandy right now. Instead, he tossed back his portion and leveled a glance at the housekeeper. "And the ladies know this about their chaperone?"

"A course they do. They are fine ones, they are," Mrs. Hutchinson said, leaning back in her chair, glass cradled in her hands. "Good gels, all three of 'em, and not high and lofty in the least. Took in Aunt Minty when her husband died. Weren't no place for her to go, and old Dingby Michaels, God rest his soul, thought she might do just fine for the girls as their new chaperone. Asked the Duchess to take Aunt Minty in just afore he died."

"Dingby Michaels?" Thatcher said. "The highwayman? I remember reading about him when I was a child. He terrorized the North Road for years and then disappeared."

"Oh, aye, a fine gentleman Dingby was. Didn't so much as disappear, but went all proper, changed his name and got himself a position with some nob. Tremont, I think his name was. That's how he met the girls—they were visiting the house where he worked and, well, they got on. So when the Duchess decided to come to London, she wrote Dingby, since he had so many connections here."

Thatcher shoved his glass out of reach. "But why would the daughters of a baron and an earl need a highwayman's connections?"

"Well, haven't you looked around? They ain't got a penny between 'em."

"But their fathers—" he protested.

"Harrumph. Scalawags, from the sounds of 'em. The earl got himself killed by smugglers, not that you'll hear that in their fine circles, but I've heard some talk. And the baron, well, there's talk he went over to the French before he . . ." She sliced her finger across her throat.

"Lord Langley would never have—"

She staved off his argument with a shrug. "Don't know

either way, just know what I hear," she said. "Not that it matters, since the money's all tucked away and that purse-tight
solicitor of theirs won't let 'em have a farthing of their inheritance. Not till they marry or come of age."

"Don't they have a guardian?"

"Did, but she died last summer. A fine lady who treated
them kindly, according to Miss Tally, but the old girl had
no more say as to their money than what they get for their
spending."

"Pin money," he supplied.

"Aye, that's what they call it. Their pin money. Not much
that, let me tell you. Been on their own since the old lady
went aloft."

"But how did they manage to rent this house, or even get
to London?"

Mrs. Hutchinson chuckled and raised her glass. "Spend
enough time with the little Duchess and you'll see. Bound
and determined to come to Town, she was, wouldn't let the
solicitor tell her different. Knew this duke of 'ers would be
here and she was afeared of letting him loose in London
without her close by to keep an eye on him."

"So this is all about the money?"

"Ain't you been listening to me? It's up to the Duchess
to get married and right quick so they have a roof over their
head and food on the table. If you haven't looked around, the
larder ain't got much in it and the coal bin even less."

"So how is it that they think they can make a Season of
it?" he asked, incredulous that three slips of muslin could
think to pull off such a feat.

Well, of course they thought they could. Because his
grandfather had all but convinced Miss Langley a betrothal
was forthcoming and therein secure all their futures.

But surely she must have realized that something might
not go right—like Aunt Minty's penchant for picking pockets, or the fact that very shortly they'd have no food or coal.

Mrs. Hutchinson leaned across the table and nudged him out of his reverie. "Don't look so worried, sir. The Duchess, well, she'll find a way to make it all work out." She filled her glass again. "I says she'll find her reward for being such a good one."

"How so?" From where he sat that was hardly the description he'd use for Miss Langley. But then as the lady explained, he realized his measure wasn't the one that counted.

"Well, she took in me and my Sally," Mrs. Hutchinson declared. "And I can say this, because she's mine, but Sally's not a bright girl, takes after her father, God rest his soul. And I drinks a bit, which ain't in my favor, but the Duchess gave us a home and for that I'm grateful. Promised me I always would have one, and Sally too."

He couldn't imagine Aunt Geneva making such a vow, let alone keeping any servants who weren't of the finest example or capable of doing their full share of labor. Who in the *ton* would?

"I can see what yer thinkin'," Mrs. Hutchinson was saying. "There's some that will promise you anything just to get what they want, but not the Duchess. She'll keep her word, bless her heart. She's the sort who'd never go back on her word. Never."

Thatcher sat back. Those words sent a chill down his spine that no amount of brandy could warm.

She'll keep her word, bless her heart.

Just as his grandfather had always averred a Sterling must, for wasn't that their motto? *Verbum Meum Jusjurandum.*

My word is my oath.

And now that promise fell on him.

Chapter 7

Aubrey Michael Thomas Sterling,
Marquess of Standon

(Addendum 28 July 1813) Notice in the Times. The 9th
Duke of Hollindrake has passed away and Standon is
now the 10th duke.
(Addendum 4 February 1814) According to a Mr. Bob
Mudgett, the duke's former valet, Hollindrake (when he
was just Mr. Sterling) had a penchant for "chasing after
any bit 'o muslin he could find and gambling without a
care for what's to feed him tomorrow." While this report is
alarming, a man who never thought to inherit is allowed
some youthful excesses. Isn't he?

—Excerpt from the Bachelor Chronicles

*Yours, sir, is exactly the attitude that leaves women—whose
fates, I might add, are entirely at the whims of men—to fend
for themselves by whatever means possible.*

Miss Langley's words, accusation really, still continued to echo the next morning through Thatcher's thoughts. *Whatever means possible.* Hard words indeed, but what they hid was a woman with a generous and loyal heart. A determined chit, surely, but there was more to his unlikely betrothed than the marriage mad miss he'd first assumed her to be.

From across the table, Aunt Geneva's insistent voice penetrated his musings. "You didn't tell her who you were?"

Thatcher shook his head. "No." Instead of elaborating, which appeared what Aunt Geneva wanted him to do, he dug into his breakfast—the ham too fragrant to ignore. Besides, he'd learned his lesson about eating with Aunt Geneva yesterday—best to fortify himself quickly.

What was he going to say? *Aunt Geneva, Grandfather betrothed me to a penniless miss, whose chaperone is a notorious pickpocket.* Then when the old girl was revived by a crate of smelling salts, he could finish her off by revealing that Felicity had gained her housekeeper on the advice of a former highwayman.

She'd think he was as mad as the fifth duke.

His aunt set down her napkin and looked across the breakfast table at him. "Your Grace, 'tis cruel to continue deceiving this poor innocent girl."

He suspected his aunt's sympathy had more to do with her desire to see them well rid of such an undesirable *parti* than for any real concern for Miss Langley's reputation.

And his sympathies? Well, they'd been shaken by Mrs. Hutchinson's revelations. After a glass or two of Stanbrook's brandy, the old housekeeper became quite loquacious, revealing far more than he thought Miss Langley would ever own up to.

The Duchess deserves more than that duke of hers. I told her to find a good man who would love her, like my Bertie loved me. But she wants her duke, she does. Well, I says, where is that top-lofty nob? He should 'ave been here to greet her when she arrived the first day. If he's done her wrong, I'll show him what a cleaver can do, I will.

Thatcher closed his eyes and wished himself out of this muddle. Honor dictated that he marry her, betrothal or not. But Mrs. Hutchinson was also right. Felicity Langley deserved someone who would love her. Passionately. Whether she knew it or not.

And there in the wee hours of the morning, as the sun started to rise over the snowy rooftops of Mayfair, Thatcher had seen a different light to this entire muddle.

What if she could love him? What if they could find some passionate accord before the chains of ducal responsibilities turned their lives as dull and lifeless as those "natural inclinations" she'd been nattering on about?

"Your Grace, are you listening to me?" Aunt Geneva was saying. "You can't continue this! You need to cry off and be done with her. Take up your responsibilities."

Thatcher put down his fork and stared at her. "That girl, like it or not, is my responsibility. How can I just cry off? Where is the honor in such an act?"

"Honor!" she scoffed. "She most likely deceived Father in some manner to ingratiate herself into our family. Well, it is scandalous, and now it can all be undone." His aunt took a deep breath and then smiled. "Your Grace, you have duties that must be seen to. Why just look at the salver! It is overflowing with cards and invitations. All pressing matters that need your attention."

He flicked a glance over at the sideboard and winced. Indeed, the salver overflowed with tidings. Invitations. Cards from families with proper daughters, respectable housekeepers, and nary a pickpocket in sight.

There it was. His future life as the Duke of Hollindrake. Obligations with little time left for skating and whatever other misadventures he had to suppose would trail in Miss

Felicity Langley's wake to the end of her days if she didn't end up as proper and stuffy as she seemed to think she must. No, if anyone could save him from a life of dull events and boring soirees, it would be Miss Langley, but only after she learned that passion counted for something.

And he suspected, given the lively light he'd spied in her flirtatious eyes yesterday, that she had enough passion to make even the most wretched recital interesting.

"The salver can wait," he told her. "I am engaged elsewhere at present."

Geneva threw up her hands. "This is beyond intolerable, Your Grace! It will be the ruin of us all! I beg of you to put an end to this. For if you won't, I'll . . . I'll . . ."

He pushed back his throne of a chair and rose. "Really, Aunt Geneva, I'm not some callow youth for you to chide. However do you propose to stop me?"

But Thatcher had underestimated the depth of Sterling blood that ran through his aunt's veins.

"I shall summon your mother."

Tugging on her mittens, Felicity stood on the steps of her "borrowed" house and took a deep breath of the icy air. It did little to clear her thoughts, which were a jumble from Mr. Mudgett's revelations from the day before.

I'll tell you, miss, he's a bounder, that one. Cut a fine swath through Town he did. A regular hound when it came to chasing skirts.

Her Hollindrake a hound? She shuddered and tried to tell herself the man who had written her such thoughtful letters couldn't be such a cad. There had to be some mistake. Even Tally had tried to look on the bright side, arguing that now that the duke was well over thirty, a veritable Methuselah according to her sister, his inclinations could no longer stray toward "drinking all night and gambling away whatever he could lay his hands on," as Mudgett claimed.

Felicity tried to blot out such an image for it hardly fit the noble and honorable one she'd imagined. Oh, could it be that she'd spent four years at Miss Emery's Establishment toiling away on every subject so as to be his perfect duchess for naught?

And the evidence went further than Mr. Mudgett. For here it was Wednesday, and Hollindrake had been in Town (if one wanted to believe Sarah Browne) since Monday, and she had yet to receive a single word from the man. Not a note, not a card, not even a carefully chosen selection of blossoms from his hothouse.

Not that such things turned her head. Not at all. But one would have thought he could have at least—

"Isn't it rather cold out to be woolgathering, Miss Langley?"

She looked up and found Thatcher at the bottom of the steps. He doffed his hat and bowed to her, but his dark, compelling gaze never left hers, as if he was searching for something.

Something that sent a shiver of anticipation down her spine.

"You'll have icicles hanging from your nose if you stay out here much longer," he teased as he straightened.

Of all the foolish drivel, she told herself, moving down the steps and dodging around him, a hint of bay rum teasing her senses. Bay rum? She slanted a glance up at him, noticing that he had managed a decent shave this morning. Unfortunately, the smooth line of his jaw only made him look less imposing and more . . . oh, botheration, handsome.

And gracious heavens, if he'd managed to find a razor, why hadn't he been able to get his hair decently trimmed? Her fingers itched to pull it out of that wretched queue he wore it in and trim it herself. Into some fashionable short cut—a side parting perhaps, or spiked forward, for she doubted his straight hair, as intractable as the man beneath it, would hardly take to being curled and fussed over. And if he were in a real suit of clothes, not their hand-me-down livery and his ragged topcoat, she had to imagine he might even look noble.

Heroic, as Mudgett had averred.

She cringed. Oh, the world had surely tipped upside down when her footman held more ducal qualities than her own nearly betrothed!

"You're late!" Felicity sputtered, then paused and glanced over him again, trying to convince herself that she'd been seeing things—that her footman was just that—a footman. "With such a deplorable sense of duty, you shall never be a *proper* footman."

"And yesterday I was a war hero," he reminded her, folding his arms across his chest and planting himself in her path. "And where exactly are you going?"

She tucked her nose up in the air. "None of your business."

He flicked a glance over her shoulder. "And without even your maid for company? *Tsk tsk,* Miss Langley."

She pressed her lips together, but only for as long as it took one of their neighbors and her maid to walk past. "You know I haven't one."

A sly smile stole over his handsome lips. "I fear you will never be a *proper* duchess, Miss Langley, if you insist on gadding about Town without an escort."

Beneath the brim of her plain blue bonnet, her brows furrowed into a single taut line. "I wouldn't be going out alone if you had arrived on time."

"Touché," he said, bowing his head slightly. "So where are *we* venturing off to this morning?"

Oh, the devilish rogue. He'd outfoxed her again. Well, if he wanted to tag along after her, that was just fine. "If you must know, I'm off to the draper's shop." She made a point of stepping around him and heading toward Bond Street. "Aunt Minty needs some red thread for darning," she said over her shoulder. "And . . . well, it's just best—for the time being, that is—if she doesn't go shopping."

"Shoplifting, you mean," he said, falling in step.

She flinched but recovered quickly. "What a terrible thing to say about an old woman in her dotage, Mr. Thatcher. What if someone heard you? I am only running this errand to save her from becoming chilled, *that is all*."

He'd caught up with her and strolled easily alongside her. "From what I understand Mrs. Follifoot has had this penchant for 'darning' for quite some time, and that she's not your aunt."

Felicity skidded to a stop and turned around slowly. "What did you say?"

"You heard me. Or do you want me to repeat it?"

She caught him by the sleeve and pulled him into Avery Row, an alley that ran at an odd angle up to Grosvenor Street. With tiny, working shops tucked along one side, it was far less traveled by anyone of consequence. "Now I know why Mrs. Hutchinson wasn't fit to cook supper last night. You got her drunk!"

Thatcher leaned against the brick wall. "Such an accusation, Miss Langley. One that implies your housekeeper is prone to drink." He held up a hand to stave her off. "And if you must know the truth, I only filled her glass once."

"'Tis all it takes to encourage her, sir."

"Tell me about it," he mused, rubbing his temple. "I thought I had a good head for spirits, but your Mrs. Hutchinson could drink Mr. Mudgett under the table."

"Serves you right," Felicity said, slanting a glance at him and realizing he did look a little paler this morning. "In the future, if you have questions about my household, I'd prefer you ask me directly, rather than encouraging Mrs. Hutchinson to consume too much brandy. We were in a sorry state last night. Tally cooked supper!"

He laughed, and the sound was so hearty, she found herself laughing as well.

"Was a dreadful affair," she told him. "But I see your sacrifice gained you a wealth of information from Mrs. Hutchinson."

"She quite enlightened me," he told her, pushing off the wall, and they continued down the row.

Felicity shook her head. "So?"

"So, what?"

Oh, the odious man. Was he going to make her pry? Apparently. "So what else did you discover?"

He scratched his chin and thought about it for a moment before he said, "That my wages won't be so forthcoming."

Felicity shrugged. That was the least of their problems. "You were bound to find that out eventually."

Now it was his turn to skid to a stop. "What? No remorse over your deception?"

"Hardly so, you are a terrible footman," she teased.

And he grinned back at her. "I also learned that you've—" He curled his hand up and coughed into it, and when he spoke again, he'd managed to catch Mrs. Hutchinson's strident speech. "'Lived in such heathen places as would curl your soul, Mr. Thatcher,' and that all that 'gadding about' has left you with some 'demmed queer notions.'"

Felicity laughed. "She thinks we are quite mad."

"I don't think there are many who would argue with her. Coming to London without any money, no dowries, and expecting to set Society on its collective ear." He paused. "I'm with Mrs. Hutchinson, you are mad."

"And you, sir? You have a patched coat, worn boots, and this is the first time I think I've seen you decently shaved. And still you continue in our service. Now who's mad?"

"That may be, but I at least am not penniless," he told her, reaching inside his jacket and plucking out a coin.

"I gave you that," she said, pointing at it, "to get your hair cut."

He doffed his hat and ran his hand over his hair. "What is wrong with my hair?"

She wrinkled her nose. "It is too scruffy."

"Then complain to my former batman," he told her. "For the last time it was trimmed, it was done by Mr. Mudgett."

"With what?" she asked. "Your saber?"

He leaned over and winked at her. "How do you think I got this scar?"

"You're teasing," she said. Still, she slanted a glance at the scar along his temple and wondered how it had gotten there. Mr. Mudgett had made some vague reference to "the captain jest about gettin' 'imself demmed near kilt at Badajoz trying to save me," but hearing such a story and seeing the evidence of Thatcher's heroism was another thing altogether. It was nearly on her tongue to ask him, but from the shadow that crossed his features and the way he tucked his hat back on, pulling it low over his scar, she doubted he wished to discuss the event.

So she took her turn at teasing. "I'm glad to see you still have my money. Tally thought you spent it on your mistress."

"Two quid? She wouldn't be my mistress for long if that was all I was willing to offer the lady."

Something akin to the feeling she had when she saw Miss Browne with another new gown slanted through her. But this time it nearly upended her. "You have a mistress?" she blurted out before she could stop herself.

He grinned at her again. "No."

"Good," she said, hoping that was the end of that subject.

It wasn't. "Why is that good?"

"I don't know," she said, not willing to look too deeply into why the thought of him with another woman, showering her with coins and flowers, made her decidedly uncomfortable.

"Would you be jealous?"

Jealous? *Oh, yes.* Would she admit to such a thing? *Never.*

"Heavens no," she told him. "And this isn't a proper sub-ject." She pulled her cloak tighter around her neck and con-tinued down the row, picking her way past the odd refuse and piled snow. That is, until she came to the last couple of shops tucked at the end of the row just before it ran into Grosvenor Street.

Felicity stopped abruptly, unable to believe the scent tick-ling her nose.

Thatcher must have been right on her heels, for he plowed into her and they skidded together on the icy cobbles, one strong arm wound around her and his sturdy legs keeping them both upright.

For a moment she marveled at the feel of him—the breadth of his chest behind her, the warmth of his body surround-ing her, instantly dashing away the chill of the day, the very masculine and indisputable muscled hardness of his arms, his legs.

So used to bustling around and being in charge, she sud-denly felt the strength that was his gift. And she would have sighed and leaned a little farther back if it hadn't been for the hand he was using to hold her upright, for it rested right beneath her breast, pressing into her so very intimately. His fingers curled slightly, rounding beneath the fullness there, and immediately her nipples tightened, sending a shock of pleasure through her. She bolted back—which was even worse, for her bottom rounded into him—into *that part of him* that was most certainly not proper. This time she didn't care if she landed on the cobbles, she twisted out of his grasp and put a decent distance between them.

"Miss Langley," he said, his hands in the air. "I apologize. I was only—"

"Yes, yes, I know," she said, feeling herself blush at the still lingering effects of his touch. *This* she decidedly did not want to discuss. Especially not since his touch had made her . . . feel so much. So vulnerable. So susceptible to the passions that a man could inspire with merely the brush of his fingers.

"You stopped so fast," he was saying, straightening his topcoat and looking as ruffled as she felt. Glancing at the narrow shops before them, their grimy windows making it next to impossible to discern what they held within, he grimaced, then queried, "Dare I ask what caught your eye?"

"Don't look," she told him. "Smell." She sniffed the air and then smiled. "Heaven!"

He sniffed, his Roman nose twitching slightly. "What? The mail coach just passed?"

She elbowed him. "No! 'Tis coffee. Don't you smell it?" She rubbed one window then the next, looking for some hint of where it was coming from.

"That one," he said, pointing to the next shop. "Is that what you are looking for?"

For the door had just opened, and a merchant strolled out, shooting a disgruntled glance at the pair of them, annoyed at having to dodge out of the path of a curious miss and her wayward footman. But Felicity didn't care—she stood rooted in place and just breathed, letting the rich, thick scent from within sweep through her suddenly starving senses. "I thought so," she declared. "'Tis Turkish coffee!"

His sniffed again and shrugged as if he didn't see the point or the difference. "One of your 'demmed queer notions' I suppose?"

"Absolutely," she said. "When other little girls were having tea parties in their English gardens, Nanny Rana was teaching us the fine art of making coffee in Constantinople."

"How very Continental of you and not at all proper," he teased.

She inhaled again. "Oh, I haven't had coffee like this in ages. Tally will be wild to come here when I tell her, so I'd best not, because I fear this shop isn't very—"

"Proper?"

"Not at all," she said, wishing it was on Bond Street or near Gunter's Tea Shop. Of course then they couldn't afford it, but at least they could *consider* going there.

"Miss Langley," he said, that teasing tip to his lips as enticing as the sharp smell of coffee wafting through the open door. "How many times do I have to remind you? You aren't a duchess yet." And he nudged her inside.

But Thatcher's plan to teach Miss Langley a lesson in living nearly ended the moment he stepped into the shadowy shop. The coffeehouse was narrow and deep, and the sight of a woman in this very masculine domain stilled every voice in the room, all eyes trained on Miss Langley. He went to tug her right back out, because there was slightly improper, and then there was *entirely* improper.

But before he could catch the back of her cloak, she'd hurried right into the thick of it, oblivious to the scandal she was causing. The owner, a tall thin man in a turban and robes, came forward complaining in his native tongue, his long finger wagging toward the door.

Thatcher could well guess the translation. *Get that female out of here.*

But he'd underestimated Felicity's "Continental" charms. Her hands went to form a prayer before her and she bowed low, murmuring a greeting that stopped the shop owner cold. Tentatively, the man addressed her, and she returned his reply with a few words in his own language, followed by another bow.

The coffee vendor stared for a few moments, then broke out in a wide grin, his white teeth sparkling in the dim light. He bowed and then escorted them, turning every few feet and speaking to her again as if he couldn't quite believe that not only was he seating a woman, but one who spoke his language. He settled them in a secluded booth in the back that

Thatcher had to guess he saved for only his best customers, for it was very private and very comfortable.

Then after a lively debate between Miss Langley and their host, the man left for the kitchens, shouting at his help in a rapid succession of fiery words.

"Should I guess as to what just transpired?" he asked. "Either you ordered us coffee or I'm about to be jumped and sold to some Eastern sultan."

She settled into her seat, pulling off her mittens and tucking her reticule atop them on table. "I ordered coffee. What could be gained by selling such a poor footman as yourself would barely fill our coffers, and therefore, hardly worth the effort."

Thatcher laughed and gave her points for being such a sharp wit. He liked that about her—and imagined she would never have been cowed by his grandfather. Perhaps that's why the old boy had settled upon her.

Meanwhile, Felicity was stealing glances around the edge of the booth at the other customers. Bright, ornamental copper pots sat on the various tables, while tiny ceramic bowls sat before them. "Oh, this is just like the coffee shops in Constantinople. And even better, Mr. Muhannad, the owner, gets his beans directly from his brother, who is a coffee merchant there. His family has been in the business for several generations. He has another brother who lives in Paris and another still in Cairo."

Thatcher shook his head as he digested all this. "You got all that in just those few moments of conversation?"

"Oh, yes! He's quite a genial fellow." Her smile dazzled, while those blue eyes that always caught his heart sparkled with joy.

As they should, he thought.

Miss Langley continued on blithely, "When we left the Ottoman palace, Nanny Rana gave us our own coffee sets. I remember one particular afternoon, we entertained the Queen of Naples and her daughters, by serving them coffee in full

Turkish dress. The next day the Queen—dear woman that she was—went down to the docks and commissioned some poor merchant about to set sail to buy her a proper Turkish coffeepot when he stopped in Constantinople."

He laughed and shook his head.

"What is so funny?" she asked.

"You say that, 'Oh, I made coffee for the Queen of Naples,' like that happens to every English miss."

"It happened to us," she said, shifting in her seat, pursing her lips.

"Now don't get mad," he told her. "But that is what makes you interesting–it isn't that you're bragging or casting about lofty names to impress anyone, it is just your life as you've lived it. And what seems extraordinary to us poor mortals was actually your everyday realm. Such a marvelous life you've led."

"I don't know if it was all that," she said, shrugging. "I always wished our upbringing had been a bit more . . . well, dull."

He laughed again. "I don't think your life will ever be dull, Miss Langley. Not as long as you have Aunt Minty about the house."

She groaned. "Oh, I had hoped you wouldn't come back to that."

"I still have Lady Lumby's shrieks rattling about in my head, so how could I forget? But what I don't understand is why she is living with you."

"Oh, I know Aunt Minty has a slight problem." She paused for a moment, then leveled her gaze at him. "With *darning*, that is."

"A slight problem?" he ventured. "She nearly landed all of us in Newgate." He leaned forward and lowered his voice, "And from what I saw, I'd say you possess much the same skill."

She blew out a breath and waved him off. "'Twas naught

but an amusement she taught us last Christmas—there wasn't much cheer to be had and Tally thought it might be fun to learn."

"Why so dour at Christmas?" he asked.

She sighed. "Lady Caldecott, our guardian, had died during the summer and Mr. Elliott, father's solicitor, was being impossible. He wanted to hire some old dragon to watch over us. Well, that would never do, and Aunt Minty needed a place to live out her retirement years. We might have stretched the truth to Mr. Elliott about her qualifications—"

"Or that she's even a relation?"

"Yes, that too." She reached over and touched her mittens. "The dear old girl knit us each mittens and the socks to match so we would have something to open Christmas morning. No one else was so kindly, and truly she's all we have." She pulled her fingers back and tucked them properly into her lap. "You won't say anything about her, will you?"

Like she had the day before on the Thames, she disarmed him utterly and completely with the silent plea in her eyes.

No one else was so kindly.

He shook his head. "No. Your secret is safe with me."

"Footman's honor?" she teased.

"Footman's honor," he promised. "Though I am still of a mind to warn the good people of Brook Street to keep a tight hold on their purses."

She sat up and shook her head. "Oh, Aunty Minty won't do it again, I promise."

"I wasn't talking about her—I meant you. I wouldn't put it past you, Miss Langley, to fill your house and larder with your newfound skills."

Her mouth opened in a wide O, but her glorious eyes sparkled just as mischievously.

Oh, hell, he'd probably given her another "perfect idea," as he had yesterday with his suggestion about finding matches for Stewie Hodges' daughters.

"You shouldn't say such things about your employer! Really, Mr. Thatcher, if I didn't need you so desperately, I'd dismiss you—you're tardy, you gossip, and let's not forget you drink on duty and you tease me incessantly!"

He folded his arms over his chest and leaned back in his seat. "You're a fine one to point out my faults. I might have been gossiping with Mrs. Hutchinson, but what were you doing, Miss Langley? Let me remind you. Upstairs pumping my former batman for information about Hollindrake."

Before she could reply, the owner arrived with two coffee-pots, cups, and a plate of some cakes. He and Miss Langley had a long discussion, and finally they both bowed and she leaned over and took a deep breath.

"Hmm. Just as I remember." Gently, she tipped the pots and poured two cups, then slid his across the table. "Wait a moment to let it all settle, then try it," she advised. Looking over her own cup, she smiled. "The crema is perfect. And I asked them to make it extra sweet."

After a few more moments, she lifted her cup and he did the same. As the earthy rich flavor struck his tongue, he felt like he'd been transported to another place. The coffee he was used to drinking was a bitter concoction, but this was rich and tantalizing. The velvet crema on the top gave way to the flavorable brew below. He looked up to find her watching him, anxiously awaiting his verdict.

"Don't gulp it down," she admonished. "It is meant to be sipped. And don't drink the bottom part—'tis nothing but the grounds."

"It is most excellent," he told her.

"Oh, good, you like it." She went back to sipping, settling into her seat, a contented look on her face.

Closing his eyes, he knew he was on the right course. For how would he ever have discovered her passion for coffee if they had met at Almack's? Or in some drawing room with all eyes on them?

They would have commenced on the typical English courtship and married as complete strangers, settling into a domestic arrangement that might possibly have never allowed them to find out if they possessed anything beyond her ridiculous natural inclinations.

"I suppose you are going to tease me about Hollindrake," she said.

A niggle of guilt tripped down his spine. "Tease you? Whyever for?"

"You might have been right about the man—"

"I doubt that—"

"No," she argued, then sighed. "After listening to Mudgett yesterday, I don't know what to think. Those stories he told, why I think—"

"Mr. Mudgett isn't the most reliable storyteller," he advised her. Though yesterday he'd half hoped that his batman's loquacious raconteur of his youthful excesses might succeed in disengaging her, now he might be regretting that course. "Perhaps you should give Hollindrake a chance to come up to snuff," he heard himself telling her. "The man may just have had matters to attend to before he can come courting."

With a clear conscience.

She nodded, then leaned forward, her hands cradling her cup. "And in the meantime, I have you."

hapter 8

Felicity didn't know what enticed her to say such a thing, but somehow this man managed to uncover her every secret wish, her every desire. He'd rescued her from Miss Browne, taken her skating, and now all but pushed her into this shop so she could indulge herself with a simple cup of coffee.

He teased her, he tested her, and he had befriended her when no one else seemed to understand her determination to secure a future that would keep Tally and Pippin from finding themselves as homeless as Aunty Minty.

What she hadn't said to Thatcher, but he seemed to understand, was that they hadn't just taken in the old pickpocket because they needed a chaperone, but because in the old lady's situation Felicity had seen their own possible future.

As they finished their coffee, Mr. Muhannad came up, bowing. "You are a most extraordinary miss," he said in his own language. "And welcome in my shop any day you wish to grace it with your beauty."

She blushed and was thankful Thatcher didn't understand a word of it.

But as they were leaving, with Mr. Muhannad holding the door for them, Thatcher smiled at her and said, "Another conquest, Miss Langley?"

"He just likes hearing his native tongue spoken."

"If you say so," he teased back. "Now where to?"

"Bond Street, to the draper's shop."

"Will your sister or chaperone be wondering where you've gone to?"

"Tally?" Felicity shook her head. "She and Pippin are trying to come up with a new play."

"They write plays?"

"Yes, dreadful things," she declared. "I fear they will try to sell this one, and then we shall be the scandal of Town. I've made them promise to use a *nom de plume*." She paused for a second, eyeing him. "You are duly warned to be cautious, lest you find yourself the hero of some wretched melodrama."

"Then you had best make them promise to take my name out of it, will you?" he asked. They had turned onto Grosvenor Street and were nearly to Bond Street.

"Whatever for, Thatcher?" she teased. "Are you hiding some great secret?"

He stumbled on the ice, and she reached out to catch him. It happened so fast, so quickly, that even later she couldn't remember how it occurred. But all of sudden she was in his arms. *Again.* And like yesterday, all of London seemed to still.

She gazed up into his dark eyes, where there was no doubt he was hiding something. But that mattered little for she found herself nearly confessing her own secret.

Kiss me, she wanted to whisper as she stared at the firm set of his lips. *Oh, please kiss me once.*

And for a moment, by the stormy light illuminating his eyes, she had to wonder if she'd said those words aloud—for his mouth moved slightly, his head began to tip down, as if ready to indulge her every wish. Her every secret.

Her body leaned into his, letting the deep heat radiating from his strong limbs surround her. She felt languid and tense and ever-so-ready to discover what it was that held so much mystery, so much power between a man and a woman.

Just one kiss, not the chaste sort of peck one might expect from a gentleman, but the rakish, sort of devouring type that one would expect from such an impossibly improper man like Thatcher.

She'd let him kiss her just this once—but even as she told herself that, a frisson of panic ran down her spine. For here he was, looking like he had every intent of indulging her. He was going to kiss her! Her common sense, every bit of propriety she possessed, rebelled.

Kissing a footman? What was she thinking?

But before she could wrench herself out of his tempting embrace, an imperious voice tore them apart.

"Dear me!" Miss Browne exclaimed as she stared with feral glee at the pair. "Shocking, but not surprising."

Felicity scrambled out of Thatcher's reach so quickly, she thought she was going to fall, but thankfully found her footing without any further folly. "I merely slipped on the ice," she told the other young lady. "Thankfully, Mr. Thatcher caught me."

"So he did," Miss Browne replied, her gaze flicking from Felicity to Thatcher and back again. "So he did, don't you think, Lady Gaythorne?"

Miss Browne's companion, a young matron in a ridiculously feathered hat, with a cloak that was trimmed out in enough fur for one to mistake her for an entire zoo full of animals, picked up the refrain. "Yes, I am all astonishment." She smiled toward Felicity, though Thatcher doubted the lady meant the gesture in a friendly fashion. "We were just coming from Madame Souchet's," she said, nodding at the shop behind them. "Fittings and such for the Season. It takes up so much of our time, doesn't it, Sarah, dear?"

"Yes, indeed," Miss Browne agreed, her discerning glance falling on Felicity's ensemble. "I see you chose to wear the same bonnet today—then again, you've always been so practical and sensible. But I think a perfect wardrobe is really the true mark of a lady."

Especially when you have no breeding whatsoever, Felicity thought, but resisted pointing out.

Lady Gaythorne, meanwhile, continued on, "Truly, when dear Sarah was telling everyone last night at Sir Nigel's soiree that she had seen you and your sister just yesterday, well, we assumed she was just trying to best Miss Spolton's news about her betrothal to Lord Varrow."

"You are a tease, Camille," Miss Browne replied, batting a hand at her companion.

"Oh, don't deny it! You *were* trying to best Miss Spolton, and thank goodness someone was, for she was going on as if she were marrying a royal duke. Had you heard, Miss Langley, that Miss Spolton had gained Varrow's favor?" At Felicity's shake of her head, the lady preened. "No, of course you wouldn't have. You haven't been out yet, have you? Of course not! You obviously haven't had time to have a decent gown made up. Then again, if you were out, you wouldn't have time to fill up those silly Bachelor Pages of yours. Or rather, to remove names, just as I assume you deleted my dear Gaythorne." She stroked the fur on her muff. "You aren't still keeping those Bachelor Pages are you?"

"*Bachelor Chronicles*," Miss Browne corrected, sincerity ringing her words, though her sly smile said otherwise.

"Oh, yes, *Bachelor Chronicles*," Lady Gaythorne said. "You don't still keep that tattered notebook, do you?"

"Well, I—"

Lady Gaythorne heaved a sigh. "I daresay you should consign those ridiculous pages to the flames—oh, what a terrible mockery could be had if those pages ever became public. Truly ruinous, and what a terrible shame."

Felicity knew it was hardly proper, but she wanted to curse. Perhaps in Russian, for she doubted that either lady spoke the language.

"Has Hollindrake called yet, Miss Langley?" Miss Browne asked.

"Well . . ."

"I can see why he hasn't," Lady Gaythorne said. "I've heard he's awash in social obligations. He was at no less than three engagements last night—"

"I heard four," Miss Browne corrected.

Her companion shrugged. "He must be overrun with invitations."

"Miss Langley," Thatcher said. "Your fitting? Have you forgotten?"

Felicity glanced over at him. "My fitting?"

He bowed slightly. "Yes, for your gown. The one you ordered for the Hollindrake ball." Then he nodded to the modiste's shop that Miss Browne and Lady Gaythorne had just exited.

What was he doing? She knew he was only trying to help—he couldn't help himself, apparently—but heroism in Spain and heroism in London society was another matter. He'd just tossed her into the ring with the lions. "Oh, *that* fitting," she said, shooting him a look that she hoped quelled any further notions of chivalry.

"Hollindrake is throwing a ball?" Lady Gaythorne asked. "I hadn't heard."

"I don't think it's been announced yet," Felicity ground out.

"Does this mean," Miss Browne chimed in, "that you and the duke have reached an understanding?"

Thatcher knew a mine field when he saw it—and demmit if he hadn't just pushed Miss Langley right into the middle of it. His aunt was right: He knew nothing about London society. At least not this side of the *ton*. Where debutantes and Originals were the generals and anyone in their path fair targets.

But once again he'd underestimated Felicity's prowess. Obviously, Lord Langley wasn't the only one in the family with a flair for diplomacy. For she rallied and dodged out from beneath the girl's question, a cannonball in disguise, by saying, "I wouldn't want to ruin the surprise. You'll have to wait and see if you are invited. I fear the invitations will be ever so exclusive." Then she nodded politely to both ladies and walked into the modiste's shop with every bit of dignity she possessed.

That ends that, he thought with relief.

He quickly discovered how wrong he was.

The moment Felicity disappeared inside, he could have been a foot scraper, for all Miss Browne and Lady Gaythorne cared.

"Did you see her gown?" the pompous little matron sputtered as she swept past him.

"I couldn't get past that dreadful cloak!" Miss Browne declared.

"Still full of herself—her and her odd ways. A duke, indeed!" Lady Gaythorne shook her head, and the pair started down the street. "Who does she think she is?"

Thatcher, unable to resist, followed. Best to keep the enemy camp in full sight, he'd always said.

Miss Browne had her nose perched in the air. *"I'll eat my hairbrush the day she marries Hollindrake."*

Right there and then, Thatcher vowed to send Miss Browne a new hairbrush—to replace the one she was most decidedly going to have to consume.

Lady Gaythorne obviously found the notion amusing for other reasons. "Oh, Sarah, how delightful you are!" She tucked her hands deeper into her muff. "You know very well she made up all that nonsense about Hollindrake just to gain attention for herself. Sad, really. And now she's taken to cavorting with her footman. Ruinous, really. I shouldn't worry about having to devour a hairbrush, for once it is known about Town how we found her, any hopes she had of making a match with Hollindrake will be . . ."

Thatcher froze and watched them continue down the sidewalk, their parting remarks floating along like an old handbill tossed in the breeze. He turned and stormed back toward the shop where Miss Langley had taken cover.

This was the society she wanted to conquer? These women were her peers? They weren't fit to share the street with her. He could hardly imagine the spoiled Lady Gaythorne or the ruthless Miss Browne helping an old pickpocket or drinking Turkish coffee, or living by their wits with no allowance but their pin money.

Not that the pair had enough wits between them to find their way out of an empty ballroom.

Miss Langley stuck her head out of the shop. "Are they gone?"

He laughed and nodded. "I thought you were fearless."

"Yes, but not foolish," she said, coming out of the shop. "I'm sure they had a fair amount to say once I escaped their clutches."

"Nothing of note," he replied.

She snorted. "I've never known Camille Hydegate—oh, excuse me, Lady Gaythorne— not to have something foul to say once your back is turned."

He laughed. "I paid little heed."

"You are lying, but it is kind of you to say so," she told him. Then her valor returned and her hands went to her hips. Better there than that wicked right she'd used the day before. "But what were you thinking? The Hollindrake ball? It will be all over Town before tea time."

"I thought I might help—"

She huffed a sigh. "And what if he does throw a ball? Then what?"

"You'll be invited, of course," he said. He wondered what she'd say when she arrived and found her footman was also the host.

Best to wear his padded waistcoat and have Mr. Mudgett at his back.

"Even if I am, don't you see how I won't be able to go? I can't afford a dress from Madame Souchet! I can't even afford a gown from the rag merchant." She paced back and forth on the pavement in front of him. "A proper footman would have kept his mouth shut."

"I was only trying to help."

"Well, you didn't," she said, chewing her lower lip and looking down the street in the direction her adversaries had gone. "And the Hollindrake ball won't be the only *on dit* being nosed about every salon and retiring room in London today. You shouldn't have held me like that!"

"Me?" he shot back. "I merely caught hold of you, nothing more."

They both knew it for the lie it was and neither of them wanted to venture back onto that slippery slope. He certainly wasn't going to admit that holding Felicity like that had held some appeal. Demmit, more than some.

And when she'd looked up at him, he could have sworn he heard her imploring him to kiss her.

Oh, please kiss me once.

Two days ago he would have declared such a notion impossible. And now? Well, he'd held a fair measure of resolve against her right up until she'd said to him, in that sultry way of hers, *I have you.* Then to his chagrin and amazement, his heart had taken a double thump, and in that moment he'd discovered he wanted this meddlesome little minx like he'd never wanted any other woman. He wanted to undo every proper lace she had wound around her passionate nature and awaken every natural inclination she possessed and then some.

"Duchess?! Is that you?" called a familiar voice from the street. "Look, Miranda, you were right, it is our fairest Felicity!"

Thatcher looked up to find a couple beaming down at the girl, which he paid scant heed, until the man seated beside a pretty redhead looked up and met his gaze.

"Jack!" Felicity called out, rushing to the edge of the sidewalk to wave at the carriage turning quickly to pull alongside her. "Miss Porter!" She blushed and then corrected herself as the curricle and smart pair came to a stop. "Lady John, I mean. Oh, dear, I fear you will always be Miss Porter to me."

"And you will always be my favorite student." Her former teacher beamed down at her, and the lady's smile warmed Felicity's heart, for it spoke unequivocally of Miss Porter's happiness in her marriage to Lord John Tremont.

A match, Felicity would point out, that had been the result of her inspiration—and some hard work.

"Whatever are you doing in Town?" Lord John—Jack to his friends, and Mad Jack to those who only remembered the libertine who had once wrecked havoc with his rakish ways—asked as he smiled broadly at her, until his gaze wandered over to Thatcher and his brows furrowed slightly. "We thought you and Tally were going to stay on with Pippin in Sussex for the time being until things could be settled."

"The opportunity for a Season came along and we were

loath to pass it by," she told him. "Besides, we couldn't wait any longer. But what are you both doing in town? Especially with your time so near, Lady John! I can't imagine that you should be bouncing around in a carriage." She shot her best admonishing glance at Jack. Really, what was the man thinking?

Lady John, the former Miranda Mabberly, who had taught at Miss Emery's as Miss Porter after a scandalous encounter with Mad Jack drove her from Society, smiled fondly at her former student. "Felicity, you dear girl. Always looking out for my welfare. But you shouldn't worry so—I am quite fit and have another two months to go." She swiped at the swell of tears in her eyes. "Botheration, I swear I cry at the least provocation these days." She patted her rounded stomach and then reached for her husband's arm, her gloved hand twining around his sleeve. "You should have seen me when we had to leave little Birdie behind."

"A veritable watering pot for fifteen miles!" Jack declared.

They all laughed and Felicity felt all the ill will that Miss Browne and Lady Gaythorne had showered down on her soul wash away.

Friends are the balm that soothes the heart, Nanny Tasha had always said, and how right their wise nanny had been.

"How big is Birdie now?" Felicity asked. "Why, she must be crawling about the place."

"Walking," Jack declared, ever the proud papa.

"Running is more like it," Miranda added. "She's got her father's determined nature."

"And her mother's sparkle—she'll lead all the bucks on a merry chase when it comes her turn to come to Town!"

Felicity grinned. "But still, why come to Town? Your last letter said you wouldn't be leaving Thistleton Park until . . ." She blushed a little. ". . . until your confinement was over and you found a new nanny."

Miranda laughed again. "Our nanny worries are over now

that we discovered why they kept departing in the middle of the night."

"I daresay Jack was regaling them with his Tremont family history and all the haunted doings about the park," Felicity scolded.

"Not at all. It was all Bruno's doing," Jack supplied.

"Mr. Jones?" Felicity glanced at both of them. "But I thought he was utterly besotted with little Birdie."

"Too much so," Miranda told her. "Apparently he was continually objecting to how the nursery was being run, convinced that our nannies didn't have Birdie's best interest at heart. The poor women were fleeing in fear."

Felicity covered her mouth with her mitten. Not that she blamed them! She held her own bit of unspoken terror when it came to Bruno Jones, Jack's secretary and man of business. A mountain of a fellow, he wasn't someone that any woman—or man—would brook easily. "He wasn't threatening to pack them off with Captain Dashwell, was he?" she teased. "Or sell them to some faraway sultan?"

"That was the least of his threats," Jack said, shaking his head. "But finally Miranda struck the perfect bargain to end our woes."

"Which was?" Felicity dared to ask, knowing her former schoolteacher had a mercantile mind that left even the most hardened smuggler in begrudging admiration of her bargaining prowess.

The couple shared a guilty smile, and then Miranda answered, "We installed Mr. Jones as the new nanny."

Felicity's mouth fell open and then she laughed. "Surely you are jesting!" The vision of Mr. Jones with a lace cap and an apron was just too much.

Miranda shook her head. "No, not in the least. In fact, he's a better nursemaid than he was a forger. And he can hardly wait to have the next one arrive." She gave her stomach another fond pat. "But I have been ordered to produce a strapping lad this time. Mr. Jones wants someone to pass on his trade to."

Felicity giggled again, only because she could well imagine what Jack's brother, the Duke of Parkerton, would say to such an idea. "Oh, if only Mr. Birdwell had lived to see such a sight. What fun he would have had teasing Mr. Jones."

Miranda's eyes welled again—as much from her pregnancy as from her fondness for the man who had done so much to bring her and Jack together.

Jack glanced at his wife and then said, "We probably would have had both of them up there arguing over the proper folding of nappies and the correct amount of fresh air!"

"You must miss him terribly," Felicity said. Mr. Birdwell had been Jack's faithful butler, having followed the madcap young lord into exile when Jack's escapades demanded a hasty departure from Society . . .

"The note you sent when he passed last fall meant much to us," Miranda told her.

"I have him to thank for our current situation," Felicity confessed, "for it was Mr. Birdwell's recommendations that helped us get settled here in London."

Jack's gaze narrowed. "Don't tell me Birdwell lent his expertise to your household?"

"Oh, Felicity, no!" Miranda exclaimed.

She waved their concerns aside. "Not to worry, he used his best judgment and found us a wonderful cook. Why, we have quite a proper household!"

Behind her there was a discreet fit of choking. Oh, no! How had she forgotten Thatcher? *Wonderful*. He'd reveal the truth of their situation to Jack and Miranda and that would end their Season before it began, with the couple insisting that she, Tally, and Pippin journey immediately to Thistleton Park until they could find a proper situation.

And by then, well, Hollindrake might have been swayed by some other young lady.

Not that she didn't trust the duke. No, it was the Miss

Brownes of the world she didn't trust. She'd rather let loose Aunt Minty in a silver shop than allow Hollindrake to wander about London's Marriage Mart without a firm and binding betrothal inked.

"And all the better to finally meet Standon—well, I suppose I should say Hollindrake now," Jack was saying. "But of course I see you have already—"

"Felicity Langley," Miranda interrupted. "Where is your maid? Your escort? My mind must be befuddled not to have noticed before! Miss Emery taught you, and I daresay I did as well, not to wander about unescorted—"

"I am not alone!" Felicity interjected.

Jack gently pressed his wife back into her seat. "Of course she isn't. Don't you see she has—"

"A footman," Thatcher said, coming forward and bowing slightly to Miranda, "At your service, and Miss Langley's."

"Yes, I have Mr. Thatcher with me," Felicity told her old decorum teacher. "I would never go out alone."

Both Jack and Miranda made a snort that was both indelicate and disbelieving.

"Thatcher?" Jack remarked, his brows furrowing again.

"Yes, my lord," Thatcher replied, and the two men eyed each other oddly, but Felicity dismissed Jack's behavior as nothing more than his overly protective nonsense when it came to their welfare. Ever since she'd managed Jack Tremont's match with Miss Porter, he'd become like an overbearing uncle.

"It is good to see you here, Mr. Thatcher," Miranda said. "You look a sensible sort, and our dear girl here is . . . well, a bit madcap."

"So I've discovered," he replied, bowing slightly.

"Enough of this," Felicity told them. "I am neither madcap nor do I require constant supervision."

The three of them shared a series of glances before they all started laughing. Miranda covered her mouth, but finally managed to ask, "Where are you living?"

"Brook Street," Felicity told her. "Right around the corner from Grosvenor Square."

"So old Elliott finally loosed the purse strings?" Jack teased.

"He was most generous," Felicity lied. And following Miranda's lead, changed the subject yet again. "You never did say why you've come to Town, and in this horrible weather! It must have been something very important to bring you all this way."

"Actually, you've mentioned the subject," Jack said. "There are rumors that our old friend Dash is here in London—he's iced in and unable to get back to his ship. By chance, he hasn't come calling, has he?"

"That pirate?" Felicity said, her hands fisting at her hips. "If Captain Dashwell does, I'll put a bullet between his eyes! He quite ruined Pippin. She still considers him the finest man alive. I'm having a devil of a time convincing her she needs to settle on a proper gentleman, not that Yankee ruffian."

"Pippin will have no choice in the matter," Jack said. "For when Dash is caught, he'll hang."

Miranda was shaking her head. "I still say that seems rather hasty. When the war ends, he'll make a good trading partner."

Jack laughed. "Only you, my dear wife, would consider that rapscallion pirate a good trading partner. But there's no getting around the fact that he'll hang, and there's nothing we can do about it."

"Bother Pymm," Miranda said, mentioning their contact in the Foreign Office. "I'll just have to talk some sense into the man."

"That ought to be an interesting conversation," Jack said. "And one that we are late for as we speak. Felicity, can we give you a ride home?"

"Oh, no, I have Mr. Thatcher with me, and it's not far. But you must come to call, and soon, Miss Porter." She paused, then smiled and tipped her head as she corrected herself. "Lady John."

"We will," her former teacher said. "We are here just through the end of the week. So we will most decidedly see you at the Setchfield masquerade."

"What are you wearing, Jack?" Felicity asked. "No, let me guess. You are going as a smuggler."

"Hades," Jack confessed with a woeful shake of his head.

"And I will be dressed as Persephone," his wife said.

"We haven't decided on our costumes," Felicity said, not wanting to reveal that unless they went as penniless debutantes, they wouldn't dare show their faces. "But we shall see you very soon."

"Yes, we shall," Jack said, sending a direct glance at Thatcher.

"Dearest," Jack said as they rolled away. He glanced back at Felicity and her "footman" and frowned. "I think we will need to change our meeting with Mr. Pymm." He looked over at her. "Besides, you look chilled."

"Botheration, Jack Tremont, don't gammon me with such flimflam. Your brows don't crease like that unless something's amiss, and I would wager it has to do with that footman of Felicity's."

He smiled at her, but the expression was merely a turn of his lips and didn't reach the furrow of his brows. "That man is no more a footman than I am honest."

"As bad as all that?" Miranda said, glancing back as well. "Then I insist you turn this carriage around and we straighten the matter out right now." She clucked her tongue. "And here I thought him quite a handsome fellow."

"More handsome than me?" Jack teased, knowing the answer to the question. Miranda's unwavering love for him was the rock of his life. Had anchored his reckless existence.

She lay her hands over her stomach and smiled. "I would

never admit how handsome you are in public, my lord. It isn't proper for a wife to be so infatuated with her husband."

"Only infatuated?" he asked.

"Besotted," she confessed. But she pressed her lips together and looked back at her former student. "You will see to her welfare, won't you?"

"Before the day is out," he vowed.

Chapter 9

Thatcher shook his head as the carriage pulled away. "Mad Jack Tremont leg-shackled," he muttered. "I never—"

"I would hardly call his situation so dire," Felicity interjected. "Jack's changed, nothing more. All men do . . . eventually." She spoke as if she had years of experience on the subject.

And her worldly air made him laugh. "Not as much as you would like to think, Miss Langley." He moved closer to her, forgetting himself and thinking only of proving how little he'd changed since his rakish days. But to his chagrin the lady just poked her nose into the air and ducked around him.

So much for his rakish charms. There had been a day when a lady wouldn't have escaped his clutches so readily. He shrugged his shoulders and set off after her, asking the question that had been on his tongue since Jack had greeted Felicity like a long lost niece. "How is it that you, Miss Langley, are acquainted with Mad Jack?"

"You shouldn't call him that. It isn't proper."

"Lord John then," he corrected.

She nodded at his concession and then answered his question. "Miss Porter—well, I mean Lady John—was our decorum teacher at Miss Emery's and when—"

Thatcher nearly tripped. "Mad Jack married a decorum teacher?" At first he couldn't believe it, then he couldn't help himself—he doubled over in laughter.

Miss Langley came to a dead stop. "I don't see what is so amusing! Miss Porter was the perfect lady for him."

Thatcher tried his best to stop laughing, but it couldn't be done.

Her foot tapped a staccato beat against the icy sidewalk. "You are making a spectacle of yourself over what is a beautiful love match."

That caught Thatcher's attention. Who would have thought it possible that such a heartless bastard as Jack Tremont could fall in love? "A man goes to war for a few years and the entire world turns upside down. I am starting to believe that the French won."

"Now you are being ridiculous," she shot back.

"Ridiculous?" He shook his head. "Just incredulous. I just can't see the man I remember—hearing about," he added hastily, "turning into a docile example of domestic bliss."

"It wasn't easy, believe me," Felicity said, pulling her cloak tighter around her neck, and starting down the street again. "It took some doing to get him to see the sense of the match, and Miss Porter, well, she all but refused to see how our plan—"

"Our plan?"

"Well, mostly me," she confessed, stopping. "But Tally and Pippin helped, so they deserve some credit."

Thatcher crossed his arms over his chest. "You're responsible for all that?" He pointed back in the direction Jack had gone.

Demmit, if she didn't puff up with pride.

"I might have come up with the idea that they may suit," Felicity said, meeting his gaze without any reservation. "Oh, don't gape at me like that. Something had to be done! Why the man was a veritable recluse, lost to society and family, while Miss Porter was—"

"You meddled!" Oh, if that wasn't warning enough, he didn't know what was. This little slip of a chit had managed to outflank Mad Jack Tremont. If he hadn't been afraid of her before, he was now. Here he'd thought all her matchmaking bluster was just that, but the minx had credentials.

Demmed impressive ones. No wonder she'd been able to hoodwink his grandfather.

"I simply helped two people arrive in the same vicinity and then perhaps ensured that they stayed that way until they saw some sense in the notion," she was saying, walking away again.

"You were matchmaking," he shot back, keeping up with her, "which is meddling, plain and simple."

"Did they look like they mind?" she said, a smug smile on her lips. "They suit, plain and simple. And best of all, they love each other."

And then it struck him. For as much as her voice filled with pride over snaring Mad Jack in the parson's mousetrap, it wasn't so much the match that she found so worthy of note, but that the two were madly in love. Something only a blind man would have failed to notice.

Yet what her words concealed, her eyes did not. When she too looked back in the direction of Jack's carriage, a tiny light of envy glowed in those blue eyes of hers.

"I don't think either of them," she was saying, "would have ever gotten married if they hadn't found each other and fallen in love." Her mitten trailed along the edge of a wrought fence, skipping along the rails.

"And you expect me to believe you just trapped those two together and they fell in love? It doesn't happen like that, Miss Langley," he said as they turned onto Brook Street.

"Someday, you'll have a different opinion on the matter, Mr. Thatcher," she was saying, once again with that smug knowing tone. "When you fall in love."

Why was it that every time a single man declared his disinterest in love and marriage, every woman within earshot considered it her personal mission to find him a bride? "No man in his right mind willingly wanders about Town with a bell on his neck like that fool Tremont."

"I think he rather likes the sound," she said over her shoulder, with that sly disarming smile that left him struggling to breathe.

Oh, the devilish little minx. She shot his defenses right out from beneath him.

And that was how they did it, he realized as he caught her taking another sultry glance over her shoulder at him. With their lithesome looks and promises of passion.

And the next thing you knew, you found yourself riding around Town like a pug dog on a silken lead, with a demmed bow stuck to your head.

Still, how was it that with just a tip of her lips and that come-hither light in her eyes, and his imagination—no, make that his demmed natural inclinations—he was seeing visions of her stripped of her plain gown, naked and lush and tangled up in the sheets of the enormous bed that took up much of the ducal suite? Beckoning him with only a glance to join her . . . join with her.

But when he looked up, she was already two houses ahead of him, as uncaring and unassuming as any regular, ordinary London miss. Good heavens, either he was seeing things or her company was driving him around the bend.

He chose to believe the latter. It was all this talk of love matches and happy couples. Why, it even had him feeling a tiny bit of envy for his old friend Jack.

Envious of Jack and his pretty bride?

Oh, good God, he was!

Thatcher tried to breathe and found he couldn't. He plucked at the first three buttons on his coat, hell, all of them—opening his coat to let the cold, bitter chill of this miserable winter ice his blood and clear his thoughts, but still they rang with her words, her voice.

I have you . . . And she did. In ways she couldn't imagine. Or perhaps she could . . . with a little help.

He took a great gulp of the freezing bitter wind but it was no use. Miss Langley made him feel rakish, and heroic, and almost ducal, but more to the point, he wanted her to look at him just as Lady John had looked at Jack.

With eyes that burned with a love no one could deny. With a glance that set his heart hammering, his loins hardening, his arms aching to cart her off to the nearest bed and bury himself inside her.

"Thatcher, are you well?" Miss Langley asked. She bustled back and glanced over him. "Well, of course you aren't. Look at you, standing out in this wind with your coat wide open." Without any ceremony or even a nod, she took hold of the lapels and tugged them together.

Pulled him closer to her. Never mind that they stood in the middle of Brook Street. With her teeth, she pulled off one of her red mittens, then the other, hardly the proper action of a lady, but it was quick and efficient. "Hold these," she ordered, shoving her mittens into his hands, and then with her bare fingers started buttoning up his coat, beginning at the bottom.

He stared down at her in wonder—years abroad hadn't made her "full of herself," as Lady Gaythorne had claimed, but had given her a freedom of spirit that called to his own unconventional nature.

Truly, the more Miss Langley tried to be the proper English miss, the more miserably she failed.

And the more he, dare he say it, loved her for it.

An odd chill ran down Thatcher's spine. He what? Loved her? Impossible notion! He didn't, he couldn't.

But life, he had learned, can change in the flash of a moment—on the battlefield or even the safe and proper confines of Brook Street. As his had in the past few minutes.

"Good heavens," she was muttering, "What were you thinking, running about with your coat open? You'll catch your death! And then where would *I* be?"

Not *we*. Not *us*. But *I*. The choice was telling. Or so he hoped.

He cocked a brow and stared down at her.

"I can see what you are thinking and you are an impertinent fellow," she chided. "Of course if you got sick, I would have to take care of you. Believe me, you wouldn't want Tally brewing your possets."

She'd finished buttoning his coat, but her hands had found an easy resting place on his lapel, her hand over his heart. He brought his own up and covered her bare fingers. "You'd take care of me?"

"Yes," she said, her voice catching slightly—and then her lips pursed and parted slightly, as they had yesterday on the ice when he'd been convinced she wanted him to kiss her. And he wasn't such a fool to miss an opportunity twice.

Madness, utter madness, he realized as he dipped his head and let his lips touch hers. They made a moue of surprise, but the real surprise was his.

Mudgett hadn't been too far off the mark when he'd said that Aubrey Sterling had once cut a wide swath through London's female population, having seduced his fair share of madams and widows and ladies of questionable character, but that hadn't prepared him for kissing the *right* woman.

She tensed in his arms, and he could tell this was her

first kiss, so instead of giving in to the need that throbbed through him, he made sure she found the experience worth repeating.

Often.

Tentatively, he slid his tongue over her lips, drawing her closer still. Oh, hell, she tasted like heaven. He deepened the kiss, longing to find himself inside her.

And thankfully, this was Felicity, for while she might have been hesitant, almost proper at first, that didn't last long. A soft moan escaped her lips and she opened herself up to him, her lips teasing his, her tongue sliding over his. Her fingers, once splayed over his coat, now tugged at his lapels, hauling him closer still.

Suddenly he could feel not only her wet, heated mouth, but her entire body as it wound up against him, her high, firm breasts, her hips rocking forward, her legs mingled and twined with his.

Desire and need assailed him, and his hand slid beneath her cloak and roamed over her well-fashioned curves. Cupping one of her breasts, his thumb rolled across the tip, and it puckered quickly, and she gasped in surprise, their mouths coming apart. Her usually clear eyes were dazed with passion. Yet just as quickly they cleared, and with that came the realization of what had just passed between them, the heat and fire that had come undone in a single kiss. And just as quickly, everything he'd succeeded in unleashing was washed away in a blinding wave of panic.

She tore her hands from his coat and stumbled back from him. For his part, he took a hasty step back as well—her lessons from Mr. Jones still fresh in his memory. They stood there, staring at each other, Felicity's brows furrowed and her mouth parted as she tried to catch her breath.

"What were you thinking?" she sputtered before turning and fleeing.

"Oh, hell," he cursed as he shot after her. He caught her by the arm and swung her back into his embrace. This time she wasn't as easily caught.

"I'm nearly engaged," she said, twisting and turning in his grasp. "I have an agreement—"

"You have nothing!" he shot back. "With a man you've never met!"

She didn't want to listen. "But he knows me, he understands me." Her now angry gaze blazed up at him. "And he wouldn't force himself on a lady when she was—"

Egads, he was sick and tired of listening to her extol Hollindrake's virtues. His virtues. Virtues he did not possess. And to prove it, he kissed her again. This time with all the pent-up passion and impropriety he could muster, letting his lips ply hers open, letting his tongue taste hers, tease her again until she was trembling and sighing in his arms. When he pulled back, she wavered in his arms. "He wouldn't force a lady when she was what?"

She stared up at him as if she was seeing him for the first time. Without his livery, maybe even without his clothes (well, a man could hope), and for a moment her lips fluttered as if she wanted to say something, but the words utterly failed to find a way out.

"Oh, heavens," she finally managed, before wrenching herself free and starting for the steps and her door.

But he caught up with her again in a few easy strides and planted himself in her path. "How can you be so sure about him?"

She set her jaw and crossed her arms over her chest. "Well, for one thing, Jack recommended him."

"Mad Jack Tremont? One would think you're mad. Hollindrake was one of his cohorts, his boon companions. *Do you know what that means?*"

She pinked, quite thoroughly, but to her credit her gaze never wavered. "He's changed, just as Jack did."

Thatcher snorted. "Men don't change."

"Yes they do. When they want to, when the right lady comes along." She rose up on her tiptoes and looked him nearly eye-to-eye. "They change because they must if they are to keep her."

This struck him. For she was right, but in his anger he wasn't willing to concede anything. "And Hollindrake has changed?" He let his skepticism drip from every word.

She stood her ground and tipped up her nose. "Yes. Of course."

"And you know this because . . . ?"

For a moment she wavered, but then her shoulders straightened back into their taut and steady line. "Because he told me he has."

Thatcher crossed his arms over his chest. "He told you?"

"Yes." This she whispered.

He paused for a moment, for he could feel the change rising between them. "And what wrought this miracle of conscience?" he asked, this time a little more carefully.

A veil of tears rose up in her eyes. "I changed him."

He couldn't help himself. He laughed. "You changed him? How could you if you've never met the man?"

"Because he told me so. He told me my letters breathed life into his existence. That before I wrote him, he'd never known what it meant to live."

Thatcher sucked in a deep breath, for her words fell with the force of a snowdrift off the eaves. She'd taught his grandfather to live? What the hell did that mean? But just as quickly as he wanted to dismiss her statement, he also in some ways understood completely.

"I changed him," she continued. "My letters changed him." Then she paused, and he saw the conflict in her eyes. "And he changed me," she whispered. "Can't you see? I must be the duchess he expects—a proper English duchess." Then she spun on one heel and this time beat a determined path toward the door.

Changed her? Turned her into a proper English duchess? Well, that was impossible, but at the same time, such a thought was ruinous. She could tell herself a thousand times she had changed, but he knew the truth—there was no relinquishing the passionate creature who lived and burned beneath her fragile facade of propriety.

"Felicity!" he called after her. "Felicity, please." No more Miss Langley. Not after that kiss. She was *his* Felicity now. But she wasn't listening to him, for if she had been he had no doubts there would have been a quick and thorough lecture about the familiar use of an employer's given name.

Damn those letters, he thought as he followed her. He cursed his grandsire for ever answering her inquiry on his behalf. What the devil had the old man written that had this once sensible woman yearning for a man she'd never met? Longing for a man who didn't exist? Couldn't exist!

And how would a real life man, a man like him, ever measure up to this fictional Duke of Hollindrake his grandfather had created? The Sterling he should have been? Just the sort of honorable man Miss Felicity Langley would find noteworthy enough to put on the first page of her blasted *Bachelor Chronicles*.

None of which he was.

A man who'd disavowed his name and family and fled into the army under an assumed identity—and all because his creditors were clamoring to have him cast into debtor's prison.

What was she going to say when she discovered the truth? That her noble and supposedly perfect duke was in truth her improper footman?

By the time he caught up with her, she was already to the door, her cloak swirling about behind her. "Felicity." He caught her hand and tried to pull her into his arms again, but this time she was wary and shook her head, refusing to look him in the eye. "Don't go inside. Not yet. There is something I must say. Something I must tell you—" But before he could test his theory, the door swung open.

"Oh, heavens, Duchess, I thought you would never return!" exclaimed Miss Thalia. "We are ruined!"

Worse than I already am? Felicity thought as she hurried into the house on her still unsteady legs.

Whatever had she been thinking, letting this all-too-handsome man pull her so close? She hadn't even fought him or resisted. At least not before it was too late.

Instead, her body had traitorously leaned toward his warmth, her tongue wetting her lips in anticipation of his kiss. And kiss her he had, leaving her breathless and wavering inside her sensible boots. Oh, the moment his lips had claimed hers, she'd felt lost.

Well, in truth, her first thought had been a fervent prayer that he kissed better than he skated.

And, oh, did he . . .

So strong and sure, he'd whispered his intent with the brush of his lips, with the tantalizing sweep of his tongue as he'd ventured forth. He'd been gentle, something she hadn't expected. But as much as she felt safe from the moment his mouth slanted toward hers, once he'd begun to kiss her, Felicity had no longer wanted that innocent harbor.

She'd wanted to sail straight into the passion he offered, cast off the proper lines and safe anchor, and be his. To let him kiss her, and touch her, and bring this fire he'd ignited to whatever came of it.

For never had she imagined that a kiss could claim one's heart, as Pippin swore.

Now she knew the truth.

Felicity closed her eyes and swore. In Russian. Then in Italian for good measure. Oh, this was what came of listening to Tally sigh over her French novels one night too many!

Truly, this entire muddle was all Hollindrake's fault, she told herself. If he had just sent his card around, she certainly wouldn't be casting herself into one of her sister's tragic plays where the sensible and respectable young lady is led astray by the mysterious, handsome stranger.

She hadn't even been that clichéd. No, she'd leapt into the arms of her ordinary footman.

Felicity glanced back to find him following her, those dark eyes glittering with passionate intent. No, he was no ordinary man, and there was enough mystery about him to qualify for an entire shelf of romantic tales.

Go back to him, some mad little voice inside her urged. *Kiss him again.*

Oh, no! She wasn't going to do that again. Never. Ever. Right there and then she vowed to keep a fair distance between herself and Thatcher. Until Hollindrake came to take her away and she could forget the compelling enigma behind Thatcher's dark eyes, the deep cleft in his chin, the curve of his lips, the way it felt when he . . .

Felicity shook off her wayward thoughts and started forward, nearly tripping over a valise in her path. When she looked up, she found the entire foyer filled with trunks and bags and packages. "Tally, whatever is all this?"

"That's what I've been telling you," her sister shot back. "If you weren't woolgathering about whatever it was that was going on outside . . ." Her sister's brow quirked upward.

"There was nothing happening," Felicity told her.

"That isn't what I saw," Tally replied, but before she could go on, a voice from upstairs stopped them both.

"*. . . and then darlings, I knew I should come here immediately! It was so obvious that my dear girls would need me . . .*"

At Tally's hem, Brutus let out a small agonized howl.

Felicity could have echoed his plaintiff cry. "Don't tell me—"

"She arrived not five minutes after you left—"

Of course she had. "She knew I wouldn't let her in."

"Most likely," Tally agreed. "I'm afraid she came with—"

"All this?" Felicity waved her hands at the maze of luggage.

"Yes." Tally pulled her along toward the stairs.

Felicity groaned as she started up the first few steps.

"Duchess," Tally rushed to explain, "I couldn't stop her. She just arrived at the door and Pippin answered it. She didn't know better, and before I could get downstairs, she was inside, trunks and all."

"Her entire retinue?"

Her sister lowered her voice. "That's the odd thing. She came with only Aziz and Nada."

"Just them?" Felicity glanced back up the stairs at the sitting room. "Not even a footman?"

"Nary a one," Tally said, reaching down to gather up Brutus, who'd gone from howling to whimpering as the voice in the salon grew louder.

"But this London! Such a cold place. I shall need new clothes. Only the best for I have delicate skin and cannot tolerate anything but silk and velvet."

"This cannot bode well for us," Felicity whispered. From the room above them wafted the scent of patchouli and other spices, while from below, a draught of icy air sliced up the stairs, drawing her attention.

Thatcher stood planted in the foyer, having finally come inside. His eyes burned with a passion that she had to deny.

Must deny, she wanted to tell him, especially now that she had more pressing problems.

More pressing than her own ruin? Well, maybe not. But right up there, of that she was certain.

"Miss Langley," he called out.

His deep voice sent a tremor down her spine. "Not now, Mr. Thatcher."

"Is that her?" came the voice inside the salon. "Is that my dearest girl?"

Felicity braced herself for the task ahead, and marched up the last flight like one condemned. "Yes, it is I, Nanny Jamilla."

Their sitting room blazed with warmth, for apparently Jamilla had ordered every last bit of coal brought up. Pippin stood behind Aunt Minty's chair, her hand on the old lady's shoulder. They both looked like they'd been run over by a mail coach.

In a sense they had.

Holding court in the middle of the room stood Nanny Jamilla, who'd looked after the sisters for the short time they had been at Napoleon's court during the peace in '01. Tall and stately, the woman hadn't changed a whit in all these years. Her black eyes flashed with the same intensity and her glorious dark hair was tucked perfectly beneath a grand, plumed hat, while diamond ear bobs sparkled from her lobes.

There was a touch of paint on her cheeks and a bit on her lips, and the kohl she loved, perfectly lined her almond-shaped eyes, making her look as exotic as a chinoiserie vase in a crofter's cottage.

"Felicity! Darling, dearest girl," she cried out, spreading her arms wide open and pulling her into a warm embrace, for the woman had yet to remove her traveling clothes and was still wearing a mink-trimmed cloak and velvet gown.

"Nanny Jamilla," Felicity said, "how kind of you to come call on us." She hoped that was hint enough for the woman.

"Call on you! Such nonsense. I am here to help. To stay." She smiled widely and reached out to snag Tally, drawing her into the embrace as well. "Now that I have my girls back, all is well. But this England, bah! It is so cold! Do they not know that I need to be warm?"

"I'll inform the King," Tally told her, as she extracted herself from Jamilla's grasp.

Felicity took the same opportunity to escape and the sisters fled to the relative safety of numbers, flanking Pippin and Aunt Minty.

"That shall be perfect," Jamilla declared. "I would love to meet him. How is that done? Would tomorrow be too soon?"

"The King is . . . well . . ." Pippin stammered.

"Indisposed. He's ill, Jamilla," Felicity told her. "So there will be no introductions to the court."

"But there must be," she declared. "For I am no longer merely the Duchesse de Fraine, but Princess Jamilla Kounellas."

"A princess?" Pippin gasped.

Aunt Minty snorted, and muttered something about pearls and swine.

Jamilla came forward, posing before the fire. "A princess. After your father abandoned me—"

"He was ordered to Vienna," Felicity corrected.

"My heart was broken," the woman replied, her hand going to her brow.

"She never did know where her heart was," Tally whispered in an aside.

Jamilla glanced at both of them, a withering stare worthy of a queen . . . or a princess. "With my life taking such a tragic turn—"

"There was the *duc*—" Felicity reminded her.

"An old man," she said with a dismissive wave. "He did not understand my passions, my needs. And your father—" She had enough sense, it seemed, to realize that few young ladies wanted to hear about their father's prowess in such matters, and changed her course appropriately. "Your father was a light in my dreary life. And then the light was gone and before I knew it, my poor de Fraine—" She sniffed, and reached out with her hand in a graceful, elegant move.

Nada, her ever-faithful maid, came forward, and deposited

a handkerchief into her mistress's hand, as if the mention of the dearly departed *duc* was always a harbinger for such a need.

The old woman then moved back to her place beside Aziz.

Felicity shot a smile of greeting at Jamilla's dutiful retainers, but the pair stood immobile like a pair of alabaster statues. Both had been with their mistress since her childhood and their loyalty to her was unstinting . . . even when she was, well . . . trying.

Jamilla sniffed into the silken cloth and then dropped it on the floor, walking past it to pose by the window. "Tragically, de Fraine died quite suddenly—as old men will—not long after your father abandoned me." Felicity didn't even bother to correct her. "Without my husband to guide me, my father decided to send me back to his homeland, for he thought his cousin, the sultan, would find me comely. Alas, en route I was stranded in Greece, and as fortune will favor those who seek it, I met my dearest Kounellas."

"The prince?" Pippin asked, her voice breathless in awe.

Jamilla, realizing she had a likely and gullible audience there, moved over to the girl and took her hand, curling it around her elbow and drawing her into the middle of the room.

Tally and Felicity shot each other knowing glances. Hadn't that been one of Jamilla's most memorable lessons?

Darlings, make sure you always take the plainest and least favorable lady in the room as your dearest companion for the evening. Thus, you give all the men the chance to see you at your finest—kind to your lessers and, of course, stunning in comparison to your companion.

And while their cousin was one of the prettiest girls they knew, suddenly she paled against Jamilla's rich and more mature features.

"Now we must see to my room," the lady announced. "My

trunks brought up and I will require three maids and at least four footmen—no, make that five—to see to my needs, for one of them will have to obtain the following items. Before nightfall." She snapped her fingers at Aziz, and he produced a list from inside his robes.

"But Jamilla, we haven't room for—" Felicity began.

"Of course you do!" the woman declared, abandoning Pippin, leaving the poor girl to list aimlessly for a moment before she recovered her equilibrium. "This house is hardly the grand palaces I am used to, but there seems to be room enough for your dear Jamilla." When no one sprang into action, she heaved a dramatic sigh. "Don't you see? I have come to help. Felicity, dear girl, why aren't you married to your *duc* as yet? Is he old? Infirm? Being difficult? Let Jamilla coax him a bit for you . . ."

Felicity tried to speak, but the horror of that thought left her throat parched and the words lodged behind a giant lump. Hadn't Jamilla once made the same offer to Josephine when Napoleon had gone straying? And look where that offer of "help" had landed the former empress! "Oh, no, Nanny Jamilla, that won't be—"

"Oh, dearest, you mustn't call me that, it makes me feel positively ancient." She smiled. "I am just your dear princess now."

"*Princess* Jamilla," Felicity said through gritted teeth, "you can't possibly think that—"

"But of course you will lend me the shelter of your hospitality, little Felicity," the woman said. "For I have had word from your father."

Thatcher had been about to march upstairs and finish his discussion with Felicity when a knock at the door stopped him in his tracks. A freight man was there with a wagonload of trunks and furniture, and it had been up to him to help the man and his sons unload them into the already crowded foyer. By the time they were finished and he'd made his way up the stairs, it was to catch the last of their visitor's announcement.

"I have had word from your father."

He staggered to a stop. Lord Langley lived?

He strode through the door, his gaze going instantly to Felicity. It struck him that it wasn't the news that her father lived that had her regarding her guest with blatant skepticism, but rather that her father would use this woman to send a message.

"And who are you?" their guest asked, sidling forward like a cat . . . one that scratched quite happily.

"Thatcher," he replied, tipping his head to avoid her gaze. He'd met enough women in Portugal and Spain like this one, ladies who used their titles and looks to gain whatever they needed at whatever cost and from whatever side currently held control.

"This is our footman," Felicity told her.

"Ah, yes, the livery!" she said, her gaze sweeping over the jacket with a bemused and calculating eye. "I remember it well."

"See, I told you it was Nanny Jamilla," Tally was saying, but no one was paying her any heed.

Felicity stepped between him and their guest. "Thatcher, this is our former nanny, the Duchesse du Fraine. And her servants, Nada and Aziz." The pair bowed slightly to him, while the duchesse looked him over from head to toe, a sly smile forming on her bloodred lips.

"Princess Kounellas," the woman purred, coming closer and bringing with her a tide of thick perfume. "Felicity forgets herself. Now I am Princess Jamilla Kounellas. I have just arrived from my dear departed husband's kingdom."

He swore he heard Thalia muttering, "Where she should have stayed."

The woman not only looked like a cat, but apparently had

the same hearing. "Impossible, darling!" she declared. "I feared for my life."

Nada's gaze rolled upward, as if she had heard this story too many times to count.

Jamilla continued, "For some reason, his people blamed me for his sudden death! I explained that he was old, that these things happen, but no one would listen to me." She gave a negligent shrug of her shoulders. "His advisors were calling for an inquiry, refusing to release my wedding settlement, calling for my arrest. Can you imagine such impertinence? So of course I was forced to flee." She glanced around her audience and then let out a long, breathy sigh. "Now, on to more important matters. Aziz, the list," she said, snapping her fingers. She took the sheets of parchment and thrust them at Thatcher. "I will need every thing here before nightfall. See to it. But before you go, send at least three of your best fellows down for my trunks."

Felicity cleared her throat. "Jamilla, Thatcher is our *only* footman."

"The only one?" Jamilla's dark eyes widened.

"Yes," Tally added. "So you see how impossible it would be for you to—"

The beringed fingers started waving them off. "Of course, of course, I see the situation now." Jamilla appeared positively distraught. The girls smiled but only for a moment. "How can two innocent and inexperienced girls be expected to run a palace?"

"Uh, Jamilla," Thalia said, edging over to the lady's side. "This is only a town house."

"I shall adjust," she declared, drawing Tally into another hug. "We all shall."

Thatcher suspected he was witnessing the Langley sisters' own version of Corunna. Yet unlike the English army with Portugal behind them, the ladies had no place to which to retreat. Thalia remained trapped in the woman's tigress-like grip, while Felicity looked up at him, her eyes pleading for help. What the devil did she think he could do? Toss the lady and her trunks back into the street?

The French he could rout, but that immense Aziz fellow, with his pair of gleaming swords stuck in the belt of his robe, looked quite capable of hacking to pieces anyone foolish enough to try such a feat.

But the plaintive look in those eyes was clear. *And she's asking you.* He had to imagine that such a request cost Felicity dear.

Jamilla made a clucking noise in the back of her throat. "Whatever are you still doing standing there, Mr. Fletcher—"

"Thatcher," Felicity corrected.

"Thatcher, Fletcher," Jamilla declared. "It matters not as long as he is standing about while my list is languishing!" She pointed one long finger at it, wagging it vigorously. "And make sure the octopus is fresh."

"Octopus?" Pippin inquired.

"For the calamari," she declared. "Your chef is French, is he not?"

Felicity groaned and covered her face in her hands, while Thalia, who'd finally gained her freedom, dropped to the settee and looked ready to be sick.

Though Thatcher had led his troops out of some really tight corners, this was one he wasn't about to wade into. He suspected Felicity, once she caught her breath, would have this faux princess packed off. But in the meantime, he had an easy escape and wasn't so much a fool as not to take it. With the list in hand, he fled from the sitting room and bolted down the steps.

Better that than be around when this Jamilla met Mrs. Hutchinson.

But when he got outside, he realized mayhap he was in

over his head. Where in the hell did one find an octopus in London?

Then it struck him as he glanced over the sheets of paper—French lavender oil, Spanish olives, a basket of lemons, a crate of oranges, along with a list of wines, cosmetics, and sundries that could break even the Rothchilds' legendary bank—that if anyone in London could procure all this, it was Staines. The bored and scandalized Hollindrake butler would most likely fall over in a joyous fit of apoplexy at the idea of being given such an impossible task.

Why, it would make Thatcher seem almost ducal in the poor old man's eyes.

Cutting through the mews, he thought he would slip into the back of his house—so as to avoid the line of carriages parading around Grosvenor Square—when from the dark shadows of an alcove sprang a figure who quite quickly and easily slid a knife under his chin.

The touch of cold steel was followed by a stern order. "Move, you rutting bastard, and I'll happily slit your throat."

Chapter 10

"Why did you let her in?" Felicity demanded of her cousin, once their "guest" had gone to tour the house to determine which rooms she would need opened for her use. Standing with her hands fisted on her hips, still wearing her cloak and hat from her trip to the draper's, Felicity shook with rage.

Pippin sat before her, nearly in tears, but not even that could assuage Felicity's ire.

"Duchess, that is hardly fair," Tally shot back. "You weren't here. One minute the bell was ringing, and the next the house was filling with trunks and she just sort of swept in on us—"

"Like the plague," Aunt Minty muttered. "We have a word for them types down in the rookeries. That's what we call a—"

"Auntie, now is not the time," Pippin whispered.

"Well, I've me opinions," she huffed, and then went back

to her knitting with an air of indignation, punctuated now by the *clack* of her needles.

"Tally, you should have sent her packing," Felicity said, turning uncharacteristically on her sister. She lowered her voice and said, "You know what she is like."

"What is she like?" Pippin asked.

The sisters shared a glance. *Should we enlighten her?*

"A vulture," Felicity replied, tugging at the strings of her cloak and then dropping it on a nearby chair, deciding it was about time that Pippin's innocence lost some of its luster. Next she pulled off her bonnet and gave her hair a quick check in the mirror. "Father always said he regretted his arrangements with her."

"A bad influence," Tally added.

"Harrumph," Aunt Minty snorted. "Could of told 'im that the first moment I laid eyes on her." She shook her head. "Men! As if they can judge these things. Probably all he saw was them pair of—"

"Enough, Auntie!" Felicity sputtered as she paced about the room. She had to think. There must be some way to evict their former nanny. "What I can't determine is how she found us. Believe me, her arrival is no mere coincidence."

"She did say she has word from your father," Pippin suggested. "And she knows he's alive."

Tally sighed and shook her head. "Even if she's discovered that his death was a ruse for the Foreign Office, I doubt Father would trust her to bring word to us."

"Exactly!" Felicity said. Their father's "death" was a trial—but she knew that Lord Langley would never have sought Jamilla's aid—no matter how dire his situation might be. "She's bluffing. Still, I can't see how she found us."

"Well—" Pippin began, then snapped her lips shut and shifted in her seat. After a few moments of squirming, she continued, "She was a *duchesse* . . . and I thought . . ." Her cheeks pinked.

"Pippin, no!" Felicity sputtered. "You invited her?"

"I didn't mean to. Well, I didn't think it would hurt. And I wrote the letter so long ago, I had forgotten that I'd even sent it." She glanced from one sister to the other. "You both spoke so fondly of her that I thought it would be like having a real mother here to help us."

"Nanny Jamilla?" Felicity said. "When have we ever spoken fondly of her?"

"'Use kindness always and keep it in your heart for it will shine from your eyes,'" Pippin quoted. "You repeat that all the time. And what about that other piece of advice . . ." She paused for a moment. "Oh, yes, 'Measure your anger as you would gold, sparingly and with a sharp eye.'"

Tally rubbed her fingers to her temples. "Pippin, dear, that wasn't Nanny Jamilla."

"It wasn't?"

"No," Felicity told her. "'Twas Nanny Tasha."

"Oh dear," Pippin whispered, glancing back toward the door. "And she didn't say, 'Modesty is the provision of the young and virtuous'?" The sisters shook their head. "Oh, heavens, I've made a muddle of things."

"You can say that again," Felicity said, throwing her hands up in the air. "That woman single-handedly caused Napoleon to set aside Josephine. Why, she caused riots when it was discovered she wanted to be the next empress."

'Truly?' Pippin asked.

"Yes," Tally said. "And I don't doubt she left Greece under similar circumstances."

Felicity snorted. "And now she's launched her latest caper. Planting herself so firmly in this house that it will take the Royal Guards to evict her. I suspect she discovered by chance that Father is still alive and decided to come here and await his return."

"This father of yours must be something for her to come all this way in hopes of having another toss—"

"Aunt Minty!" Felicity protested.

Apparently, Pippin wasn't willing to concede defeat just yet either. "What if she is here, as she said, to help us. She has had two husbands after all, one of them a prince."

"Dead husbands," Felicity pointed out. Oh, wait just a moment. *Dead husbands?* Which left Jamilla in need of a . . .

Not another lover, as Aunt Minty avowed, but something else. She hurried over to her desk, pulling open the drawer and retrieving her *Chronicles*. When she found the entry she wanted, she stuck her finger on it.

Tally came and stood by her elbow, Brutus sitting down at the hem of her gown. "You can't mean to—"

"I do."

"But—"

"This is war," Felicity declared. "I must find her a new husband immediately so she won't—"

"You don't think she'd—"

Felicity turned and looked at her sister, one brow cocked. Hollindrake needn't be handsome for Jamilla to set her sights on the man. He'd need only a pulse and a hefty bank account, and that much Felicity did know about the man.

Tally nodded in concession. "Yes, I suppose she would."

"Perhaps you've misjudged Nanny Jamilla," Pippin offered. "I don't think she'd intentionally interfere with your arrangements with Hollindrake."

Both sisters shot her a withering stare. Then Felicity said, "Shall I tell our cousin about the incident with the Archduke of Prussia and Jamilla or should you? Or how about the envoy from Rome? Or the Russian prince?"

Pippin's color drained, leaving her already fair features as white as muslin. "Oh, what have I done?"

"Quite possibly handed my Hollindrake over to her!" Felicity said. "Well, she can't have him. He's my duke."

"Your duke!" Aunt Minty snorted. "Heard enough about him to fill me ears, I have. Starting to wonder if this fella's even real." She got up and bundled up her knitting, Pippin leaning over to help her. "And don't particularly care to hear any more." She left, Pippin taking the opportunity to slink out as well, under the guise of carrying the lady's work basket.

With the room cleared, Tally spun around and faced her sister. "But the real question is, do *you* still want Hollindrake?"

Felicity's head swung up. "Of course I do!" she snapped. "Why would you say such a thing?"

"Because I saw you from the window before I opened the door."

Now it was Felicity's turn to pink.

"Duchess, whatever were you doing letting poor Thatcher kiss you?" Tally caught up Brutus and held him to her chest. "And from what I could see, you had no objections to the arrangement."

"You're lucky I didn't kill you back there," Thatcher told his adversary as they settled down in a back booth of a nearby pub.

Mad Jack Tremont grinned at his old friend. "You're lucky I haven't slit your throat. What the hell are you doing posing as Felicity Langley's footman?"

His friend's fierce protectiveness took Thatcher aback. But only for a moment. "From what I understand, I should be the one emptying your gullet for setting that little marriage mad chit on me. 'Try Hollindrake's heir,'" he quoted.

Jack didn't even look embarrassed to be found out. "You'd be lucky to have her."

"Lucky to have that little title mad, managing, conniving—" he stammered, resorting to his original supposition about his nearly betrothed.

"Smart, brave, demmed good to have at your back in a fight," Jack countered. "You want some simpering miss, then you've come to the right place, London is full of them. But a girl like Felicity . . ." Jack shook his head. "You should hear

Temple on the little duchess! He's quite mad about her."

"Why doesn't he marry her then?" he asked, taking a long drink from his glass.

"You haven't heard?"

"Heard what?"

"Temple's married. Ran off to Gretna, what, five years ago. Got hitched to Lady Diana Fordham."

"Temple's married?"

"Contentedly."

"I never thought—"

"No, no one did," Jack said. "But he and Diana suit."

"Like you and your bride?"

Jack laughed. "Wouldn't be the happy man before you if your little duchess hadn't worked her mischief."

"She seems to have a talent for it," Thatcher agreed. "And she's not my duchess." *Not yet, anyway.*

"She will be." Jack pushed his glass out in front of him. "But if you are toying with her, I'll be the first one in line to meet you at dawn. So you had better convince me that whatever you have planned won't break her heart."

Thatcher glanced up at the man who was more brother to him than his own two siblings had ever been. "I don't know what I am doing with her, quite honestly," he admitted. "I went to cry off and she mistook me for a footman candidate from an agency."

Jack, who had been taking a sip from his glass, sputtered. "She truly thinks you're a footman?"

"Aye."

Jack shook his head. "You have to tell her the truth immediately. She'll shoot you if she discovers from someone else that you've been misleading her."

"A Bath miss with a pistol?" Thatcher mocked. "You must be joking." But in the back of his mind he still hadn't forgotten that punch from yesterday.

Then Jack sobered him up further by telling him the story

of how Felicity had once aided him in regaining the freedom of two English agents from a rogue privateer, Captain Dashwell. Not that he was surprised—Felicity truly was the most unique miss he'd ever met.

"You should have seen her," Jack was saying, "down on that beach, pistol in hand. Believe me, Felicity will put a bullet between your eyes, or lower still, if she thinks you've played her false."

"I've been shot at enough to know when to duck," Thatcher replied. "I was just wishing my grandfather was still alive. Because if he knew that the lady he'd chosen for me could shoot the ballocks off a man, I'd have the pleasure of seeing him drop dead yet again at the very thought of such a chit as the next Duchess of Hollindrake." He took a swig from his glass.

Jack sat back, a smug smile on his lips. "He knew."

Thatcher stilled. "What?"

His friend glanced up and looked him in the eye. "He knew."

A shiver ran down Thatcher's spine. He wasn't a man who believed in fate or coincidences, or any other such superstitions. A practical man who'd looked death down the barrel of a rifle and tip of a sword more times than he could count, he'd never once considered that his grandfather could have known.

And still given his consent.

"You're telling me my grandfather knew that the bride he chose was a reckless, conniving—"

"Oh, yes. All that and more," Jack told him. "Two years ago he summoned me and Miranda to Baythorne for a full reckoning. He'd already interviewed Temple, and I believe even their teacher, Miss Emery, was trundled up north for an interview. That was in addition to what that secretary of his—"

"Mr. Gibbens," Thatcher supplied.

"Yes, Mr. Gibbens. Efficient fellow, that one. He'd managed to gather quite a volume on Lord Langley's work for His Majesty."

"That should be interesting reading," Thatcher commented, thinking of Lord Langley's questionable liaisons with his daughter's "nannies." Jamilla alone would give poor, fussy Gibbens nightmares for a month.

"Your grandfather wasn't a man to leave anything to chance . . ." Jack paused. "He wanted to know Felicity."

"I still can't see how he could have chosen her if he—"

"Thatcher, he knew. Miranda gave him a complete accounting of Felicity. Her faults, her penchant for matchmaking, her meddlesome, high-handed, sometimes illegal—"

Thatcher shook his head. "The man I knew would never have—"

Jack stopped him again. "But he also knew the truly important things about her."

All Thatcher had ever heard his grandfather go on and on about was honor, and duty, and proper decorum. He hardly saw how Felicity fit into that mold. "Such as?"

"That you'd never find a more brave, intrepid, determined, and loyal bride, no matter how far you roamed, no matter how far you fled. He knew someday you would have to come home and he hoped that . . ." Jack paused and shrugged. ". . . that you'd forgive him."

Thatcher's throat caught. Forgive his grandfather? He didn't think he even knew who the man was any longer. The Duke of Hollindrake had been like a dragon in the family cave, ruling over the finances and proceedings with a fiery personality that had singed anyone who crossed him. Everything he did was measured toward keeping the family firmly afloat and in its rightful place in English society.

"And *he* told you all this?"

Jack nodded. "Good man, your grandfather. Knew he'd made mistakes in his life. Confessed to them one night over too much whisky and some fine cigars." He smiled at the memory, then leveled his gaze at Thatcher. "He envied you. Your honesty, your bravery."

Thatcher blew out a long breath. "I don't think—"

"He did. He was especially proud of your courage. Said he'd never had the chance to make such choices, and he envied you for them. He also knew the weight of the responsibilities and expectations he was leaving you and what they could do to a man. Thought perhaps someone like Felicity might . . ." Jack grinned. ". . . keep you on your toes."

And suddenly that odd voice in the back of his head, the one that had urged him to play this masquerade, to save Felicity from Lady Lumby's threats, and more to the point, to kiss her, sounded more like that of the domineering old man who he had spent the last twelve years putting an ocean and a war between them.

Still, it was hard to fathom that his grandfather had chosen *her*—a reckless, too-smart-for-her-own-good, meddlesome, and barely proper chit.

"Funny, eh?" Jack mused. "But he was quite adamant about you marrying her. Wrote me not a year ago and made me swear that I'd see you brought to the altar if Felicity didn't do it herself."

"So he did, did he?"

Jack nodded. "Your grandfather wasn't leaving anything to chance. Suppose he figured if I'd been brought to heel, you could be too." He laughed and rubbed his chin. "Must have been some courtship. Miranda tried cautioning Felicity last summer about putting too much stock in a man she'd never met, and the little chit sent back a scathing defense of her 'Aubrey.'" He sat back and laughed. "I'd give my best shipment of brandy to find out what she and Hollindrake wrote about for the last four years."

"You and me both," Thatcher agreed, wondering how many more days it would take Gibbens to arrive.

"I have to ask this," Jack said, "because if I go home and not have an answer for her, I fear my wife will be after you, and her temper makes Felicity's look quite docile." He took a deep breath. "When are you going to tell her the truth?"

Thatcher reached for his glass. "Do you really think she'll shoot when I do?

"If you're lucky."

Thatcher had arrived back at the house on Brook Street to find that Staines had done his work well—the kitchen overflowed with baskets, from Jamilla's shopping list and more.

"Well, finally," Mrs. Hutchinson was muttering as he'd come through the back door. "Something what to cook with." She fluttered a knife at him. "But if that foreign tart thinks she's going to bring some sea monster into this house and 'ave me cook it, well, I don't care if she's the Queen herself, I ain't letting some foul thing into me kitchen." Slamming the knife down in the carving board, she crossed her arms over her chest. "What are you doing just standing about? That princess wants her trunks brought up. Seems she's taken the entire second floor."

"Why hasn't her man done it?" Thatcher asked, suddenly seeing the world of footmen in a new light. Haul those trunks up three flights of stairs?

"Apparently he doesn't lift things, so get a move on."

Thatcher thought to protest, but if he wanted to keep up this masquerade for a little longer, he needed to do the tasks set out before him. He'd helped move cannons, tugged stubborn pack mules across swollen rivers, and done his fair share of hard labor in the army, so there was no reason he couldn't haul a trunk or two up a few flights of stairs. Right?

Well, he hadn't considered that Jamilla would make moving an army look like a country picnic.

After the sixth flight, he was convinced he was about to

meet his maker, but triumphantly he hauled the last piece into her room.

That was his first mistake.

The princess had reappeared and arranged herself on her bed—worse yet, her servants were nowhere to be seen. At his arrival, she rose like Venus from the sea foam. "Ah, the footman," she said, her eyes flicking over him like a cat's. She circled him and before he knew it was between him and the door.

Good God, not even Bonaparte was this deadly. "Yes, well, here are your trunks," he said, trying to dodge around her.

Her hand came out and her fingers splayed across the braid on his livery. "Darling, I don't know what game you are playing with those dear girls down there, but it won't work on Jamilla."

"Game?" he gulped, feeling a bit like a fox in the hunt.

The princess moved even closer. "They think you are the footman."

"I am," he told her, backing away, but well aware that with a few more steps, he'd find himself backed up against the bed, which was the last place he wanted to be.

She laughed. "The footman. Dear man, I know footmen. Believe me, I do. And you are no footman. So tell Jamilla who you really are and she will see if you are worthy of her assistance."

After the chaos of the morning, Felicity had quite forgotten that she'd sent a note over to Lady Stewart and her daughters inviting them to call.

Then much to her shock, it wasn't the lady who ventured to ring their bell, but her husband, Lord Stewart Hodges.

Oh, not Stewie Hodges, Felicity cursed silently as Tally brought their guests upstairs, and Pippin hurried off to tell Mrs. Hutchinson to prepare a tea tray—a decent one, she prayed as she led her guests to the upper salon. The Hodges might not be in the upper crust, but Stewie—as he was known about the *ton*—was invited everywhere, and where he went, so did the latest *on dit*. A badly set tea tray would be just the sort of *bon mot* to keep Stewie going for days.

Following in Lord Stewart's self-important wake were his sister, Lady Rhoda Toulouse, and all three of the Miss Hodges: Margaret, Frances, and Eleanor—whom their father introduced as Peg, Fanny, and Nelly, much to the cringing embarrassment of the young ladies, who were doing their elegant best to make up for his lack of social graces.

The second son of the Marquess of Kennings, Stewie had neither valor nor intelligence to recommend him, but by a stroke of luck had married Miss Alice Simons, a coal heiress worth five thousand a year, and therefore secured his continued standing amidst society with a simple "I do."

"Lady Philippa, Miss Langley, Miss Thalia, how prodigiously kind it was for you to send around a note to my Alice," he began. "She was quite taken with your well-written words and sincere expression, and was overwrought this morning when a cold—a trifling matter, really—prevented her from coming to call straightaway. So I said, 'Alice, I will call on those dear girls, for their father, bless his soul, was a most excellent fellow.'"

Felicity opened her mouth to respond, but Lord Stewart was off and running again.

"And zounds! As we were about to hie off to see you all, who should arrive but my dearest sister." He beamed at Lady Rhoda, who sat on the settee beside him. "Right there and then, I had such a capital idea. I said to her, 'Rhoda, you love a good visit, and those poor motherless girls could use your sensible advice.' So here she is with us."

"And it is very nice to meet you, Lady Rhoda," Felicity interjected before the loquacious lord had a chance to take another breath.

"And you ladies as well," the matron said. "I remember

your mothers . . ." She smiled at Pippin and Tally. "They were such blithe spirits and so well liked. I can see the three of you take after them."

"Ah, yes!" Lord Stewart added. "The Hawstone sisters! Oh my, I see the resemblance now! What a lucky bloke Langley was when he caught the elder Miss Hawstone's eye. Caused such a scandal when they eloped." He sat back and stuck his thumbs in the pockets of his waistcoat. "Have to imagine the three of you will find a way to set all the tongues wagging just as your dear mothers did when they first came to Town."

"I assure you, Lord Stewart," Felicity rushed to tell him, "none of us have any intention of causing a whiff of scandal."

Aunt Minty, who up until now had appeared to be dozing in her chair, snorted and coughed.

"Don't see how you can avoid it," he said, puffing up his chest. "'Tis in your blood. Besides, as much as you protest, my dear Miss Langley, there is already much talk about you and *a certain fellow*." His brows waggled up and down.

"Me?" Felicity shot her sister a look.

How would I have told anyone what I saw? Tally's wide-eyed expression said.

No matter, Felicity realized. Any gossipy cat who'd been looking out her window this morning might have caught sight of her with a footman dangling over her like an erstwhile Lothario.

And if Lord Stewart already knew about it . . .

Felicity shuddered. She might as well have had an engraving done and put it on the front page of the *Times* with a description underneath that read, "The Ruination of Miss Felicity Langley," for the popular paper was decidedly more discreet and had far less range than Stewie Hodges.

"And you other two," he said, grinning at Tally and Pippin. "Come along as well for the Marriage Mart, I venture," he said. "The girls are here for your second . . . no, make that third go 'round. Come as long as it takes, I tell my Alice. We'll find them some likely lads."

"Papa!" Miss Eleanor Hodges protested, her cheeks pinking.

Her father didn't notice her distress in the least, and continued on until he had all of his daughters sinking into the settee and looking as if they wished themselves in the farthest reaches of Ireland. "Of course that's what the fillies do in the spring! But those young rapscallions out there are crafty devils—you'd best watch your step, Miss Langley. I was quite the young buck in my day, and I was forever—"

"Papa!" the eldest, Miss Margaret Hodges, protested. Nut brown hair and plain brown eyes left her without any remarkable features, but Felicity could see she shared her aunt's intelligence. "You promised quite faithfully—*no stories*."

"And so I did, poppet, so I did." He winked broadly at Felicity. "No stories about how Hollindrake and I were rakish devils in our misspent youths."

"You know Hollindrake?" Tally asked, moving to the edge of her seat.

"Oh, now you've done it," Lady Rhoda laughed. "He was hoping one of you would ask. Been all but bursting at his buttons to regale you with his lies and exaggerations."

Stewie grinned broadly, having succeeded in finding an eager audience. "Hollindrake? Of course I know him. Wasn't even the heir back then, why not even an Honorable, just plain old Aubrey Sterling, and a rare spirit he was. Rare, indeed!"

Now perhaps, Felicity thought, she could get to the truth of the matter. Lord Stewart might natter on, but he was known to be honest. Oh, finally she'd get to the bottom of all the mystery surrounding her nearly betrothed. Yet much to her chagrin, Jamilla chose that moment to come floating into the room, interrupting the man's discourse.

There was, Felicity grudgingly admitted, something to the

way their former nanny entered a room that left every man in the vicinity gaping. She took a glance over at the Hodges sisters and had to imagine they wouldn't make it to their fourth Season if they were to perfect Jamilla's grand style.

"Darlings! I thought I heard new voices in the house! Especially such a deep masculine one—for it held such a divine noble tone to it, I was drawn, I tell you, drawn here!" She'd come to a stop in the middle of the room, wearing a gauzy sort of gown with a length of purple silk wound through her dark hair, the ends trailing down her back. It was if the Queen of the Desert had just arrived in their midst.

Stewie's mouth flapped, his eyes nearly popping at the sight of this unprecedented lady before them, and after a moment of shock, he rose hastily to his feet.

Lady Rhoda's face held a bemused look of begrudging admiration, while the Hodges sisters, like their father, gaped.

Felicity heaved a sigh, for there was nothing left to do but introduce her. "May I present our guest, Jamilla—"

"Princess, darling," she corrected. She held out her hand to Lord Stewart. "Princess Jamilla Kounellas."

Stewie stumbled forward, taking her fingers as if he'd been presented gold, and with great flourish brought them to his lips. "Madame, you are a divine presence, a flower amidst—"

Jamilla glanced over at the Hodges sisters and then back at Stewie, her calculating gaze obviously noting not only the family resemblance but the plain and serviceable gowns. It took the lady but a moment to realize there was no future for her here. Jamilla had never really relished a man with children—inheritance issues and all, though Lord Langley had been the exception—and as such she dismissed Lord Stewart from her affections before he had a chance. "Yes, yes I am," she said, plucking her hand back and settling down on the nearest chair. She turned her head toward Felicity. "Why aren't there any refreshments for our guests?"

Felicity smiled perfectly, while at the same time grinding her teeth together. "I've rung for the tray."

"Perfect, darling," Jamilla purred. "And whatever were you saying, Lord Stewart, when I dared to interrupt you?"

"Interrupt? I say not, Madame." He was still standing in the middle of the room staring at her as if he'd never seen a woman before. Lady Rhoda caught him by his coattails and tugged him back down on the sofa. He didn't appear to notice, rambling on with his story. "My dearest, radiant princess, I was just telling these girls about my acquaintance with Miss Langley's future . . . oh, shall we say, her future betrothed, the Duke of Hollindrake."

Jamilla's dark eyes glittered. "You know of him? Delightful! I would hear more, for the little duchess has been quite, how you say, closed in the mouth about her *duc*."

"I daresay she would be, especially if she knew some of the things I do. The tales I could tell you of Aubrey Sterling—" He was interrupted by Brutus, who chose that moment to sit up and start barking. Unfortunately for the little dog, Lord Stewie's half boots presented little appeal, so he'd been keeping an eye out for Thatcher's return. "Yes, well," Stewie stammered, before he tried to continue, "let me tell you all about old Aubrey Sterling—"

"Ah, here he is with the tray!" Jamilla announced. "You naughty fellow! Where have you been? Nada says the kitchen has yet to see any sign of my octopus!"

Jamilla's complaints held little weight, for Thatcher was too busy trying not to drop the tray and make a complete, and cowardly, retreat to, say. . . . Scotland. For of all the people to come face-to-face with in Felicity's salon, the last person he wanted to see was Stewie Hodges. Gossipy, running at the mouth, indiscriminate Stewie Hodges.

"Yes, well let me tell you all about old Aubrey Sterling—" the man was saying.

Oh, demmit, this was a nightmare.

Jack's warning rang in his ears. *She'll shoot you if she discovers from someone else that you've been misleading her.* No, Scotland wouldn't be far enough, he reasoned wildly. Siberia, perhaps. Or maybe China would be well out of Felicity Langley's furious range.

Not only was Stewie there, but his sharp-eyed sister, Lady Rhoda Toulouse. Stewie barely noticed his arrival, for the man's gaze was fixed in a glazed sort of fashion on the princess, but not so with Lady Rhoda.

"If you would put the tray here, Thatcher," Felicity told him, and he did so, keeping his head down and counting the seconds until someone said something. But nothing came and he glanced over at Lady Rhoda.

After a flicker of recognition, she coolly turned her gaze toward Felicity. "I see you have settled quite nicely into London. However did you find such a perfect address?"

"And costly," Lord Stewie said. "When all the talk is that you three haven't a coin between you, seems demmed odd you'd have such a fine house. Why, I'd say you'd have to commit treason to manage such a splendid address!"

While Thalia sputtered, Felicity rushed in to explain, "Our solicitor, Mr. Elliott, assisted us. He was quite adamant we find suitable lodgings."

"A lovely room," Lady Rhoda said. "Interestingly appointed." This she directed at Thatcher.

He took a deep breath and turned to flee, er, leave.

"No, no," Jamilla protested. "Thatcher, is it not?"

"Yes, ma'am."

"You must stay. I may have need of something. Stand over there," she told him, waving her hand toward the drapes.

And so he had no choice but to plant himself in the corner. But the advantage was that he could observe everyone with little notice being sent in his direction.

Certainly Stewie had changed little in twelve years. Still the same toady, garish buffoon he'd always been.

"You have a fine hand at pouring, Miss Langley," Lady Rhoda was saying.

"Miss Emery was an exacting teacher," Felicity demurred as she finished and began handing out the cups and saucers.

"An extra lump for me," Stewie said. "Not unlike the lumps I used to get when I went out in Town with Aubrey and Mad Jack."

The mousy-looking girls on the settee all groaned. "Papa!"

Ah, the Misses Hodges, he realized.

"Come now, poppets, Miss Langley needs to know the sort of man she's aligned herself with. I wouldn't be doing my duty to Lord Langley if I just let her attach herself to such a rapscallion fellow without fair warning!" He smiled at his daughters. "As much as I would love to see one of you wearing a ducal coronet, I wouldn't have a daughter of mine marrying such a fellow. No, indeed!"

Oh no. Not again, Thatcher silently cursed.

"I am certain you have the current duke confused with someone else," Felicity said politely.

"Confused? I daresay I'd know the man in the middle of Japan!"

"Which," Lady Rhoda pointed out, "would be quite simple, Stewart, for he would be the only Englishman around."

Stewie slapped his knee, sending his napkin flying. "Well, I daresay you're right, but still, I know the man. That I do!" Flicking a glance over at Thatcher, he said, "Be a good fellow and fetch that for me, will you?"

"Yes, milord," Thatcher said, catching the napkin up and dropping it into the man's wide lap.

Stewie glanced up at him and blinked. For a moment Thatcher thought he was about to be unmasked, but whatever thoughts tumbled through Stewie's madcap mind, making the connection wasn't one of them, and he continued, "Now where was I? Oh, yes! Hollindrake! Fine fellow if you are looking for someone to prowl about with. But marriage? Ridiculous notion! Can't see him falling into the parson's snare—not and take to it, if you know what I mean."

"Lord, I hope not," Lady Rhoda muttered.

"He's a demmed rake, Miss Langley. Cut a swath a mile wide when he was in town. Flirted with Rhoda a bit afore I ran him off."

"I believe *I* flirted with *him*," she corrected. She turned to Felicity to explain. "I used your poor betrothed quite shamefully, but a few dances with Mr. Aubrey Sterling was enough to get my most excellent Mr. Toulouse to propose." She shot an apologetic smile at Thatcher, her eyes a-sparkle with her trademark intelligence and mischief.

Thatcher felt his pride crack a little. So much for his legendary prowess and charm.

Stewie still wasn't convinced he hadn't had a hand in all of it. "Disappeared right after that. Probably feared I'd have him eating grass for breakfast."

One of the Miss Hodges groaned, and Felicity glanced from Lady Rhoda back to Lord Stewart.

"The duke is not the same man he was back then," she announced. "He is quite a changed man."

Lord Stewart laughed. "That's how they all appear when they go courting. But mark my words, we rakes never change."

Thatcher began to choke. Stewie thought himself a rake? Had the man ever owned a mirror? Unfortunately, his sputtering drew nearly everyone's attention.

"Are you well?" Felicity asked.

"Yes, miss," he said.

The pompous little fellow continued. "No, Hollindrake

hasn't changed. I remember a night when ol' Aubrey, Mad Jack, and I were out on one of our prowls—liked to prowl about Town, we did—and I bet Aubrey a ridiculous amount that he couldn't steal Lady Fanshaw's yellow petticoat—"

"Stewart!" Lady Rhoda protested. "That is hardly—"

He waved his sister off. "Oh, now don't get miss-ish on me, Rhoda. Miss Langley needs to know the sort of man that she's aligning herself with. Besides, demmed if Sterling didn't show up the next day at White's with the petticoat. Caused a fine *on dit* that week."

Thatcher had all but forgotten that escapade but flinched at the memory. Why was it Stewie wouldn't be able to tell you the capital of France, even if he were standing on the front steps of Notre Dame, but he had a memory for gossip that would put the *Morning Post* to shame? Not only that, his indiscreet nature let him blather on without a care for his audience.

And one of those, namely Felicity, didn't appear to share Stewie's enthusiasm for the tale. With her jaw set and her eyes narrowed into two dangerous slits, a smarter man would have shut his mouth.

No, not Stewie, he took her silence to mean she was ready for more. And more he had. "Though that was a fine lark, I always liked the time Aubrey got so drunk he fell in the Thames and we had to pay a ferryman to fish him out. Middle of May, but you couldn't tell that by the way he was shivering. Thought he'd catch his death that night. Lucky for him, Lady Babcock came along and offered him a ride back to Mayfair, but once she caught a whiff of him, she made him strip down to his small clothes afore she'd let him into the carriage." Stewie laughed. "And demmed if old Aubrey didn't offer to—"

"More cakes," Thatcher said, having picked up the tray and shoved it under the man's flapping lips.

"Well, yes, I don't mind if I do," he said, looking slightly befuddled at having been prevented from finishing his story.

Felicity took the opportunity to jump into the conversation and steer Lord Stewart in a new direction. "I must confess, I did have a purpose behind my invitation to all of you."

"Do tell, Miss Langley," Lady Rhoda urged her. "*Please do tell.*"

"Well, it is just that I am so happy in my situation"—this she directed at Lord Stewart—"that I thought perhaps to share my joy with your daughters by suggesting the following . . ."

Thatcher closed his eyes, for what man wanted to witness another hapless bachelor—no, make that three poor souls—about to meet their fate in the form of one determined Felicity Langley.

But then again, he had to admire her for one thing.

She'd gotten Stewie Hodges to shut up. Something he doubted anyone in the *ton* had ever succeeded in doing. For when she announced that she intended to see the eldest Miss Hodges become the next Countess Lumby, the poor fool keeled over in a dead faint.

After Jamilla provided a vial of her smelling salts and Lord Stewart was brought around, the visit with the Hodges went off better than Felicity could have imagined. All and all, her suggestions had been met with great enthusiasm by the Misses Hodges, but strangely, Lady Rhoda had remained the only one not to voice an opinion—and considering her reputation as a forthright matron, it was more than a little odd.

Lady Rhoda was not only forthright, but also astute, and she'd kept her questions to herself until everyone else was bundled into the waiting carriage. There on the curb, the woman, still beautiful and stately, stopped and turned to Felicity. "It is most kind of you to help my nieces . . ." She paused as she adjusted her gloves. "But I must ask, why?"

Felicity would have expected as much from someone as smart and experienced as Lady Rhoda. "I will be perfectly frank," she told her. "I have two reasons. One being, I wish to vex Miss Sarah Browne, and helping your nieces find advantageous marriages will do that."

Lady Rhoda nodded, a sly smile on her lips. She was too much of a lady to express her approval of such a plan, but one could see that she knew of Miss Browne's slights toward the girls. "And the second reason?"

Taking a deep breath, Felicity knew the only course was, again, the honest one. "We are out of coal."

Lady Rhoda laughed. "That is it? That is the boon you seek in return?"

She nodded. There was no use beating about the bush, they needed coal, and apparently everyone in Town knew they were up the River Tick. Blast her father for not leaving them in better straits before he'd gone off on this fool's assignment for the Foreign Office.

"Miss Langley, you will never survive in Society if all you ask for is a lump of coal! You are living in an empty house, having obtained it by Lord only knows what means—"

"As I said, our solicitor—"

The woman waved her off. "Please, no more of this gammon about your solicitor. Everyone knows what a pinch purse Mr. Elliott is. I only ask that one day you tell me how you managed it, for I suspect it is a marvelous story."

Not so much marvelous, Felicity would have told her, but rather a rare stroke of luck. She'd spotted a notice in a newspaper she'd picked up to pass the time while waiting in Mr. Elliott's office. There, amidst the notices, she'd spotted the following:

Notice to all Claimants: The disposition of all possessions and properties of the late William Burbage, esq. late of Brook Street will be handled by Mr. Georges, esq. All inquiries and disputes should be directed to his attention, including but not limited to claims on the property at No. 4 Brook Street. All claims must be entered before the end of the year . . .

It had only taken a little prompting—and flirting, Tally would have added—to get Mr. Elliott's clerks to explain the case to her, one of them having had a pint or two a few nights before with Mr. Georges's unfortunate clerk. Apparently, several "heirs" had come forward, all with different versions of the late Mr. Burbage's will. Each was clamoring for the right to live in the house, and a judge had recently ruled that until the matter was sorted out, the house could sit vacant.

"Of course, that could take months," the tall, skinny clerk had informed her in his most professional of opinions. "These sort of matters do."

And to Felicity's way of thinking, it had seemed an awful shame that such a perfect address should sit vacant while the proceedings languished, so they'd . . .

"I don't need to know how you came by this house, but I think you need more than coal." The lady let her words fall gently, for they held an offer for so much more.

But Felicity had her pride, and she wasn't going to take more than was necessary. "No, I ask only for enough coal for the month. By then things should be settled—"

"With Hollindrake?" There was a disapproving lilt to her query.

Felicity nodded. "I know your brother means well—"

Lady Rhoda drew her away from the carriage. "My brother barely knows his waistcoat from his trousers, but I want you to think well on the subject before you jump into marriage with a man you know so little about. You've put much thought into the matches for the girls, but I wonder if you've done as much to discover who it is you are about to marry?" She tucked her hands into her gloves and shivered in the winter chill. "I'll ask Alice to have the coal sent around directly. And in the meantime, I might suggest you find a man you can love, Miss Langley. One who will warm you for far longer than any amount of coal." She glanced up and over Felicity's shoulder and smiled, then turned and climbed into the carriage.

Felicity shivered as Lady Rhoda's words struck a chord inside her. *I wonder if you've done as much to discover who it is you are about to marry?*

And then there was Thatcher's angry peal as well. *You have nothing . . . with a man you've never met.*

She wavered on the curb as Mr. Mudgett's voice added to the cacophony. *He's a bounder, that one. Not fit company for a good lady, if you know what I mean.*

And finally, there was Lord Stewart's laments. *He's a demmed rake, Miss Langley. Cut a swath a mile wide when he was in Town.*

Oh, heavens! This was a disaster. Suddenly, her duke didn't seem so perfect after all. Rather, it seemed her betrothed was the worst sort of dodger.

Here she had prided herself on knowing every detail of so many men's lives, but had she ever really pried that deeply into Hollindrake's? Truthfully? No. And she knew the reason . . . for fear she'd discover exactly the sort of things that Lord Stewart had recounted. Or Mr. Mudgett had willingly offered.

She'd wanted Hollindrake to be her perfect duke and looked no further, certain he would love her for having worked so hard to be his perfect duchess.

But could he love her? This libertine? This rake? This petticoat-stealing lounger? How would she even know how to keep such a man?

And finally, it was Lady Rhoda's voice of reason that left her trembling from head to toe. *Find a man you can love.*

The wind curled down the street, whipping at Felicity's

skirts and chilling her to the bone, but she barely noticed, for her world seemed to be over. How could she ever love Hollindrake? Love such a terrible man?

Then for some reason, she turned around and discovered what had caught Lady Rhoda's attention. Or rather, whom.

Thatcher.

To her chagrin, and then relief, an odd, comforting sort of warmth spread through her limbs at the sight of him. Before she knew what she was doing, she stumbled up the steps and into his arms. And there she started to cry.

And she didn't care who saw her.

Chapter 11

I grew up living abroad—in palaces, in castles, in grandly appointed houses—like a princess, yet I've always wondered what it would be like to have a home. And now that I have lived here, in England, I know what I was missing. A house of yellow stone, surrounded by gardens. And my own rosebush—one that I could wake up each day knowing that it could continue to grow in its own sunny spot and would grow year after year right there, blooming in well-rooted contentment. Yes, I know that roses can grow just about anywhere—even in Russia—but nowhere do they grow and flourish as they do here, in our beloved England.

*—From a letter to the Marquess of Standon
by Miss Felicity Langley*

"Duchess?" Tally whispered gently to her sister. "Duchess, are you well?"

Felicity barely heard her, hardly nodded her head to respond as Thatcher led her into the sitting room. He settled her onto the settee, and she looked up at him, expecting to find him bemused by her distress.

But there was no mirth there in his eyes, only concern, and

that made her unhappiness all that much more distressing.

Of course *he* was concerned. He was honorable and noble and loyal and everything a man should be. Everything her duke was not.

"Thatcher," Tally was saying, "could you please fetch us some more tea?"

"Certainly," he said. "Is there anything else you need, Miss Langley?"

Felicity shook her head. She couldn't even look at him. He'd held her on the steps as she cried and hadn't said a word of remonstration. As he could have, most likely should have.

When she glanced up, he was gone and Tally and Pippin sat opposite her, their expressions mirroring her own shock over Lord Stewart's revelations. Aunt Minty sat near the fire, knitting furiously, while Jamilla lolled on the other end of the settee, glancing wistfully at the picked over tea tray.

Hollindrake a wolf in sheep's clothing? How could this be? Certainly she'd heard some rumors about his past, but hadn't Mad Jack Tremont been much the same in his youth? And he turned out to be noble and heroic.

There are things a man can't undo, that a man can't disavow. But time has a way of making one see what is important, what is necessary and how change isn't always the bitter potion it is made out to be.

Hollindrake had written her those words, hadn't he? She rose absently and moved to her desk.

"Felicity, are you sure Thatcher can't get you something more?" Pippin said. "Some nice jam and bread, perhaps?"

"A bit o' warm brandy?" Aunt Minty suggested.

"Another footman?" Jamilla offered.

She shook her head and settled into her familiar chair. Pulling at the chain around her neck, she drew out the key that hung there and tried to work it into the lock of her writing box. But her hand shook so badly, she couldn't manage it.

Instead she slumped and started to cry again. Oh, what had she done? Aligned herself to the man who was quite likely the worst libertine in the history of London.

Why couldn't he be more like . . . *like Thatcher.*

This made her tears flow even harder. How was it in two days' time she'd gone from being singularly confident in her choice to this? Curses on Lord Stewart and Mr. Mudgett. And Thatcher as well. He shouldn't have insisted she go skating. Or drink Turkish coffee. Or worst of all, kissed her and turned her world upside down.

No, she thought, mustering what remained of her pride and confidence. There was still time to prove them all wrong. Prove to herself that she was right about Hollindrake.

"What do you need, dearling?" Tally asked, having moved softly to her side.

She pointed at the writing box that held all of her letters.

His letters. They'd prove her point. Make everyone see the truth as she did.

Tally pulled a pin from her hair, tucked it into the lock and opened the box faster than if she had used the key. With a mildly apologetic shrug, she hastily opened the box, lifted the writing tray out, then moved the blank sheets of paper aside. With a quick tap on the hinge, the hidden compartment opened and she retrieved the bundle of letters tied in a blue ribbon. "Are these what you are looking for?"

Felicity nodded, catching hold of them and shuffling through the worn and well-read pages until she came to the one she was looking for.

Swiping at her tears, she scanned the lines, searching for the paragraphs she remembered. "Here, Tally, read this." When Tally read it silently to herself, Felicity shook her head. "No, aloud."

"If you think I should," her sister said.

Felicity nodded for her to begin, so she did:

"'I suppose by now you have heard the rumors of my misspent youth. They are mostly true.'" Tally stopped and glanced up at her sister, wide-eyed.

Felicity waved at her. "Read on."

Taking a deep breath, Tally did just that. "'But my sweet girl, you must realize that such days were well before I met you. And that your letters, your vivacity, your innocence, your spirited discourse have left me with only one thought— to make amends where I can and attend to my obligations with nothing less than an equal measure of your determination. I stand in awe that one as young as you should use your time to such better use—'"

She stopped and glanced at her sister.

"I had written him about our campaign to have mandatory knitting hour each evening," Felicity explained, "so we could make socks to send to Wellington for his troops."

Pippin laughed. "Did you also tell him that you begged Miss Emery to let us do that so you didn't have to spend the hour reading aloud from *Fordyce's Sermons*?"

Felicity laughed as well, swiping the last of the tears from her eyes. "No, I neglected that point. But don't you all see? He isn't the same man as the one Lord Stewart described."

Biting her lower lip and not willing to look her sister in the eye, Tally lowered her voice and said, "That may be true, but the point is that you have never met him and Lord Stewart has. He sounds rather . . ."

"Rakish," Pippin offered.

"A devil to boot," Aunt Minty added.

"Divine!" Jamilla declared. "Your Hollindrake sounds absolutely divine! A man with experience, he shall please you, little Duchess! He will know how to carry you to the heights of heaven—and such a man is—" She made a purring noise in the back of her throat and ended her discourse with a drawn-out, breathy sigh.

"Well, there is that," Tally agreed.

"Yes, so he can please a woman, but how will I ever please him?" Felicity shot back. Then her mouth dropped open as she realized what she had just said. "Oh bother, I don't care how improper that sounds. What if the duke finds me dull in the marital sense and decides to seek solace elsewhere?" She began to cry again, this time in great choking sobs. "I won't know what to do."

"Well, you kissed Tha—" Tally started to say, then clapped her hand over her lips to stop from blabbering her sister's secret. But it was too late.

"Thatcher?" Pippin finished, hurling herself off the settee and coming to sit on the footstool beside Felicity. "You kissed him?"

Felicity covered her face with her hands and started to cry again. She didn't know why she was turning into such a watering pot other than the fact that kissing Thatcher had most likely ruined any chance she had at securing Hollindrake. Why, if he found out . . .

"Did you really kiss him?" Pippin asked again. After a few more sobs, Felicity nodded. "That's wonderful! Why he's perfect! And so much better than Hollindrake, for Mr. Thatcher is likely ten times more handsome and so very heroic."

"Perfect? Perfectly unacceptable," Felicity shot back, her hands dropping to clutch two fistfuls of her gown. "I am nearly betrothed! What was I thinking when I let him—" A devilish warmth ran threw her limbs and she wished with all her heart she could forget his kiss.

But she doubted she ever would, curse the man!

"He is a handsome devil," Tally noted.

"Very handsome. I wouldn't be surprised if he has some

noble blood in him," Pippin said. "For he's been nothing but kind these past two days—saving us from Miss Browne and then helping us with Lady Lumby. It's almost like he can't help himself but be heroic." She paused and her eyes grew wide, her mouth opening into a wide moue. "Oh, Tally, that can be our new play—'The Lost Duke.' The man is working as a footman when it is discovered that he is actually a duke who was kidnapped as a child . . ." Pippin paused and her fingers fluttered against her lips as she considered the next point.

"By pirates," Tally provided.

"That's perfect," Pippin agreed quite readily. "And he has utterly and completely forgotten his aristocratic beginnings."

Oh, yes, Felicity thought. Just as she'd predicted. They'd found a way to use Thatcher in one of their ridiculous plays—and had just as quickly forgotten her very important and very real plight.

As if to prove the point, Tally leaned over and grabbed up a dozen or so sheets of writing paper and nudged Felicity out of her chair. "Oh, I have the perfect subtitle: 'The Noble Spirit Uncovered.'"

Pippin clapped her hands together. "'Tis perfect! The first act must take place at sea."

"No, no, no! A prologue—of his kidnapping, his mother begging the pirates not to take her precious child, her only son." Uncorking the bottle of ink, Tally hastily dipped the quill and began to scratch away at the pages. Pippin turned and brought over the plate of leftover cakes, settling them on her lap and happily dictating between bites of currant scones.

Felicity threw her hands up in the air. "Oh, you two are incorrigible! My life is in ruins and you want to write another one of your foolish plays?"

Neither of them heard her, but there was a gentle tug at her elbow. She turned to find Jamilla leading her away from the engrossed pair.

"They cannot help you, little Duchess," she said. "But I

can see you are troubled by all this. Why, I am not so sure, but you are worried and Jamilla is here to help."

Help yourself to our unwitting hospitality, larder, and social standing, Felicity thought. But then again, right now she'd take any advice she could get.

Besides, if there was one subject Jamilla could be called upon to offer advice, it was men.

"The duke has so much experience—"

"And that is a good thing," Jamilla assured her, leading her to the settee before the fire and settling them both down before the warmth of the coals.

Their last bit of coals, Felicity thought, but at least she needn't worry about them freezing now that Lady Rhoda had promised them enough to get them through the end of the month.

"There is nothing wrong with a man who has experience in the arts of *l'amour*," Jamilla told her.

"But I have none," Felicity said. "And what if he expects—"

"He will expect nothing of you," she said. "These Englishmen are fools—they want their brides to be innocent and wide-eyed and then they are bored. And you Englishwomen, you want love and fidelity. Bah! How can you accomplish such a thing when you are dull and unwilling to explore your own passions. But you, little Duchess, shall be the exception for your duke."

Felicity shook her head. "However will I do that?"

"Your footman, darling!" Jamilla declared. "It is how all women of the world practice their arts."

"Thatcher?" she sputtered "You want me to kiss him again?"

"Not just kiss him, little Duchess," Jamilla announced. "Your footman has a wicked gleam in his eyes—believe me when I tell you this, he will know what to do. Let your Thatcher love you and you will go to your duke a woman with experience."

* * *

Thatcher stood in the hallway, his mouth hanging open. What had he just heard?

He needn't have asked, for that demmed woman repeated herself.

"Felicity, so unbecoming—you resemble a fish at market when you gape so. You heard me correctly, let this Thatcher make love to you."

This was how the princess thought to help? He could well imagine the ruin of London society if all nannies were like this Jamilla.

"Do you think so?" Felicity said with a curious, dare he say it, hopeful, note to her voice that had his head shooting up and staring at the open door in shock.

In that same instant, he saw exactly that. *Felicity atop his bed, naked, splendidly so, her blond hair released from those infernal pins that held its honeyed depths imprisoned. Lithe, long limbs reaching out for him, welcoming his hard body, his ragged needs.*

But as fast as his fantasy had his blood pounding through his veins, he realized something else. Despite having listened to Stewie's dire warnings about Hollindrake's character, Felicity was still intent on marrying her "noble duke," so much so that she'd ruin herself with a footman to ensure she was capable of satisfying her rakish husband.

He turned quickly and marched down the steps, for the irony that he was one and the same didn't escape him.

It wasn't until he was out of the house and in the middle of the alley that he finally came to a stop. The twist in his gut was something he'd never felt—well, not over a woman— and he knew exactly what it was. Jealousy. Jealous of himself. Or rather that wretched Hollindrake his grandfather and Mr. Gibbens had created and could never exist. Certainly no man could be such a paragon of virtue and nobility.

He certainly wasn't. Look at him now! Standing in the middle of an alleyway, having fled the house like the greenest of recruits. Then again, what sort of man wanted to stand about eavesdropping as his almost betrothed plotted her seduction of another man?

Now, that wasn't done. Wasn't proper. The eavesdropping or the seducing part.

Raking a hand through his hair, Thatcher began to laugh. He doubted even Thalia and Pippin could contrive such a misadventure.

Oh gads, he was in a terrible muddle. Taking a deep breath, he looked up at the darkened skies, the snow twirling hypnotically down from the heavens. And as the snowflakes fell around him, so did images from the day.

Felicity urging him to try his Turkish coffee.

The keen pain in her eyes when Miss Browne and Lady Gaythorne had done their worst to cast their poison upon her.

The taste of her lips when he'd kissed her.

Jack's revelation about his grandfather.

Stewie falling over in a dead faint.

The incredible feeling of having her seek solace in his arms.

Oh, it was a day worth recounting.

"Cap'n?"

Thatcher glanced over to find Mr. Mudgett standing before him.

"You well, Cap'n?" the man said, his head cocked to one side as he studied him. "You look funny."

"I'm well, Mr. Mudgett, just surveying the field a bit."

"Oh, aye, Cap'n," the man replied, though his skeptical glance suggested he didn't understand in the least.

"Mr. Mudgett?"

"Aye, Cap'n?"

"Do you remember the warning you gave me?"

"Which one?" the fellow asked, sticking his hands into the pockets of his trousers.

"The one about Miss Langley."

"Oh, aye."

"When was it that you said I was going to end up in briars if I wasn't careful?"

"Yesterday, sir." Mudgett shuffled his feet in the snow. "Sir?"

"Yes, Mr. Mudgett?"

"Are you?"

"Up to my neck," he confessed, looking up at the sitting room, where a few candles had been lit. He wondered if Felicity was already at work amending her *Chronicles* entry about Hollindrake. About him.

"Hmm," the older man mused. "You kissed her, didn't you?"

Thatcher swung around. "How did you—"

"I've a cousin. Had the same thing happen to him."

The man didn't elaborate, but Thatcher's curiosity nudged him. This was, after all, entirely new territory for him. "What happened to your cousin?"

"Oh, sir, I don't think you—"

"That bad, eh?"

Mudgett hung his head, then nodded it in a forlorn bob.

Thatcher glanced back up at the window where the light shone like the first star of the night. "Was your cousin happy, Mr. Mudgett?"

"Never stopped smiling, sir." His batman glanced up at the window as well. "Are you going back in there and tell her the truth?"

The truth? That she deserved to be loved and love a man in return. Felicity Langley was so far gone with the idea of marrying a duke—a real one— that if he went in and told her the truth, first of all he doubted she'd believe him.

And more important, he feared she'd send him packing, with or without the musket ball.

Thatcher shook his head. "I've been warned that she'll shoot off my ballocks when she finds out. That, and I'm hardly the man she deserves."

"Don't see how you can't be good enough for any lass, sir, iffen you don't mind me saying. As for your miss there," he nodded toward the house, "too bad you can't just marry her afore you tell her the truth. She might still be madder than a hornet, but she'll be married and a duchess to boot. She'll hardly shoot you then."

Thatcher stilled. "What did you just say?"

"She won't shoot you once she's a duchess."

He shook his head. "No! The other part—"

"Why can't you just marry her afore you tell her the truth?" Mudgett blew on his hands. "Seems it won't matter much then."

Thatcher laughed. "Mr. Mudgett, you old matchmaking dog, you! That's perfect!"

Mudgett looked none too happy. "Don't you be telling anyone this is my idea. 'Specially if that miss can shoot. I like me ballocks right where they are."

Thatcher clapped him on the shoulder and led him down the alley. "Say, whatever are you doing out here, my good man?"

"Looking for you," Mudgett replied. "You told me to keep watch for that Gibbens fellow and he arrived not five minutes ago. So I was coming around the corner here to find you."

The letters. Thatcher caught his breath. "Gibbens? He's made it to London?"

"Aye, sir."

He took off on a fast march across the icy cobbles, Mudgett bringing up the rear. He flew through the gate in the back and into the kitchens. The cook and scullery maids gaped at the sight of their master rushing past.

"Gibbens!" he bellowed, even as he came up the kitchen stairs. "Gibbens, where are you?"

The poor man, still rumpled and icy from his journey, sat on a chair to one side of the grand foyer looking miserable. "Yes, Your Grace. Here, Your Grace."

"Where have you been, my good man?" Thatcher said, glancing around for his secretary's trunks.

"The roads were—"

"Yes, yes, Quite so. Terrible. Do you have my grandfather's correspondence with you?"

The man blinked. "Correspondence?"

"Yes, his letters."

"Letters? Oh, I brought what I thought you would need, the books, some newly arrived reports from your stewards, and since the former duke kept a rather voluminous exchange, I brought only the more recent and relevant—"

"His letters, man!" Thatcher bellowed. Then he looked around and realized that Staines, Mudgett, and the rest of the staff were staring at him as if he'd gone mad.

Perhaps he had.

Still, he lowered his voice and leaned forward. "The letters, Gibbens. The ones from Miss Langley."

His secretary blinked again and then blushed. "Oh! *Those letters.*"

"Yes, yes, those letters," Thatcher said.

"Yes, of course."

"Give them to me. At once."

A slightly ruffled Gibbens turned and surveyed the luggage around him. Then his owlish eyes lit on one of the trunks and he fumbled in his pockets, finally removing a key and moving with agonizingly, exacting precision that had Thatcher wishing for his old rifle. He'd have that lock open and the contents spilled without any of this painstaking agony.

Finally, after what seemed an eternity, the man opened the chest and retrieved a stack of correspondence, neatly tied with a blue ribbon. Even before he held them out, a note of Felicity's perfume tantalized his senses.

But to his amazement, Gibbens wasn't quite the lackluster fellow he appeared. When Thatcher reached out to snatch the letters away, the secretary snapped them back, his eyes narrowed, and looking for all intent and purpose like Thalia's little mutt of a dog, Brutus.

"Gibbens, give those to me," he ordered, pushing his open palm forward.

The man shook his head. "Not until you give me your word, Your Grace. Will you be careful with them?"

Careful with them? He was acting like he was holding the only copy of Magna Carta, not the romantic musings of some chit. But the stubborn glint in Gibbens's eyes said only too clearly he wouldn't be naysaid, not by anything.

"Yes," Thatcher ground out. "I will." After another moment of détente, he added, "I promise."

Gibbens's brow furrowed and then, after another long moment, he ever so slowly extended the bundle into Thatcher's eager grasp.

With what he was positive was the key to all this mess, Thatcher turned on one heel, marching toward the study that overlooked the garden. "Staines, I'll need the fire in the study stoked, extra candles . . . and, oh yes, a bottle of my grandfather's best brandy. The good French stuff he always kept. And then I don't want to be disturbed. Not by anyone—especially not my aunt. No one is to bother me." He was nearly down the hall when he heard a hasty patter following him. He turned to find Gibbens at his heels.

"Your Grace?" the man said.

Stopping at the door to the study, Thatcher bit back an impatient curse. "Yes?"

The man shuffled his feet and cast an anxious glance at his new employer. "Do you want the replies?" His question sounded more like a confession.

"The what?"

"The replies." His owlish eyes blinked again and he swallowed down an anxious breath. "As a matter of course, I always made a copy of His Grace's correspondence in case it was needed for future reference."

Thatcher shook his head. "You have not only all her letters, but my grandfather's as well?"

"Yes, but his are only copies."

He waved his hand at the man. "Well, what are you doing standing there? Go get them."

Again the little man's brows furrowed. "I must advise, Your Grace, that they are the *only* copies."

"I don't care if they contain the King's own secrets, get them!" This he thundered, and when he looked up after his secretary who was now scurrying with all haste to fetch the letters, he caught Staines beaming from ear to ear.

As if the old duke himself had made an appearance from the choirs above.

Finally, Gibbens returned with an equally thick bundle, tied just as the first was, with a worn blue ribbon. He glanced down at the letters in his hands, then said, "While His Grace dictated most of these letters, I should tell you I added my own sentiments from time to time." He took another wheezy breath. "Miss Langley is a most excellent lady and I—"

Thatcher reined in the explosion that threatened to erupt, and carefully pulled the letters free from the man's grasp. "You needn't say more, Mr. Gibbens. I understand." He turned to enter the study, where a fire was already waiting for him.

Ah, Staines. This is why you are the finest butler in all of London.

"Your Grace?"

Thatcher turned back. "Yes, Gibbens."

"The ribbon . . ." he stammered.

Thatcher looked down at the silken bit. "What about it?"

"She—that is, Miss Langley—sent it because she said it was the same color as her eyes." He glanced one last time at the bundle then up at Thatcher. "Is it?"

So Felicity had made a conquest of his grandfather's poor secretary. Heaven help the besotted fellow when he finally met her—the troublesome minx would bowl him over like a regiment of cavalry, leaving him lifeless in the ditch.

Yet he couldn't help himself, he looked down at Gibbens's prized letters where the poor faded ribbon conveyed none of the blue fire of Felicity's fierce gaze. Yet he knew what his secretary wanted to hear.

"Yes, Gibbens, it is."

The man fairly beamed. "I'm glad of it, Your Grace."

When Thatcher arose for breakfast the next morning, he looked out at the snowy garden below his window and knew exactly what he had to do.

What he *must* do.

It wasn't a matter of duty or honor. If he hadn't already been half in love with Felicity, after spending the night reading her letters, he would have been. And in those letters he'd received a far greater gift.

He'd discovered his grandfather through pages on politics, on social questions, and on the subject of women's rights—surprisingly, his grandfather had even conceded a few points to Felicity's well-formed answers. Amidst those lines, he found himself in the middle of conversations, wishing he could have joined in on the discourse, for they were often lively and always engaging. But there were moments of depth in there, where for once he saw the man his grandfather truly was, the man his title and position had masked.

And that was the message he'd found from his grandfather laced and twined between the lines—not to let being Hollindrake take away from the passions and important things in life.

A mistake he was not going to make. At least not after he'd won Felicity's heart, he mused, as he pressed his forehead to the icy windowpane and let the chill of the morning clear his thoughts.

An hour later when he came downstairs, he thought he saw tears in Staines's eyes at the sight of him in a perfectly fashionable dark green jacket, buff breeches, and gleaming Hessians. As he entered the breakfast room, he found his aunt in her new chair, and on the opposite side of the table, his mother, Lady Charles Sterling.

Mudgett had forewarned him about her arrival, but nothing could have stopped him more than her enthusiastic welcome.

"Aubrey, my dearest, dearest son!" she said, crossing the space between them so she could wrap him in a tight embrace. Then she held him out and looked at him. "Home at last! How I have worried and prayed for your safe return."

"Yes, well, it is good to see you too, Mother," he said, trying to recall the last time Lady Charles had ever shown him any warmth. His childhood? Not that he could recall. When he'd been sent off to school? Nay.

Then again it struck him—perhaps he knew as little of her as he had his grandfather. He smiled at her, tentatively, and lent her his arm as he led her to her chair.

"We've held breakfast for you, but first let me look at you!" She stepped back and admired him. "Why you look positively ducal. Quite surprising, for who would have ever thought that *you,* of all the family, would ever have inherited?" She made a *tsk tsk* under her breath and sat down in her seat.

Now *that* was the mother he remembered.

She took another sharp glance at him and sighed, then turned to his aunt. "Geneva, dear, I hardly see what you were nattering on about." She shook her head and turned back to Thatcher. "Some nonsense about you posing as a footman. Geneva, I think you should start avoiding the sherry bottle.

He doesn't look at all nicked in the nob—though that scar doesn't help. Really, Aubrey! Whatever were you doing in Spain?" She sighed and waved to Staines to begin serving as if she were the mistress of the house. "Why, your aunt had me believing you were as mad as Dick's hatband, which wouldn't be surprising given how you spent your youth, but I can see for myself you're no worse for wear."

Thatcher heaved a sigh as well. No, his mother hadn't changed, but perhaps that wasn't such a bad thing. She did have a way of getting Aunt Geneva's ire up, and now his aunt wouldn't spend the morning pestering him.

At least so he hoped.

"I see you've finally found the coats Weston delivered," Aunt Geneva said, wresting the conversation away from his mother.

"Yes, madam, and I thank you."

She nodded to the footman to fill her teacup. "Am I to understand it that you've ended your association with Miss Langley and are now going to make your entry into good society?"

"Miss Langley?" his mother asked. "Who is she?"

Thatcher looked down at his now filled plate and sighed. So much for eating in peace. "My grandfather saw fit to betroth me to Miss Felicity Langley, the daughter of the late Baron Langley."

His mother blew out a quick breath. "A baron's daughter? You must be joking! Your grandfather would never be so plebian." Lady Charles was the daughter of an earl, and considered anyone less than that beneath mention. "Besides, the Langleys? What nonsense! Such low sorts. Wasn't he a clerk for the King?"

"A diplomat."

Aunt Geneva added her opinion to the discussion, "Traveling about to God knows where. Bringing home all sorts of foreign notions. Dear heavens, Lady Kingsmill went to

Vienna with her husband and came back positively odd."

He considered pointing out that he'd just spent the last ten years crisscrossing Portugal and Spain, but didn't want to listen to the discourse that was sure to follow on the folly of those endeavors.

"So you have broken this entanglement, haven't you?" Aunt Geneva pressed.

"No, I have not."

"What?" both women said. They glanced at each other like wary cats, for the two sisters-in-law had never agreed on anything since the day Lord Charles had brought the former Lady Rosebel Redford home as his bride.

"But, Your Grace—"

"Aubrey, I must protest—"

"Enough!" he told them, sharply enough to set them both back in their seats. "This matter is mine and mine alone."

After a few tense moments, his aunt ventured a new subject. "I have come up with a preliminary invitation list to the ball, and your mother was making some additions to it when you came in—"

"What ball?" he asked.

"The one for the evening after your investiture."

"Oh, yes, excellent idea," he said, before taking a hasty bite of ham. Well, if anything, this ball of Geneva's could double as his marriage ball, but he wasn't going to tell them that. Their surprise that night would be nothing compared to Felicity's when she arrived and found him the host. He only hoped she didn't make a habit of attending balls armed.

Then something else occurred to him. "Where is the list?"

"The what?" Lady Geneva asked.

"The list . . ." He waited a moment and then added, ". . . of the guests you intend to invite?"

"Whatever for?"

"Because it is my house, my money paying for all this, and as such I will have a say in who you invite."

The two ladies shared a glance that bordered on rebellion, but after a few moments Geneva nodded to Staines, who brought forward a stack of parchments. At first he brought them to her, but she shook her head and gestured toward Thatcher.

It didn't take much of a glance for him to see that this ball was meant for only the finest families of the *ton*.

"Mrs. Browne and daughter?" he asked.

"Mrs. Browne is the Marquess of Saxby's cousin and well thought of."

"Her daughter is a pretentious nit, and not welcome in my home." Shaking his head, he glanced over at Staines. "Bring me a pen and ink."

"Whatever do you mean to do?" Aunt Geneva said, rising to her feet.

"Amend this list."

Staines brought forward the necessary implements and Thatcher set to work. Drawing a thick line through the Brownes, he also eliminated Lord and Lady Gaythorne. Then he added some names to it.

"But Aubrey," his mother protested, "you can't just invite whoever you want."

"I can and I will."

His mother leaned over and looked at the names he'd just scratched onto the page. "Lord and Lady Stewart Hodges?"

"And all their daughters," he added.

Aunt Geneva paled and then collapsed into her seat.

His mother stood her ground. "Stewie Hodges? Whatever are you thinking? He's a veritable mushroom and his wife is the daughter of a coal merchant. We'll have no peace all evening."

Aunt Geneva's nose wrinkled. "Why, his daughters haven't even been granted vouchers to Almack's—and after two Seasons, I might add—and you want *them* to grace *our* house?"

"Yes," he told her. "But if the lack of vouchers is a problem, then get them some."

"Get them . . . ?" His mother's mouth flapped impotently.

"Vouchers. Before the ball," he repeated.

"We can't just—" Aunt Geneva protested.

He glanced over at her, his brows arched, a look he remembered his grandfather used to great effect. It quelled Aunt Geneva, for the moment, but not his mother.

"Aubrey Michael Thomas Sterling, if you think I will go prostrate myself to Sally Jersey or Mrs. Drummond-Burrell, you are quite mistaken on the matter." Lady Charles shook out her napkin as if that finished the matter. "I have no desire to go pandering after the patronesses of Almack's like some *cit's* wife in search of bargain silks."

He glanced over at his aunt to see if this rebellion had spread.

His mother's stubborn refusal must have given Aunt Geneva a bit of hope, for she shook her head as well. "Your Grace, you've been away for some time, and these matters are best left—"

"Vouchers for all of Stewie's daughters or I will close the house on Bedford Square," he said, quietly but firmly.

"My house!" his mother said. "You wouldn't dare. Where would I live?"

"At Baxton Park with Aunt Geneva," he replied, offering one of the duke's minor properties. In Cumberland. About as far away from London as he could banish them without sending them to the hunting lodge in Scotland.

"I will not be tossed from my own house because I refuse to ruin myself socially," Aunt Geneva said, defiance in every word, her Sterling blood boiling.

But Thatcher was Hollindrake now, the head of the Sterling family, and his word was law. Like it or not. "If these arrangements aren't satisfactory to you, Aunt Geneva, you can return to your husband." He rose to his feet. *"Where you should be."*

She gasped, as did his mother.

"Vouchers, ladies. It should be a trifling thing for the two of you to do." And then he strode from the room.

"Aubrey . . . I mean, Your Grace," his mother said. "Where are you going?"

"I have obligations elsewhere."

"You aren't going back . . . there," Aunt Geneva said, a note of protest and hesitation in her voice. "I forbid it!"

He shook his head. "Aunt Geneva, you needn't get into such a lather. I'm not going over there."

She heaved a sigh. "Thank God!"

Then he winked at his mother. "Not until I've changed." Then he left the room, which had fallen into shocked silence.

Aunt Geneva fell back into her chair. "I told you," she said. "He's come back utterly mad! Whatever is to be done with him? He can't seriously expect us to single-handedly raise up Stewie Hodges's daughters like they are diamonds of the first waters. They are beyond the pale, and we will be as well if we do as he suggests."

Lady Charles wasn't listening, her gaze was fixed on the empty doorway and then down at the edited list.

"Rosebel! Are you listening to me?" Geneva heaved a sigh. "You must do something."

She did. She began to laugh.

"Whatever is amusing about all this?" her sister-in-law asked. "Now it appears we will have to endure an afternoon of listing to Patience natter on about some nonsense if we are to gain those vouchers."

But Lady Charles's thoughts were hardly on an ill-spent hour in the company of Lady Jersey. "Did you see him?"

"See who?"

"Aubrey! I never would have thought it. Truly, I am beside myself."

"Mad!" Aunt Geneva declared. "Completely mad!"

"Oh, no, not at all, Geneva, dear," she said. "Did you hear him? Threaten to move us both into exile? And together, no less." The lady heaved a sigh and positively beamed. "I thought he appeared quite ducal. In fact, I couldn't be prouder."

Chapter 12

"Oh, heavens! There you are! You really should invest in a watch," Felicity told Thatcher as he came through the door. She took a glance at the bracket clock behind her. "You'll never keep a position if you don't show up in a timely fashion."

Since he had no intention of remaining a footman for much longer, he made a contrite bow. "My apologies, Miss Langley," he said, looking around at the vast array of crates and trunks surrounding her. Simply gowned in a plain gray dress, her delightful red socks poked out from beneath the hem of her gown.

He looked at her this morning with a new understanding—for her letters to his grandfather had been revealing. In as much as his grandfather hadn't been honest with Felicity, he knew she hadn't been all that forthright in her correspondence. She'd done her best to cast herself as the perfect duchess, but like her red socks, her wit, humor, and independent spirit had shown through. Like when she'd written:

> *Why is it that young men are granted their fortunes when they are one and twenty and we women must wait another four years? What makes a young man—who is more inclined toward drink and gambling—a better hand at finances, than a young, modest woman who has no such inclinations? Do not tell me that I haven't the mind nor the capacity to understand such matters, for I understand them well enough. Women aren't allowed their portion until they are five and twenty because by then the men have run through their wealth and suddenly even the plainest of ladies begins to look quite comely . . .*

Yes, there was no repressing Felicity's opinions. He still couldn't quite believe his grandfather's choice, but he was more thankful every day that she wasn't some Miss Browne.

He rather liked this irrepressible minx, in her red socks, and wielding (as she was right now) a pry bar. "Thinking of pawning the princess's belongings?" he asked, looking over the collection of boxes he'd help unload the day before.

She let out an exasperated sigh, arms crossed over her chest, her toes tapping a staccato beat. "If they were her things, I would never have let them in."

Thatcher laughed, as did Felicity, and for a time that tenuous thread wound around the two of them. She was studying him . . . well, looking at his mouth, and he wondered if she was seriously considering Jamilla's advice from the afternoon before.

Let your Thatcher love you . . .

Demmit, if the little chit wasn't considering that woman's advice! And that meant if she was looking for a kiss, some experience, then she was still intent on marrying her mythical Hollindrake. Not that he didn't understand her reasons. Between the lines of her letters he'd seen her very real need for security and respectability, at any price. Especially with a life spent being uprooted and tossed about as she and her sister followed their father to his various postings. Not to mention having a father who was nearly as notorious as the Prince Regent for his liaisons.

Yet how could she still want Hollindrake? Even after everything that Stewie had told her, or rather, warned her about. Flying in the face of Mudgett's advice. Not caring a whit about the passionate kiss they'd shared the day before.

Perhaps putting his plan into action wasn't going to be as easy as he'd hoped . . .

"Dare I ask what is all this?" he inquired, edging around a particularly large box, putting it between them.

"My mother's things. They've been in the attics at Langley House forever, and I finally convinced the current tenants to send them to me. I was starting to think they'd never arrive."

But Thatcher was still fixed on another statement. "Your father's estate is leased?"

"Yes. Has been for ages. He always thought it impractical for the house to sit vacant. It's been rented out for as long as I can remember." Her fingers trailed over the top of a crate. "I've never even seen the place."

Her wistful words reminded Thatcher of what she'd written about the rosebush and having a home in the country. That ache for roots, a place to bloom, he understood. He wouldn't have all those years ago when he'd been a reckless youth, but he did now. After so many years of following the drum, sleeping in tents, in sheds, and even under the stars when there was no other shelter. Of praying to live yet one more day in the midst of a hail of musket fire, the desire for a home he understood.

He itched to tell her that now, quite conveniently, he had seven residences, as well as a castle, and that wasn't even counting the hunting lodge. She could have rose gardens at all of them if she so desired.

"Why aren't Lady Philippa and Miss Thalia here to help?" he asked, looking at the monumental task before them. "I would think a treasure hunt would appeal to that pair."

"You'd think," Felicity said, eyeing one crate then another. "But they are in alt over their new play and not even the French army could rout them from their 'art.' They'll be closeted away for the next week or so, at the very least. 'The Lost Duke'! Such falderal."

Thatcher flinched. *If they only knew* . . . "Don't you think a duke could go about without people knowing who he is?"

She snorted. "I'd know!"

It was his turn to laugh. "You would? You mean to tell me that if Hollindrake came to your door, you'd know the man?"

"Of course," she replied, shaking the pry bar at him like one would wag a finger. "He'd be the one in the Weston jacket, with a gilded carriage, a matched set of horses, and footmen in the blue and white livery."

"Here, let me do that," he said, catching up the rod in her hands. "Which one first?"

She shrugged. "Matters not. I haven't the vaguest notion what is in any of these. I'm just hopeful there is something we can use."

So he set to work opening the one closest to him. "Use? What do you need?"

"Haven't you looked around," she said, glancing around the empty foyer and nodding toward the empty study behind him. "There isn't much in the way of furnishings in this house, or decorations. We can't keep fobbing off our empty house as an oversight for much longer. People will start to suspect."

He looked up from the crate. "I think they already do."

"Exactly. So you can see why the contents of these boxes are so important. I'm hoping my mother had some silks or sateens tucked away that we could use to have some new gowns made up. The colors won't be fashionable, but the right styles will keep most of the gossip at bay." She nodded toward the crate, urging him to continue.

"Why don't you apply to your solicitor?" he asked as he reset the bar and put his weight into it to get the lid off.

"Harrumph! Don't think I haven't," she told him. "Mr. Elliott has a very frugal sense of budgets and even less regard for the necessity of a Season. He considers the pin money that father authorized in his last letter far too extravagant, but at least he can't naysay that poor amount." She eyed his work. "I think if you try that corner, you may get the lid off a little more easily." Walking around the box, she tried to peer in, but still there was nothing as yet to see. "Truly, if Mr. Elliott had his way, we'd still be in Sussex." She made a low growl. "Sussex, indeed!"

Thatcher shook his head. "What did Mr. Elliott say when you came to London?"

"Something about being headstrong lassies without much more sense than a bowl of oats. He's of the opinion that once we run out of coal and food, we'll go back. I'll use his desk as kindling before I go back to Sussex."

Thatcher laughed, but when he caught a glare of indignation from his employer, he stifled it as best he could.

"There is nothing to laugh about. I had thought if we came to London, he could hardly refuse us, but he's a stubborn man and is steadfast against giving us anything beyond what we are allocated by Father's instructions."

"And this house? However could you afford such an address—even if it is empty?"

She winced. "Do you really want to know?"

"Yes, of course," he said. In for a penny, out for a pound. But in truth he was more focused on getting this last nail to pop free, and even as he pressed all his weight against the bar, she made her confession.

"We aren't really renting it, more like borrowing it without permission."

The nail gave way with a great *pop* and the lid came flipping off. The bar flew next, and Thatcher went pitching head first onto the floor.

"You should be more careful," Felicity told him, pointing at the floor. "I don't want that marble chipped. Looks Italian."

Thatcher propped himself up. How the devil did one borrow a house without the owner's consent, unless they were . . . "You're squatting in someone else's house and you are worried about the floors?"

"Squatting? What an ugly word. Borrowing sounds so much more . . ."

"Proper?" he teased.

She brightened considerably. "Exactly." Pulling at the straw, she burrowed into the crate and came up with a set of pall-mall mallets, followed by a large urn, and then another smaller box of carefully wrapped books. Taking a cue from Tally, she cursed in Russian. "This will never do. I need something to make costumes for the Duke of Setchfield's ball." Hands back on her hips, pry bar in hand, she attacked another crate.

But Thatcher was still stuck on the notion that they were living in a house that belonged to someone else—without the owner's permission. He rose to his feet and marched over to where she was—and with some skill, he noted—wielding the metal bar on another hapless crate.

He reached over her shoulder and gingerly took it from her. "Whose house is this?"

"Does it matter?" she asked, trying to retrieve her bar, but to no avail. "Suffice it to say, the previous occupant is not going to show up, since he has gone aloft." She tugged again at the bar. "Give that back."

"Not until I get some answers," he told her.

She let go and stepped back from him. "Sir, you no longer command a troop of men. You are my employee and if you don't like the arrangements then you can leave."

They stood face-to-face in stubborn silence, and finally Thatcher shrugged and walked toward the door.

"Where are you going?" she asked.

He paused and turned slightly toward her. "So you want me to stay?"

Her lips pursed together. "You can't leave with my pry bar."

Holding it up, he asked, "Is it yours or did you 'borrow' it?"

"That's beside the point," she told him, but that twinkle of amusement rose in her stubborn gaze. It was one of things he found intriguing about her. She could be fired with stubborn passion one moment and then when she realized her own folly, just as bemused as if the joke were on someone else.

"You wouldn't leave me without any means to open all these crates, would you?" she asked, tipping her head just so and casting that look that always left him upended.

From the come-hither light in her eyes to the way her lips turned, as if they were just waiting for a kiss—and not just any chaste peck, but one that asked, no, *begged,* to be ravished.

"Don't do that!" Now it was his turn to shake the bar at her.

"Do what?" Her eyes might be wide with innocence, but the light dancing in their blue depths was pure mischief.

"Look at me like that." He groaned and went over and attacked the box closest to him. "Who the devil taught you that? Surely not your sainted Miss Emery, I have to imagine."

"Oh, heavens no. Miss Emery would probably have put us to darning socks for the rest of our lives if she saw one of her students pulling such a face." She cast another look in his direction. "Nanny Jamilla taught it to us."

"Figures," he muttered.

"Does it bother you?" she said, moving around the box, floating really, just like her courtesan mentor.

"Not . . . at . . . all," he ground out as he sidestepped her and went to work on another box. "Now tell me how you came to 'borrow' this house, so I know who to watch for when they arrive at the door expecting Holland covers and the curtains drawn."

She sighed. "If you insist—"

"I do," he said, pry bar clenched in his hands.

"The house is part of a property dispute amongst heirs. I spotted the notice about it in a legal newspaper I found at Mr. Elliott's office. Apparently when the former owner died it wasn't quite clear who was to get the house—there is more than one will. While they continue to squabble over the details, it is ours to use."

He suspected there was more to it than this simple explanation. It was far too proper to be the truth. "And who says it is yours to use?"

"I did," Felicity told him. "Can't you see how wasteful it would be to have a perfectly elegant house sitting empty during the Season? And I do intend to pay rent—to whoever ends up as the rightful owner—once I am—"

Married.

Thatcher closed his eyes. "Do I dare ask how you got into a house that isn't rightfully yours?"

Felicity eased around the crate, her hands covering his as she helped him set the bar. Her fingers were cold and for a moment she left them atop his—and he might have thought it was because his were warmer or that she was testing Jamilla's advice, but when he looked down at her, he saw something different in her eyes.

That same awareness, that same disbelief that had lit her eyes the day before when he'd kissed her. The warmth moving between her fingers and his was more than just heat, it was a joining, for her hand felt right atop his—as if that was where it belonged.

And as he realized that, a spark moved between them. He edged closer to her, ready to forget that she was innocent, ready to forget that she considered herself promised to another.

Immediately wary, she plucked her hand away, breaking the spell. Then she nodded to him to continue his task. "Surely this box has something useful. Don't you think?"

"It could," he replied, straining to open it. But she still hadn't answered his question. "However did you get inside this house if you hadn't the keys?"

"Do you really want to know?"

Every time she asked him that question, he always regretted hearing the answer. But it was like rum to a sailor—he couldn't resist listening to her runaway plans.

"Yes," he said, waving his hand in permission. "Do tell."

"Tally picked the locks."

He didn't know why he was surprised—or even shocked—but there it was. The daughter of an English diplomat was a clever Kate, a lock pick of the finest order.

Still, he couldn't quite believe it. "Your sister?"

Felicity nodded. "She's quite adept. If you ever have need of a lock—"

He shook his head. "No, I don't think—"

"Well, if you do," she offered.

Oh, but there was more to this tale than just their larcenous entrance, he wagered. And demmed if he didn't want to hear it. "And once you got in?"

"Mrs. Hutchinson has a cousin who put new locks in for us," she admitted.

That harridan would have such a relation.

"And then," she continued, "we moved in with what little we could bring from the house Pippin's mother left her."

"The one in Sussex?"

"Yes," Felicity said with a delicate shudder. "We certainly weren't going to make our way in Society out in the country! Sussex, I will have you know, is a veritable desert."

"But whatever possessed you to think you could attempt all this? Did you ever once consider what would happen if you were caught?"

Felicity glanced up at him as if he had just questioned the color of the sky or the King's paternity. "When in doubt, a lady always appears to be completely in the right," she said with her usual air of supreme confidence.

"What?"

"When in doubt—"

He shook his head. "No, I know what you said, but wherever did you hear such nonsense?"

"Nanny Tasha."

He was starting to wonder if an ounce of morality could be found amongst all these nannies of theirs. "I doubt she meant for you to steal a house."

"Stealing? I prefer to think of our residency as maintaining the house's character. Why, it would be going to damp if we weren't here keeping it warm."

He glanced around at the empty and shuttered rooms. It was a weak argument at best since they only had three rooms open, and with meager fires in those, but leave it to Felicity to already have her defense at the ready.

"Let me get this straight," he said, pausing in his labor and ticking off on his fingers the points he understood thus far. "You've stolen this house—"

"Borrowed."

"Fine. Borrowed this house."

"Yes."

"Haven't any money for gowns or servants—"

"Or coal or food," she admitted. "But the baskets the princess provided yesterday will tide us over for a few more days."

The princess had provided? Thatcher didn't bother to explain that her servant had instructed him to buy it all on credit as the lady was still waiting for her draft to clear with the bankers. "So you haven't any coal or food, save what you can scrimp by on with your pin money—"

"Correct so far—"

"And you think you can pull off a Season for all three of you?"

"We only need one good betrothal," she explained. "And I already have—"

"Hollindrake."

"Yes, exactly." She brushed her hands over her skirt and sighed. When she found him studying her, she quickly glanced away. "Really, this is all for Tally and Pippin, though they hardly appreciate my efforts."

Was it him, or was her enthusiasm for her perfectly titled and noble spouse waning?

"Now that you know everything, can you finish getting that box open?" She was leaning over and looking into the crack he'd created. "I'm convinced this one shows some promise."

Thatcher stepped back. "No, I don't understand. Why do you have to sell yourself into marriage with a man you don't love?"

"Whoever said I don't love him?"

"Demmit, Felicity, you don't love the man. And how could you love him? Didn't you hear a word Stewie Hodges said yesterday? Hollindrake is a regular bastard, and here you are, ready to continue on with this betrothal like he's some prince."

"A duke—"

"Top a bastard with any coronet you want and he's still a bastard."

"I'm not going to listen to—"

"You will listen," he told her, catching her by the arm. "Why don't you deserve the happiness you insist your sister and cousin have?"

"Because . . ."

"Because what?"

"Because they believe in love!" she shot back. "And I never have, at least not until—" Her eyes widened, but it was her lips that snapped shut, cutting off her confession.

"Not until what?" he said, pulling her closer.

"Until nothing. I don't believe in love," she said, not looking at him. "All that passionate nonsense and . . . feeling helpless . . . and making one's knees go weak and wanting . . ."

"Wanting what?" he growled.

"I don't want anything from *him*."

From Hollindrake. But that didn't answer the real question between them. "What do you want from me?"

"Nothing." A lie not even Felicity could gammon, but that didn't mean she wasn't going to try. "They can have their romantic matches, for I am not affected by—"

Oh, he'd heard enough. Thatcher swooped down and let his lips have the final say.

The kiss that had started as an impetuous stolen moment deepened until it became evident that the passion between them hadn't merely been a passing lark.

"Circe, my dangerous little Circe," Captain Dashwell whispered into Pippin's ears. "You drive me mad." And as his body pressed her into the stone wall of the garden, she realized just how far such madness could spread.

What was she doing? She was Lady Philippa Knolles, not some dockside tart to have her head turned by a rakish kiss.

But it wasn't just her head that turned, it was her entire insides, as Dash tugged her up against him, the very heat of his body as tantalizing as a plate of fresh scones. *Her Dash.*

"What are you doing here?" she managed to gasp once they pulled apart. Taking a guilty look up at the house, she added, "If you were caught, I could never—"

"Never forget me?" he teased.

Never, she wanted to tell him, but she feared that would only encourage the reckless American. "If you are found, you'll be hung."

"That's a large 'if,'" he told her. "They have to catch me first." Nuzzling her neck, he added, "Besides, you would come and rescue me, wouldn't you, Circe?"

Pippin swallowed. It was like a scene out of her third play, "The Pirate and the Lady," wherein the lady rescues the pirate from the hangman's noose. But what if she couldn't rescue him? On the pages of her plays it sounded easy, but her only brush with danger had been on the beach near Hastings, the same night she'd met Dash, and that had ended with her nearly getting her head blown off.

If Dash hadn't saved her . . . kissed her . . .

As he was now, his lips eager and warm, beckoning her to open up to him, which she did, with a willingness that shocked her. And when the kiss deepened, his tongue sweeping over hers, her knees buckled beneath her.

He held her up, one arm wound around her waist, the other cupping one of her breasts, his thumb rubbing against her nipple, leaving it in the same torrent of fire that was brewing in her belly.

"You'll come with me, won't you, Circe?"

"Come with you?" she whispered.

"To sea. Come with me," he asked. "I've thought of you, all these years. Thought of nothing but you. Never thought I'd find you again, my beautiful little goddess."

"Me?"

He grinned at her. "Yes, you. Who else?" His fingers toyed with a stray strand of hair. "Come privateering with me. You'll be my pirate queen."

For a moment the smell of salt air piqued her imagination, tar and ropes and the flap of the sails. And every starry night, Dash. Dash kissing her. Carrying her off to his berth below. Teasing her, touching her, leaving her as breathless and reckless as she felt right now.

More so.

"Pippin? Pippin? Are you out here?" came Tally's cry, breaking into her reverie, piercing the spell Dash had wound around her.

"I have to go," she whispered. "Please, Dash, leave London. Tonight. Don't stay for me—I won't have you hung on my account."

The handsome privateer laughed. "I can't go, not until this bloody ice melts. But don't fret, I shan't be far. I'll come back the night after next for you."

She shook her head. "I won't be here—there's a ball. The Duke of Setchfield's masquerade ball."

"Setchfield? You mean Temple?"

Oh, demmit, she cursed, using her brother's favorite expletive. She shouldn't have said anything. "Dash, you cannot go! You know who Temple is—and if he were to spot you—"

"He wouldn't dare—we go back too long," Dash told her.

"But you held him captive—he still holds you accountable for Mr. Grey's death."

"I can hardly be responsible for what—"

"Pippin, are you out here?" Tally called again. "Mrs. Hutchinson, are you sure she was out in the garden?"

"Oh, aye," the housekeeper's voice could be heard. "That fellow asked me to fetch her 'round."

"What fellow?" Tally's question darkened immediately with suspicion.

"Oh, dear," Pippin whispered, pushing Dash away from her. "Go! Now! If Tally sees you, she'll tell Felicity, and believe me, Felicity will call not only the watch, but the Home Guard and the entire 95th."

Captain Thomas Dashwell leaned over and stole another quick kiss, and whispered in her ear, "Tomorrow night. You'll recognize me quite easily." He dashed across the yard and vaulted atop a barrel, up the toolshed and then atop the wall. With a wave and a flourish of his hat, he said, "I'll be dressed as a . . ." But he jumped before he said the final word.

But Pippin didn't need to know what it was. It was burned into her imagination.

A pirate.

And for some inexplicable reason, his departure tore at her heart, for despite all Dash's confidence, she knew something terrible was about to happen to him. So it was that when Tally found her, Pippin burrowed her face in her cousin's shoulder and cried.

Felicity's world tilted the moment Thatcher's lips touched hers. Everything she'd planned for, studied for, lied and borrowed for, fell from the perfect platter of propriety she'd constructed and shattered as if it had hit the fine Italian floors beneath her stocking-clad feet.

And along with it, every desire she'd ever held to be a duchess. Would a proper and lofty duke ever kiss her thusly?

For today Thatcher claimed her with a ravenous hunger that sent her senses reeling, even as he swept her across the room, carrying her to the curtained window seat. He'd deposited her onto the cushions and come crashing down atop her.

Thank goodness the shutters are drawn, she thought, for they would be giving Brook Street a spectacle she doubted the top-lofty residents had ever seen.

Even so, her hands balled up, ready to protest such liberties, but all too quickly, as his tongue swept over hers, inviting her to join him in this passionate foray, her fingers unfurled and then splayed across his coat, finally ending up tugging at his lapels and pulling him closer.

Their mouths fused in a torrent of a kiss. Like the snow swirling outside, Felicity felt her insides whirl about, chased on the relentless winds of passion he was unleashing.

Whatever it was he was doing to her, there was no stopping it. It was as if he'd uncorked these desires and now she'd never be able to cap them back into the tidy bottle from which they'd come. She should be cursing him, stopping him, but oh, how she loved the way he felt atop her, covering her, devouring her. Here in this little enclosed world of theirs—with the shutters cutting them off from the city beyond and the curtains behind them giving them privacy from the household.

Her nipples puckered as his hands roamed over the tips of her breasts, her hips rose in invitation—as if begging his touch to come lower. And in the very heart of her desires, in that place between her thighs, she ached. Ached and twisted with need. Need for this man, and this man only.

His fingers twined in the hem of her gown, skimming past her red socks to her bare knees, slowing only to tease her now quivering thighs.

Oh, gracious heavens, he was going to touch her *there*.

Oh, yes, please, she thought most improperly. *Please.*

His fingers parted the way, stroking first her nether lips, then delving deeper until he came to the nub and ran his finger over her, leaving her breathless at such a sensation. She would have moaned loudly, but his mouth covered hers in a kiss that matched what his fingers were doing, exploring and stroking her.

A wisp of cold air wafted over her, and she realized he'd found a way to free her breasts, having opened her gown with his other hand.

Dear heavens, her footman wasn't just honorable and nearly noble—he was also a devilish rake!

His mouth pulled away from hers and for a moment he looked down at her. Oh, the wicked light in his eyes left no doubts he wasn't done making his case—or that she'd lost her argument, utterly and completely. And for once, she didn't care, especially not when his lips covered her nipple, his tongue running over it, his hand cupping it from beneath.

Her body turned languid and tense at the same time, her hips rising to meet his fingers there and the rest of her stretching like a cat, seeking her pleasures wherever she could. His fingers slid over her, and she was wet and slick. Then he slid a finger inside her, and she arched and knew what she wanted.

For all he did was make her ache. Ache for more.

Touch him, a wild, provocative voice whispered inside her head. *Touch him.*

Tentatively, her hands left the safety of his lapels and began to follow the lines of his arms, thick and strong, across his chest and down over his stomach. She reached the top of his breeches and stopped.

She couldn't. She couldn't do this. Then he kissed her again, and she found herself lost in the wildness of it, his mouth fused to hers, his fingers sliding over her pulsing nub, inside her, awakening every desire a woman could possess, and she knew she had to answer in kind.

Over the waistband her fingers forged, and down until they came to the hardened length of him. Oh, it was so hard and stiff . . . and ready.

She closed her eyes and sighed. In a flash she saw what would happen next: She'd free him, explore him as he had her, but not for long, for her body was ready. As hot and ready as he was, if his ragged breathing and erection were any evidence. He'd fill her, love her, ruin her. And there would be no turning back.

Her eyes sprang open. For as much as she wanted to urge

him on, she wasn't so lost that she hadn't forgotten entirely where she was.

Or who she was. And what her future held.

As much as she wanted this man, there was another who'd claimed her first, and despite all of Jamilla's assurances of Englishmen, Felicity wasn't inclined to go to Hollindrake's bed anything else but innocent, well at least in the narrowest and most important definition of the word.

This wasn't about what was right for her, but also for Tally and Pippin, and there would be no hope for them if she did this. None whatsoever. She wouldn't be just ruining herself, she'd be destroying their chances at making any sort of good marriage.

"Stop," she whispered.

"Not until you admit that you would rather kiss me than him." He cheated by kissing her again, leaving her utterly breathless and unable to answer.

At least for a wild, tangled moment. But there was more to question than just admitting what they both already knew. He was asking too much.

For her to give up everything. All her years of hard work. Of preparation. Of dreaming and wishing for a life free of insecurity and the whims of society. He was asking her to give up everything and leave Tally and Pippin to fend for themselves.

"No," she gasped, struggling out from beneath him, away from the lure of his heated body, no matter that she ached to be back in his embrace. "I cannot."

They sat on either end of the window seat, glaring at each other, their bodies both trembling with need—one that Felicity now stubbornly refused to give in to.

"Demmit, Felicity, this isn't a game," he told her, coming forward. "Just admit that you want me. You want me to be your duke." His hands reached for her.

Yes. From the first moment I met you I wanted you to be

him. How easily those words would solve everything. But she could no more admit that than tell him the rest of it.

She had fallen in love with him.

So she shook her head and did what had recently come so easily to her. She lied. "I only wanted to know how to kiss." And then she cast Jamilla's look at him, smiling as she did it, as if it was all just a great lark.

She rose from the bench and turned her back to him.

"Do that again, Miss Langley," he said, spinning her around and hauling her up against him. She thought he was going to kiss her, but to her shock and disappointment, he didn't. "And I will strip you of your gown and ruin you utterly. Completely."

Do it, clamored every part of her body. *Let him ruin you. Utterly.*

For one trembling moment she nearly put his promise to the test, but the light in his eyes told her that such folly would have her on her back before she could draw another breath. So she looked away and masked her desires. Closed her eyes and wished she'd never let him into her life, let him ruin everything—even without taking her innocence.

For he had stolen her heart, and that, she imagined, had to be worse.

After a few moments he let her go and stormed away, stalking toward the back of the house, his footsteps rumbling through the empty corridors like rolls of thunder.

"Oh, Tally, please promise me you won't tell Felicity. You mustn't. Can't you see that?"

Tally wasn't as convinced, for as much as she loved a good romance, she was worried about her cousin. If anyone suspected that Pippin was helping Captain Dashwell, there would be consequences, and they hadn't the connections needed to save Pippin from the fate that would await her.

"You must promise me not to see him again," Tally told

her. "If he comes around, you must send him packing. 'Tis best for you and for him. You see that, don't you?"

Pippin nodded, swiping at the lingering tears on her cheeks.

The two girls turned to go back into the house when all of a sudden the kitchen door swung open and a great oath exploded from the opening.

"Damn that woman to hell!" Thatcher came marching out into the garden and went striding down the path as if his boots were on fire. As he approached the grotto where they stood, they shrank back, concealed from his sight by the tangle of weeds and a rickety arbor, heavily laden with untrimmed rose canes.

"Oh, Duchess has him riled," Tally whispered.

He sailed right past their hiding spot, muttering, "Deny me, will she? I'll teach her a lesson she won't forget." He strode out the doorway and into the alley in the blink of an eye.

"That was odd," Pippin said.

Tally nodded in agreement. "That's exactly what I was thinking—it usually takes Felicity a good half an hour longer to have someone storming off in such a huff."

"No, not that. Didn't you notice? He went to the right, not the left," Pippin said, nodding to the doorway. "If he were going out to the street, he should have gone left. To the right there are only the other houses on the square. There's no other way out."

"Perhaps he just needs to pace a bit. Papa always did that when one of our nannies was being—"

But Pippin wasn't listening, she was already tentatively opening the garden door to peer out. There in the alleyway she spied their footman, pounding on one of the other gates.

"Let me in, demmit!" he was calling out. "Let me in now!"

Tally came up behind her and looked as well. "Oh, that does it for certain. Felicity has driven the poor man over the cliff. Why, he's acting like he owns that house." She paused for a moment. "Whose door is that anyway?"

They both shared a look of recognition. *Hollindrake.*

Slipping out and moving quietly and furtively along the wall, Pippin and Tally drew closer.

There was some benefit to reading and writing so many tragic romances—they knew how to lurk about. But to their benefit, the object of their spying was otherwise occupied trying to gain the attention of someone in the duke's house.

But what happened next left them both feeling as light-headed as if they'd spent the morning matching Mrs. Hutchinson brandy for brandy.

The heavy latch on the door creaked as it cracked open, and from within someone said two fateful words. "Your Grace?"

Whatever else the man said, neither Tally or Pippin cared.

"Hollindrake," Tally whispered. "It cannot—"

"It is," Pippin said, and whirled around, about to bolt back toward their house. To Felicity.

But Tally caught her by the back of her cloak. "Don't."

"Don't what?"

"Don't you dare go back and tell Felicity that . . ." That their footman was her nearly betrothed. That *he* was *her* duke. Hollindrake. Neither of them dared say it aloud.

"But we must," Pippin argued.

Tally shook her head. "Don't you see? He *is* the lost duke. 'Tis the ending we've been looking for."

"You can't mean to suggest we allow him to continue to gammon her—"

"I do indeed."

Pippin straightened to her full height. Tall and lithe, she towered over her more petite cousin. "I will not keep this from her." She pulled her cloak free and began to march determinedly toward their own door.

Tally held her ground. "If you say one word to her about Thatcher, I will tell her about Dashwell."

Pippin spun around. "You wouldn't dare!"

But Tally was her father's daughter, not so much gifted in diplomacy, but brimming with his infamous audacity. "Care to wager his life on that?"

The first person Thatcher ran into as he stormed through his house was his mother. "Madame, whatever are you still doing here? I would have thought—"

"That I had engagements elsewhere?"

He nodded. "I thought you preferred your social calls to family obligations." His words came out sharp and arrogant and he regretted it immediately. Hadn't his grandfather's letters said over and over, not overtly but between the lines, that he wished he'd forged a different life, a different outlook?

Not that the footman who'd been stoking the fire appeared all that alarmed by his employer's foul mood. Why, the man appeared positively giddy with delight.

"I did, but I cancelled them," she said, ignoring his tone and barely noting the other footman, who brought in a bottle of whisky and glasses.

"Leave us," Thatcher told them, and the pair of grinning fools nearly tripped over each other in their haste to depart. "Whatever is wrong with the staff in this house?"

"I believe they are just happy to have an overbearing brute back in charge. You've turned out to be quite ducal, you know."

"I'm hardly ducal. Grandfather must be rolling over in his grave at the thought of me, of all the Sterlings, inheriting."

"I'd say given your current mood and your performance at breakfast, you've quite mastered the position." She settled down comfortably on a sofa and patted a spot next to her for him to sit. He shook his head and strode over toward the tray, where he poured himself a drink. "Suffice it to say your Misses Hodges have vouchers, as do the Misses Langley and their cousin, Lady Philippa."

This took him aback. "What?"

"Well, I assumed you'd want your Miss Langley to have vouchers, so I went and called on the Countess Lievin. When I told her about the unusual nature of your courtship, she declared you the most enlightened man alive and most likely would have given vouchers to my butcher's daughter if I'd asked, for she was utterly delighted with my story. Russians! They do love a star-crossed love affair."

He held up an empty glass for his mother, the decanter of sherry in his other hand. "Why?"

She nodded for him to pour. "Why did the countess find your story so amusing?"

"No. Why are you helping me?" He was more than a bit shocked that his mother had gone to such lengths for him. As the third son of a third son, he had never thought he warranted much notice from his family, let alone this outburst of parental aid.

"Because I realized something this morning." She reached for the glass he held out for her.

"Which was?"

"I've been a selfish creature for too long. First your father died, and Archie and Aldus were all grown up and living their own lives, and then, before I knew it, they were both gone. Of course, you were off God knows where with never a line or a note to tell me if you were still alive." She pursed her lips together and studied her sherry for a moment.

Thatcher felt a frisson of guilt. Quite honestly, he hadn't thought anyone would want to hear from him. But in this, like so many other things, he'd been wrong. Terribly so.

Lady Charles continued, "I've been alone for a long time, and had quite forgotten what it was like to be a mother—not that I was ever a very good one. I can't take any credit for the man you've become—which I must say you've done a fine job of it. Your father would be proud, as your grandfather was of you when he learned about your promotions, the accounts of you in the field." She held up her hand and staved off the questions he was about to ask. "Today, you reminded me of Charles. Of why your grandfather always said he regretted that he'd come third instead of first. Not that he didn't think highly of Michael and Edward, but . . ." She paused again, but this time she glanced away, and he thought she might even have tears in her eyes. But with a quick swipe of her hand, she made short work of them. "I've done you a disservice all these years. I suppose it was because you reminded me of your father so much."

"Father?"

"Yes, your father. Charles was an impetuous devil as well. Do you know when he courted me, my parents were quite opposed to the match—a third son after all—but that didn't stop your father. He arrived one night at a soiree they were throwing—one he had not been invited him to, so he dressed as a waiter and stole me away."

Thatcher blinked. "I never—"

"No, of course not. By the time you came along, our lives were quite different. We were different. Obligations, our place in society, I don't how it happened, but sadly, we changed." She took a sip from her glass. "Your grandfather always kept the best cellars in London." She took another sip and glanced up at him. "Now, where was I?"

"Father?"

"Ah, yes. He would find it quite amusing that you've inherited. As for me, I'm glad you're the duke, and I'm even more thrilled that you've found your duchess."

"Miss Langley is hardly my—"

"Pish posh," his mother said with the wave of her hand

that was her trademark. But there was none of the coldness in it, for her eyes shone with a light he'd never seen before. "If you have half of your father's resourcefulness, you'll win her heart."

He took a deep breath. "So, how did Father finally win your heart against your family's objections?"

She laughed, a magical, warm sound that left him stunned, for suddenly she was young again and full of the brilliance that must have caught his father's eye. She leaned over and kissed his cheek, then patted his arm. "My dear, dear boy, he did what any man in your situation does." She rose and went toward the door. Then she turned around and smiled at him. "Why, he seduced me, of course."

Thatcher choked and sputtered on the gulp of whisky he'd taken.

She laughed again. "Oh, yes, and then he sent over diamonds. And don't even ask which one I preferred more."

Chapter 13

The very next morning, in all his ducal glory, Thatcher did not call on the *ton*'s favorite jewelers, Rundell & Bridge. At least not at first. For his mother's confession, nay, her suggestion, had haunted him all night long.

Seduction. He was starting to think his mother and Princess Jamilla had gone to the same finishing school. Yet, if he wanted to prove his point to Felicity—that she deserved love above all else, that passion was more vital to living than any coronet—then finishing the seduction they'd started was the order of the day.

But this wasn't just about teaching Felicity a lesson, there was also his pride. After all, he was still a Sterling.

If he was going to spend the rest of his life with this opinionated, hard-headed, overbearing little chit, he wanted to know for certain that she'd chosen him, Thatcher the lowly footman, over all the titles and wealth a duke could offer.

If she chose from her heart, then perhaps they could learn the lessons his grandfather had tried to impart in his letters, and that his mother had shared—not to let the obligations of Society, the outward appearances, matter more than one's heart. If Felicity could see that, then they might have a chance at real happiness.

That is if she didn't, as Jack had warned, shoot off his ballocks for his troubles.

And to accomplish all this he needed the perfect setting for his plan to work, and for that he needed Felicity at the Setchfield ball. And for Felicity to get there . . . well, it would take a little bit of magic . . . and a fair amount of overbearing ducal privilege.

Her mother's old pall-mall mallets and musty books weren't going to do it.

So with his gilded carriage, the coat of arms shining in the meager winter sunlight, he called on no less than Mr. Archibald Elliott, solicitor. The previous night he'd given Mr. Gibbens the task of locating the man before morning, and by first light his ever-efficient secretary had the directions at the ready, along with a list of the man's other well-heeled clients, including an old friend of his and Jack's, Alexander Denford, Baron Sedgwick, as well as Jack's brother, the Duke of Parkerton.

This would make the task a fair bit easier and decidedly more fun, Thatcher thought as he traveled to the respectable building near the Inns of Court.

When they arrived, his footman shoved the door open so it banged on the hinges and Thatcher strode into the middle of the room and stopped, taking in the entire scene with a flick of a glance.

He found Mr. Elliott's reception room sparsely furnished and well-ordered, much as would be expected of a man who, as Gibbens put it, was known to be excessively frugal and cautious with his clients' affairs. Two clerks manned the long desk in the outer office, staged as if it was their lifelong duty to protect their employer against any onslaught.

Apparently, they had never been faced with a living and breathing duke.

"I am Hollindrake," he announced, affecting a pose that he'd seen his grandfather use on many an occasion. As a boy, he'd likened the stance to that of a bored yet hungry lion looking for some tired, hapless game upon which to lazily pounce.

The two clerks shot up from their chairs, one of them sending his skittering across the floor.

"Hollindrake?" the taller one squeaked. "I don't think the master had any appointments with—"

Thatcher flicked off his gloves and let the ruby and diamond crusted signet ring on his hand light up the dim room. "Perhaps you don't realize who I am. I am the *Duke* of Hollindrake," he said, narrowing his gaze on the first fellow. "And I never need an appointment."

Gaunt and fair, the man paled further beneath his rimmed spectacles, looking as white as his cravat. "No, no, Your Grace," he stammered. "Of course you don't, I'll just get—"

They were saved when the door to Elliott's office opened and the man himself came barreling out. "Mr. Fishman, what is the meaning of—" Of course, his words got no further than the sight of the obviously elevated person in his office.

"'Tis the Duke of Hollindrake to see you, sir," the shorter clerk managed, before he took refuge behind his chair.

Archibald Elliott hadn't gained an aristocratic clientele for nothing. "Your Grace, my apologies. I wasn't expecting you," he said, casting accusing glances at his employees as if this unexpected arrival was entirely their oversight. Swiftly he swept aside his clerks, rather like a set of bowling pins, and ushered Thatcher into the warmth of his private office.

The clerks might have no heat and only a shared candle, but the inner workings of the solicitor's office had Mr. Elliott cozy and warm in an elegant room that spoke of a prosperous practice. A mahogany desk, a thick Turkish carpet, a lamp on the desk, and a polished tall clock in the corner. Bookshelves lined one wall. He waved Thatcher toward a large leather chair opposite his desk and without asking went over to a cabinet in the corner, unlocking it and retrieving a decanter from the far reaches within, along with two sparkling cut lead glasses.

The rich, thick amber liquid could only be Scottish whisky, Thatcher thought. And the man's best, if the dust on the bottle was any indication as to the rarity of its arrival upon the desk. Elliott poured an unstinting glass for his unexpected guest.

"Your Grace, I am deeply honored you have chosen to call upon me. But you had only to send a note around and I would have been happy to save you the trouble of—"

Thatcher waved him off. "No need. I prefer to partake in business when the mood strikes me."

"Yes, of course. Then let us get on with it," Elliott urged him, pulling forth a sheet of paper and picking up his quill.

"I am here regarding a young lady," Thatcher began.

The pen dropped to the blotter as the middle-aged man colored. "Your Grace, I am sure your own solicitor would be better able to—"

"This lady is a client of yours."

Mr. Elliott shook his head. "I generally don't do business with—"

Thatcher arched his brow and let his dark glance bore into the flustered man.

It only took a moment longer for the light of realization to illuminate the man's features. "Lord Langley's daughters."

"Precisely," Thatcher told him, looking up from the glass

in his hand. "You will release their funds. Immediately."

The solicitor coughed and sputtered. "I will do no such thing."

Thatcher had to give it to this Mr. Elliott. He had a measure of backbone. But he was about to find himself like a salmon on the hook. He could fight all he wanted, but eventually he was going to be netted and headed for the frying pan.

"I think you shall, and quite willingly, I wager." He smiled. "The ladies would like a Season in London, and by all accounts it seems a necessity."

"A necessity!" The man snorted. "A fine waste of money, is what it is. I dinna know how it is Miss Langley has convinced you, Your Grace, to come here and plead her case, but I will not release her funds. Not now, not until she's of age, and then only under duress—which I am sure is why you are here. That headstrong lass has most likely badgered you to come plead her case. I don't hold it against you, Your Grace, for in time you will grow, as I have, quite immune to her endless harangue."

"Quite the contrary, sir. The lady doesn't know I am here. And for the record, I find her determination admirable."

Reaching for his handkerchief, the solicitor cleaned his spectacles and set them back in place, studying Thatcher anew. Seemingly satisfied that the man before him was nothing more than a pampered fool, he continued as if he were lecturing one of his secretaries. "Females such as Miss Langley haven't the sense for such matters. 'Tis all shopping and expenditures and more shopping, and for what? To find some foppish fellow to marry." He sat back in his chair, arms folded over his chest. "'Tis nothing but good money being poured after bad."

"That might be so," Thatcher told him, leaning forward, "but perhaps you aren't looking at it from the right perspective, sir." Elliott sputtered some more and looked ready to argue the point, but Thatcher continued before he could. "If

Miss Langley took her money and invested it soundly and at the end of three months showed not only a solid return, but so successful an investment that the lady would never have to worry about her security again, would you consider her plans ill-conceived?"

Elliott's brow wrinkled. "I don't deal in speculations. Not with my clients' concerns."

"Certainly, but if it were true, that in three months time—nay, make it a week—the lady would have outdone her initial investment beyond even your wildest dreams, would you hold the same opinion?"

He snorted. "I'm not inclined to such fancies, Your Grace. I am a man of business, but if—which is a very big if—Miss Langley had such an investment at hand, I might take the matter under consideration."

"Excellent! For she has such an opportunity," Thatcher told him.

The solicitor shook his head. "Impossible."

"Hardly. For once you release her funds, she will be able to launch herself properly into Society, and before the end of this week she will be a duchess—her future more than assured and her father's legacy quite trifling compared to the riches that will be at her disposal."

"A duchess? Who but only a fool would—" the man started to say, then his eyes grew wide. "Nay, Your Grace, you don't mean to say that *you*—"

"I do. But her funds will be released so she can come to this decision of her own accord. If it is a matter of risk that worries you, I have a note here that states I will reimburse any and all of her expenditures if she decides not to agree to my suit."

The man studied Thatcher and then sighed. Thatcher thought for certain Elliott was going to capitulate—for really, what harm was there now that Thatcher had guaranteed the funds?

However, to his surprise, Elliott refused. "Nay, sir. I have a duty to Lord Langley. And I consider my obligation to his daughters equal to what I would want done for my own lasses. I will not release her funds, for if she refuses you, the barn door will be open, if you understand me. I'll never be able to get that filly back into any sort of fiscal responsibility."

Thatcher had to admit this Mr. Elliott had an agile mind; that, and he obviously knew Felicity.

However, he still had one last card to play.

"Sir, you have a fine list of clients," Thatcher said, glancing down at his signet ring, going for his grandfather's favorite leonine pose yet again. "Including, I believe, Baron Sedgwick."

"Yes, yes, Lord Sedgwick trusts my judgment on all his business dealings."

"And the Duke of Parkerton," he offered, naming Jack's brother.

"Yes, yes," Mr. Elliott said, shifting in his seat.

"Good friends of mine. All of them. I would hate for them to remove their business and legal dealings from your office—"

"Sir, that is most high-handed!"

Thatcher shrugged. "That and a few comments dropped at White's in a fashion that would make them heard by one and all—"

"Uncalled for! Why you'd ruin me!"

"Sadly, yes. You'd be left with no clients at all. Definitely would make this whisky out of your reach," Thatcher pointed out, draining his glass and smiling. "Release the funds, Elliott, and you have nothing to worry about." He rose to his feet and flicked at an imaginary bit of lint on his sleeve.

Elliott scrambled up as well. "No good will come of this! She'll spend it all before the week is out."

"She'll be the Duchess of Hollindrake before the week is out and it will matter not."

Elliott's brow furrowed again, for it appeared the man

found this possibility more alarming than losing all his clients. "She'll be insufferable," he warned.

"I have every hope she will be," Thatcher told him. "Here is the initial list of what she requires. I have taken the liberty of having the staff and household requirements sent over. But the rest of it, the notes of credit for her modiste and other necessities, I leave in your capable hands."

"Mark my words, this is utter folly," Elliott complained, his face growing mottled with rage as he looked at not only the first page but the three that followed. "If she were my daughter—"

"Yes, quite right, you mentioned a daughter," Thatcher said. "And is Miss Elliott out in Society?"

This personal turn of questioning seemed to set the solicitor on edge. Pry as he might into the affairs of others, apparently he wasn't used to having his own privacy scrutinized. "Yes. In our own limited circles, of course she is," he said. Yet the man wasn't ready to concede any further points. At least so he thought. "However, she hasn't the ridiculous expectations that Miss Langley seems to suffer under—"

"Does Miss Elliott have sisters who are also out?"

The man's jaw worked back and forth. "Four, Your Grace."

"You have five daughters at home waiting to find husbands?" Thatcher whistled. "No wonder you work such long hours. But tell me, why aren't any of them married?"

The question was so blunt, so personal, that it left Elliott nearly speechless. "They are modest young ladies. Not prone to prancing about—"

Thatcher didn't let him finish. "Perhaps if you were to loosen the purse strings a bit, let the fillies out of the stable, as you so eloquently said earlier, they might have a chance to find a man—"

"Dear God, sir, you sound like my wife," Elliott interjected, having recovered from his shock.

It was most likely meant as an insult, but Thatcher could only grin. "Perhaps, Mr. Elliott, you should listen to your wife more often."

"Give regard to my wife's opinions? Are you mad?"

Thatcher moved to the door and there he paused, his hand on the latch. "Perhaps. But maybe not. I'll make you a deal, Elliott. You loosen the purse strings for the Langley sisters and follow my instructions there"—he nodded to the list still clenched in the man's hand—"and I'll invite you, your wife, and all five of your daughters to the ball my aunt is throwing at the end of the week. I will instruct my mother to obtain vouchers for the young ladies as well. She has a talent for these things." He glanced down at his ring again and then back up at the man. "Then I suggest you meet with Miss Langley and beg her forgiveness over your pigheadedness, as well as seeking her assistance in seeing your daughters properly matched."

"You want me to ask—"

Thatcher shook his head. "No, I said 'beg her.' Grovel if you must. Think of it, my good man, a household without daughters. Think of the peace and financial freedom you could gain. If you were inclined to approach her with an open mind, you might find that Miss Langley is your salvation. She'll have your daughters matched before the month is out."

Now these were arguments Elliott could understand. And catch hold of with the tenacity of a terrier. "It would be quiet around the house," he mused.

"As the grave," Thatcher whispered back.

The solicitor sighed, his eyes half closed as he considered such a fate. But like all good men of the law, he was one argument ahead of the conversation. "And when Miss Langley asks for the reason for my sudden change of heart, what am I to say?"

Thatcher nodded. True, Felicity wouldn't trust this sudden

turn around. "Tell her Princess Jamilla was your inspiration."

Elliott's brow furrowed again. "Princess who?"

"Jamilla something. Don't worry about the rest of it. You'll meet her when you call." Thatcher almost wished he could be there to see the proper and prim Elliott when Jamilla strolled into the room and happily took credit for Felicity and Thalia's newfound fortune. "Oh, and Elliott?"

"Yes, Your Grace?"

Why, Thatcher would have sworn the man was cringing. "Send around a case of that whisky, will you? For my troubles, as it were."

When the bell rang at the Langleys' borrowed house not an hour later, Felicity flew down the stairs. Not that they were expecting anyone.

Except Thatcher, and he certainly wouldn't use the bell. She glanced at the door and pressed her lips together. Since he'd stormed out of the house the day before, she'd been on pins and needles awaiting his return.

If he would return. Worse still, she'd spent a restless night, her dreams haunted by the passionate knowledge he'd awakened in her. Of him touching her, kissing her, filling her, her body shivering and quaking beneath him.

Oh, if only . . . she'd wished more than once.

As much good as that did! For the man hadn't shown up for work this morning—not that he was overly punctual to begin with—but much to her surprise, in his place arrived three footmen, four maids, a cook's assistant, and no less than a butler. All knocking properly at the kitchen door with the explanation that they'd been hired to work, their wages for the quarter already paid.

Yet, no sign of Thatcher.

So as the bell rang, Felicity found herself on the first floor landing, clutching the railing and holding out hope that her unconventional lover had returned. That was until their new butler, Rollings, pulled open the door to admit none other than Mr. Elliott.

At the sight of their parsimonious solicitor, her stomach sank.

"Miss Langley!" he called out, smiling up at her. Felicity was immediately wary, especially since his jovial countenance bore a startling resemblance to Brutus when he spied a particularly good pair of Hessians. "I see the staff has arrived, good, excellent," he said, clapping his hands together before he handed Rollings his hat, gloves, cloak, and walking stick. "I have letters of credit and some other business we need to see to, so you can make your proper bow. I believe that is what it is called, is it not?" He smiled again, and Felicity found herself taking a step back from him as he came up the stairs. "Your receiving room is on the second floor, correct?"

She nodded and followed him. Letters of credit? Had she been struck by a coach and not known it? Or rather, had Mr. Elliott?

At the next landing, Tally caught up with them and whispered in Felicity's ear, "What is *he* doing here?"

"Seems he's responsible for our newfound staff."

"I don't believe it," Tally scoffed.

Felicity nodded in agreement. "Makes absolutely no sense. But I mean to get to the bottom of it."

When they entered the room, Pippin bounded up from the window seat, while Aunt Minty continued her morning snooze, her soft snores competing with Brutus's as he too took a nap in a basket near the lady's feet.

Mr. Elliott wasted no time getting to business. "Miss Langley, it is with a sincere heart that I've come here today."

Sincere? The man didn't even know what the word meant.

"For you see, I was most keen to see how I could help you, bound as I am by your father's instructions—"

"He never would have wanted us living in destitution," Tally shot back, and looked to continue, but Felicity staved her off with a sharp shake of her head.

"No, certainly not, Miss Thalia, but I am a man of the law and as such cannot go against a client's express wishes, as I know them to be."

"You've heard from our father?" Felicity asked. For certainly that could be the only explanation for the man's change of heart.

His jaw worked back and forth. "Not exactly—"

Just then, Jamilla arrived, floating into the room like a butterfly, still in her morning *dishabille*, a fur-trimmed wrapper tied loosely over her night rail—a lacy confection of black silk and satin. "Darlings, here you are! And entertaining yet again." She eyed Mr. Elliott, and apparently his well-cut, albeit plain coat, stiff white cravat, and polished boots, didn't leave her cold for she smiled as a cat might, a tempting feline curl to her lips that had wrecked havoc on more than just Napoleon's marriage.

It also didn't hurt that Mr. Elliott had bounded to his feet and produced an elegant and courtly bow. Who would have thought the stuffy solicitor capable of such social prowess?

Then again, Elliott was well off, and that alone was enough to put the man in Jamilla's good graces.

"Princess Jamilla," he said. "To meet you *again*, and so soon, is an honor and a privilege."

Again? "You know our nanny?" Felicity asked.

"Nanny?" He took his glasses off and cleaned them before taking another glance at the exotic and glamorous lady before him.

"'Tis more a term of endearment than an actual title," Jamilla said, taking the man's arm and pulling him down on the settee beside her. "But you were saying something about a meeting and I—"

"I know you didn't expect to see me again, but I wanted to

know that the arrangements you requested for these young ladies met with your approval. The servants, and now I've brought over the letters of credit—"

"Letters of credit?" Jamilla scooted closer. "I think I know what these are, though my English is not always perfect. They are used for shopping, no?"

"Yes. Exactly," he told her, extracting himself from Jamilla's grasp and smoothing out his wrinkled sleeve. Reaching inside his valise, he plucked out a packet of papers. "Ah, yes, here they are. The financial matters, as well as the staffing arrangements. I think you will find them all in order." But instead of showing them to Jamilla, he held them out for Felicity— though for a second he seemed reluctant to release them.

After a momentary tug-of-war, she discovered why. "You've released father's money!"

The man's eye twitched nervously. "Yes." He dropped back down to the settee and mopped at his brow with a hand-kerchief he'd plucked from his waistcoat pocket.

"You mean we have access to our funds?" Tally asked.

His eye twitched again before he answered. "Yes. I believe you will find the amount more than adequate."

Felicity thumbed through the papers she'd finally managed to wrench from his grasp, and realized they had been handed everything—everything Elliott had claimed not a fortnight earlier he would never surrender to them before they came of age (and some good sense to boot), and then only over his dead body.

No, this was too good to be true. She handed the letters back. "I don't believe this."

"Duchess, don't be foolish," her sister hissed, reaching over and retrieving the documents—their very freedom— before Mr. Elliott recovered from whatever mental break-down had caused this miraculous reversal.

"Why this sudden change of heart, sir?" Felicity asked.

"Um, I had an unexpected visitor." He glanced over at Jamilla, his gaze wandering from her darkly kohled eyes to the bounty of cleavage sitting nearly level with his nose. "And when they . . . I mean, when the princess appealed to my sense of honor—"

What a pile of rubbish, Felicity thought, dismissing the man's fustian and trying to determine who might have exerted enough force and influence over their solicitor to get him to release their funds. She rose from her chair and wandered toward the window, only to find a line of wagons pulling to a stop before the house—laden with furnishings and rugs and crates. Along with the servants and the foodstuffs that had been arriving by the basketload since dawn, there was only one explanation.

Only one person who could have wrought this miracle.

Hollindrake.

But how would the duke have known of their financial woes?

". . . and then when the princess related the terrible conditions you had been reduced to live in, and with her guarantee against your father's estate for any excessive expenditures—"

"Oh, Jamilla, you've done all this for us?" Tally exclaimed, rushing over to their former nanny and embracing her like a beloved long lost relation.

"Yes, yes, darlings, it is all my doing," the lady said, smiling over at Mr. Elliott as if they were old friends.

Felicity bit her lips together. Obviously Jamilla had no idea what "guarantee against your father's estate" meant. For if she had, she might not have been so willing to take all the credit.

Not ones to look a gift horse in the mouth, Pippin, Tally, and Felicity set to work immediately, ordering gowns and shopping well into the late afternoon. Dusk came early in the winter, and it was nearly dark as they cut across Grosvenor Square toward Brook Street.

Felicity paused across from Hollindrake House. "I would wager my new garters that *he* had something to do with all this." They had debated all day whether Jamilla could truly be the source of their newfound riches and were divided on the issue. "I have half a mind to march up there and demand an explanation—"

Much to her sister's horror, she did just that, starting off toward the palatial stone mansion.

"Felicity, what are you thinking?" Tally said, catching hold of her arm and towing her to a stop. "Have you thought for a moment what a fool you will look if it wasn't Hollindrake?"

"Gammon! It must be him, there is no other explanation. Who else do we know who has the influence to force Mr. Elliott into submission? And not just influence, but a bank account large enough to act as a guarantee? Mr. Elliott would never have released a ha-penny of father's money without some way of covering the amount." She glanced again at the duke's residence, suddenly unsure she wanted to be the recipient of his largesse. For with it came an obligation . . . one she wasn't as keen upon as she had been a few days ago.

"What if it was someone else other than the duke?" Pippin ventured. "Like Mr. Thatcher?"

"Thatcher?" Felicity ignored the pang in her heart. "Wherever would he get such a princely sum?"

"Perhaps when he sold out his commission," Tally offered. Pippin nodded enthusiastically at this suggestion.

"And he's using every farthing he has to see me marry another?" Felicity shook her head. "Even if he was worthy—which I am not saying he is—I would cross him off my list for being such a fool!"

"Who's a fool?" a deep voice behind her inquired. "Or rather shall I say, whom?"

Felicity spun around. *Thatcher.*

Tally and Pippin shared a glance and then like a pair of traitors retreated, leaving an indecent amount of space between her and him . . . this man she'd fallen in love with.

"Whatever are you doing here?" she asked, still furious over the disaster his kiss had wrought . . . and furious that he'd left her.

"I'd ask the same of you, but I'm sure the reason is obvious." He sent a glance over her shoulder toward Hollindrake House.

"You're late for work," she said, not knowing what else to cast at him and feeling foolish at saying even that.

"I assumed that after yesterday I'd been dismissed." He drew closer to her. "That is, unless I was mistaken . . ."

She shook her head. No, he hadn't been mistaken. She couldn't . . .

"Actually, I just came from your house—"

He'd come to see her? She pressed her lips together. Botheration, why did such a thing fill her heart with hope?

"What did you do, Duchess?" he said, using her nickname, his dark eyes alight with mischief. "Pick every pocket in Mayfair to affect such a transformation?"

"Hardly," she said, knowing she should be offended at such a suggestion, but rather delighted down to her toes to be teased. *By him.*

But looming behind him stood a reminder of why she shouldn't be delighted or even mildly amused. Hollindrake. And now she owed the duke so much more . . . That was, unless . . .

"Mr. Elliott released our money. He claims that Jamilla convinced him to do it, but that's absurd."

Thatcher crossed his arms over his chest as he eyed her. "You don't believe him?"

"Oh, I believe we have the money, but because of Jamilla? Only a fool would believe such a clanker." She paused, and decided to test the other theory. "Tally and Pippin think you did it."

He glanced up at her sister and cousin, then back at her. "And you don't think me capable of such a gesture?"

Felicity let out the deep breath she'd been holding. "Why would you? Now I can go out in Society and meet—"

"And meet your duke like the duchess that you will one day be," he said, drawing closer and reaching out to take her hand in his. She'd replaced her red mittens with a fine pair of leather gloves, but in truth, Aunt Minty's plain home-spun mitts were far warmer than the elegant ones gracing her hands now, just as Thatcher's hands, callused and broad, were so very warm and masculine. No pampered prince of society was he.

"Are you so sure it wasn't me?" He drew her closer still, until the warmth of his body enfolded hers.

She shook her head. "How could you? More to the point, why would you?"

"But it was, Felicity," he whispered into her ear. "I can give you everything you desire, everything you ever deserved."

Desire. Oh, he had helped her discover her desires. And not just the kind from kisses and tumbled moments behind a curtain, but for the things she loved, like the fleeting joy of skating in winter, and the cozy, comforting warmth of a cup of Turkish coffee. That her life and travels and "odd notions" were to be celebrated, not hidden behind a proper veneer.

"Come with me, Duchess," he offered. "Come with me, right now. Marry me."

Felicity staggered back, out of his arms. "Wh-a-a-at?"

"You heard me. Marry me. Tonight. I know a chaplain who can obtain a Special License for us. We can be wed tonight and away from here on the morrow." He closed the distance between them and swept her into his arms. "There will never be another man who will understand you like I do. Love you like I do. Who will make you feel like this—"

And without any more ceremony, he kissed her. He kissed her tenderly, passionately, and of course, he kissed her perfectly, his lips strong and firm, his tongue tempting her to open up to him, to yield . . .

Oh, everything she desired seemed wound up in this kiss. The freedom he held before her, a life of desires unchecked and happiness.

But just as quickly as his lips had captured hers, he released her, and she staggered back from him.

"Marry me, Felicity. I do have some money. Enough for us to live on. We'll live by our own rules, our own choices. And we'll skate every winter and drink your wretched coffee in bed every morning—"

"I thought you liked the coffee—"

He pulled a long face. "Horrible stuff, yet for you I would drink it every day if I must. But first you'll marry me."

She shook her head. "You know I cannot. I—"

"Don't answer me yet, wait until tomorrow night."

"The answer will be the same then as it is now. I cannot—"

He put a finger to her lips and stopped her. "Don't say anything yet. I have every intention of changing your mind tomorrow night."

He was changing it by standing so close, she would have told him, but she feared speaking. This is what he did to her—he stood too close, he was too tall, and he was far too improper.

A gentleman would have taken her at her word. But not Thatcher. Of all the arrogant, ill-mannered . . .

"Until tomorrow," he was saying, leaning down as if he meant to kiss her.

Oh, that would never do. It would be her ruin. Felicity hastily backed away. "I will be at the Setchfield ball, so you needn't bother calling. Really, Thatcher, how you can think such a thing is possible—"

"Nothing is impossible," he told her. "Besides, I plan on attending the ball, if only to be with you. Oh, I nearly forgot. This is why I came to see you." Carefully he opened his coat and pulled out a single orange blossom. "I brought this as a peace offering."

The exotic fragrance and beauty of his gift nearly left her blindsided to his other plans. Nearly.

He thought to go to the ball? "You can't go to the duke's costume ball," she said. "You weren't invited."

"For you, I would find a way."

His promise sent a shiver rippling down her spine, left her knees wavering beneath her. But didn't he know the humiliation he would cause? The scandal? Yet, worst of all, she would have to refuse him. "I won't have you there. You'll be cast out." Then she tried another tack. "I shall not speak to you, so don't even dare come."

He laughed and leaned forward, whispering in her ear. "Yes, you will, because I've a surprise planned for you."

A surprise? Felicity opened her mouth to ask what it was, but then clamped her lips shut. She didn't care what he had planned, she would have none of it. A surprise, indeed! Of all the supremely overreaching notions.

"I have no need of surprises," she told him, even as her heart hammered with an unsteady beat that left her reeling. If she stood here much longer and listened to him any further, she knew she'd find herself wavering like some romantic schoolgirl. And that would ruin everything. "You needn't bother, for I shall refuse you, mark my words." Furious, more with herself because his promise sent a current of desire jolting through her, she whirled around and stormed past Tally and Pippin, marching for home, where she could order Mr. Rollings to load her pistol and bar the doors. Where she could be a proper lady and live the life she'd planned—with a proper, noble gentleman, she would add.

And yet when she glanced over her shoulder as she was

about to round the corner onto Brook Street, there he was, standing in the last vestiges of sunlight, so tall and proud and nearly noble that her heart made an odd, tremulous skip. For he might not be a duke or even a knighted merchant, but he was, as he smugly claimed, the right man for her.

Marry him, a voice urged her. *Marry him.*

Of all the impertinent notions! Marry him? Why it was ridiculous. Preposterous.

So why was it then, that by the time she reached her front steps she'd dissolved into a complete watering pot?

"Miss, are you well?" Rollings asked as she stumbled inside.

"I—I—I—" she sniffed. "I—I—I am perfectly fine." But she wasn't. She was miserable and anyone who looked at her could probably see that.

"Then I have something that will most decidedly cheer you up," he said. Holding out the salver, a single card sat atop it in regal glory, engraved with the four words that, instead of righting her world, turned everything upside down.

THE DUKE OF HOLLINDRAKE.

Instead of following her sister, Tally turned and raced after their former footman, for there was no doubt after that completely improper kiss that Felicity was a tangled wreck. Tally loved a star-crossed romance just as much as everyone else, but this was her sister's heart that was being broken.

Reaching inside her reticule, she plucked out the one thing she possessed that would bring this wretched charade to an end. She knew she'd made Pippin promise not to tell Felicity, but that didn't mean she couldn't discover what Hollindrake was doing—especially when it was so evident that her sister's heart was being torn apart. "Your Grace!"

And when he turned to acknowledge the greeting, he found himself looking down the barrel of a small but deadly enough pistol.

Tally held it with steady assurance. "Now, Your Grace, you are going to tell me what game this is you are playing with my sister's affections or I will—"

"Shoot off my ballocks?" he inquired calmly.

This took her aback. "Well, yes." So much for the element of surprise.

He smiled at her. "So I was warned."

Chapter 14

The following evening, Felicity stood in the middle of the Setchfield ballroom feeling as if she'd been dropped into a sandstorm. The *ton* had turned out *en masse*, for everyone knew that Hollindrake was to make his bow tonight.

Oh, this should have been her triumphant evening. The culmination of all her plans and hard work. The duke would arrive, resplendent in some perfectly cut jacket—no costume for such a dignified person—and a regal mask trimmed in gold braid that marked his social preeminence even further. Then he'd request an introduction to the lovely Titania in the corner, and they'd dance the opening set. Her future—her very place in society—would be assured in just those few minutes. Soon after there would be an announcement in the *Times* of their betrothal, and finally a grand wedding in the late spring at the duke's Kent estate.

She'd had this entire evening mapped out for four long years, and now that it was here, she wished herself far from every speculating glance and sly comment.

Felicity took a deep breath and tried to tamp down the butterflies rattling about in her chest. But instead of composing herself as she intended, all she could think of was what Thatcher had offered her.

To live by their own rules, their own choices.

And passion. The passion of his kiss, the warmth of his body. His very heart.

What had she done? She'd run away from him.

If there was anything to be thankful for, it was her wide mask, for it hid the tears that threatened to spill down her cheeks.

"Miss Langley?" came an inquiry from amidst the crowded Setchfield ballroom. "Is that you?"

"Lady Rhoda," Felicity replied as she turned to find the matron approaching her, a Diana and pair of young wood nymphs behind her. "You found me!"

"A battalion of French couldn't have stopped us." Lady Rhoda blew the feathers dripping down from her turban out of her eyes. "I took your advice," she said, "and had the girls go see Madame Ornette for their costumes. I only wish I'd done myself the same favor."

So did Felicity. She'd let Tally and Pippin choose her costume and they dressed her as the fairy queen, Titania, wings and all, though Cordelia in *King Lear*, might have been a more apt choice.

"Do you like our costumes?" Miss Eleanor Hodges, the youngest of the three, asked.

"Most excellent!" Felicity told her, admiring the trio. The

little known modiste had transformed the usually mousy trio into three striking young ladies. "When you are all brilliantly married, you should use Madame Ornette for all your gowns, for no one has a better eye for style and color. You will make her famous."

Eleanor gasped. "Do you truly think so?"

"Decidedly," Felicity declared.

"I understand your fortunes have reversed," Lady Rhoda said softly. "I'm glad for it." And from the ring of sincerity in her words, Felicity knew she meant it.

"Thank you," Felicity said. She rather liked Lord Stewart's sister. But then she glanced around and asked, "But where is your brother and Lady Stewart?"

"Alice is still unwell, and I convinced Stewie to stay home and keep her company." The elegantly clad matron, dressed as Ceres, leaned forward and whispered, "I thought my nieces might get on better without their father loitering about and running off any likely suitors. I love my brother dearly, but he is a dreadful buffoon."

Felicity smiled and let the obvious reply pass, for she felt a fondness for Lord Stewart—even with his outspoken bluster—but agreed that he could be . . . well, a bit overwhelming.

"I suppose you are quite nervous tonight," Fanny said as she glanced around the room. She was, unfortunately, more like her father than her more discreet mother or aunt.

"Whatever for?" Felicity asked, trying to avoid the obvious.

Not Fanny Hodges. She dove in with both feet, just as her father would have. "Why Hollindrake, of course! It is on every tongue. He's to make his first appearance tonight."

"I hadn't heard," she lied, trying to act nonchalant about the entire situation, for however could she come face-to-face with him now? She'd sat up most of the night rereading his letters, trying to discover a spark of what had made her so certain he was the perfect man for her, and had found nothing. Not a single line that made her heart flutter as it did when that wretched Thatcher just walked into a room.

"Oh, Fanny, leave Miss Langley alone," Margaret Hodges chided. The oldest of the three girls, Peg was a sensible and unflappable young lady. "Leave such chatter and gossip to those it better suits."

As if on cue, a Pocahontas and a Queen Elizabeth wandered by, and the long, disapproving glances they tossed at Felicity and her party left no doubt as to who was behind those masks.

The sight of Miss Browne and Lady Gaythorne was enough to prod Felicity back into action. While she no longer needed the Hodges coal, she'd given her word to help the sisters, and after enduring another of Miss Browne's slights, she was ready to settle the score.

"As I said before, I believe Lord Lumby would make a brilliant match for you, Miss Hodges," she told Margaret. "Now, for Frances and Eleanor, you two would do well considering Lord Dalderby and Lord Sprotley."

"You've still got your sights set on an earl for our Peg?" Lady Rhoda shook her head. "Seems a bit top lofty for a gel who"—again the voice lowered—"prefers a day in the country riding, and if she can, a bit of fishing."

"I think you'll find Miss Hodges and Lord Lumby are well-matched." Of this, Felicity was certain, for the countess had bemoaned that her son would never find a bride when he spent most of his days out riding and fishing.

Tally and Pippin came rushing through the throng, having scouted out the room for her.

"Ho there, Duchess," her sister called out.

Tally had chosen to come in full Turkish costume, having badgered Jamilla into opening her trunks and loaning one of her more exquisite gowns. Pippin wore a Grecian-inspired robe with a mask that evoked all the symbols of Circe, a golden sun rising over her blond hair. Thankfully, Felicity had talked her out of finding a small pig to bring with her.

"We found Lumby—he's dressed as Robin Hood. Dalderby is a harlequin—" Tally shuddered. "I do believe his mother chose it—he really needs to send her to a dower house somewhere in Scotland." Taking a quick breath, she added, "And Sprotley is dressed as Hamlet." She leaned forward and whispered, "Are you sure you want to remove him from the list by casting him in Nelly Hodges's direction? He's quite well-favored."

Felicity smiled, for her sister was always falling in love with a handsome man without any thought as to how he might suit. "You'd stand in the way of true love?"

Tally's mouth pursed, but she was far too romantic by nature to stand in the way of something dictated by the Fates.

With that settled, Felicity turned her attention to the Hodges. "Ladies, if you were listening to my addlepated sister, you know who you are looking for—Robin Hood, Hamlet, and unfortunately, a harlequin. The Duchess of Setchfield told me yesterday that the waltzes are to be lady's choice, so you must make sure when a waltz is about to begin that you are in the position to ask your future husband to dance."

"Ask him?" stammered Margaret, suddenly loosing her usual self-assurance. "Oh, I couldn't do that!"

"Oh, Peg, don't be such a ninny!" her sister Fanny said. "Didn't you hear what Miss Langley said the other day? Lumby rides *and* fishes."

That was enough to renew her sister's courage, for with her quiver in hand, Margaret Hodges now scanned the crush like the huntress she'd chosen to portray.

Felicity had no doubt that by the end of the evening Lord Lumby would be well struck. But not to leave anything to chance, she added, "I hear tell that Lumby Park sports a fine trout pond, and that the earl just bought Lord Vere's best hunter."

"Tiburon?" she gasped.

"Yes, I believe that is the beast. He might even be inclined to let you ride him; that is, if you can catch his eye." Felicity looked up and waved Jamilla over from where the princess stood nearby. "And I know exactly how to do it."

"Darling girls, how pretty you look!" the princess said with a great flourish of her manicured hands. She had come dressed in a regular gown, disavowing a costume as so very distracting and. . . unnecessary. Truly, Jamilla stopped men by just walking into a room.

"Jamilla, they are here to meet their future husbands," Felicity told her, "their true loves, and I thought you might share a secret or two as to how to catch a man's eye. To seal their fates, as it were."

The princess preened. "But of course! For the friends of my little Duchess, I will show you how. Come with me . . ." She rose up on her high-heeled shoes and spotted an alcove. "Yes, over there. Come, this will but take a moment, and for the remainder of your lives you will have these men in your thrall." With that, Jamilla had the Hodges sisters bundled off.

"When is someone going to teach me that look?" Pippin complained.

"I daresay you don't need it," Tally remarked.

The two girls shot each other furious glances and Felicity flicked off their odd behavior as more of their artistic temperament.

"Are they safe?" Lady Rhoda asked as she watched her nieces being led off by the exotic and questionable lady.

"Perfectly," Felicity assured her. "Oh, and there is Lady Lumby." She pointed at a lady dressed in a Spanish mantilla. "Might I suggest, Lady Rhoda, you begin forging a more practical bond between your two families? I believe you will find her very amenable to a possible alliance."

"Thank you, Miss Langley," Lady Rhoda said, taking one last speculative glance in Jamilla's direction.

"I wish your nieces all the best," she replied before Lady Rhoda made her way to Lady Lumby's side. Then she swiped her hands together and looked about the room, her gaze eventually settling on her sister and cousin. "Now that we have that done, I have names for both of you—"

Tally and Pippin groaned, but Felicity was immune to their protests.

"I would think you have enough to do tonight without worrying about us," her sister said.

"Yes, Felicity, please don't go to any trouble over me," Pippin added. "But do promise me, when you meet the duke, you will give him a chance—"

"I thought you wanted me to fall in love with Thatcher," Felicity said, crossing her arms over her chest. Really, her cousin was turning into a regular scatterbrain.

"I do," Pippin said. "It's just that—"

Tally nudged her and again there was a series of furious glances back and forth.

Felicity had seen enough. "Really, whatever has you two at odds, you need to settle it, immediately."

"But Felicity—" Pippin began.

"Cousin, you fret too much," she told her. "I have every intention of meeting Hollindrake and falling completely in love with him. Why wouldn't I? He has done so much for us, how could I not?"

"Aubrey," the Duke of Setchfield called out in greeting. "Good to see you, old friend. Or should I say, Captain Thatcher?"

Thatcher laughed. "And you as well, Temple," he said, using

the duke's old nickname. "I must assume you've seen Jack."

"Seen him?" Temple shook his head. "He raged at me for over an hour at White's last night as to how you were playing the little Duchess false. Made me promise to be his second if he had to call you out."

"Well, I intend to marry the chit, so there is no need for Jack to get in a lather."

Temple held up his lorgnette and studied Thatcher's plain costume. "Still incognito, I see."

"Yes. And I'd appreciate it if you didn't announce me."

"Done, but I'll have you know that if it is discovered that I concealed you this evening, I will most likely be found hanging from Tyburn in the morning, having been lynched by every marriage-mad mama in London."

Thatcher shook his head. "I prefer to remain this way until I've gained Felicity's consent."

"Not quite the usual courtship, I'd say."

"Not the most usual of ladies," he replied.

Temple laughed. "Excellent! You've discovered the little gem that shines beneath that determined exterior." He bowed to a countess who had just arrived and waited until the lady passed to say, "Diana is in alt over Felicity. When the little chit came over yesterday and demanded to see the guest list in order to ensure that she could make matches for Stewie's daughters, I declare she had my usually unflappable wife bowled over—happily so, for Diana has a soft spot for Stewie as well, and was touched that Felicity would befriend his daughters when so many others have snubbed them."

"Speaking of wives, what's this about you and Lady Diana Fordham?" Thatcher asked. "Wasn't she engaged to that rapscallion cousin of yours?"

"Danvers? Well, yes. But she had a change of heart," Temple told him, with a proud, sly grin on his lips.

"Quite a lady, your wife," Thatcher continued. "Demanded I call on her yesterday and then spent a good hour outlining how she thought I should steal away my bride tonight."

"My wife? Meddling? Preposterous." Temple laughed, and said, "If anyone knows a thing or two about stealing away, it is Diana. Follow her advice to the letter and you shall win the little Duchess."

"If only I had your confidence. I still wonder if she will let herself find happiness by giving her heart to a footman."

"Is the test necessary?" Temple asked, sounding more like Jack. "Why not just tell her?"

"Because I want her to realize that she is worthy of the same love she seems determined to find for everyone else."

Temple nodded. "Then I see you have discovered her frailties as well, and for that I am thankful. The Duchess is loyal through and through—by her word and deeds—but I've always worried that her top-lofty aspirations would leave her little but a shiny coronet. She deserves a measure of happiness." He paused. "But you do know she will most likely shoot you when she discovers the truth."

"So I've been warned. Besides, I've already had a run-in with her sister and Lady Philippa."

Temple laughed. "That's well and good, but remember, Felicity is the better shot."

Through the crowd two men came forward, Jack Tremont and another fellow who Thatcher didn't know.

"Have you met Lord Larken?" Temple inquired.

Thatcher's gaze rose to meet that of the man before him. Larken? Why, the fellow had been legendary amongst Wellington's intelligence officers. "Only by reputation. I am honored to meet you, sir."

"Captain Thatcher?" Larken asked, holding out his hand. "Yes."

"And I have heard of you as well." The two men shook in greeting, and Thatcher liked the fellow immediately. "You were at Corunna, were you not?"

Thatcher nodded.

"Saved your entire unit from capture, I heard, and then ended up capturing the French pursuing you. You've a devious mind, sir. Have you considered a career in the Foreign Office?"

Temple laughed. "Don't even try recruiting him, Larken. He has obligations enough now that he's come home."

"Yes," Jack said moodily. "Obligations he needs to get on with." He nudged Thatcher in Felicity's direction.

Standing his ground, Thatcher shot back, "Speaking of obligations, why aren't you with your wife?"

"Working," Jack replied. "Still haven't found our man."

"And you think this Dashwell fellow will be here tonight?" Thatcher found it hard to believe the cheeky American, no matter his legendary daring, would show his face here with Temple, Jack, and Larken all in attendance, all hunting for him.

Jack crossed his arms over his chest. "You don't know Dash. The man would love nothing more than to come here and leave some impertinent message for Temple to find or to steal a kiss from some innocent miss and ask her to pass a note to one of us."

"Not if we find him first," Larken said with a deadly assurance that made Thatcher all too glad his only plans for the night were finding Felicity and convincing her to marry him.

Then again, perhaps his friends had the easier task.

The Setchfield ball always promised the *ton* a night of surprises, and on more than one occasion, scandal.

Felicity had no interest in either. She wanted only to meet Hollindrake and get on with her life. And forget Thatcher. And his dark eyes. And the way he made her laugh.

As the third set ended, she tried to still her tapping foot, for impatience, as Miss Emery liked to tell them, "was not the sign of a lady." Well botheration, she wouldn't be in this state if Hollindrake would just make his entrance and get all this over with!

But there was another element to her nervousness. What if Thatcher made good his promise and arrived? Oh, whatever would she do then?

Then suddenly there was a murmur through the crowd, and a whisper of excitement raced across the room.

Hollindrake.

Felicity took a deep breath and tried to tamp down the nausea that threatened to make her the first *on dit* of the night. She couldn't toss up her accounts on the man! She just couldn't. So taking a few more breaths, she turned toward the grand entrance, but in her path stood a man in a simple black suit, a plain domino on his face. She barely slanted him a glance as she strained to see who was about to be announced, that is until the stranger took her hand and without asking her favor or preferences hauled her out toward the dance floor where the strains of a waltz, the first of the evening, were beginning.

It was then she saw the glittering dark eyes, the hot, rakish gaze devouring her, felt the familiar heat of his hand running up and down her arm.

Thatcher! Dear heavens! And worse, her traitorous body trembled in rapture. Oh, why did he have to make her feel so . . . wonderful?

"What are you doing here?" she asked as he continued to guide her toward the dance floor, farther and farther from Hollindrake. "I told you not to come."

"So you did." He took her other hand, set it on his shoulder and began the waltz without saying another word.

"I'll have you know the waltzes are lady's choice and I don't recall choosing you," she told him, trying not to melt into his chest, doing her best to ignore the way her body swayed happily with his. Oh, she should be furious with him, but instead she realized she was . . . well, relieved.

"Then you were quite neglectful in that regard for you would have missed your chance to dance with me." He swung her around.

"How did you ever get in here?" she asked.

"Walked. Right through the front door."

"As if you were invited? Of all the cheek—" Though she supposed that was what she loved about him—he cared naught for Society's dictums.

"Yes, exactly as if I'd been invited." He pulled her closer, and her breasts grew heavier as they brushed against his chest, sending tendrils of desire spiraling downward.

"Stop that," she protested.

"Stop what?" he asked, tugging her closer still.

"You are holding me too tight. What if someone sees me?"

"Sees what? A fairy queen dancing with her footman?"

"Is that what you are? You look like a highwayman."

"Shall I steal you away? Shall we chart our own lives, Duchess? By our own rules?"

"I—I—I—" she stammered. "I cannot."

"Let me love you tonight, Felicity," he whispered; no, he promised. "As you should be."

As they continued to whirl around the floor, Felicity caught glimpses of other couples. Margaret Hodges—her smile bright and dazzling with joy as she danced with her Robin Hood. In another moment she caught sight of Pippin, her eyes starry with wonder as she danced with a tall, disreputable looking pirate.

Felicity saw it then. Love. Her cousin and Margaret Hodges had found it tonight, so why shouldn't she?

He spun her again, and Felicity grew dizzy. Oh, it wasn't from the waltz, but the terrifying power those words held.

Let me love you.

What if Hollindrake never truly loved her? The staid, proper marriage she'd planned for all these years seemed a dull and wretched existence now. Natural inclinations, indeed! She'd been a fool. But what could she do now?

Not that she had a choice in the matter, for she'd been so lost in her practical musings, she hadn't noticed Thatcher maneuver her quite easily to the far side of the ballroom. In the blink of an eye he tugged her through an opening in the crowd, and through a door that was cleverly fitted into the wall. In an instant they were out of the lively buzz of the ballroom and in the soft muted silence of a dimly lit hall. But her abductor didn't stop there—with his usual audacity, he continued to tow her deeper into the house.

"Thatcher, what the devil are you doing?" she finally protested. If they were found like this, so far from the ballroom, her reputation would be . . .

He didn't speak, he just stopped, so abruptly that she slammed into the wall that was his chest. Her arms wound immediately, automatically, around his neck. She only glanced up at him for a moment, but what a moment it was. His gaze held and trapped hers, and suddenly the world spiraled down to just the two of them.

Slowly, tantalizingly, his head tipped down and his lips covered hers.

And Felicity was lost. Lost in his arms, lost in his kiss.

He steadied her when she swayed by pressing her up against the wall, where her body came alive, her hips moving up against his, coming up against that hardness that left her quaking with need. In the foyer the other day it had been like a game, but now . . . now there would be no turning back if they were to continue this hazardous play. "We shouldn't . . . I can't."

But she didn't mean it. For something about the light in Pippin's eyes, the joy in Margaret Hodges' smile, left her envious—because she too could have that same bliss if only she would let herself.

And then she knew why she loved matchmaking. It wasn't

the satisfaction of two good and proper families uniting in marriage. Or the alliance of noble lineages.

It was the chance to see love happen. From that first spark of attraction to the happiness that shone in the eyes of a bride and groom.

Or as in Jack and Miranda's case, a love that blossomed and grew into a family, filling the world around them with the happiness and affection they shared so openly.

"Thatcher, I—" she whispered, starting to tell him what she'd discovered. What this spark had ignited in her heart.

"We shall, and you will," he told her, thinking she was about to issue another protest and staving her off by sweeping her up into his arms, then carrying her up a nearby stairwell. He continued to kiss her until they were up to nearly the top of the house and they'd arrived at a doorway. Pushing it open, Felicity found herself in the most magical room she'd ever seen, and knew without a doubt that her ruin was upon her.

"Your kingdom, my fair queen," he whispered.

Felicity didn't know what to say. Here, hidden away was an orangery built into the attics at the back of the house. A glass roof and two walls let in the starry night above, the snow having been swept away. In the corner a small stove kept the room warm, while around them orange trees grew in large pots. Candles had been tucked in all sorts of corners and nooks, giving the place an ethereal glow.

The smell of orange blossoms spiced the air, as if they had indeed stepped into a fairy kingdom.

"How did you know this was here?" she asked.

"I have my sources," he told her, his hands warm upon her shoulders. "I wanted some place private . . . and perfect." He led her to a wide lover's couch that sat nestled amidst the trees. Obviously this spot had been designed for trysts, for the rich velvet cushion and wide width were more like a bed than a bench.

She shouldn't, she couldn't, she wouldn't . . . but when she went to protest, she inhaled the fragrance in the room, and more so smelled him—a rich masculine scent that whispered unthinkable notions, incited her passions. She wanted to feel him, inhale that scent, taste him.

And when she looked up into his eyes, peered into those dark, mysterious depths, she realized something else. That all the ducal coronets in the world would never give her this—her heart's desire.

"Thatcher, I—" She tried again to tell him how she'd changed her mind, how she wanted him and only him, but he took matters quite into his own hands.

He hauled her into his arms and kissed her anew. His lips didn't just cover hers, they demanded a response.

And she gave it to him, winding her arms around his neck and clinging to him, letting the dizzy passion of his kiss build inside her. His kiss plundered her lips, her neck, behind her ear, until she moaned, if only to release some of the pent-up desire inside her.

Her feminine sigh was just the urging he needed to continue further—and not one to waste any time or chance, his rakish and expert fingers undid her costume. Her wings, her wig, and shoes were soon flung to the four corners, tangled as they were with his jacket, waistcoat, and shirt. Her hair tumbled out of its pins, and he opened the laces at the back of her gown and slid it down, so first one, then the other breast were freed.

Her knees quaked as his fingers teased her nipples into tight, taut buds. Oh, dear heavens, how was such a thing possible? To feel as if one's very soul was being coiled up. He kissed her anew, sweeping her up, her gown falling away, and then he laid her down on the settee wearing only her chemise and stockings.

"You are the most beautiful creature alive," he whispered, before his mouth caught hold of one of her nipples and began to suckle at her, the rough surface of his tongue laving over her until that coil she'd thought impossible to endure tightened even further.

Then quickly, he tore her chemise open, exposing her to him. She should have been shocked, outraged, but when she saw the covetous light in his eyes, the way his breath stilled, she wished she had a hundred more of them for him to tear asunder.

His fingers trailed up her leg, over her thigh and delved into the curls there, stroking them apart. Her legs fell open shamelessly, for she wanted him there, to touch her as he had before.

And he did.

She moaned, without any thought of propriety, as his finger traced a lazy circle around her sex. Was such a feeling possible?

"Please," she panted. "Do that again."

"Do what?" he asked, even as his fingers drew that devilish circle once again.

"Oh, yes, that," she said, her hips rocking upward.

"I think I would rather do this," he told her, then lowered himself, letting his mouth blaze a hot trail over her stomach, down past the rumpled remains of her chemise.

Before she realized it, his lips nuzzled her, his breath hot upon her, and then his tongue made a long, slow swipe over her.

She trembled beneath him as she thought she was going to explode. And there was only one thing she could say. "Oh, yes, again."

And he did. Again his tongue teased her, tormented her, in careless circles, coming atop her and suckling her. Her hips rocked and bucked and she thought she was about to fall from the very rooftop where they were perched.

How she ached, how she wanted . . . something . . . to end

this torment, to make it go on forever. And then she knew what she wanted.

"Thatcher," she gasped as she felt herself growing tighter and tighter. But what she wanted wasn't this hot and fast passion. No, she knew with a woman's own reckoning what she wanted to end this ache, to fill her needs. "Thatcher, please make love to me."

And so he did.

Thatcher had never heard those words uttered with such passion, such need. His own body was ready to burst, and if he got much harder, he had to imagine he would.

Felicity's lush, gorgeous body tempted him like no other woman's ever had. From her fair silken skin, to her round, firm breasts, to the curve of her hips, to the tantalizing taste of her sex. She was a woman of passion and he wanted her.

"Thatcher, please make love to me," she whispered again, her hands coming to his breeches, tugging impatiently at the waistband.

He rose and tugged them off, his erection rising out. At first she stared at him, her eyes wide, but then a slow smile spread across her mouth and her hips rose up to taunt him. Her rosy nipples were tight and pointed, and her thighs parted just a little farther, as if opening the gates for him. He wasted no more time, and came down atop her, pinning her to the cushions, his penis thick and hard, and ready to plunge inside her and find the release they both craved.

But he stilled for a moment, for he had no idea if she knew what this meant.

"It might hurt," he told her.

"Yes, I know," she said, but looking unafraid. "But then it will be all joy."

She sounded just like . . . Jamilla. Perhaps her old nanny wasn't such a bad influence after all.

Her legs wound around him, drawing her cleft right up to the tip of him. "Please, Thatcher. I need you. I want you."

And so he did, entering her slowly, moving back and forth, like gentle waves on the beach, ebbing and flowing as she opened up to him, stretching to meet him. He kept moving deeper and deeper until he came to the evidence of her innocence, but she gave him no time to reconsider or reconnoiter the barrier before him. She caught hold of his hips and held him as her hips thrust upward.

And he suddenly he found himself completely sheathed inside her, surrounded by her, buried inside her, and he knew he'd found heaven.

Felicity wondered at first how she would ever find her way back to that hot, ragged place, but the moment he began to stroke her, the length of him moving in and out of her, pressing against the nub of her sex, she found herself spiraling once again out of control.

His mouth came crashing down on hers and they kissed, their tongues wild to taste each other, their hands exploring every inch they could claim. They were a tangle of passion, the two of them, bound together as he continued to make love to her.

And when the first wave hit her, her eyes sprang open. For it was like finding a secret inheritance or a title or some other grand prize. No, better, she realized as her body quaked and rocked. She cried out his name as every desire in her body seemed to rush to her very core, then explode outward, like a Chinese rocket, sending sparks and showers and bright colors down around her. She trembled again, and realized it was because Thatcher too was finding his release, for his body slammed into hers, pushing her further along, and they rocked together through this stormy, tempestuous moment.

And then it was over and a quiet, sated feeling fell over

both of them, and Felicity could only stare up at the stars in wonder.

"What have you done to me?" she whispered sometime later.

"Ruined you," he teased.

"You have," she agreed. "Quite thoroughly, I'd say. That is, in my limited experience in these matters."

He rolled her beneath him. "I could do it again, if you so order me, my dearest queen."

Felicity sighed. *Again, a hundred times,* she would have so ordered, but Thatcher was already continuing, "First," he said, reaching for his coat, "there is something I need to ask you—"

"Ask me?" she gasped, wiggling out from beneath him. Oh, dear! He was about to propose. Again. When would this man take the time to stop doing things so impetuously? First, she'd let him ruin her—which most decidedly had not been in her plan—and secondly, she'd never envisioned herself in her altogether when she received a marriage proposal!

"We are to be married," he told her. "Tomorrow."

"Tomorrow?" Why, she barely had time to revise her *Bachelor Chronicles* and obtain a decent gown, let alone get decent dresses for Pippin and Tally. "Oh, I cannot do it to-morrow."

Really, there were some things that must be done in proper order.

And when she glanced up to explain it to him, she realized he was taking her hesitation all wrong. For he'd risen to his feet and was jerking on his pants, muttering under his breath. "I have taken rooms at the Ransomed Cat. 'Tis the posting house for the Kent road. I'll be there until noon tomorrow—"

"Noon? But I can't, I have—" From the tilt of his brows, she could see he was taking her objections all wrong. Of course she was going to marry him, if only he would just do things properly.

"Noon, madam," he repeated, once again all imperious and overbearing. "Meet me there. For after that I will never ask you to marry me again."

Felicity wasn't quite used to being in love, and a very practical part of her made a determined leap to the forefront of her rattled sensibilities.

More to the point, she lost her temper.

"I don't recall you asking me tonight," she sputtered back.

"I just did," he said, crossing his arms over his chest.

"No, you did not," she shot back, tossing aside her ruined chemise and pulling her gown over her head. "You ordered me about and you certainly didn't ask."

"I don't think I need to 'ask,'" he claimed, catching up his shirt. "The answer was implied when we came up here."

As if she'd had a choice in that . . . Well, she had, but . . .

Thatcher wasn't done. "Tell me, Miss Langley, are you going to marry me or not?"

Felicity's tart reply was cut short as the sharp report of a pistol rang out, followed by screams and the panic of a house in complete uproar. More shots followed, and true to his former profession, Thatcher finished dressing faster that Felicity thought possible.

"Demmit—it must be that Dashwood fellow," he said as another round of shots rang out.

"You mean Dashwell?" Felicity corrected, the image of a pirate dancing with Pippin flitting through her thoughts.

"Aye, Captain Dashwell. An American privateer. Jack thought he might dare to show his face—"

"Oh, no!" Felicity cried as the dire truth dawned upon her. How could she have been so blind when she saw Pippin earlier dancing with a . . . *pirate*. Of course. Why hadn't she realized it then? She caught up her shoes and hopped toward the door, putting on one, then the other, clinging to Thatcher as she went. "He's with Pippin."

"Your cousin?" he said, faltering to a stop.

"Yes," Felicity said, heading toward the stairs without any hesitation that she was headed straight into what sounded like a dangerous commotion downstairs. "We must save her."

Chapter 15

Felicity flew down the stairs ahead of Thatcher, ignoring the fact that her gown was barely on and her hair fell loose, or that her wig, wings, and the remaining pieces of her costume were either lost or ruined.

When she stumbled through the same door from which they'd escaped the crowds, she found herself in the middle of the now nearly empty ballroom. Thatcher arrived moments later and skidded to a stop behind her.

The members of the *ton* who hadn't been able to escape cowered against the walls. Felicity glanced to her right and was shocked to find three men—Jack, Temple, and a fellow she didn't know—with pistols leveled at her. Their gazes never wavered from their target, which lay beyond her.

"Let her go, Dashwell," Temple ordered. "Release her so she isn't harmed."

A chill ran down Felicity's spine as she turned to see her cousin pinned against the devil's own chest.

Dashwell. And worse yet, the pirate held a pistol to Pippin's head.

"Release her?" Dashwell laughed. "Not until I've had a chance to kiss her."

"Pippin," Felicity gasped. "Oh, dear God, no!" She tried to move forward, but Thatcher caught her by the back of her gown and held her fast.

Pale, but unwavering, her cousin managed a wan smile.

Looking around, Felicity spied Tally tucked in next to Lady Rhoda. The Hodges sisters were being protected by Robin Hood, a harlequin, and a rumpled-looking Hamlet.

Well, at least one thing was going right tonight, she thought, turning her attention back to her cousin. "Let her go," Felicity ordered, having tugged her gown free from Thatcher and starting a determined march toward the pair. "I will not allow you to—" But before she could get any farther, Thatcher caught her around her middle and dragged her back until they were both behind Temple.

"Come now, Dashwell," Jack coaxed. "Can't you see you've caused enough scandal and excitement tonight? There is no escape. Let the girl go and no harm will come of this."

"No harm you say?" Dashwell shook his head. "None but to my neck, I'd wager. No, my sweet Circe comes with me."

"Lady Philippa isn't one of your doxies," Temple told him. "My God, man, hasn't your arrogance killed enough good people?"

"My arrogance? Coming from you that's a fine one! As for killing good people, what have you to say about your fine navy? They strung my father up after they pressed him into service—hung him for trying to get home to his family after they'd stolen him off his own ship. And can you tell me what has become of my little brother? He was on that ship as well and there's been nigh a word of him since." The pistol in his hand wavered but then steadied as it came to rest up under Pippin's chin. "Perhaps that's a blessing right now."

Temple and Jack shared a glance. *What next?* it seemed to say.

Well, Felicity knew exactly what needed to be done. "Shoot him!" she cried out. "Shoot that devil! I demand it!"

"Felicity," Thatcher told her, "leave this be. He's surrounded."

"But they don't have Pippin," she sputtered. "Shoot him, Jack. Why don't you just shoot that devil?"

"He could hit your cousin," Thatcher told her, still holding her fast.

"They might, but I won't," she said, wrenching herself from his grasp and in a flash snatching up the extra pistol in Larken's belt.

Thatcher watched what happened next with an air of disbelief. He'd thought in ten years of war he'd seen everything. But he'd never seen a lady shoot like Felicity Langley.

She fired like the finest trained rifleman, cocking as she brought the weapon up, taking her mark with a glance and pulling the trigger before anyone could stop her. The retort blasted through the room, and for a moment it appeared that she'd missed.

Temple, Jack, and Larken all turned, slowly and in unison, gaping at her.

But Thatcher's eyes never left Dashwell's. He'd seen where the shot had gone and knew it had hit its mark. Dashwell's eyes opened wide and the arm holding the pistol dropped away, revealing the growing stain of blood in his shoulder. He glanced down at his wound and then whispered something to Pippin before he raised his weapon and aimed it at Felicity.

Thatcher moved without a thought, shoving Felicity to the floor and following on top of her, his body shielding hers.

And when the shot rang out, he readied himself to be hit, but the only thing that he felt was plaster falling down on him. For Pippin, realizing the danger her cousin was in, had twisted out of Dashwell's grasp and shoved his arm up, so the shot went wild, lodging into the plaster ceiling, blowing a large hole into the French design.

For the longest moment silence reigned over the room as all eyes fixed on Captain Dashwell, the scourge of the Atlantic, England's greatest enemy at sea. He teetered with Pippin in his arms as his eyes grew glassy and finally rolled closed. Then he pitched backward, falling through the French doors behind him.

Felicity tried her best to struggle out from beneath Thatcher, but he refused to let her up until he knew it was safe. He watched as Jack and Temple rushed forward, while Larken gingerly retrieved his pistol from Felicity's grasp.

"He's still alive," Temple called out. "Looks like the ball went right through his shoulder."

"Demmit," Felicity cursed when Thatcher finally let her up.

"Pardon?" Thatcher asked her as they crossed the room to where the privateer lay.

"I missed."

"Missed? You shot better than the King's own riflemen."

"Through his shoulder, indeed! I was aiming for right between his eyes." She turned to Larken. "Your sights are off."

The young lord opened his mouth to argue, but when Thatcher shook his head in warning, Larken thought twice and made an apologetic bow to Felicity.

Tally had rushed to Pippin and pulled her cousin away, even as Temple ordered a footman to fetch the surgeon.

The Duchess of Setchfield came forward. The former Lady Diana Fordham, having once been abducted herself, knew exactly what needed to be done. Winding her arm around Pippin, she drew the girl away. "I think it best that you three come with me. Away from any further gossip and speculation." But this latter part she directed at Felicity, her gaze sweeping over the girl's *dishabille*.

"But Dash is hurt—"

"Shh, dear," Diana told Pippin, turning her attention back to the matters at hand. "Temple is a man of honor and he'll see that the captain is cared for."

Lady Rhoda came forward to add her assistance, catching the Langley sisters in her matronly net and towing them along as well. Her sharp gaze didn't miss Felicity's transformation either. "Well, this is a pretty mess. I daresay it is going to take more than a wagonload of coal to save you three now. I have to wonder if even Hollindrake's title and money will be enough to salvage your reputations."

"Hollindrake?" Felicity whispered, the truth of the lady's words sinking into her chest. Into her very heart.

"Of course," Lady Rhoda said, looking over her shoulder at Thatcher and then back at Felicity. "You'll have to marry him now. 'Tis the only way!" She started to shoo her and Tally after Lady Diana and Pippin, but Thatcher stepped into her path.

"Felicity, there is something we need to discuss," he told her. "Tomorrow, we will, we must be—"

"I—I—I—" she stammered. "Please forgive me. I can't. Not now. I have no choice but to marry *him*."

She sounded utterly miserable at the prospect, and Thatcher would have been delighted if she wasn't talking about marrying *him*.

Oh, Temple was right. He'd made a mess of things by not telling her the truth.

Lady Rhoda came marching back. "Miss Langley, *now*," she ordered. "Before there is more scandal out of this evening than even the *ton* can swallow."

"Thatcher, I—" she said, before she was led away.

"Tomorrow, Felicity," he whispered after her, looking around the ballroom at the stunned faces staring back at him. Oh, the scandal would be torrential, but she'd have his title and the protection of his name.

That is, if she didn't put a hole in him as effectively as she'd taken down Dashwell.

Felicity dressed the next day for the Duke of Hollindrake's investiture with great care. His note had arrived first thing in the morning, apologizing for not finding her at the Setchfield ball and insisting she and her sister and cousin attend the ceremony at the House of Lords. His carriage was coming around at one for them and the ceremony would start precisely at two.

This invitation was tantamount to a betrothal announcement. Either the duke hadn't heard about the scandal of last night or . . . he didn't care, so true was his affection for her.

The Duchess of Hollindrake. The lofty title would be hers, and she, Pippin, and Tally would be shielded from any and all damage to their reputations last night.

If only she could say the same for herself. Overnight she'd changed. Thatcher had given her a great gift—he'd helped her discover her romantic side.

While she might not be as foolish as Tally or Pippin, now she understood what they seemed to just know and to believe. But believing also came at a price, one she wished she didn't have to pay. But there was no going back now.

The door behind her opened and she glanced over her shoulder.

Her cousin stood there, elegantly dressed, but her face

held the strain of the night's horror and she hadn't said a single word since Dash had been carried away.

"Pippin," she whispered, tears welling up in her eyes. "I am so sorry. I shouldn't have shot him, but I was afraid for you." She crossed the space between them and then hesitated. "You love him, don't you?"

She nodded, then burst into tears. The two girls clung to each other, crying, each in her own state of misery.

Tally came rushing in, took one look at the scene and gazed up at the heavens. "It's a very poor day indeed when I'm the one with the level head around here."

Felicity and Pippin both stopped crying, wiping at their faces, both of them finding a small smile at Tally's jest.

"Now, that's better," she told them. "I'm glad to see that you two have come to your senses. Really, Duchess! Shooting Pippin's pirate. Poorly done, indeed. But he's alive, and that's the good news."

"He is?" Pippin's hands covered her mouth.

"Aye. Jack just came by to tell you. He wanted to see both of you, but I sent him packing. He's really quite overbearing since he's turned respectable."

"Thank you," Felicity said. The last thing she needed was a lecture from Jack on her conduct last night. Botheration, there was nothing worse than a reformed rake! Well, perhaps a rake in footman's livery . . .

Tally reached over to the dressing table and caught up the hand mirror, holding it up to the both of them. "Look at you two! Red eyes, and those noses! I dare say not even Jamilla has enough paint and powder to put you to rights."

"Oh, dear, I do look a fright," Felicity admitted.

"Yes, and the carriage is here," Tally told her. "Are you sure you want to go?"

"Yes," she said. Now that she and Pippin were embroiled in scandal, the only way for any of them to regain a place in the *ton* was for her to marry the duke. There was no other way as far as she could see. But, oh . . . it made her heart break even further . . . if such a thing were possible.

Tally leaned over and studied her twin's reflection in the mirror. "I do say, Duchess, you look odd this morning. Different. I can't put my finger on it, but you look different."

"She's in love," Pippin said from behind them.

Tally spun to her cousin first and then back to her sister. "Are you?"

Felicity nodded, then before she could help herself, began to cry again. "Oh, what is to become of me! I've turned into a watering pot!" She took the already damp handkerchief that Pippin offered and blotted away her newly sprung tears. "I used to be so sensible, so proper, and now . . . well, I'm ruined!"

Both Tally and Pippin stepped back. "Truly?"

Felicity looked up. "You needn't sound so pleased! This is a disaster. I love Thatcher, but I'm promised to Hollindrake."

"Well, you aren't really betrothed," Tally pointed out.

"Close enough," Felicity wailed. "And now I must marry him, for we are all ruined."

Her sister waved off her lament. "Oh, Duchess, you are overwrought. 'Tis only a little bit of scandal, and we are Langleys after all. I do believe a little bit of scandal is expected."

"No, Tally. *We are ruined.* All because I fell in love with our footman." There it was. She'd said it out loud.

And much to her shock, the world didn't come to a stunning end.

She loved Thatcher. Oh, demmit, yes she did.

"You love him?" Pippin whispered.

Chills ran down Felicity's spine. She looked down at her hands, where once she dreamed of seeing a huge ring, and now would give anything to have a plain gold band, as long as it meant she could spend the rest of her life with him.

"Are you truly in love with him, Duchess?" Tally asked.

There was no other answer to give, she realized. "Yes. Yes, I am."

Pippin grinned. "Oh, Felicity that is wonderful!"

"You think so?" she asked.

Tally and Pippin both nodded.

"What did Nanny Rana always say?" Tally tapped her lips. "Oh, I remember. 'We are all on our own paths.' You cannot bear the burden of my mistakes or Pippin's. You have only your own heart to follow. So, please, Felicity, follow your heart. You will never regret it.

"It couldn't be more perfect," her sister went on. "You must tell him so. But I suppose now you will have to wait until after the ceremony."

Then, as if to punctuate the problem, the bracket clock on the mantel chimed once for the hour.

But it wasn't the clock she heard so much as Thatcher's vow from the night before. *Noon, madam . . . Meet me there. For after that I will never ask you to marry me again.*

Noon? Oh, heavens, it was already an hour past. Her only hope was that he wouldn't be entirely true to his word. Surely he was always late—he'd forgive her for being less than punctual. He must.

Felicity sprang into action, dashing about the room, catching up her valise and putting a change of small clothes, stockings, and her hairbrush inside. After a moment of hesitation, she tucked her *Bachelor Chronicles* in, then caught up a cloak, hat, and gloves.

"Is Hollindrake's carriage still outside?" she asked.

Pippin crossed the room and glanced out the window. "Yes."

"I must take it," Felicity told them. "You'll have to take a hackney to the House of Lords." She rushed to the door and flung it open. Before she went flying down the hall, she turned to her gaping cousin and sister. "Give the duke my apologies. That's terribly inadequate, I know. But I'll send him a letter later explaining everything." Then she rushed out before either of them could stop her.

Pippin stared at Tally. "Am I missing something?"

"She still doesn't know," Tally told her.

"How can that be?" Pippin asked.

"'Twas why I urged her to follow her heart. If she's wed to Thatcher, she'll eventually forgive him."

Pippin sighed. "It would be nice if one of us found a happy ending."

Tally wound her arm around her cousin. "Dash will recover. You'll see."

"And when he does, Tally, what then?"

"That's another story altogether. I daresay we'll have to wait for the Duchess first."

"Good things come to those who wait," Pippin whispered.

"So said Nanny Tasha," Tally told her. "So said Nanny Tasha."

Well into the evening, the door to the private suite at the Ransomed Cat crashed open and Thatcher strode in. "Felicity? Felicity? Where are you?"

When he'd looked up to the galleries from his seat in the House of Lords and seen the empty spot between Miss Thalia Langley and Lady Philippa Knowles, he'd nearly bolted out of the long-winded ceremony right there and then.

Felicity hadn't come!

Dear God above, she hadn't come! And if she wasn't in the House of Lords seeking her duke, that could only mean she was waiting for her footman at the rooms he'd told her about at the posting inn.

Waiting for him.

With no regard for appearances, the moment the ceremony ended he'd barreled past all the well-wishers as well as his family, commandeered a horse from a young lordling in the street, and ridden straight for the inn. Only to find the suite he'd taken cast in shadows, a low banked fire in the grate, and Felicity nowhere to be seen.

He was too late. She'd left.

"Demmit!" he cursed.

"That-der?" came a sleep-slurred voice from the bedchamber to his right. "Is that you?"

"Yes, 'tis me!" He crossed the room and stopped in the doorway, stunned at the sight before him. There was Felicity clumsily untangling herself from the sheets and climbing out of bed.

"Yer late," she slurred, taking a distracted swipe at her tumbled curls. "Must get you a pocket watch. A wedding gift."

"I need no gifts, you are here," he declared, coming toward her until his foot sent something clattering across the floor.

"Oh, that's where that demmed thing got to!" She giggled. "Don't worry about it. I have a 'nuther one!" She rustled around under the pillows and produced a wine bottle. Peering into it with one squinty eye, she frowned. "Empty as well." She tossed it back into the sheets, then looked up at him. "Can you get some more?" she asked as she tried to get up and out of bed, but ended up tumbling forward into his arms.

The thick, sweet smell of wine assailed his senses. *She was drunk.* Completely and utterly pissed.

"Thud you weren't comin'," she slurred into his shoulder.

"So I see," he said, holding her out at arm's length.

"Thud you'd left me," she continued, waving her hands in the air.

"Well, I am here, and just in time, I see." He glanced around the room. "What were you thinking, drinking all this wine?"

"Well, Nanny Bridget once told us to have a glass or two of good wine before our wedding night. Well, this inn hasn't very good wine, so I drank two bottles instead. Maybe three." She wavered in his arms. "I don't think Nanny Bridget had the right of it, for the wine is making the room pitch quite violently."

"That's not the only thing that's going to pitch violently, I'd wager," he laughed.

She blinked and looked at him. Really, more at something over his shoulder, before her gaze steadied and she met his eyes as if surprised to find him standing where he was. "Whatever do you mean?"

"You'll find out, soon enough." He hoisted her up and set her back on the bed. "Whatever am I to do with you now?"

She shook a finger at him. "You'll marry me. Right now. Here. Tonight. I'll not be ruined anymore. I want to be a proper wife."

He laughed. "Felicity, you will never be a proper wife."

"But I'll be your wife. Dear Thad-her, I want to be your wife. I love you. I really do. I realized it today. When I told Tally and Pippin that I loved you, I knew it must be true. And I wouldn't trade you for all the ducal coronets in the world. Not a single one."

"You love me?" he asked. He couldn't quite believe it. Yet here she was. And she'd come to him of her own free will. By following her passion.

"With all my heart," she told him, her lips forming a lop-sided smile.

"And this isn't the wine talking, but you?" he asked, kneeling down before her.

"No. I was quite definite on that fact before I drank too much." She paused and blinked, looking around the room as if seeing it for the first time. "Am I drunk?"

"Corned, pickled, and salted," he told her. Right now she'd give Mrs. Hutchinson a run for her money.

"Will you still marry me?"

"Yes."

She brightened, her winsome smile lopsided. "Now?"

"Well, I don't know—"

"Yes, now! Marry me please." She glanced up at him. "You still have the Special License, don't you?"

Thatcher sat back on his heels. Special License or not, there wasn't a clergyman in England who'd marry a nearly insensible lady of good breeding to him. Not even with the bribe he could now afford.

"Oh, you don't want to marry me!" she cried out. Apparently the Langley dramatic streak wasn't confined to Thalia, for Felicity was now giving a performance Mrs. Siddons would have envied. "I've ruined it all." She started to keen and wail, as if the room had been turned into an Irish wake, and before he knew it, the innkeeper was pounding on the door.

"Ho there! I don't run this sort of house! Whatever is going on in there?"

"I want to get married!" Felicity wailed. "I'm ruined. Ruined, I say!"

Thatcher opened the door and eyed the short, squat innkeeper, whose hand was stuck out awaiting compensation.

Thatcher filled it with a few gold pieces. "Is there someone around here who can marry us?"

"What sort of wedding you want?" the man asked, not even bothering to look at the coins in his hands, having hefted them and knowing them for what they were—good gold.

"The kind that can be performed quickly, before the bride is . . ." He glanced back at Felicity, who stood wavering beside the bed, her hand on her forehead and her cries taking on new levels of slurred indignation.

"This was to be my wedding bud . . . no, bad . . . no, bed."

A curse in something that might be Russian followed. "Thad-her, you'd best find a vicar fast, I don't feel so well . . ."

"A hasty wedding it is, guv'ner," the man told him, lending a broad wink to his instructions. "Bring 'er down in about five minutes. Got a fellow who can do the job right, though not altogether proper, if you know what I mean." The innkeeper took a glance at Felicity. "Not that she's likely to notice."

Thatcher didn't care. They'd rectify all this first thing in the morning with the Special License he'd procured, but for now, all he wanted was to placate his insensible bride.

And five minutes later the Duke of Hollindrake married Miss Felicity Langley before a mixed crowd of dubious onlookers in the common room of the Ransomed Cat.

And it was a good thing that the marriage was performed with such undue haste.

For right after the vows were finished and the couple were declared married, the bride discovered exactly what her groom had meant earlier by "pitch violently."

For she did. All over his new boots.

Chapter 16

Felicity's eyes fluttered awake, what time she knew not, but when the light from the window struck her, she closed them immediately, covering her face with her hands and sinking beneath sheets and coverlet.

Oh, dear heavens! When had it gotten so bright out? And why did her head throb so?

Gingerly, she pulled the covers down again and let one eye crack open. The meager winter sun streaming through a window on the far side of the room was like a knife through her aching head.

Yet, two things were at once apparent to her. This wasn't her room, and she hadn't any clothes on.

Botheration, what had happened to her?

She tried to recount the night before, but a jumble of voices tangled her still murky thoughts.

There was a smoky, dark room. And the smell of ale everywhere. And people. She'd been surrounded by strangers.

"Such a pretty lady. My, don't they look fine."

"Wish you well, missus."

"Egads, who'd of thought such a wee thing could hold so much?"

Getting up, she dragged a sheet along with her and wavered toward the washstand, where she rinsed out her rancid mouth and washed her face. It did little to help her.

"Oooooh," she groaned. "Whatever is wrong with me?"

"First day as my wife and already complaining?" came a familiar voice from another room.

Thatcher? What was he doing in her bedchamber? Oh, hold the coach—what had he said?

Wife?

Frantically, she glanced down at her left hand and there it was: a plain and simple gold band around her third finger.

She straightened and regretted immediately moving so fast, but that didn't stop her from staggering to the doorway and asking, "We got married?"

"Yes. You insisted, I'll have you know." Thatcher sat reclined in a chair near the fireplace, his long legs stretched out toward the grate. A white shirt and black breeches were all he wore, the shirt open at the neck revealing a triangle of dark, crisp hair on his chest, while an open book sat in his lap.

"Then last night . . ." She glanced back toward the other room where the large bed, its sheets a tangled mess, spoke of a night spent . . . "Did we . . . ?"

He laughed, loudly and thoroughly. "If you are asking if we consummated our marriage, the answer is no."

She tugged the sheet higher. "But I haven't anything on," she whispered.

"Yes," he whispered back. Then he glanced around the room. "Why are we whispering?"

"Because I'm naked!" she told him indignantly. It wasn't every morning a proper young lady awoke naked, feeling completely dreadful and having no memory of her—Felicity gulped—wedding night. "I haven't any clothes."

"I know. I removed them," he said, rising from his chair and crossing the room.

Felicity still was having a hard time believing she was married, and she backed away from him, colliding with the wall behind her. "Improper rogue!"

"Drunken wench," he teased back.

"I do not drink!" Yet even as she made her indignant statement, her legs wobbled beneath her and she thought she was going to fall over. Thatcher came to her rescue, yet again, catching her up and carrying her to the bed, gently settling her back down on the mattress. "I feel wretched. And how is it I don't remember a thing about last night?"

Thatcher leaned over and rolled first one, then a second, and finally a third empty wine bottle out from under the bed. The clatter was like having an entire regiment of soldiers marching through her head. "I found that last one this morning. You really shouldn't mix port with burgundy."

"Oh, heavens! Did I drink all that?"

He nodded, but his eyes sparkled. "You said something about it being Nanny Bridget's recommendation."

She snorted. "She always did smell like brandy."

Sitting down beside her, he said, "Then I would strike good Nanny Bridget from the advice book I am sure you will write some day." He smiled at her. "You have a deft hand for comedy. I think your sister and cousin should draft you into service."

"Whatever are you talking about?"

"Well, since I was cheated out of my wedding night—"

Felicity's cheeks heated.

"—and there wasn't much else to do, for you'd drank the inn nearly dry, and I discovered that you snore—and quite indelicately, I might add—"

"I most certainly do not," she said, rising up farther.

One brow arched, but he didn't argue the point. "Suffice it to say I decided to partake in a little light reading." He nodded toward the volume on the bed.

She glanced down and recognized it immediately. "My *Chronicles*? You were reading my *Chronicles*? Those are private." Scrambling down the length of the bed to retrieve her journal, she got halfway there when she remembered she was naked. She froze and glanced at him.

His face was a study of innocence, but there was nothing but mischief in his dark eyes.

She caught up the sheet and hauled it with her. Taking hold of her journal, she pressed it to her chest. "This is private."

He plucked it out of her grasp. "And now entirely unnecessary, because you are mine."

"I am, aren't I?" She sighed. If there was any good in all this mess, it was that they were married. "I'm quite relieved."

"Make that two of us," he laughed, his fingers cupping her chin. "You are the only woman for me."

"I fear I haven't been much of a bride," she said, glancing at the bed around them.

"Then let us get on with it," he told her, catching hold of her and kissing her thoroughly as he pinned her to the mattress with his body.

"Of all the arrogant, top-lofty—" she sputtered. "I'm beginning to think I did marry a duke. You've become quite overbearing since we met."

"Thank you," he said, nodding politely. "I have you to thank."

She batted at him. "Oh, you odious fellow!" Then she paused, her gaze falling to her hand. "Are we really married?"

"You're wearing a ring, aren't you?"

She nodded. "But I don't remember a thing about the ceremony. Was it beautiful?"

"It was everything you wanted."

"I wish I could remember tossing my bouquet," she said, still gazing down at her ring.

"I think it's better that you don't remember the tossing part," he said, before he pulled her into his arms and made damned sure their marriage was consummated. Utterly and completely.

Felicity had felt wretched a few minutes ago, but the moment Thatcher hauled her into his arms, she forgot all about her megrims.

For to find herself enfolded in his warm embrace, to feel the heat of his breath on the nape of her neck, she gave into the sinful pleasures twining through her naked limbs.

There were advantages to waking up without her clothes, she realized. For it meant there was nothing standing in the way as Thatcher's hands roamed over her skin in a heated exploration. Her shoulders, her arms, the curve of her hips, the roundness of her breasts. His fingers left a trail of fire in their wake. He'd caress her, stroke her in one place, kindling her desires, and then move on, leaving her breathless and anxious.

And if his hands were leaving such dangerous trails, his mouth was even more hazardous. His lips teased the nape of her neck, sending delicious shivers down her spine. His breath trailed over her shoulders, until his head sank to her breasts, capturing a nipple with his teeth. They grazed the pebbled flesh, and her entire body rose up to meet him.

He caught her by the hips and brought her right up against his breeches, so she could feel that as much as he was pleasuring her, she was doing the same to him.

Felicity sighed as the hardness there rubbed up against her.

Well, it certainly wasn't going to do either of them any good trapped in his breeches.

With a boldness she'd never imagined she could possess, her fingers tugged his breeches open.

Thatcher laughed. "In a hurry?"

"Yes," she said, a newfound huskiness to her voice.

"We have all day," he told her, rolling her beneath him, covering her with his body.

"I won't have you crying off."

"Crying off?"

"Now that you have a clear head, I don't want you changing your mind—about us, and about marrying me."

"Felicity, I never have a clear head when I am around you," he teased. "And certainly not when you haven't got a stitch on." His head dipped down and his lips teased hers.

She arched like a cat, her hands finding the waistband on his breeches and working them down over his hips. "Is this all I have to do to have my way with you?"

"'Tis a good start," he told her, his voice thick with need. His manhood sprang free, hard and erect, and she arched against him again, enthralled by the very feel of him against her sex.

He made a low growl of a sound, and reached down impatiently to finish tugging off his breeches. His shirt followed, and then he was atop her again, their bare skin meeting, the crisp hair on his chest rough against the soft silk of her breasts.

He drew her closer and his hand reached down and slowly stroked the curls at the apex of her thighs. Ever so slowly he parted her nether lips and began to tease her.

Felicity sighed, the heat of his touch sending a dizzy rush of desire running headlong through her body.

She moaned softly, even as he touched her again, his fingers circling the tight nub there and then dipping inside her, drawing out the wetness.

She was slick and hot, and had started to pant. Her heels dug into the mattress, raising her hips up to meet him. Her hands caught hold of his shoulders, twined in his hair, stroked his back—as if trying to find someplace to hold onto.

"Please, Thatcher," she whispered. "I need—"

She couldn't even manage to say it, her breath catching in her throat.

He grinned down at her, a wolfish light in his eyes as he shifted and the torture his fingers were plying from her were replaced by a new tormenter.

She gasped as he entered her, both from the size of him and the pure bliss of having his entire length slide over her sex. He was heavy and thick and he fit her ever so perfectly.

"Now you are mine, always and forever," he told her, the possessive tone to his words sending a thrill down her spine.

Mine. And hers as well. "I wouldn't have it any other way," she whispered back, her hips rising to meet him as he stroked her softly, gently.

For a time they made love slowly, letting the depth of the act surround them.

There was no one else in the world but the two of them, and they let their bodies join into one passion.

So lost in the rhythm, her climax caught her by surprise— as Thatcher's caught him unaware. Their gazes met, and she watched the joy in his eyes as he found his release, his body thrusting deeply into her as his seed spilled out, even as her very core tightened around him, sending waves of pleasure washing over her.

He held her tightly afterward, so close they remained joined together, and Felicity knew she'd made the right choice.

For such bliss was theirs—to find and discover with each other, and only each other.

This was her path, and she surrendered herself to her destiny and to this man who made her life complete.

Sometime later, Felicity awoke and glanced over at the man she'd chosen. With her heart.

"'Twas the right thing to do," she whispered. He snored softly, and she pressed her lips together to keep from laughing. "I'm not the only one."

But for all her happiness, there was something left undone, and if there was one thing she detested, it was unfinished business.

Hollindrake.

She needed to tell him what had happened and of her change of heart. Perhaps she could even find him the right bride, she thought cheerfully, as she slipped silently from the bed.

She found her clothes, cleaned and pressed, hanging from hooks near the door. After donning her gown and pulling on her stockings, she glanced back at the bedroom.

She couldn't just leave without letting Thatcher know where she was going. But if she told him, he'd most likely insist she stay with him. Or persuade her quite effectively to remain. She blushed and then shook her head, for there was also another consideration. He might insist on accompanying her.

At that thought, Felicity shuddered. She had forsworn great wealth and privilege to marry him, and there was no point in rubbing it in.

No, better she go alone and end her attachment to Hollindrake once and for all, and then she could rush back here—to Thatcher, to her new life.

Pulling a blank page from her journal, she found a stub of a pencil on the desk and wrote a quick note explaining her absence in case he awoke before she got back.

And then, silently, she fled, not realizing that Thatcher was standing in the doorway watching her leave. He crossed the room, read the note, and tossed it onto the coals in the grate.

"There's no putting it off now," he muttered.

Felicity arrived back at the house on Brook Street to find her sister and Pippin making their final finishing touches for the Hollindrake ball.

"Duchess, there you are!" Tally called out, crossing the room in a thrice and drawing her sister into a warm embrace, not caring a whit for wrinkles to her silk gown or damage to her elegant coiffure. "Thatcher sent around a note that he had found you, but I am glad to see you well." She paused and then held her sister out to study her. "All is well, isn't it?"

Felicity nodded and then grinned. "We are wed."

"Then you aren't mad?"

"Mad? Whatever for?" Felicity asked. "Certainly it wasn't the ceremony I had envisioned, but I don't care for that any longer. I love him, and he loves me, and we are man and wife. For now and forever."

"Married! Oh, Felicity, that is glorious news," Pippin said, coming to join in as the three of them danced in a circle, Brutus barking happily as he darted between their ankles.

When they came to a dizzy stop, Felicity glanced at the two of them in their finery. "How pretty you both look! Madame Ornette did a beautiful job. And I see Mr. Betchel's services as a hairdresser weren't exaggerated."

Both girls grinned, twirling around to show off their finery.

"You must see your gown," Tally said, pulling Felicity toward her old narrow bed, where a blue-hued gown of changeable silk lay shimmering on the mattress. "Pretty enough, even for a duchess."

Duchess. Oh, that nickname would never do. Not any longer.

"You have to stop calling me that," Felicity admonished her.

"Whatever else would I call you?" Tally laughed. "Mrs. Thatcher?"

Both Tally and Pippin laughed, until her cousin asked, "I never did know, is Thatcher his given name or surname?" They both laughed again, this time until Tally had to swipe at the tears running down her cheeks.

Felicity stepped back, feeling both stung and dismayed. "I don't see anything funny. Just because I chose to marry a footman doesn't give either of you the right to make sport of it."

"Oh, Duch—" Tally began, until she spied the hot fire in Felicity's gaze. "Well, we were just teasing, and we are sorry if you don't find it amusing."

"Oh, yes," Pippin added. "Please don't be angry."

"I suppose I am just tired," Felicity admitted, "and a little apprehensive about tonight."

"You'll be fine," Tally told her. "And you'll look stunning in that gown. Every tongue in Town will be wagging tomorrow."

"Oh, heavens, I hope not!" she declared. "I don't want any more scandal."

"I daresay, with a runaway marriage, you won't be able to avoid it," her sister said, soothing her. "But you'll have the two of us there with you, so you won't really be alone."

"No, this is something I must do alone," she insisted.

Tally tipped her head. "Do what?"

"Tell Hollindrake I've married someone else." Felicity crossed the room and picked up her hairbrush.

"Tell what to who?" Tally sputtered.

She let out an aggrieved sigh. "Tell the duke that I've married someone else. I hope I don't break his heart." She settled down at the table and started to brush her hair.

Pippin looked about to say something, but Tally caught her by the hand and said, "We'll leave you to get ready," as she towed her cousin from the room.

Felicity muttered her thanks as she went about her hurried toilette.

"Tally, we have to tell her!" Pippin insisted as they huddled on the second landing. "Since he obviously has not."

"Not me. She'll be furious."

Pippin snorted. "Furious? She is going to murder us both for not telling her earlier."

"Not if she loves him as she professes," Tally argued. "Oh, she'll be mad, but let the first wave of wrath rain down on Hollindrake. This is all his doing." She paused and looked up the stairs. "But I have to wonder why he hasn't told her yet. And how they can be wed if he didn't use his real name." She shook her head.

"I still think we should tell her before she ventures into that ballroom and discovers the truth."

Tally stepped aside and waved her hand toward the stairs. "Be my guest. But don't blame me if she tosses the powder pot at you and ruins your dress."

Pippin glanced down at the moss green silk and considered her chances.

"Besides," Tally said, "you heard her. They are man and wife, now and forever. She'll forgive him, as she will us." She glanced up and over her shoulder. "Eventually."

The first person Felicity ran into at the Hollindrake ball was the last person she wanted to see.

"Uncle Temple," she said, smiling up at the man who was like a second father. "How nice to see you!"

"And you as well," he said, his brows furrowed together.

"You must tell Her Grace that I thought the costume ball

was wonderful—with the exception of the shooting, of course," she said. "I do hope the damage wasn't extensive."

"So glad you found it to your liking, little duchess," he said. "Considering how little you saw of it—with the exception of the shooting, of course."

Felicity winced.

"You'll never believe what one of the maids found up in the orangery . . ."

"The orangery?" she asked, trying to sound innocent.

"Apparently a fairy forgot her wings up there, as well as some rather unmentionable pieces of clothing. I can't imagine what she was doing up there. *Undressed*." He made a *tsk tsk* sound under his breath. "In the absence of your father, I suppose I will have to call him out, for I will not see you—"

"Oh, you mustn't, Uncle Temple. For we are married!" she rushed to explain. "And I understand why you are angry, but I do so love him. And he loves me. I would think that of all people, you would understand."

"Married?" he asked. "You're married to—"

"Excuse me, Miss Langley," a footman intoned.

"Yes," she replied, sending an apologetic smile to Temple.

The man bowed low and then passed along his message. "If you would follow me, the Duke of Hollindrake requests your attendance in the library."

"I just bet he does," Temple muttered.

"Do be a gentleman," she scolded. "He has every right to summon me." And with that she followed the footman through the crowd and then deep into the vast house.

Steeling herself for what was to be a difficult interview, she entered the softly lit library and launched immediately into the speech she'd been practicing for the last two hours.

"Your Grace," Thatcher heard Felicity say, which could only mean she didn't recognize him.

Not yet, anyway. It helped that he wore the ducal finery befitting his station and was standing before the hearth, facing it, not her. Cowardly perhaps, but he had good reason. Just as he'd had when he'd chosen the library because it lent itself to the shadows so well, and because there were no firearms or weaponry close at hand.

Though he had to imagine Felicity could render quite a bit of damage with only a volume of Johnson's dictionary.

"Your Grace," she repeated. "Please just let me speak and get this out before I lose my nerve."

He bowed his head slightly and waved his hand, giving her permission to continue.

"It is just that we have had an unusual understanding—"

How much so, she had no idea.

"—and from the start, I know I was quite forthright in my desire to marry well, to marry apart from love."

He said nothing, just waited for her to continue.

"But as it usually happens, at least so my sister and cousin say, I've met someone else. And while you and I share an intellectual partnership, I fear with him it is an altogether different story."

"You love him," he whispered, wondering if she still would when he turned around.

There was a soft sigh from across the room. "Yes, I do. Ever so much so. He makes me laugh. He loves skating and Turkish coffee. And when he kisses me—" There was a moment of abrupt silence, and then she continued. "When he kisses me, I cannot think of anyone else but him." Her slippers pattered softly on the carpet as she drew closer.

Thatcher tensed.

"I am so sorry, but I cannot be your duchess," she told him.

Realizing she'd just given him the opening he needed, he took a deep breath and slowly turned around. "I am sorry to hear that, for I fear the title is yours, whether you want it or not."

Her eyes widened, then blinked. But her shock wore off quickly enough. "Thatcher? What the devil are you doing here?" Her hands fisted to her hips as she glanced over her shoulder at the door. "Hollindrake is going to be here any moment, and I certainly don't want you here when I—"

He stalked toward her. "My wife goes to meet another man and I'm supposed to turn a blind eye to such an indiscretion? And less than a day after we're wed. Really, Felicity."

She blew out a loud, disgruntled breath. "Don't be ridiculous. I had to do this. Besides, *he* summoned *me*. 'Tis all quite proper." Her gaze was still fixed on the door.

"Proper? Meeting another man in such a secluded romantic setting?" he said, drawing closer. "I disagree."

She turned, her mouth opening to make some hot retort, but her gaze narrowed and then her mouth fell open, impotently. *"Where did you get that jacket?"*

He glanced down at the dark green wool, trimmed with silver. "Weston, I believe."

"Weston?" She shook her head. "I mean, where did you find it?"

He pointed to the ceiling. "Upstairs. There is an entire closet of them." He held out his arms so she could take a better look. "What do you think? The cut is good, but the fashion is a bit ostentatious for me." He glanced at the cuffs. "What really matters is if you like it. Do you?"

She gaped at him. "Not in the least!"

"That's too bad, for I fear this and the others are all I have right now. But I am sure Mr. Weston can be enticed to make something more to my taste, and more importantly, to yours."

She trembled, then outright shuddered with anger. "You stole this from the duke's closet? Thatcher, this is dreadful.

He's going to be here any moment, and I doubt he is going to be very understanding—"

"How do you know that he isn't here already?"

"Here?"

"Yes."

"Where? Atop the mantel?"

"No, standing right before you."

She eyed him, his words sinking in, but he could see her discard the conclusion he'd been trying to prod her toward. "You've gone mad. Now please take off that jacket before someone—" She starting tugged at the sleeve but was stopped by a scratching at the door.

Thatcher looked up. "Come in."

A footman came in, bowing formally to them. "Your Grace, your mother begs your attendance downstairs." The man bowed slightly to Felicity. "That is to say, Lady Charles asks that you bring Her Grace as well, so the formal announcement of your marriage can be made." He paused and bowed to Felicity again, more deeply this time. "Many happy returns, Your Grace."

Thatcher nodded. "Tell my mother that my wife and I will be down momentarily."

The footman bowed and left, closing the door behind him.

He looked over at Felicity, to find she'd gone completely pale.

"Thatcher—" she managed to whisper. "It cannot be . . ."

He reached out for her, but she backed away from him as if they had just been introduced.

In truth, they had.

And so he did what he knew he should have done from the start. He bowed, then rose and straightened. He was his own man now. Because of her, he would tell her, that is if she'd listen to him.

"Aubrey Michael Thomas Sterling, the tenth Duke of Hollindrake, formerly Captain Michael Thatcher of His Majesty's 95th Rifles, at your service."

"You lied to me—"

"It was a mistake at first, and then—"

"How could you have done this to me? I thought you loved me. I thought you were—"

"I do. I am," he managed to wedge in.

She paused and looked up at him. "Are we really married?"

Oh, he had been hoping to avoid that subject, at least until she'd gathered her wits about her . . . and managed to forgive him. "Felicity—" he said as he reached for her.

But she'd dodged out of his reach, then did something that was far worse than Jack and Tally's dire predictions.

His duchess didn't shoot him.

She left him. And took his heart with her.

Chapter 17

"Ahem!"

Thatcher cracked an eye open and groaned. His mother. "Go away."

"I have to say," Lady Charles said, entering the drawing room anyway, "that if your intention was to come to Town, assume your grandfather's title and take your place in Society in an unassuming and stately fashion, you've failed utterly." Strolling through the room in an elegant day dress, she didn't wait for an invitation, and ignoring the fact that he had yet to rise to his feet, sat down on the chair nearest to him. "Lawks! Haven't you even changed since last night? I do say, find a decent valet."

"Good afternoon, Mother," he said with a wave of his hand. "'Tis lovely to see you, now leave."

"You could see me better if you sat up and opened your eyes."

He obliged, and she winced as she took a better look at him.

"You might want to call a doctor as well. You look like the devil's own." She glanced over her shoulder. "Staines? Is that you?"

The butler, who'd been lurking in the hallway, came in immediately. "Yes, madam?"

"Order up tea for His Grace, and have a basin of hot water and soap sent as well."

"Mother, I am certainly capable of—"

"And I'd like a glass of Madeira. I've had a morning like no other."

"Yes, ma'am," Staines said, departing quickly.

Thatcher struggled to sit up. He'd been out all night trying to find Felicity and had yet to locate her. "I'll warn you if you are here to lecture, Geneva's near to blistered my ears already."

"Better that than the morning I've endured! I have to say I haven't had so many callers since . . . well, since I can remember. Every old and dear 'friend' come to see how I am surviving the scandal." She plucked off her gloves and plopped them down on the small table beside her. Then she laughed, the merry sound startling him out of his fog of despair. "Quite honestly, I haven't had so much fun since your father was alive. You've quite made my Season, and it's just begun."

Thatcher shook his head. Had he heard her correctly? "My life is in shambles, and you call it 'fun'?"

"Fun? Why it is a most delicious scandal, my dear. I'm taking full credit for it. None of your stuffy Sterling nobility. This smacks of something one of my Redford relations might have done in their better days before that wretchedly dull brother of mine inherited."

Thatcher closed his eyes again and rubbed his aching skull. "Excuse me if I don't see the humor in all this. I am at present worried about my wife. Who, if the news has yet to reach you, has yet to be found."

"Oh, that," she said, adding a *tsk tsk* to the end of her dismissive statement. "Perhaps you wouldn't have lost her if you'd been a little more honest with her. Though I am a little surprised by her defection considering her well-known intention to marry a duke. I would think that she would have found your deception a great lark."

"She did not."

"Then she is a ninny, and I can see that my work is as yet not done for the day." She heaved a sigh and rose, retrieving her gloves. "And I was so looking forward to that glass of Madeira. Oh well, I shall have it upon my return." She leaned over, pecked a kiss on his cheek, and went to leave.

An uneasy ripple ran down Thatcher's spine. "Where are you going?"

"To do what you seem unable or unwilling to do," she told him from the doorway. "I am going to retrieve your wife."

"Retrieve my—"

"Wife," she said, with all the confidence that was her trademark. "Now I would suggest you start packing."

That got him to his feet. "Packing? Whatever for?"

"For your honeymoon, of course. 'Tis a terrible time to travel, but I doubt the two of you will get much farther than the first decent inn after Ludgate, given the gossip being bandied about regarding the Setchfields' orangery." She paused, her elegant brow arched and a wicked smile on her lips.

Thatcher choked. "Wha-a-t?"

"That was my reaction at first, but I told Lady Jersey that to me, the entire setting sounded delightfully romantic." She paused. "Though next time you decide to make love to Felicity in public, take better care not to leave so much evidence behind. Really, Aubrey, her wig and stockings?" Tugging on her gloves, she shot him one more glance.

"Yes?" he asked, almost afraid to.

She wiggled her fingers at him. "The packing? Please have it under way in about . . ." She glanced over his shoulder at the standing clock in the corner. ". . . an hour. That should set the stage very well. Very well indeed."

Thatcher gaped at her and wondered how it was he'd never seen this side of her before. "Mother, I wish you wouldn't interfere."

"Apparently someone must."

He groaned, crossing his arms over his chest. "And how exactly is it that you know where Felicity is, when I haven't been able to locate her all night?"

"Because you didn't ask me," she replied smugly, and then left just as smartly.

"Oh, this is perfect," he muttered. His mother knew where his wife was. He could just imagine what Lady Charles might say to her errant daughter-in-law to fetch her home. Most likely put Felicity in such a fine humor, it would take the entire British army and some French legions as well to keep him from being drawn and quartered by his fiery wife.

"Pardon, Your Grace," Staines said from the doorway, where he was directing a legion of footmen to bring in the tea tray, a wine bottle, glasses, and decanter, and behind that the requested wash basin and toilette items.

"My mother," he said, waving his hands toward the door. "She's gone off to fetch my wife, or so she claims."

"About demmed time," he thought he heard the proper old butler mutter.

Thatcher glanced up at Staines and studied the man carefully. First his mother was full of surprises, and now Staines

as well? Certainly his first official day as the Duke of Hollindrake had set the *ton* on their collective ear. As Aunt Geneva
had said over and over, "A Sterling never . . ."

Then again perhaps Lady Charles had the right of it—he
was only half Sterling—and though he was forever more the
Duke of Hollindrake, something he couldn't escape, suddenly he didn't want to. He'd put his own stamp on the family
legacy. With Felicity's able assistance and madcap ways.

"Staines," he said, rising to his full height.

"Yes, Your Grace," the man said, meeting his level gaze.

"Order my carriage. No, make that carriages. And then
pack everything I will need for a honeymoon. And fetch my
wife's belongings from her house on Brook Street. They no
longer belong there."

Staines nearly grinned. Or as well as he could manage
such a feat. "And when do you want to leave, Your Grace?"

"In an hour, my good man," Thatcher proclaimed.

If ever a London butler looked giddy, it was Staines.

Felicity sat in the Duke of Parkerton's well-appointed London mansion surrounded by friends and family and feeling
as lost and alone as if she'd been tossed into the deepest well
in India.

Lady John Tremont and Diana, Duchess of Setchfield, sat
opposite her in a pair of matching chairs. Tally and Pippin
held their post on a sofa against the far wall.

"I say, this entire situation is a scandal, but not one without sympathy, my dear," Lady Rhoda was telling her, having
just arrived from a morning spent gleaning gossip from one
and all. She sat down next to Felicity and sighed.

From the corner where Jamilla sat happily lounging on a
love seat, a fine pekoe having been procured for her, as well
as a selection of Turkish candies, she spoke up. "He is a
duke, is he not? And so very rich. I do not see what the fuss

is all about." She shook her head and went back to looking over the tray of delights the awed Parkerton butler had delivered, having never entertained a real princess before.

Out in the hall, Jack paced up and down the marble corridor, all but banished from the female confines of the parlor. But still he remained, for Felicity had declared she wanted nothing to do with Hollindrake, and that much Jack could offer—for he was still wavering between shooting his old friend and wondering if he wouldn't have done something just as foolish to gain Miranda's hand.

The bell clamored and everyone in the room stilled as they waited to see who was to be announced.

"Lady Charles Sterling," the Parkerton butler intoned.

Thatcher's mother sailed into the room and took in her surroundings in one easy flick of a glance. "My, such a mournful looking party, but I can see you have chosen your compatriots well, my dear girl."

Miranda rose, as was her duty as the *de facto* hostess for her absent brother-in-law, the Duke of Parkerton. "Lady Charles, I don't mean to be impolite, but I don't think now is the time—"

"Now is the perfect time," the lady said, blithely ignoring the cut she'd been given and settling down on the settee, nudging aside Lady Rhoda in the process. "Now, we can properly meet," she said to Felicity. "I am Lady Charles, your mother-in-law. But please, call me Rosebel." Her words were warm and full of enthusiasm. "Let me take a look at you."

Felicity glanced over at the woman, having heard tales of her less than congenial nature, and was surprised to find her smiling in welcome.

"My, you are as pretty as your mother was. She and I were friends, of a sort. You have her hair and her eyes, but I think your fire speaks more to your father, that devil of a man."

She sighed and glanced over at the tea tray, sending a broad hint that she might like some, but none was offered. Nonplussed, Lady Charles continued. "Now I have come to tell you that I think you have every right to be furious with my son. He's made a complete muddle of things, but that's a man for you."

Jamilla laughed, but no one else did, and so thus chastened, she went back to picking through the candy box.

"Lady Charles, he isn't the man I thought he was," Felicity told her. She felt foolish enough, for she loved Thatcher with all her heart—but he'd lied to her, deceived her. First with his letters and then letting her think that he was someone else. "The man who wrote to me all those years would never have—"

"But my dear girl, Aubrey never wrote any of those letters," Lady Charles said, obviously tired of waiting for someone to pour her a cup and helping herself to the excellent pekoe.

Never wrote any of those letters? But then . . . Felicity's stomach quaked. "Who did?"

The lady took an appreciative sip of tea before she answered. "'Twas all Hollindrake's doing—Aubrey's grandfather. I fear my father-in-law had an entirely underestimated romantic streak. And while I believe he composed most of the letters himself, he also had help from his secretary, Mr. Gibbens, of all people." She shook her head. "They were responsible for the letters you received. I'm afraid the man you thought was Hollindrake's heir wasn't Aubrey, for my son has been in Spain all these years."

It was as if the air suddenly left the room, and Felicity stammered to find the words to say.

But there were none.

And yet for some reason she felt an overwhelming sense of relief. Though she'd always thought herself in love with the man of her letters, she hadn't truly known what it meant to love someone, passionately and thoroughly, until she'd met Thatcher.

Not that she needed to say anything, for Lady Charles blithely went on as if she were just relating some innocuous *on dit.* "Quite honestly, when Aubrey found out about his grandfather's deception he was none too pleased." She turned to Felicity and looked her straight in the eye. "And he came to London the moment he discovered the truth to cry off."

"Cry off!" Tally said. "Why that's—"

Lady Charles glanced over at the girl and smiled. "Exactly. But that was what he intended to do the day he arrived on your doorstep."

"And I thought he was—" Felicity began, replaying those first few moments when she'd first met him. And how she'd wished he was Hollindrake. Wished with all her heart.

And now he was, and everything was a terrible tangle. She paused for a moment, a tingle running down her spine.

Perhaps there was a way . . .

Lady Charles sighed. "Yes, you thought he was the footman. Dear heavens, I can see why you made that mistake. Geneva claims he looked a fright, that I would have probably mistaken him for the dustman, and he's my own son." The lady glanced around at her audience. "Well, there's no need to gape and stew about it. It was an honest mistake. And Aubrey's fault for not correcting the situation immediately. But I fear my son has always had a rather poor sense of humor." She paused and shook her head. "Inherited from his father's side of the family, I assure you." Then she looked at Felicity and smiled. "But then something quite miraculous happened. He came to cry off and found himself quite taken by you, dear girl. And why wouldn't he be?"

The woman reached out and cupped her chin and smiled at Felicity with a warmth she'd never known. Felicity, who could not remember her own mother, and who'd had all kinds of nannies who tried to be just that to her, a mother, found in that brief moment a woman who could be that—a mother-in-law in name, but a mother to fill that empty place in her heart.

Rosebel patted her cheek fondly and then reached for her teacup. "In the end his curiosity and his heart won out—though he did bungle things utterly."

Felicity let the lady's words sink in. Oh no, she was the one who'd made a complete muddle of things! She shouldn't have let her temper get the better of her when she discovered the truth. So she'd married the man she loved and he was a duke. She could hardly hold that against him—even if his courtship had been conducted so very improperly.

But wasn't that what she loved most about him? His complete impropriety?

She shrank back on the settee in shock, while the others in the room rose to her defense.

"Yes, Lady Charles," Diana said, using her rank as the Duchess of Setchfield to exert some influence over this entire debacle. "Now that you've pled your son's case, I can advise you that you've wasted your time."

Felicity felt a tremor of hope. If Thatcher's mother had come to plead his case, did that mean he would take her back?

"Plead his case?" Lady Charles made an inelegant snort. "Why of course not. Why should I? No, I've simply come to bring my daughter-in-law home."

Diana wasn't one who was naysaid easily. "Miss Langley doesn't want to return to Hollindrake. This very moment my husband is consulting the archbishop to see what remedy can be made, for he is certain there are grounds for annulment and—"

"An annulment?" Felicity sat up. She didn't want her marriage annulled. She might have mentioned it last night as she cried her eyes out to Jack and Miranda and Temple, but she'd never thought . . . never meant . . .

Temple's wife wasn't finished. "After what he has done to her—"

Lady Charles snorted. "And she should listen to you, Your Grace? How many years did you spend casting covetous glances at Templeton before you finally got the nerve to make him come up to scratch?" She cast her gaze around the room and stopped at Miranda. "Or you? How many years did you hide from society because Mad Jack Tremont kissed you? " She blew out a breath. "If it was such a bad kiss, why did you marry him in the end?"

"My husband's kiss isn't—" Miranda began, then blushed deeply at such a confession, her hands folded over her ripe belly, proof that she found her husband's kiss quite adequate.

Lady Charles glanced over at Jamilla. "I haven't the vaguest notion who you are."

"I am the Princess—"

"Yes, yes, whatever. Whoever you are, I doubt it has any bearing on these matters." Turning to her right, her discerning gaze fell on Lady Rhoda. "And what say you, *Mrs.* Toulouse. Shall my daughter-in-law remain stubborn and proper or should she come home with me to the man she loves? How many years did it take you to make up your mind and marry Mr. Toulouse over your father's objections to his lack of title and nobility? Fine man that he is, I can't believe he waited for you, but you should be thankful he did." She wagged her finger at the rest of them. "You should all be thankful."

Lady Charles rose and held out her hand to Felicity. "You can be like these foolish, prideful women who hate to admit they were wrong, *even when it nearly cost them their splendid marriages*, or you can listen to me, a woman who loved her husband every day of his life and misses him terribly." She paused, and Felicity felt the weight of her measure falling on her shoulders. "Go home to my son before he leaves London. For good."

Panic ran down Felicity's spine. "He's leaving?"

She sighed. "Yes. He was ordering Staines to pack his things not thirty minutes ago."

Felicity bolted to her feet. "Where is he going?"

"How should I know?" Lady Charles said. "He's in a terrible temper."

Oh, no. Thatcher couldn't leave. Not yet. Not without her. "Do you think he will forgive me?"

"Of course he will," Jamilla said, glancing up from her tea. "The look, darling girl. Use the look."

Yes, the look! She would use that, and if she failed there, well, she'd just beg. Felicity rushed toward the door, then came to a halt. "Oh, I will never get there in time."

Thatcher's mother smiled and nodded for her to continue on. "Take my carriage. It is right out front."

"Oh, thank you, Lady Charles," she said. "How will I ever thank you?"

"Give me grandchildren. Plenty of them for me to spoil."

Felicity nodded, having not even thought of such a thing. Then her eyes widened and her hands went to her very flat stomach. "Children?"

"A houseful, please," came the cheerful order.

Dashing out the door, Felicity whispered a word of thanks up to the Fates for bringing Lady Charles just in time.

Fate, it turns out, had little to do with it.

Even after the door slammed shut and the carriage rolled away at a frantic clip, the ladies waited. Then Lady Charles sat down on a chair and beamed at her audience.

"Oh, well done, Rosebel," Lady Rhoda said. "I loved your entrance, darling! Splendid. So very dramatic. And Diana, darling, the annulment part was a stroke of genius. Did you see how pale she went?"

Diana grinned. "Yes, I thought it all went perfectly!"

Miranda leaned forward, or as much as her pregnancy would allow, and said to Lady Charles. "I take it your son was just as unsuspecting?"

"Utterly taken in," Lady Charles declared.

Everyone in the room applauded, except of course for Jack, who stood in the doorway, gaping at them. "You staged all that?" It wasn't a question, but a statement of masculine horror. "You let Felicity think . . ."

The ladies all nodded.

"And now those two are headed on a collision course?"

"A perfectly charted one, dear boy," Lady Charles told him.

He shook his head, as if still not quite sure he could believe it. "And whose balmy idea was that?"

From the far corner, two hands went up. "Ours," Tally said, nodding toward her coconspirator, Pippin. "'Tis from the final scene of our new play, 'The Lost Duke.'"

Jack groaned. "I should have known."

When Felicity arrived at the house on Grosvenor Square, the entire front curb was taken up with carriages—it seemed nearly everything Hollindrake owned was in the process of being loaded. And a legion of footmen, clad in the blue and white Hollindrake livery, scurried about carrying trunks and crates and all sorts of valises.

It was, simply put, chaos.

As she waded through it, a footman hurried past with a familiar looking traveling bag. *Hers.*

"Wait just a moment," she called out to the man. "What are you doing with that?"

"Putting it in the wagon, miss."

"You will not, that is mine."

The man snorted. "It belongs to the Duchess of Hollindrake."

Felicity's hands went to her hips. She might still be wearing the same gown she'd worn the night before, her face still puffed and red from the buckets of tears she'd shed, but she hadn't been practicing and planning her elevation all these years for nothing.

"*I am the Duchess of Hollindrake,*" she said.

The man looked skeptical, but only for a moment, and then his face fell. "Pardon, Your Grace. Where would you like this, Your Grace?"

Having moved households constantly throughout her life, with her father's rather unorthodox assignments requiring they leave with all haste, and sometimes in the middle of the night, Felicity was in her element. "In the main carriage," she declared.

Then she glanced around, realized nothing was being packed correctly and set to work to righting it all.

"No, no, no," she was saying, as one of the hapless fellows came down the steps with a trunk. "That shouldn't go in the wagon, but behind His Grace's carriage—for what if he decides to ride his horse rather than inside the carriage? He'll need his riding clothes close at hand!"

From the top of the stairs came a question, a voice that sent shivers down her spine. "And why would I want to leave your delightful company?"

Felicity spun around. "Thatcher!" She went to rush into his arms, but ended up skidding to a stop on the step below him, still unsure, despite the rakish gleam in his eyes.

"I'm not the man who wrote those letters," he told her. "Not the man you fell in love with."

"I know," she said, so very glad of it.

"But you fell in love with *him.*" There was a fierceness to his words. A jealousy that made her smile.

"I've only ever truly loved one man," she confessed. He stiffened and stared at her, until she playfully slapped him on the chest. "Oh, don't be such a cabbage head. I mean you. I fell in love with *you*."

"You did?"

"I did. I am," she confessed.

He looked down at her, his eyes filled with a light that seemed brimming with hope. "I wanted to tell you last night, but you—"

"I left," she finished for him. "I was being the cabbage head then. But I'm back now. That is, if you want me . . ."

It seemed every member of the Hollindrake staff froze, as if their fates too were about to be decided.

And in a thrice Thatcher gave them their answer. He caught up his bride in his arms and kissed her soundly, and quite improperly.

And sensing a fresh new wind blowing through their lives, the staff responded just as uncharacteristically, cheering, "Huzzah! Huzzah!"

Felicity melted in Thatcher's arms, marveling under the spell of his kiss. And when he finally—and reluctantly—pulled away, she sighed. "I'm so glad you're my Hollindrake. Though I'd nearly gotten used to the idea of being poor and unfashionable."

"I fear you'll have to make do with being excessively rich and terribly spoiled."

Felicity grinned. "Then why don't you start right now by kissing me again, Your Grace. Improperly, and before all of Mayfair, so we might add to our infamy before we go on our honeymoon and someone else has a chance to scandalize society." She glanced at the carriages still being packed. "We are going on a honeymoon, aren't we?"

He nodded and bent over to kiss her thoroughly yet again, planning all the ways he was going to make love to her in the coming days, weeks, and years. And much to his delight, no one disturbed them, allowing the Duke and Duchess of Hollindrake to kiss for as long as they wanted.

And in those moments, Thatcher realized two things.

He'd forgiven his grandfather for his high-handedness.

And it wasn't so bad being a duke.

Epilogue

Several hours later the Duke and Duchess of Hollindrake set off for their honeymoon, having taken their public and improper display of mutual affection inside and continued it in the privacy of the duke's bedchamber.

But the journey got no farther than Bond Street, where Thatcher ordered the carriage stopped and dashed inside a shop, without so much as a "just a moment" to his bride.

Felicity waited for about a minute or so, before she caught up her cloak and marched inside to discover what was so urgent that their honeymoon must be delayed.

When she entered the tidy little shop, the bell overhead rang with a sweet jingle and both Thatcher and the owner turned toward her. The man behind the counter held a lady's hairbrush for the duke's inspection.

"Yes, yes, that is perfect," he said. "Please wrap it up and send it along with this note." He was bent over the counter scribbling on a sheet of paper.

Felicity glanced over his shoulder. "A wedding gift?"

"Of a sort," he murmured as he tipped his shoulder to hide what he was writing.

"For me? For I already have a hairbrush, and don't need another."

"I know," he said, his back still to her.

She arched a brow. "You are buying a gift for another woman?"

"Exactly," he said, blowing on the paper to dry the ink, then folded it up and handed it to the man. "Thank you, sir, and good day." He caught Felicity by the elbow and led her from the shop.

"Who is that hairbrush for?" she asked as he all but pushed her inside the carriage and nodded for his driver to get under way.

"Miss Browne."

Felicity dropped to her seat, but her gaze flew to his, where his confession had left a smug, satisfied smile on his handsome face. "You bought a gift for who?"

"You heard me," he said, leaning back in the seat opposite hers and propping his boots up on the seat beside her. "Miss Browne."

"Harrumph."

"I can tell you why, if you're curious," he offered. "But you'll have to come sit next to me." His brows waggled invitingly, and oh so very improperly.

Felicity knew exactly what would happen if she took him up on his offer and joined him on his side of the carriage—he'd kiss her, and then he'd . . . well, suffice it to say, he'd distract her utterly and then there would be no getting her answers.

"I am not curious and I am quite comfortable here," she said, but in truth she was dying of curiosity and wanted nothing more than to curl into the warmth of his arms. But as much as she wanted her answers, she'd rather have had her name struck from the social registry than ask.

"Suit yourself," he said, crossing his arms over his chest and closing his eyes, as if he'd like nothing better than a little nap.

If he wanted to act like there was nothing wrong with him buying gifts for the lady she considered her worst enemy, then she could as well. And so she crossed her arms and closed her eyes.

But all that danced through her thoughts were visions of Miss Browne's delight at receiving such a personal and intimate gift from no less than the Duke of Hollindrake.

She peeked at him and found him peeking at her, and knew he would tell her only if she took another course. "How I wish . . ." She let her question float through the carriage.

"What is that, my dear?" he asked, shifting in his seat.

"Oh, I'm sorry," she said, glancing up at him, handsome devil that he was. "Did I disturb you?"

He shook his head. "No, not at all. You said something about a wish?"

"I did," she told him. "I was just thinking how delightful it would have been if we could have had a big wedding, you know, in the country with our families and friends around and a large house party. I could have carried a bouquet of orange blossoms and had a new gown from Madame Ornette's. With Tally and Pippin as bridesmaids, of course."

He nodded and closed his eyes again. "Well if that is what you wish . . ."

"Well, the house party certainly, but we are already—" she began, even as a vague memory from the night at the Ransomed Cat flitted through her hazy recollections.

Got a fellow who can do the job right, though not altogether proper, if you know what I mean . . . Not that she's likely to notice.

"Oh, dear heavens!" she gasped. "We aren't—" She couldn't even say the words.

"No. No, we aren't," he agreed, still feigning his sleep stance.

"You rakish, improper, devil of a—" Felicity blustered for a moment, then continued, but in Russian and some Italian and even a bit of French, which obviously Thatcher knew, because he flinched when she impugned his parentage as well as his manhood.

"Now, that's a lie," he pointed out. "I believe I proved that quite to the contrary earlier today." Then he grinned like Brutus in a boot shop. "If you want, I can prove it again."

"You will not! We aren't married," she replied. "Dare I ask when exactly were you planning on telling me?"

He leaned forward and looked out the window. "I suppose in about five minutes. When we got to the archbishop's house, but now you've gone and ruined the surprise." Then he reached over and tugged her into his arms, that passionate, smoky light in his eyes telling her that her outburst had been like an aphrodisiac to him. "I had Gibbens send around a note asking the good man to see us this afternoon." And then he kissed her, plundering her lips and teasing her until nearly every bit of her anger had fled.

Nearly all.

"Marry me, Miss Langley, for you are the only woman I will ever love."

"I will not," she told him, her gown askew and her hair tumbling down from its pins, her body trembling from his touch. "Not ever."

"You will when I tell you why I sent that hairbrush to Miss Browne," he said, nuzzling her neck with his lips.

"I doubt it," she replied.

And so he told her.

And as he predicted, she married him. Again.

Because a man so thoughtful, so very scandalous, was worth marrying. Twice.

Even if he was a most improper duke.

Bad girls who can be so good . . .

Admit it. Women have known since they were teenagers that a sultry look, some flirtatious banter and perhaps a quick coat of lip gloss is often all the arsenal they need to get what they want. It's really quite unfair . . . But there's nothing more dangerously seductive than a bad girl who knows exactly what she wants and how to get it. Our heroes don't stand a chance!

In these thrilling Romance Superleaders, meet four sexy and unstoppable heroines who are determined—by any means, legal or otherwise—to get the man of her dreams.

Love Letters From a Duke

Elizabeth Boyle
September 2007

Felicity Langley had set her sights on being the next Duchess of Hollindrake. But then she hires a mysterious footman and finds herself reluctantly drawn to him. Whatever is a girl to do when all she ever wanted was to marry a duke and suddenly finds herself falling in love with the unlikely man at her side?

As the bell jangled again, Tally groaned at the clamor. "Sounds as presumptuous as a duke, doesn't it? Should I check the window for a coach and four before you answer it?"

Felicity shook her head. "That could hardly be Hollindrake." She nodded toward the bracket clock their father had sent them the year before. "It's too early for callers. Besides, he'd send around his card or a note before he just arrived at our doorstep. Not even a duke would be so presumptuous to call without sending word."

Sweeping her hands over her skirt and then patting her hair to make sure it was in place, Felicity was actually relieved it couldn't be her duke calling—for she still hadn't managed a way to gain them new wardrobes, let alone more coal. But she had a good week to solve those problems, at least until the House of Lords reconvened . . . for then Hollindrake would have to come to Town to formally claim his title and take his oath of allegiance.

"So who do you think it is?" Tally was asking as she clung to a squirming Brutus.

Taking another quick glance at the clock, Felicity let out a big sigh. "How could I have forgotten? The agency sent around a note yesterday that they had found us a footman who met our requirements."

Tally snorted. "What? He doesn't need a wage and won't rob us blind?"

Felicity glanced toward the ceiling and shook her head. "Of course I plan on paying him—eventually—and since we have nothing worth stealing, that shouldn't be an issue."

The bell jangled again, and this time Brutus squirmed free of his mistress's grasp, racing in anxious circles around the hem of Tally's gown and barking furiously.

Well, if there was any consolation, Felicity mused as she crossed the foyer and caught hold of the latch, whoever was being so insistent was about to have his boots ruined.

Taking a deep breath, she tugged the door open and found herself staring into a dark green greatcoat, which her gaze dismissively sped over for it sported only one poor cape. The owner stood hunched forward, the brim of his hat tipped down to shield him from the wintry chill.

"May I help you?" Felicity asked, trying to tamp down the shiver that rose up her spine. It wasn't that she'd been struck by a chill, for this mountain of a man was blocking the razor cold wind. No, rather, it was something she didn't quite understand.

And then she did.

As this stranger slowly straightened, the brim of his hat rose, revealing a solid masculine jaw—covered in a hint of dark stubble that did little to obscure the strong cleft in his chin, nor hide a pair of firm lips.

From there sat a Roman nose, set into his features with a noble sort of craggy fortitude. But it was his eyes that finally let loose that odd shiver through her limbs with an abandon that not even she could tamp down.

His gaze was as dark as night, a pair of eyes the color of Russian sable, mysterious and deep, rich and full of secrets.

Felicity found herself mesmerized, for all she could think about was something Pippin had once confessed—that from the very moment she'd looked into Captain Dashwell's eyes, she'd just known he was going to kiss her.

A ridiculous notion, Felicity had declared at the time. But suddenly she understood what her cousin had been saying. For right now she knew there was no way on earth she was going to go to her grave without having once had her lips plundered, thoroughly and spectacularly, by this man, until her toes curled up in her slippers and she couldn't breathe.

She didn't know how she knew such a thing, but she just did.

"I'm here to see Miss Langley," he said. His deep voice echoed with a craggy, smoky quality. From the authority in his taut stance, to the arch of his brow as he looked down at her—clearly as surprised to find a lady answering her own door as she was to find him standing on her steps—he left her staggering with one unbelievable thought.

And her shiver immediately turned to panic.

This is him, her heart sang. *Please let this be him.*

Hollindrake!

She struggled to find the words to answer him, but for the first time in her life, Felicity Langley found herself speechless. She moved her lips, tried to talk, tried to be sensible, but it was impossible under this imposing man's scrutinizing gaze.

Yet how could this be? What was *he* doing here, calling on her? And at such an unfashionable hour?

And no wonder he was staring at her, for her hair wasn't properly fixed, her dress four years out of fashion, and her feet—dear God, she'd answered the door wearing red wool socks!

Tally nudged her from behind. "Felicity, say something."

Reluctantly wrenching her gaze away from his mesmerizing countenance, composing herself, she focused on what it was one said to their nearly betrothed.

But in those few moments, Felicity's dazzled gaze took in the coat once again—with its shockingly worn cuffs. *Worn cuffs?* Oh no, that wasn't right. And where there should be a pair of perfectly cut breeches, were a pair of patched trousers. *Patched?* But the final evidence that cooled her wayward thoughts more thoroughly than the icy floor that each morning met her toes was the pair of well-worn and thoroughly scuffed boots, one of which now sported the added accessory of a firmly attached, small, black affenpinscher dog.

Boots that looked like they'd marched across Spain and back, boots that had never seen the tender care of a valet. Boots that belonged to a man of service, not a duke.

And certainly not the Duke of Hollindrake.

She took another tentative glance back at his face, and found that his noble and arrogant features still left her heart trembling, but this time in embarrassed disappointment.

To think that she would even consider kissing such a fellow . . . well, it wasn't done. Well, she conceded, it was. But only in all those fairy tales and French novels Tally and Pippin adored.

And that was exactly where such mad passions and notions of "love at first sight" belonged—between the covers of a book.

"You must be the man we've been expecting," Tally was saying, casting a dubious glance in Felicity's direction. Obviously unaffected by this man's handsome countenance, she bustled around and caught up Brutus by his hind legs, tugging at the little tyrant. "Sorry about that. He loves a good pair of boots. Hope these aren't your only pair."

A Touch of Minx
Suzanne Enoch
October 2007

Samantha Jellicoe and Richard Addison are at it again! Sam knows Rick wants more of a commitment from her—it's just so hard for a barely reformed thief to resist a golden opportunity to test her skills. But is she willing to risk losing her sexy billionaire lover?

For a second she hung in the air before she smacked into the palm's trunk and wrapped her arms and legs around it. That would have hurt if she hadn't worn jeans and a long-sleeved shirt. Black, of course; not only was the dark color slimming, but it was the clothing of choice for disappearing into shadows. Sucking in another breath, she shimmied up the rough trunk until she was about four feet above the house's roof.

The roof here at the back of the house was flat and had a very nice skylight set into the ceiling of the room she needed to get into. Glancing over her shoulder to make sure she was lined up, she pushed off backward, twisting in midair to land on her hands and knees on the rooftop. Keeping her forward momentum going, she somersaulted and came up onto her feet.

Normally speed wasn't as important as stealth, but tonight she needed to get into Richard Addison's office before he tracked her down. And for an amateur, he had a pretty good nose for larceny. Of course she was a damned bloodhound, if she said so herself.

With another smile she crouched in front of the skylight and leaned over to peer into the dark office space below. Just because he'd announced that he would wait for her to show up outside the door didn't mean that he'd done so. The padlock he'd put on the skylight stopped her for about twelve seconds, most of that taken up by the time it took her to dig the paper clip out of her pocket.

Setting the lock aside, she unlatched the skylight and carefully shoved it open, gripping the edge to lean in headfirst. The large room with its conference table, desk, and sitting area at one end looked empty, and her Spider-Man senses weren't wigging out.

Pushing off with her feet, she flipped head over hands and landed in the middle of the room, bending her knees to cushion her landing and cut down on any sound. A small black box topped by a red bow sat on the desk, but after a glance and a quick wrestling match with her curiosity, she walked past it to the refrigerator set into the credenza and pulled out a Diet Coke. Deliberately she walked to the office door, leaned against the frame, and popped the soda tab.

A second later she heard the distinctive sound of a key sliding into a lock, and the door handle flipped down. "Surprise," she said, taking a swallow of soda.

The tall, black-haired Englishman stopped just inside the doorway and glared at her. Blue eyes darkened to black in the dimness, but she didn't need light to read his expression. *Annoyed.* Rick Addison didn't like to be bested.

"You used the skylight, didn't you?" he said, making the sentence a statement rather than a question.

"Yep."

"I padlocked it an hour ago."

"Hello," she returned, handing him the Diet Coke. "Thief. Remember?"

"Retired thief." He took a drink and gave it back to her before he continued past her to the desk. "You didn't peek?"

"Nope. The thought never crossed my mind." Well, it had, but she hadn't given in, so that counted. "I wouldn't ruin your surprise."

When he faced her again, his mouth relaxed into a slight smile. "I was certain you'd attempt to get around me in the gallery hall."

"I went out through the library window. If I'da been a bomb, you would have been blowed up, slick."

Grabbing her by the front of the shirt, he yanked her up against him, bent his face down, and kissed her. Adrenaline flowed into arousal, and she kissed him back, pulling off her black leather gloves to tangle her bare fingers into his dark hair. A successful B and E was a lot like sex, and when she could actually combine the two, hoo baby.

"You smell like palm tree," he muttered, sweeping her legs out from under her and lowering her onto the gray carpeted floor.

"How do you think I got in here?"

Rick's hands paused on their trek up under her shirt. "You climbed up the palm tree?"

"It's the fastest way to go." She pulled his face down over hers again, yanking open the fly of his jeans with her free hand. She loved his body, the feel of his skin against hers. It amazed her that a guy who spent his days sitting at conference tables and computers and arguing over pieces of paper could have the body of a professional soccer player, but he did. And he knew how to use it, too.

He backed off a little again. "This was supposed to be fun, Samantha. Not you climbing up a tree and jumping onto a roof thirty feet in the air."

"That *is* fun, Brit. Quit stalling. I want my present." She shoved her hand down the front of his pants. "Mm, feels like you want to give it to me, too."

Halfway to the Grave
Jeaniene Frost
November 2007

Catherine Crawfield has more than a few skeletons in her closet. She's a vampire slayer with a big attitude, who makes an unlikely alliance with a vampire named Bones to track down an even more menacing evil. Though their chemistry is sizzling hot, how long can their dangerous association last?

"Beautiful ladies should never drink alone," a voice said next to me.

Turning to give a rebuff, I stopped short when I saw my admirer was as dead as Elvis. Blond hair about four shades darker than the other one's, with turquoise-colored eyes. Hell's bells, it was my lucky night.

"I hate to drink alone, in fact."

He smiled, showing lovely squared teeth. *All the better to bite you with, my dear.*

"Are you here by yourself?"

"Do you want me to be?" Coyly, I fluttered my lashes at him. This one wasn't going to get away, by God.

"I very much want you to be." His voice was lower now, his smile deeper. God, but they had great intonation. Most of them could double as phone-sex operators.

"Well, then I was. Except now I'm with you."

I let my head tilt to the side in a flirtatious manner that also bared my neck. His eyes followed the movement, and he licked his lips. *Oh good, a hungry one.*

"What's your name, lovely lady?"

"Cat Raven." An abbreviation of Catherine and the hair color of the first man who tried to kill me. See? Sentimental.

His smile broadened. "Such an unusual name."

His name was Kevin. He was twenty-eight and an architect, or so he claimed. Kevin was recently engaged, but his fiancée had dumped him and now he just wanted to find a nice girl and settle down. Listening to this, I managed not to choke on my drink in amusement. What a load of crap. Next he'd be pulling out pictures of a house with a white picket fence. Of course, he couldn't let me call a cab, and how inconsiderate that my fictitious friends left without me. How kind of him to drive me home, and oh, by the way, he had something to show me. Well, that made two of us.

Experience had taught me it was much easier to dispose of a car that hadn't been the scene of a killing. Therefore, I managed to open the passenger door of his Volkswagen and run screaming out of it with feigned horror when he made his move. He'd picked a deserted area, most of them did, so I didn't worry about a Good Samaritan hearing my cries.

He followed me with measured steps, delighted with my sloppy staggering. Pretending to trip, I whimpered for effect as he loomed over me. His face had transformed to reflect his true nature. A sinister smile revealed upper fangs where none had been before, and his previously blue eyes now glowed with a terrible green light.

I scrabbled around, concealing my hand slipping into my pocket. "Don't hurt me!"

He knelt, grasping the back of my neck.

"It will only hurt for a moment."

Just then, I struck. My hand whipped out in a practiced movement and the weapon it held pierced his heart. I twisted repeatedly until his mouth went slack and the light faded from his eyes. With a last wrenching shove, I pushed him off and wiped my bloody hands on my pants.

"You were right." I was out of breath from my exertions. "It only hurt for a moment."

Much later when I arrived home, I was whistling. The night hadn't been a total waste after all. One had gotten away, but one would be prowling the dark no more. My mother was asleep in the room we shared. I'd tell her about it in the morning. It was the first question she asked on the week-ends. *Did you get one of those things, Catherine?* Well, yes, I did! All without me getting battered or pulled over. Who could ask for more?

I was in such a good mood, in fact, that I decided to try the same club the next night. After all, there was a danger-ous bloodsucker in the area and I had to stop him, right? So I went about my usual household chores with impatience. My mother and I lived with my grandparents. They owned a modest two-story home that had actually once been a barn. Turned out the isolated property, with its acres of land, was coming in handy. By nine o'clock, I was out the door.

It was crowded again, this being a Saturday night. The music was just as loud and the faces just as blank. My initial sweep of the place turned up nothing, deflating my mood a little. I headed toward the bar and didn't notice the crackle in the air before I heard his voice.

"I'm ready to fuck now."

"What?"

I whirled around, prepared to indignantly scald the ears of the unknown creep, when I stopped. It was *him*. A blush came to my face when I remembered what I'd said last night. Apparently he'd remembered as well.

"Ah yes, well . . ." Exactly how did one respond to that? "Umm, drink first? Beer or . . . ?"

"Don't bother." He interrupted my hail of the bartender and traced a finger along my jaw. "Let's go."

"Now?" I looked around, thrown off guard.

"Yeah, now. Changed your mind, luv?"

There was a challenge in his eyes and a gleam I couldn't decipher. Not wanting to risk losing him again, I grabbed my purse and gestured to the door.

"Lead the way."